CHAPTER ONE

THE CRUISE LINER 'OSTENTANIA' — OFF THE CANARY ISLAND OF LANZAROTE, NORTH ATLANTIC —
SUNDAY, SEPTEMBER 9 . . .

Andy Green's lungs were bursting, his head exploding, his eyes burning, his arms and legs flailing in one final, desperate attempt to regain the surface before the inescapable urge to breathe ended his young life. But he was trapped in the maelstrom created by the death throes of the sinking ship. The surging waters were sucking him ever downwards, buffeting him with debris and spinning him like a rag doll in a washing machine.

"And me still just a laddie," he lamented as he succumbed to the cruel inevitability of his plight, "and wi' a great future in the police force an' all."

Then, through the raging turbulence, he heard a voice — his mother's voice, calling his name, pleading with him to return to her. Yet, even as the black hole of unconsciousness began to envelop him, he knew that his mother's beckoning was only oxygen deprivation playing tricks with his mind. His mother was over two thousand miles away, back in Haddington, the little town in the midst of the rolling East Lothian countryside, the heart of the "Garden of Scotland", that had been his home since birth. Exhausted though he now was, the thought of never seeing his parents and that beautiful landscape again somehow gave him the strength to kick once more for the surface with what he realised would be the last vestige of breath in his body. He closed his eyes and made the supreme effort.

"Andy!" his mother's voice called out again as his head collided with something — something firm, yet sensuously soft. He opened his eyes and saw a leg — a shapely female leg, dangling down in front of him. It was naked. A distinct absence of varicose veins told him that this leg certainly didn't belong to his mother. He wasn't *that* befuddled. Instinctively, he grabbed at the leg's thigh and frantically pulled himself upwards.

"Andy!" the voice yelled again, a shrill note of protest distorting it this time.

Suddenly, he felt two hands grabbing him under the armpits. The feel of the hands didn't match the look of the leg. These were strong hands, a man's hands, and they were yanking him roughly up and away from the shapely limb.

"Oo-oo-ooh!" the voice of the leg woman warbled when Andy's head finally emerged from the depths. "Oo-oo-ooh," it giggled, "that *was* a bit up-close and personal, wasn't it?"

"What the *hell* do you think you're playing at, Green?" the voice of the hands man growled. "You're an even bigger bloody idiot than I ever gave you credit for, and that's *really* saying something, believe me!"

Taking great, shuddering breaths of air, Andy blinked the stinging water from his eyes and shook his head in an effort to clear his mind.

BOB BURNS INVESTIGATES

The Cruise Connection

Peter Kerr

First published in Great Britain 2008
by
Accent Press Ltd.

Published in Large Print 2009 by ISIS Publishing Ltd.,
7 Centremead, Osney Mead, Oxford OX2 0ES
by arrangement with
Pollinger Limited

British Library Cataloguing in Publication Data
Kerr, Peter, 1940–
The cruise connection. – Large print ed.
1. Burns, Bob (Fictitious character) – Fiction
2. Police – Scotland – Fiction
3. Cruise ships – Fiction
4. Detective and mystery stories
5. Large type books
I. Title
823.9'2 [F]

ISBN 978–0–7531–8282–6 (hb)
ISBN 978–0–7531–8283–3 (pb)

Printed and bound in Great Britain by
T. J. International Ltd., Padstow, Cornwall

"Wh-what happened?" he gasped. "Wh-wh-where am I?"

"You're in a Jacuzzi — a whirlpool spa bath, you bloody half-wit!"

Andy's senses were rapidly recovering from their watery ordeal. He cringed inwardly as the identity of the voice of the hands began to dawn on him. His rapidly re-focusing eyes now confirmed the worse. "Boss?" he said sheepishly. "Is, ehm — is that *you*, boss?"

Detective Inspector Bob Burns didn't bother to reply, but stood slowly up from where he had been kneeling, fully clothed, at the edge of the pool. He glared menacingly at his hapless subordinate, then motioned with a jerk of his head in the direction of the owner of the shapely thigh, which he was still clinging to as though his life depended on it.

Hesitantly, Andy followed his boss's stare.

"You're a bit lanky for a koala bear, Detective Constable Green," the owner of the voice of the leg crooned into his eyes. She was sitting in the Jacuzzi right beside him. "And, uhm, by the way, sunshine," she added in that seductively posh Glaswegian accent that Andy always found to be a grade-one turn-on, "no one *ever* mistook me for a eucalyptus tree before."

"So, Randy bleedin' Andy," Bob snarled, "get your horny mitts off Doctor Bryson's leg — NOW!"

Mortified, Andy Green swiftly did as instructed. "Aw listen, Ah'm really sorry, Doc. It was the — Ah mean, Ah thought Ah was goin' down wi' a sinkin' ship — all that bubbly water and the jotsam and fletsam swirlin' about and everythi —"

"The only flotsam and jetsam swirling about," Bob cut in, "was the beer bottle that fell out of your hand, and . . ." He paused to point to the bottom of the Jacuzzi. "And the pair of Jesus boots that fell off when you tumbled arse-over-tit off the bench in the water there."

Julie Bryson sniggered.

Bob glowered.

Andy stared forlornly into the pool. "Aw, jeez," he groaned. "The fancy leather flip-flops ma mother gave me. She said ye're supposed to keep them dry, like. Aw, no," he moaned, "she'll kill me if Ah've ruined them."

"Bloody pathetic," Bob muttered, sitting down on a sun lounger.

"Never mind, Andy," Julie smiled, "we'll fish your flip-flops out and, once they've dried, I'll rub some shoe cream into the leather. They'll be good as new, never fear."

Andy's head hurt, his mouth tasted (in his own words) like the saddle of a nudist's mountain bike, and he was still struggling to get his half-drowned thoughts together. He cast Julie an exaggerated little-boy-lost look. "B-but what happened, Doc?" he pleaded. "How did Ah come to fall into the water?"

"Because," Bob snapped, before Julie could reply, "because, Green, you were as pissed as a fart — sound asleep when Dr Bryson and I came along the deck here — sitting slumped in the Jacuzzi there with a bottle in your hand, your head lolling about as if your neck was

broken, and snoring like a hippopotamus with wind."
Bob tutted in exasperation, then lay back on the lounger. He shot Julie a reproving glance, then mumbled, "What took Doctor Bryson to go in there beside you, I'll never know."

"Oh, come on, Kemosabe," Julie scolded, "don't be such an old misery guts. Andy deserved to have a wee celebration last night. We all did. I mean, the case is solved now, and just think, it might still be dragging on if young D.C. Green here hadn't done the things he did. Yes, and he *is* off duty, after all."

Bob gave a grudging grunt, closed his eyes and let his thoughts drift back . . .

TWO WEEKS EARLIER — OUTSIDE THE CASTLE INN, DIRLETON VILLAGE, SOUTH-EAST SCOTLAND . . .

"This is the life," Bob grinned, then took a luxuriant gulp of his beloved Belhaven Best. He sat back and gazed lovingly at the tawny beer in his pint glass. "Saturday morning, off duty 'til Monday, Andy Green away on secondment to the Customs Department, Julie here to spend a quiet weekend with me . . ." He allowed himself a sly smirk. "Well, not *too* quiet, I hope. Yeah, life doesn't get much better than this."

He looked out from the table where he was sitting in front of the old whitewashed inn. He had known this scene for as long as he could remember — the little stone church by the footpath leading away to the coast; the village green flanked by pantiled, roses-round-the door cottages; the shady old trees along the perimeter wall of the castle. Dirleton, regarded by many as the most beautiful village in Scotland. So many fond memories came flooding back every time he looked at that view. Priceless. And now, after years of living in the hurly-burly of Edinburgh, while his career in the police flourished and his marriage disintegrated in sympathy, he was back in the village of his birth, and with one of those pantiled cottages to call his own. Even the grind of the twenty-mile daily drive into Edinburgh was bearable when there was this to look forward to at the end of the day. Then, of course, there was Julie's flat in Forth Street — right in the centre of the city — where he could retreat to for the night when they had indulged in some homely Italian food and a little too much Italian wine in the *Ristorante Mamma Roma*, just round the corner in Antigua Street. Yes, he reflected, nowadays it was too risky to drive even slightly over the limit the way he had once done, even occasionally using his police siren and flashing blue lights to speed his way through the traffic on the way home after a night in the pub with some of the other young coppers. Those daft days were over.

His eyes wandered over the village green to the ruins of the ancient castle, from which the inn took its name. "The pleasantest house in the land," was how someone had described Dirleton Castle in the dim and distant past. That was before Cromwell had marched up from the south over three centuries ago and knocked the stuffing out of its walls with his heavy cannon in a crude effort to impose his will on the people hereabouts. Cromwell's troops had done exactly the same to every other magnificent old fortress in the area — the heritage created by generations of master craftsmen shattered for ever by the brute force of an autocrat bent on domination.

Bob glanced at the headline trumpeting the latest Middle East crisis on the front page of his newspaper. "Some things never bloody change," he mumbled. "When will we ever learn?"

"Talking to yourself again? First sign of senility, as I've told you many times before." Julie gave Bob a peck on the cheek, then sat down beside him. She handed him a picture postcard. "This was lying inside your front door when I came out of the shower."

Bob looked at the card. "It's from Green. Lisbon postmark. Addressed to Detective Inspector Robert Burns and signed Detective Constable Andy Green." He shook his head and sighed. "So much for the lessons I gave him in C-R-A-P."

"Crap?" Julie enquired with a puzzled frown.

"Clandestine Research And Probing. The essence of hush-hush investigative work. I've told you about that many times before." He gave her a commiserating look, then added, "Memory loss — first sign of senility."

"Touché," Julie shrugged. "Anyway, why does he have to be secretive about being in Portugal?"

"Simply because he's working undercover for the Leith Customs bods — all part of his police education. He's posing as a trainee barman on a cruise ship that's doing a trip to the Canary Islands. Supposed to be trying to get inside info on some cigarette-smuggling caper or other."

Julie raised her eyebrows. "Nice work if you can get it."

"Bloody cushy number, if you ask me," Bob replied. "Never had any perks like that when I was —"

"When you were young?" Julie gibed.

Bob took another sip of his beer.

Julie then flashed a big smile at a young waiter who had appeared at the doorway of the inn. "'Morning, Vincent."

"The usual rosé spritzer, is it, Doctor Bryson?"

"A bit early for anything alcoholic, I think." Julie took a disapproving gander at Bob's pint. "No, Vinny, just a glass of fresh orange juice for me, thanks." She flashed him another smile. "Oh, and, uhm, no need for the formal Doctor tag. Julie will do fine."

"You certainly know how to wind the young guys round your little finger," Bob dryly remarked after the waiter had left with a cat-that-got-the-cream grin on his face. "Don't you think you're getting a wee bit long in the tooth for the flirty sixth-former stuff?"

She tweaked Bob's cheek. "I'll remember that the next time you ask me to dress up in my old school uniform."

Bob looked around furtively. "Keep it down, for Pete's sake," he hissed. "The last thing I need is for folk in the village to think I'm some kind of perv."

Julie gave him a reassuring pat on the hand. "Don't worry, Kemosabe, your secret's safe with me."

"Yeah, yeah, yeah — very droll."

"Anyway," Julie bristled, "enough of the long-in-the-tooth stuff. I'm still in the flush of my twenties. You're the one who's about to hit the age when life begins — supposedly!"

"Bollocks! I won't be forty for another couple of years — almost."

"Oo-ooh! Getting a bit defensive about that now, are we?" Julie patted his hand again. "Never mind, deary," she said, aping the patronising manner of the stereotypical nurse in an old folks' home, "I'll make sure your eggs are *softly* boiled in the morning, once you're at the chewing-with-your-gums stage."

"Aye, well, I'll probably have turned you in for a newer model long before that happens, darlin', so don't count your chickens, *or* your soft-boiled eggs."

"And don't you get too cocky, or my gymslip goes up for sale on eBay." While Bob signalled her to keep her voice down, Julie added for everyone within earshot to hear, "That's the skimpy gymslip *and* my St Trinian's black stockings and suspenders I'm talking about, OK?"

Bob half turned his head towards two middle-aged men who'd started chuckling at an adjacent table. "Glaswegian humour," he said through a fake smile. "A bit crude at times, but even posh Weegies like her can't resist it."

"Aye, well, we're Weegies wurselfs, like." one of the men replied. "Hunner per cent Glesca, so no problem for uz, like, eh?"

"No," the other man said, "and if the lassie wants to stop dressin' up for ye, ye cannae force her, unless ye want to get yersel' arrested, like."

"Mind you," his friend told Bob with an air of confidentiality, "Ah'm in the rag trade masel', pal, so if ye want kitted oot in a nice school blazer, short troosers and a wee schoolboy's cap yersel', Ah can do ye a handy price for cash."

General laughter and merriment, in which Julie was delighted to participate.

Bob cleared his throat, directed another wooden smile at the two men, then resolutely returned to reading his newspaper.

Just then, everyone's attention was drawn to a black Rolls Royce, with dark tinted windows, purring to a halt in front of the inn. Even in this well-heeled corner of East Lothian, a gleaming limo like this was a fairly rare sight.

"Maybe it's the Queen arrivin' tae lay that knighthood on ye at last, Tam," one of the Glaswegian men said to his mate.

"Aye, that *will* be the day, Eck!" his friend replied.

And he was right, because the first figure to emerge from the Roller couldn't have been mistaken for any female member of the British Royal Family. Although the person was built like a 1970s East German shot-putter of indiscriminate gender, a full beard confirmed his masculinity, and his accent was certainly *not* of the upper-class House of Windsor variety.

"Werry nice place," he growled to one of the two glum-looking henchmen who followed him out of the car. He paused to take in the view towards the castle, then added loudly, "Maybe I go buyink da whole fockink willage as vell!"

At that, he draped a camelhair coat over his shoulders and swept into the inn with his two sidekicks following closely behind, sullenly eyeing those seated at the outside tables as they went.

Bob scowled back at them. "Who the hell's that?" he asked Julie out of the corner of his mouth. "Arnold Schwarzenegger's cultural envoy to Scotland or something?"

Julie pulled an indifferent shrug. "Search me."

"He's Boris Kaminski," one of the two adjacent Glaswegians informed Bob. "Ye'll see the story in yer paper there, pal. Back page — sports."

"Yeah," his mate confirmed. "Stinkin' rich Russky — across here tryin' tae buy Glasgow Rangers Football Club. Fat chance o' that happenin', by the way."

"Aye, unless he's in the Moscow lodge o' the Masons, of course," his chum quipped.

The two Weegies had a wee chuckle about that.

"He's Balgonian, actually," Vincent the waiter discreetly revealed as he put Julie's glass of orange juice on the table. "He was in here for lunch yesterday as well. Says he's looking for an estate to buy near here. Huntin', shootin', fishin' — all that stuff. Oh, and all the golf courses round here are a big attraction, too. Likes his sport, he says."

"Hmm," Bob murmured as he scanned the sports page of his paper, "he's from Balgonia *now*, it says here, but he claims he's originally from the Ukraine."

"Either way," Julie chipped in, "it means that, technically speaking, he isn't really Russian."

"Near as dammit," Bob retorted. "Whatever, he's yet another mystery man from the old communist east, with a rare talent for suddenly being able to teach us so-called capitalists how to amass huge fortunes overnight. Bent as chocolate frogs, the lot of them." His interest in the Boris Kaminski story instantly over, he returned to the general news section of his paper.

Whereupon, a fourth figure, squat and well-upholstered, emerged from the black Rolls Royce. Despite the warm August sunshine, she was clad head-to-toe in fur, her high-cheekboned, Mongoloid features suggesting, Bob mused, a direct line of descent from Genghis Khan. She waddled unsmilingly into the inn.

"That'll be Mrs Kaminski," Glasgow Tam reasoned. "Her photie's been in one o' the papers an' all, like. Supposed tae have been Miss Pan-Siberia or somethin' back in the Sixties."

"Pan-Siberian pie-eatin' champion now, by the looks o' things," his companion Eck opined.

"Aye," Tam agreed, "and available for hirin' as a mobile bouncy castle between contests as well, eh?"

No sooner had their third bout of chuckling subsided than Boris Kaminski emerged through the inn door, closely followed by his wife and their two minders. His expression indicated that Boris was not a happy man.

"If no can makink borscht soups vid *pampushki* dumplinks here," he snarled as he stomped towards his car, "I go eatink some odder fockink place!"

Julie leaned in close to Bob. "Wherever he comes from, he's certainly mastered the fluent use of the English F-word."

"Hmm, well, that would be a natural spin-off from attending all those Scottish football matches the paper says he's been busy with recently."

Boris interrupted his march carwards to directly address Julie, whose visual attributes he had blatantly assessed on his sweep into the inn a few minutes earlier. He assessed them even more blatantly now.

"I am delightful to meetink you, *baryshnja*," he smarmed, ignoring Bob completely while he clicked his heels, bowed and offered Julie his hand. "Boris Kaminski, beink please to service you."

Julie nodded demurely. "Charmed, I'm sure."

Boris gestured towards his car. "You likink big Rolls Royce, *baryshnja*? Vell," he flamboyantly continued without waiting for a reply, "I havink four. I also havink big ocean-goink yatt vid helicopter on it — big von — and I havink four big willa vid svimmink pool — and I havink private execute yett at airport vid Rolls Royce engines — two big vons — and —"

"You also have a big shadow," Bob butted in, "and you're blocking out the sun, so kindly move yourself out of my way."

Boris saw red, and his cheeks reflected it. "You tellink me fock off?" he spluttered.

Bob was niggled, and he didn't disguise the fact. "Also, your car's illegally parked, and if you don't move it immediately, I'll . . ." He instinctively made to reach into the pocket that contained his police ID card. "I'll have you for —"

A sharp knee-nudge under the table from Julie stopped him short.

"C-R-A-P," she whispered behind a cupped hand.

Bob got the message. No point in revealing his profession to this guy — not for the worth of a measly parking ticket at any rate. Judging by his bulldozing demeanour, it could turn out that there would be an opportunity to nail Boris Kaminski with a bigger rap in future. Bob knew the type. Stranger coincidences happened in the police game, and anonymity was the ace in the policeman's hand if and when they did.

Mrs Kaminski gripped her husband's clenched fist. "Come, Boris," she urged. "Ve must to goink now."

Boris took a slow, deep breath and nodded his head in agreement — though with patent reluctance. "But," he growled at Bob, screwing his eyes into a menacing squint, "I no beink forget you. *NOBODY* can tellink Boris Kaminski fock off!"

"Aye, well, ye certainly made a new pal there, son," Glaswegian Eck said to Bob after the Roller had rolled away.

"Bloody arrogance," Bob muttered, as much to himself as anyone else, "coming over here with their misbegotten loot and acting like they own the place." He glanced sidelong at Julie. "Yeah, and everybody in it, too."

"Ah couldnae care less masel'," Glasgow Tam stated blandly, "just as long as he doesnae invest his misbegotten Russky loot in Rangers Football Club."

"So, you don't like Russians?" Julie enquired by way of keeping the small talk going.

"Nah, nah, nothin' against them, doll. Nah, it's just 'cos we don't like the Glasgow Rangers."

"That's right," Eck concurred. "See, we're Glasgow Celtic supporters wurselfs, like."

Bob hid his face behind his newspaper. How the hell, he silently pondered, could whole countries be at peace, in the Middle East or anywhere else, when supporters of two football teams at opposite sides of the same bloody city were only interested in doing the other lot down at every opportunity? Religion — that, of course, was the common root of both evils. "God help us and save us!" he cynically mumbled.

"Talking to yourself again?" Julie sweetly smiled.

Bob didn't rise to the bait. "More to the point, what did that barry-whatever thing the Russky called you mean? Sounded a bit over-familiar to me."

"*Baryshnja*? Oh, nothing to get excited about. It's just Russian for 'young lady', that's all." She held up the third finger of her left hand and wagged it in front of Bob's face. "*Unmarried* young lady, to be exact!"

Bob's mobile phone rang, providing him with a timely excuse to get up and cross over the road to the village green, ostensibly for the sake of manners, but equally to escape Julie's less-than-subtle hint about wedding rings. "Once bitten in the nuptials, twice shy," was still his motto in that regard. It also helped him avoid — for the present at least — the ribbing that Julie would relish giving him for almost forgetting the basics of the "C-R-A-P" principle that he'd originally dreamed up to confuse and control poor Andy Green.

As Bob talked on the phone, Julie watched his body language change from expectant to tense and on to round-shouldered despair.

"What's the name of that cruise ship on Green's postcard?" he asked her when he returned to the table.

Julie picked up the card and checked. "The *Ostentania*."

"Just what I bloody well thought," Bob grumped. "And just my bloody luck!"

CHAPTER TWO

ONE HOUR LATER — THE OFFICE OF DETECTIVE SUPERINTENDENT BRUCE McNEILL, LOTHIAN AND BORDERS POLICE HQ, EDINBURGH . . .

Bruce McNeill was one superior officer with whom Bob got along just fine — usually. Too many of the other brass hats, in Bob's opinion, were lazy pension-hatchers, who regarded delegation of duties as a euphemism for sitting on their arses while colleagues lower down the food chain shouldered the workload, relinquished plaudits to them when things went right *and* took the rap for them when things went wrong. Bruce didn't fit into that category. Like Bob, he was a hands-on copper, who never asked anyone to do anything he wouldn't willingly do himself. Unlike Bob, though, his independent nature hadn't held him back in the career-advancement stakes. For all that, he'd once told Bob that the only real difference between them was that he knew how to keep his mouth shut on occasions when opening it would risk swallowing a fly — or, more professionally painful, a wasp. Bob readily conceded that he'd left himself open to being stung in this way a tad too often, but that was his nature and nothing was going to change it now. Bruce McNeill knew that, respected Bob for it and, whenever possible, demonstrated that respect by assigning Bob to cases that would benefit from his individualistic ways. Which made it all the more difficult for Bob to understand why he was being lumbered with such a lousy job now.

"Come on, Bruce," he said, "you know that skiving off on a wild goose chase like this isn't my style. I mean, do me a favour — there are plenty other guys here who'd jump at the chance to go through the motions of checking out a man-overboard case that can never be solved. It'd just be an excuse to ponce their stuff with the idle rich on a big boat, which appeals to me like contracting leprosy. And anyway, I can't see why you'd want to stretch police resources on such a pointless exercise in the first place."

Bruce McNeill smiled a crafty little smile. "It'll only be pointless if we *waste* these resources, Bob, and that's precisely why I'm putting you on the case. You won't just swan about cruising on police exies — you'll get stuck in and do the business."

Bob wasn't convinced. "Yeah, but you could get any rookie dick to handle this for you. And, don't forget, we've already got our very own rookie dick-cum-dickhead on the tub in question."

"I haven't forgotten that — far from it. And *you're* forgetting that DC Green is working undercover for HM Customs on that ship, so it would defeat the purpose if he suddenly morphed into a gumshoe, wouldn't it?"

Bob acknowledged the logic of that with a shrug.

Bruce McNeill gave him a wry smile. "Not like you to forget the basics of your famous C-R-A-P principle, is it?"

Bob responded with a rueful sigh. "Twice today, as it happens, and both times involving Detective Constable Andy Green — indirectly or otherwise. The bane of my life, that laddie."

"You're too hard on young Green, Bob. OK, he may not be the sharpest knife in the drawer, but you were the one who gave him his break in the CID, and he's already put his life on the line to help you out of a couple of *very* sticky situations."

"More by accident than good intent," Bob retorted. "Anyway, if we must put somebody on this case, it'll be a test of initiative for one of our *other* rookies. Should be a walk in the park."

"How come?"

"Simply because this man-overboard mystery, like most man-overboard cases on cruise liners, would've been over by the time the guy was reported missing. You read about it all the time. He committed suicide — that would've been the line-of-least-resistance decision made by the ship's security, and that's the verdict that'll have been swiftly accepted by all interested parties."

"Not quite. You see, it turns out that the bloke's life was insured recently for a hefty amount of money, and his —"

"Don't tell me. And his insurance policy states that the company won't pay out on successful hari-kari efforts, right? Yeah, and his wife's claiming that it wasn't suicide, but foul play, resulting, no doubt, from some sort of negligence on the cruise line's part. Right again?"

"Yup, that's it in a nutshell — more or less."

"But why do we need to get involved? If, as you say, it was off the Portuguese coast the bloke topped himself, or somebody topped him, surely it's up to the Portuguese police to sort it out."

Bruce McNeill shook his head. "As you surmised a moment ago, they're regarding it as just another man-overboard case that happened outside their twelve-mile limit, and they're only too pleased to leave it at that."

"All the more reason for us to keep out of it as well, no?"

Bruce opened a file on his desk, took out a photograph and handed it to Bob. "Does that mug shot ring a bell?"

Bob's facial response was a curious mix of disapproval and affection. "Wee Rab Dykes. Self-styled king of the Edinburgh underworld. Which is a bit like claiming to be the leader of a gang of notorious hamster rustlers. Oh yes, *many*'s the brush I've had with wee Rab in the past. Even nailed him to a couple of wee stretches in the slammer for selling bootleg DVDs at Ingliston Sunday Market." He smiled reflectively for a moment, then went on, "But he's a bigger danger to himself than anybody else. Thick as a bottle o' shite, soft as a Ken Dodd tickling stick, but still determined to go down in history alongside the Al Capones of this world." Bob couldn't resist a chuckle. "So, what's the daft wee bugger been up to now?"

Bruce arched a name-that-tune eyebrow.

It took Bob but a couple of seconds to collate the metaphorical minims and crotchets. "You're saying *he's* the suicidal plank-walker?"

"You named it in one."

Pensively, Bob stroked his chin. "Hmm, I'd never have figured wee Rab for a terminal high-diver, though."

Bruce pulled another picture from his file. "What do you make of that?"

"It's one of wee Rab's over-the-top signet rings. I recognise the zodiac sign — Pluto, the idiot."

"Pluto?"

"Yeah, Walt Disney cartoon characters are — were — Rab's main heroes in life — apart from Al Capone, that is. He had weird astrological-type signs made up for Mickey Mouse, Goofy, Donald Duck and so on. Had them inscribed on these huge fake-gold rings. Wore them on four fingers of each hand, would you believe?"

Bruce McNeill invited Bob to take a closer look at the photograph. "You'll notice, however, that the finger this ring encircles is no longer attached to anything — hence the surrounding cotton wool. The detached digit is, according to Mrs Dykes, the middle finger of her deceased husband's right hand."

Bob smiled again, wistfully this time. "The last time I saw that finger was when wee Rab raised it to me from the dock in the sheriff court after I'd had him sent down for peddling cannabis-spiked rock cakes to school kids in Leith. Spin on it, pig, were the words he mouthed, if I remember right."

A frown creased Bruce McNeill's brow. "The finger's come a long way since then, though. It was found in a slice of quiche lorraine by a very shocked passenger while she was dining aboard the good ship *Ostentania* on the same night Rab took a farewell dip several miles out in the Atlantic Ocean."

"Well, he *did* always like to keep a finger in a few different pies, that's for sure," Bob quipped, "but maybe this *is* taking it a bit far."

If Bob had been expecting his boss to be amused by that glib remark, he was in for a disappointment. He looked Bob admonishingly in the eye and said, "This is a man's life we're talking about here, all right?"

Bob took the point. "Fair enough," he replied, adopting a suitably more sober tone, "but I still can't see why Lothian and Borders Police need to be involved."

Bruce McNeill exhaled a slightly exasperated breath. "Just look at it this way . . . the dead guy's a citizen of Edinburgh, OK? His wife — who, incidentally, is shouting blue murder aboard the ship — is a citizen of Edinburgh, and the insurance company concerned has its head office here as well. On top of that lot, the local media here will make a meal of this when they get wind of it, so who do you reckon is more liable to be involved than us, huh?"

"Right, I'll give you that, but why pass the ball to me? I mean, I'm not even a good sailor. In fact, I had to pop seasick pills every time I took a ten-minute ferry trip on that recent Mafia case up in the Hebrides. And besides, I don't fancy the idea of being cooped up in some floating booze palace with swarms of the nouveau riche and their pretentious bloody —"

DS Bruce McNeill held up a silencing hand. "OK, OK, Bob — nice try, but no dice. This job has your team's stamp all over it, and everything's set up for you to get started."

Bob half closed his eyes. "My *team*?" he charily enquired. "I wasn't actually aware I had one."

"Don't come the coy one with me, Bob. For all your moans and groans about young Andy Green being a thorn in your flesh, you aren't kidding anyone — least of all me. Dim as he may be, when the chips are down, the bond the pair of you have comes good and the job gets done, irrespective of the risks involved." He raised his hand again to stave off Bob's imminent objection. "Add to that Doctor Bryson's forensic brain, feminine guile, multi-linguistic skills and, for want of a better word, *athleticism*, and if that isn't what constitutes a team . . ."

"So, uhm," Bob hesitantly interjected, "are you saying that Julie, I mean *Doctor* Bryson would be joining me on this cruise ship stint?"

Bruce nodded emphatically. "Essential cog in the wheel. After all, you haven't got the usual luxury of being able to bugle up the full force of forensic troops when you're at sea, so the next best thing is to take your own — even if it's only a one-woman platoon."

Of a sudden, this open-and-shut, man-overboard case was taking on a distinctly more attractive aspect for Bob. In an attempt to hide the smirk that was playing at the corner of his lips, he stroked his nose and asked, "And, uh, am I to take it that we — that's Doctor Bryson and I — would be travelling in, ehm . . . ?"

"The same cabin? Oh, yes," DS McNeill replied with a half wink, "Lothian and Borders Police resources could *never* be stretched to coughing up for two singles."

"Well, that *does* put a different complexion on things," Bob readily conceded.

"Yes, quite. I had a suspicion that the cutting-down-on-police-costs angle would win you over in the end." Bruce McNeill returned the two photographs to the file, then pushed it over the desk to Bob. "So, now that you're officially on the case, I can tell you that we reckon there could be more to this business than meets the eye."

"Yeah, I was wondering when a fly would enter the ointment," Bob said with a resigned sigh. "All right, Bruce, tell me the worst."

There wasn't really anything *that* bad to tell, McNeill assured him. Nothing that set particularly loud alarm bells ringing, at any rate. No, it was just that this cruise ship, the *Ostentania*, had first attracted the attention of the Customs people down the road in Leith when, several months earlier, they'd received an anonymous phone call, supposedly from a crew member, tipping them off that a large quantity of smuggled cigarettes was stashed away on board. At the time, the ship was approaching Leith on the last leg of a cruise that had taken it to the Canary Islands. However, despite a thorough search of the vessel when it docked, not one packet of hooky fags was found. Nevertheless, just a few days later, there had been a marked increase in the amount of contraband cigarettes changing hands in the usual pubs and corner shops of the city. Exactly the same thing had happened on the two subsequent occasions that the *Ostentania* had returned to Leith from a cruise to the Canaries.

"Which is why," Bob said, "our mates at HM Customs sent one of their guys, along with our DC Green, on an undercover mission on this current trip. Right?"

"Again, that's it in a nutshell — more or less."

Bob shook his head in despair. "Well, we can only hope the Customs bloke has a lot more savvy than our mole, or there's bugger all chance of anything being found out about anything."

Bruce McNeill dismissed that with a swat of his hand. "That's a Customs problem, not ours — not at this stage, anyway. No, if it isn't stating the bleedin' obvious, the way I see it is that the phone tip-offs about these non-existent stashes of smuggled fags on the *Ostentania* are only a smoke screen."

"To conceal what?"

"That's for you to find out. But it could just be that the disappearance at sea of Rab Dykes, a known pusher of hot ciggies around here, has something to do with it."

"And that's *all* I've got to go on?"

DS McNeill pointed to the file that he'd pushed over the table to Bob a bit earlier. "Such as it is, all the background stuff we have is in there, so Doctor Bryson and you had better familiarise yourselves with it fast. Oh, and better look out your dinner suit and swimming pants as well as seasick pills. You're on a flight first thing in the morning — booked on a fly-cruise package aboard the Ulanova Line's *Ostentania*, sailing from Palma Mallorca tomorrow night and bound for the sunny Canaries."

This was beginning to move a bit too fast for Bob. "But what about our cover?" he frowned. "Yeah, and how about one or two contacts in the Canaries? I mean, it's a big bunch of islands and it's a helluva long way from home."

Bruce got up and ushered Bob towards the door. "Create your own cover and make your own contacts," he smiled. "Standing on your own two feet — that's what you and your team are good at, and that's why you're going on this assignment." He shook Bob's hand. "Safe journey . . . *amigo*!"

NEXT MORNING, ON A CHARTER FLIGHT FROM EDINBURGH, SCOTLAND, TO THE MEDITERRANEAN HOLIDAY ISLAND OF MALLORCA . . .

Bob was fizzing mad.

Julie was highly amused.

"If that damned kid behind me doesn't stop screaming like a banshee," Bob fumed, "I swear I'll turn round and stuff one of my socks in its mouth!"

"You surely couldn't inflict that on *any* fellow human!"

"That kid isn't human."

"The same could be said for the pong that comes off your socks."

Bob chose to ignore that. "Nah," he grouched, "this sort of airborne nightmare is the reason I've always avoided these package holidays like the plague. Crammed together in a tin tube seven miles up with badly behaved brats and their couldn't-care-less parents. Should be a law against that type being allowed to breed!"

"Well, you'll only have to put up with it for another hour or so."

"How do you make that out?"

Julie had been reading through the schedule of the cruise they were booked on. She showed the relevant detail to Bob. "Look — says here it's an adults-only trip — no sprogs allowed."

"Thank God for that!"

"Anyway, you were going to clue me up on your master plan for this mission, so just relax and fill me in — figuratively speaking, of course."

He'd had precious little time to work out anything at all, Bob admitted. And this, he declared, was another reason for his irritable mood. Bloody Bruce McNeill and his "great little team" bullshit. Should never have allowed himself to get sweet-talked into this stupid boat trip. Fishing for for red herrings, that's all they'd be doing. Waste of bloody time.

Julie ordered him a beer from the passing trolley dolly. "Maybe this'll get your creative juices going *and* calm you down." She turned on her old-folks-home nurse's voice again. "There, there, there — just think of your blood pressure, deary."

Bob flashed her a humourless smile.

"OK, Kemosabe, let's start with what kind of cover you're considering for us," Julie chirped in an attempt to goad Bob into some positive thinking. "We can't just own up to our fellow cruisers that we're on a mission from Lothian and Borders Police."

Bob couldn't disguise his growing disenchantment with the entire project. "Well, I suppose," he sighed, "it'd have to be something that would allow us to ask a lot of questions without arousing suspicion. Easier said than done, though."

Julie snapped her fingers. "Newshawks!"

Bob gave her a you-must-be-joking glare. "I'd rather pose as a male stripper in that CC Bloom's poof pub at the top of Leith Walk than pretend to be one of that degenerate bunch of scandal ferrets."

"No, no, I wasn't meaning tabloid hacks. No, I was thinking more about us making out that we're freelance feature writers for glossy magazines, that sort of thing. We could say we always use noms de plume for our bylines. That way nobody could say they'd never heard of us by our real names."

"They'll never have heard of us by trumped-up noms de plume either, though."

"Nonsense! No, we just say that we do all of our articles for overseas mags — in Australia, Canada, South Africa, places like that."

"And what if there are Australians, Canadians and South Africans aboard?"

"Slim chance, but even if there are, I'm sure we can bluff our way out of that."

Bob stroked his jaw pensively for a while. "Yeah," he eventually conceded, "maybe the freelance writer thing could be a possible cover at that." He thought about it again, then, with an air of mounting enthusiasm, said, "That's right — we could be researching a piece on how different people see cruising in different ways. Get them to talk about their individual experiences. Guide the conversations round to what they think about how wee Rab Dykes might have met his end. Find out if they've got any suspicions. We'd also be able to pump members of the crew. The Captain as well, maybe. Hmm," he nodded, smiling broadly now, "the freelance writer thing will be a *really* good cover. Yep, and I dreamed it up only just in the nick of time."

Julie punched his arm. "What a snake in the grass! Honestly, you're no better than those credit-grabbing brass hats you're always decrying!"

"If you can't beat 'em, join 'em," Bob grinned. "Now, I reckon I'd better have one last look through this case file Bruce McNeill gave me. Not that it'll do any good," he added, the smile fading from his face, "'cos there's nothing much in it I didn't already know about wee Rab."

Julie looked on as Bob flicked through the notes. "Seems to have been just another ten-a-penny, small-time crook," she said. "I mean, none of the things he's been nicked for even involved a lot of money. A bit of a numpty, if you ask me."

"Yeah, but a likeable enough wee fella, for all his lack of smarts. Fact is, I've never known anybody say a bad word about wee Rab."

"What about his wife? What sort of character is she?"

Bob hunched his shoulders. "I haven't a clue. She never appeared at any of Rab's court cases I was involved in, so I don't even know what she looks like."

From the file, Julie took a sheet of paper emblazoned with an insurance company's letterhead. "Well, according to this summary," she smiled, "whatever she looks like now, she'll look a helluva lot better when she gets the pampering this sort of money will buy her."

Bob shook his head in undisguised wonderment. "Yeah, two million quid. I'm amazed wee Rab Dykes could even afford to pay the first premium on a life policy worth that kind of dosh."

Just then, the infant behind him started to scream again, this time venting its ill-humour by hurling a plastic truck at the nearest target, which just happened to be the back of Bob's head.

The kid's youthful father leaned over Bob to retrieve the toy. "Aw'right, big man?" he said in a broad Glasgow accent, while affording Bob's nostrils an opportunity to have a close encounter with his armpit. "See bairns — pure, dead pain in the arse, eh?"

"Yeah, and if that bairn was mine," Bob replied through gritted teeth, "a sore arse is exactly what it would have right now."

Instantly, the young parent looked as though he was about to aim something a lot more malevolent than a plastic truck at Bob's head.

Time, Julie decided, to pour oil on potentially troubled waters. "Ach, don't mind him," she said to the Glaswegian lad in his own brogue. She gave him a smile that was as melting as it was sympathetic. "He's Edinburgh, like. Nae sense o' humour an' that, eh no?"

Prudently, both adversaries were content to leave it at that.

ONE HOUR LATER — THE INTERNATIONAL ARRIVALS HALL AT PALMA AIRPORT, ON THE SPANISH ISLAND OF MALLORCA . . .

"According to the schedule," Julie told Bob while they struggled out of the melee in the baggage-reclaim area, "we're supposed to look for a rep holding up a sign with Ulanova Cruise Lines on it."

Bob nodded towards the exit. "And that'll be her right over there."

"You'll be passengers Burns and Bryson," the harassed-looking girl said as they approached her.

"Clever trick," Bob remarked. "How'd you guess?"

"Easy. You're the only two booked on that Edinburgh flight. The rest of our fly-cruise clients joining the *Ostentania* here are coming in from other UK airports at different times throughout the day. Phew," she puffed, then fanned her face with her clipboard, "It's been one sod of a job trying to find overnight hotel accommodation for you all!"

"Hotel? Overnight?" Julie queried. "But the schedule says we go straight to the ship, all ready to set sail for the Canaries later today."

The rep cast her a quizzical look, then repeated it in Bob's direction. "You mean you — you haven't seen the TV news this morning?"

"We've hardly had time to think," Bob curtly informed her, "never mind look at the telly. What's the problem?"

The rep heaved a beleaguered sigh. "Norovirus outbreak on the *Ostentania*. The Spaniards won't allow her to dock at any of their ports, so she had to head back to Gibraltar. The British health officials there will have to sort it out."

"Norovirus?" Bob asked Julie. "What the hell's that?"

"Norwalk-like virus, to give it its proper name. Named after the American town of Norwalk — in Ohio, I think it is. Yes, the first recorded outbreak happened in the local school's dining hall, if I remember correctly."

"Skip the history lesson," Bob said impatiently. "Just give us the highlights."

"No highlights, I'm afraid — just lowlights. The effects are particularly nasty — projectile vomiting, diarrhoea, stomach cramps, severe headaches, sometimes accompanied by fever. Can last for two days or so."

"Contagious?"

"Very. And in an environment with a lot of people living in close proximity . . ."

"Yeah," Bob nodded, "I seem to remember reading about it now. A year or so back — an epidemic on one of those huge, new superliners, wasn't it? Pulled into Southampton with hundreds of its passengers hit by the bug."

"It's the scourge of the cruise business," the rep dolefully concurred, "and it had to happen on one of our ships right in the middle of one of our busiest times of the year."

Detective Inspector Robert Burns could see his best-laid plans going severely agley. "So, what happens now?" he asked the rep, apprehension writ large on his face.

Oh, there was no need to worry, the rep assured him, swiftly adopting an everything-in-the-garden's-lovely approach. The company was trying to accommodate as many as possible of the new fly-cruise arrivals on the *Ostentania*'s sister ship, the *Hedonia*, which would be arriving in Palma the next day. It wouldn't be bound for the Canaries, however, but embarking on a truly wonderful tour of the Mediterranean islands — Corsica, Sardinia, Malta, Sicily, Corfu and so on. If anything, it would be an even *better* itinerary than the one they'd have to forfeit on the *Ostentania*.

"Forfeit?" Bob frowned.

"Yes, the *Ostentania*'s going to be withdrawn from service at Gibraltar until a thorough sanitisation is completed. Could take a couple of days, could take a week. Depends on the Gib health officials."

"All right, we'll wait," said Bob. "OK, it's an inconvenience for us to hang about here in Mallorca, but I presume the cruise line will cover our expenses?"

The rep gave a derisory little laugh. No, that wasn't company policy, she bluntly informed him. It was a big enough headache for them to try and fit the fly-cruise clients into the *Hedonia*, but that's what had been decided, and any passengers who didn't want to comply would be given vouchers for a future, equally priced cruise of their choice. Meantime, the cost of their flights back to their home airports in the UK would be the clients' responsibility. Noting Bob's deepening frown, she quickly added, "It's the terms of your booking, sir, as noted in the schedule. The cost of repatriation of passengers, when caused by circumstances beyond the company's control, will be borne by the passengers themselves."

"Yeah, but I'm not bothered about all that," Bob came back, "because we've no intention of going home. No, it's essential we take the trip aboard the *Ostentania*, and I'm going to hold the company to the booking we made."

Wearily, the rep checked her watch. "Look, I'm sorry, but I haven't got time just now, all right? I've another three flights to meet, one after the other." She handed Bob a piece of paper. "This is your hotel reservation for tonight. You'll get a taxi outside here, and we'll refund the cost. But, first thing tomorrow morning, you'll have to tell me whether you're going on the *Hedonia* or going home. There's no other choice."

CHAPTER THREE

MEANWHILE, ABOARD THE CRUISE LINER 'OSTENTANIA', *ANCHORED OFF THE BRITISH DEPENDENT TERRITORY OF GIBRALTAR, ON THE SOUTHERN TIP OF SPAIN* . . .

Andy Green had really been enjoying his training as a barman — or a "mixologist", as he'd been told to refer to himself during the early-evening "Cocktail for Today" Happy Hours in the Stardust Lounge. Even when at sea, this time of day could be a bit quiet in the bar. Most of the passengers were either doing things like sunbathing, playing deck quoits or shuffleboard, watching ice-carving demonstrations, attending keep-fit classes, still sleeping off post-lunch strolls round the promenade deck, or were already sprucing themselves up for the first sitting of dinner. Consequently, the company's stratagem was to plug a different "Cocktail for Today" in the daily shipboard newspaper, *The Ostentania Times*, a copy of which was placed outside every cabin in the ship before the occupants got up in the morning.

Between the hours of 4p.m. and 5p.m., special half-price offers were available in the Stardust Lounge for such exotic alcoholic concoctions as *Hawaiian Dream-makers* (Malibu, Curaçao and pineapple juice), *Caribbean Sundowners* (white rum, Tia Maria and grenadine syrup), *Montezuma Massages* (tequila, Bailey's Irish Cream and Cointreau), *Napoli Gloom-lifters* (grappa, Crème de Menthe, Zambucca and soda), *London Knees-ups* (gin, dry Martini, cold tea, lemon juice, milk and sugar) and — but only when there was a sizeable contingent of Scots aboard — *Glasgow Kisses* (Scotch whisky, Drambuie, Southern Comfort, brandy, gin, vodka, tequila, Pernod, sweet sherry, port, cherry brandy, Archer's Peach Liqueur, Carlsberg Special, Coke, Buckfast Tonic Wine and Irn Bru). This latter potion had to be pre-mixed in a stainless steel bucket and carefully dispensed into glasses via a large hypodermic syringe at the point of serving. The Glasgow punters in particular appreciated this delicate final touch.

There was more to this mixology job than met the eye, however. As well as memorising the ingredients of the cocktails, which Andy had found difficult enough, you also had to be familiar with all sorts of little side issues, like what glass to use for which particular drink, whether to include cubed or crushed ice, whether or not to dip the rim of the glass in salt or sugar, which fruits (if any) had to be used to decorate what, and, of course, whether to shake or stir. There was always at least one half-blootered Sean Connery impersonator at the other side of the bar ready to give you grief about that one. Yes, there was much for a trainee cocktail barman to learn, but Andy was picking up the ropes reasonably well, under the expert tutelage of Pedro "Speedy" Gonzales, the diminutive head barman.

Speedy was in his early forties, fancied himself as a Julio Iglesias look-alike and, as such, saw himself as the flower of Spanish manhood, albeit of the semi-dwarf variety. He had been "on the boats" since shortly after he left school in his native Mallorcan village of Porto Cristo, starting out as a deck hand on a little cargo ship that plied between the Balearic Islands and North Africa. Before long, he had graduated to washing dishes on one of the big Mallorca-to-Barcelona ferries, got promoted to assistant barman, then worked his way up to his current position after landing his first cruise ship job some twenty years ago.

What Speedy didn't know about the bartending game wasn't worth knowing. He was master of all tricks, and then some. An essential component of his stock in trade, of course, was juggling with bottles and cocktail shakers, and he'd delight in showing off his flashy mixologist's skills to the customers whenever the mood took him — which was frequently. He had picked up the basics of the English language from below-decks Liverpool "swabs" in his early cruising days. That was before cruise line companies latched onto the economies that could be derived by crewing their ships with "oriental" personnel. His grounding in English, then, had been courtesy of a distinctly foul-mouthed school of linguistics. Indeed, Speedy Gonzales could curse and blind in English like a Pioneer Corps squaddie, even if his accent did betray his Mallorcan origins. In any case, he knew better than to borrow from his bilge-pit vocabulary when serving customers.

Behind the bar, Speedy was the epitome of Latin charm and civility.

As all drinks aboard a cruise ship are put on the customer's tab, to be paid for at the end of each voyage, no cash changes hands and, consequently, there's no opportunity for a cruise ship barman to skim off any till takings for himself in the time-honoured manner of land-lubbing members of the same noble profession. Being extra nice to the cruising punters, therefore, is mandatory, if any financial gratuities are to be forthcoming. Speedy had put Andy wise to this early doors.

"*Hombre*!" he'd said, "you gorra smile like a fookin' Cheddar cat at the bastids, even if you no like 'em more than a lumpa dog crap in a fookin' swimmin' pool!"

He'd then gone on to advise Andy that, contrary to popular reasoning, it wasn't usually the dedicated bar flies who parted with the big tips. No, no, no, skin, he'd insisted, it was more likely to be little-old ladies getting tiddly on a cream sherry or two who'd come good with a decent back-hander of the folding kind. Lace her second sherry with a shot of vodka, that was the secret, then it was just a matter of turning up the flattery and waiting for the old *puta*'s purse to open. It wasn't as easy as this to patsy the younger bints, of course. Too used to downing a right gutful of bevvy without turning a hair, that lot. No, but with a load of bullshit and a few outsize measures of hooch, you'd occasionally manage to entice one of them back to your cabin for an after-hours shag.

"*Madre de Dios*!" Speedy had said with the customary upsweep of a phallic fist, "no every fookin' perkyshit for a sailor boy is for spendin' ashore on his fookin' missus, eh!"

Andy could only take his word for that, since all his own attempts at perquisite-milking had met with abject failure. So far, his bung bucket — both financial and carnal — had remained conspicuously empty. God knows he'd tried often enough in the two weeks since he'd boarded the *Ostentania*, but neither variety of perk had come his way. Truth to tell, his best efforts to score in both fields had resulted only in a reversal of the accepted norms, in so much as an offer for a hump *had* been forthcoming, but from a gin-sodden old slag that even his grandfather would have knocked back — and his grandfather had been dead ten years. On the tips front, meantime, the only one he'd received had been from a curvy Essex girl of sophisticated mien, who, on being served a wrongly mixed *Freddy Fudpucker* cocktail for the umpteenth time, had told him, "I'll give you a tip, mate — take early bleedin' retirement — soon!"

Such disappointments aside, Andy was enjoying the experience of working on a cruise ship. It was a complete change from being a rookie detective, although the purpose of his being here at all *was* essentially to detect if contraband cigarettes were being shipped on the *Ostentania*, and if so, how and by whom? However, to do this effectively, he had to depend on being given advice and instruction from his superior undercover agent, James Alexander of Her

Majesty's Department of Revenue and Customs. To date, no advice and instruction had come Andy's way. "Gentleman Jim", as Officer Alexander was covertly referred to by fellow members of the ship's company, was a widower nearing retirement age and, Andy suspected, had been shooed off on this mission to keep him from getting under the feet of other more career-motivated officers in their Leith HQ. Jim's cover on this case was to act as one of the *Ostentania*'s small group of dance hosts; middle-aged-to-elderly gentlemen, whose job it was to take to the floor with any unaccompanied, middle-aged-to-elderly female passengers at ballroom dancing events on board.

"Fookin' dance hosts?" Speedy Gonzales had growled on the first occasion Andy witnessed one of these "hosted dancing" sessions from behind the bar. "Fookin' male hoors, more like. Fookin' wrinkly giggleohs, tryin' like fook to get their fookin' mitts on a lorra lolly offa the old bints through their fookin' knicker elastic! Fookin' deesgoostin'!"

Gentleman Jim certainly had the air of an old charmer about him. Andy had to admit that. And he had to agree with Speedy's observation that he dressed so fookin' sharp you could shave with his underpants.

Andy sighed as he pondered the unfortunate downturn in bar business that had resulted from the current outbreak of norovirus. Today was even quieter than usual in the Stardust Lounge, as most of the passengers who hadn't been laid low by the bug seemed to prefer taking the air on deck, now that there was the majestic Rock of Gibraltar to gaze out at. And that's as near to sampling the charms of Gib as they'd get, for the present at least. No one was to be allowed ashore until all aboard had been declared healthy and the ship thoroughly decontaminated.

It was probably this last-mentioned activity that had turned people off coming indoors today. The whole ship reeked of commercial disinfectant. According to Speedy Gonzales, it hummed like a knockin' shop karzi in fookin' Algiers. Again, Andy could only take his word for this, as he'd never been to Algiers and the nearest he'd been to a knocking shop was when he'd helped investigate a robbery at a door-accessory retail outlet in Edinburgh's notably respectable New Town.

In an attempt to lure punters inside and, accordingly, ginger up bar sales, Mike Monihan, the effervescent, enjoy-yourselves-or-else Cruise Director, had even roped in the Sunbeam Band, the ship's general purveyors of dance music, to play an earlier-than-usual session in the Stardust Lounge today. This Happy Hour musical shift was normally manned by old Enrique Molinero, the lounge's resident cocktail pianist, but he, like a few dozen others, was still cabin-bound and quarantined in the grip of "the fookin' pukin' and dihoria-hi-hay," as Speedy so eloquently put it.

Mike Monihan, a blarney-blessed, fifty-something, failed rock star from Tipperary, was responsible, in his capacity as Cruise Director, for just about everything aboard the ship that the Captain and his officers were not. The onboard entertainment of the passengers was top of his priority list, with the overseeing of shore-excursion arrangements coming a close second.

There was good money to be made for Mike, derived from kickbacks from the owners of onshore "attractions" that he and his small team elected to guide the punters towards, so the current confined-to-ship decree was giving him a pain in the pocket. To make matters worse, his company bonus, related to punters' onboard bar spending, was taking a severe hit as well. Mike Monihan and norovirus outbreaks were not good shipmates.

His voice rang out over the ship's Tannoy system, cheerfully advising everyone of the special treat about to commence in the Stardust Lounge. A few moments later, he strode in, resplendent in sky-blue blazer and white slacks, his face radiating perma-tan, his bleached locks billowing in his own slipstream. He proceeded directly over the small dance floor to the stage, where he instructed the leader of the Sunbeam Band to wick up the amplification and hit the punters with something that would be bright and catchy enough to pull them in. A selection of Abba hits would do it, he advised, before striding back towards the door on his way to inflict, in the flesh, his persuasive verbal powers on the meek and vulnerable.

He paused at the bar. "Knock anodder twenty-five per cent offa duh price a' today's cocktail special for duh next half hour, why don'cha?" he muttered to Speedy. "Oy'll plug it over duh PA. Yeah, what we're needin' in here is a bunch a' die-hard ravers ta get tings goin'. Oh," he said as an after-thought, "and don't be forgettin' ta water down duh booze ta compensate for duh reduced price. Extra fruit juice, less alcohol, dat's duh game."

The musicians who comprised the Sunbeam Band were, in common with the majority of the "non-executive" members of the ship's company, natives of the Malay Archipelago. "The National Youth Orchestra of Indonesia" was how they were referred to by "Laugh-a-Minute" Lex McGinn, the bagpipe-playing comedian with the *Ostentania*'s troupe of entertainers on this particular cruise. Lex's allusion to "youth" was, to say the least, somewhat cynical, in that the Sunbeam Band's members had shed the bloom of juvenescence several decades ago. His describing them as an "orchestra" was not without a deliberate touch of irony either, as their line-up totalled but five. He was correct, however, in saying that they were Indonesian; a people not noted, if the Sunbeam Band were anything to go by, for the musical gift of perfect pitch. In Laugh-a-Minute's view, even his comedy bagpipes routine sounded more in tune than the racket produced by this bunch of old buskers from the streets of Jakarta. But, like the rest of their good countrymen and women who manned the Ulanova Cruise Line's engine rooms, kitchens, laundries, dining rooms, maintenance squads and cabin-servicing departments, they came a helluva lot more cheaply than their "western" counterparts, and that suited the bean-counters in company headquarters splendidly. Any connoisseurs of musical intonation who found themselves partaking of a cruise aboard an Ulanova Line ship, therefore, could take their tuning forks and stuff them where it's been said that bean-counters, retentively, stuff their beans.

And so it came to pass that, while the tortured strains of Abba's *Mamma Mia, Dancing Queen* and *Fernando* Tannoyed discordantly from the ship and bounced off the majestic cliffs of Gibraltar, the bar of the Stardust Lounge remained woefully devoid of customers.

"Even the fookin' monkeys has shot the crow," Speedy Gonzales observed as he gazed forlornly out of the window towards the bare summit of the Rock. "*Sí*, and who the fook can blame the fookers?"

CHAPTER FOUR

LATER THAT EVENING, IN THE SWISH FOYER OF THE "HOTEL PALAS ATENEA", OVER-LOOKING THE PALM-FRINGED BAY OF PALMA, MALLORCA . . .

About eighteen months previously, Bob, Julie Bryson and Andy Green had found themselves rather bizarrely thrown together on the island of Mallorca during the course of an investigation into a murder that had taken place back in Scotland. On that occasion, Ian "Crabbie" Scrabster, a keyboard-playing entertainer in a Mallorcan holiday hotel, had helped them in their enquiries, though not entirely of his own free will. However, Ian and Bob were from the same corner of Scotland and had known each other at the local North Berwick High School in their youth. So Ian, a few years Bob's junior, had allowed sentiment and a lingering sense of respect for a senior pupil to get in the way of what he had at first considered to be his better judgement. He was soon to regret it.

But all's well that ends well, and that adventure had ultimately been concluded to the definite benefit of all concerned. This happy state of affairs had resulted, in no small measure, from the fact that Ian Scrabster was a gregarious, go-getting type of fellow. He had made the most of his years in Mallorca to familiarise himself with the "mechanisms" and machinations of island life and, in so doing, to establish as many potentially useful contacts as he could. There wasn't much or anyone of importance that Ian didn't now know, and his ability to use this knowledge to the benefit of his friends and acquaintances (particularly if there was a concurrent buck to be made for himself) had earned him the reputation of being the "Mr Fixit" of the English-speaking expat community of the island.

Who better than Ian "Crabbie" Scrabster, then, for Bob Burns to turn to now?

"I won't beat about the bush, Crabbie," he said, ushering his old friend up the sweeping stairway towards the residents' lounge. "We're here on police business — undercover business — investigating another *possible* murder."

For a bulky big chap, Ian Scrabster was surprisingly nimble of foot. He could get off the mark extremely sharply when circumstances dictated, and he could *stop* in his tracks equally quickly when the occasion suited him. It was the second of these two abilities that he employed now.

"No way, Bobby, man!" he exclaimed, his hands held palms-forward and shoulder-high. "Nah, nah, school days o' auld lang syne are one thing, but no way am I gonna get inveigled into another one o' your loony police capers. Nah, nah, I was lucky to come out o' the last one alive, so no way am I gonna —"

"Now, now, Ian, no need to get your breeks in a fankle," Julie soothingly interjected. She was smiling one of her most melting smiles. "We're not expecting you to get involved — just to give us the benefit of your advice, that's all."

"That's right," Bob verified, inspired to attempt a melting smile himself, "we just want to ask if there's maybe a string or two you can pull for us." Noting Ian's distinctly unmelting reaction to his smile, he promptly decided to resort to flattery.

But Ian was one step ahead of him. "And don't bother trying any of your soft-soap baloney on *me*," he said with a stern look. "I used to watch Kojak on telly as a kid, so I know how you sleekit cops operate. Do the big buttering-up act, then hit the victim with the pre-planned whammy once his defences are down."

Bob couldn't argue with that, and, consequently, he couldn't conceal a self-satisfied little smirk either.

Julie, not being strictly a cop and, therefore, not prone to feeling chuffed at receiving such backhanded praise, turned up the melting temperature instead. She patted Ian's ample midriff. "You've lost weight," she fibbed, "but a big boy like you shouldn't really diet. You, for one, can carry a fair amount of weight." She eyed him up and down — twice. "Hmm, you look a lot better with a bit of beef on you, I've always said."

Ian's defences dropped like a clown's baggy trousers. "Pfwah!" he pooh-poohed, lowering his eyes in feigned bashfulness. "Well, you know how it is — I wouldn't want to risk catchin' anorexia or somethin'."

Julie linked arms with him. "So, then, how does a nice, big, slap-up seafood dinner appeal to you? I'm told they do a *fabulous* lobster *a la plancha* in the El Laurel restaurant here."

Ian cocked a tell-me-more ear.

Julie duly told him more. "As a guest of Detective Inspector Bob Burns's expense account, naturally."

"*Yeah*?" Ian checked, grinning hopefully.

"Yeah," Julie nodded, pouting positively.

"Wait a minute," Bob objected, scowling worriedly.

But it was too late. Julie and Ian had already resumed their ascent of the sweeping stairway, arm-in-arm en route to the first-floor restaurant.

No sooner had they been shown to a window table by the maître d'hôtel, than Ian excused himself and headed for the gents' toilets.

"That'll be the big gannet going to make room for as much scran as he can stuff down his cakehole — and at *my* expense," Bob hissed at Julie. "What the hell got into you? Don't tell me you've never noticed how much that bloke can eat!"

Unruffled and manifestly unconcerned, Julie sat down at the table and smiled politely at the waiter as he unfolded a napkin on her lap. "*Muchas gracias, señor. Muy amable*."

"Yeah, thanks," Bob said askance, after the waiter had afforded him the same courtesy. Financial prudence — or rather the impending lack of it — was taking priority over dining room niceties in his league table of essentials right now. He waited until the waiter had left, then grouched, "I mean, Julie, one lobster between the three of us is gonna cost me more than I can justify on exies, but that bottomless pit Scrabster will probably gobble *three* all by himself." He countered her look of amused uninterest by adding,

"You're forgetting that the cruise line is only covering us for the cost of bed and breakfast here tonight, you know."

Pointedly ignoring that, Julie smiled up at the waiter as he arrived at Bob's side with the wine list. There would be no need for Señor Burns to study *la lista*, she informed him in perfect Spanish. Because, she went on, they had already decided. *Sí*, she affirmed, a bottle of the house's best *Cava* would do nicely — for starters, *por favor*.

Although Bob's knowledge of Spanish was on the sparse side of modest, he did know what *Cava* meant, and he also knew that the "best" qualification Julie had attached thereto translated into "expensive" in any language.

"Top-of-the-range Spanish champers!" he fumed. "What the hell are you ordering *that* for? This is a beer-and-crisps murder investigation we're on, not a swanky picnic by yon bonny banks o' Loch Lomond with your toff-Weegie chums from Whitecraigs bloody Tennis Club!"

Espying Ian emerge from the gents' toilets, Julie quietly but firmly reminded Bob that it had been his idea to phone his old chum as being the only person even remotely likely to be able to find a way for them to join the *Ostentania* cruise. "Nothing for nothing" was Ian's maxim, she stressed, even for auld-lang-syne school acquaintances, and if Bob could think of a more economical way of connecting to Ian's do-a-good-turn bone than through his stomach, then he should say so now, or forever hold his peace.

"But," was as far as Bob got in an attempt to reason with her.

"But," was also the first word in her rebuttal. "But," she told him behind a cupped hand as Ian homed in, looking ominously refreshed and ravenous, "if my theory doesn't work, I'll gladly cough up for tonight's posh nosh out of my own toff-Weegie pocket!"

"Phooh! Well now," Ian puffed, after he'd pulled up a chair, "I've turned fair peckish all of a sudden. Do you, ehm, do ye maybe fancy something to pick at before we get stuck into the lobsters?" He flipped open a menu. "They do a fair-to-middlin' line in angels-on-horseback oysters in here, if I mind right." His eyes lit up as they lighted on the relevant entry on the bill of fare. "Yeah, there they are! *Fabuloso*!" Frowning expectantly now, he scanned the menu further. "Hmm," he hummed, "I wonder if they've got any of the, uhm . . . now, let me see." His eyes followed his forefinger hungrily down the list of seafood goodies. "Bingo!" he barked. "*Raoles de jonquillo*!" He glanced momentarily at Bob and Julie. "That's fritters made with these tiny-wee transparent fish they call gobies or something in English. Very rare here now — very expensive, so ye've *got* to order them up if ye ever get the chance."

Bob blanched.

Ian continued to study the menu, his facial expression indicating a growing sense of disappointment. "What a drag," he muttered, "I was hopin' they'd have some *chipirones* and *angulas* as well." He beckoned the waiter and spoke solemnly to him in Spanish.

Bob's expression grew darker while Ian's glowed sunnier with each word of the waiter's reply.

"Magic!" Ian grinned at Bob. "They've just had a delivery. A bucket o' each. No time to put them on the specials menu yet. You'll love them — the wee baby cuttlefish, deep-fried 'til they're nice and crispy, and the wee baby eels, served in bubblin' hot olive oil wi' a rake o' garlic. Great delicacies, ye know."

Bob also knew that the "baby" word usually translated into "expensive" in all things epicurean. Any ailing appetite he might have been nursing was now receiving the last rites from his police credit card.

"*Oiga*!" Ian called after the departing waiter.

Bob understood just one word in Ian's ensuing question — *Caviare*, which everyone understands means *very* expensive in any language.

Ian gave Bob a hearty slap on the shoulder. "We-e-ell, Bobby," he drawled, "may as well have a few wee nibbles up front to keep us busy, know what I mean? Can sometimes take them a wee while to dish up the lobsters." He laughed a bonhomie-promoting laugh. "Got to catch the buggers first, eh?"

"Mm-hmm," Bob droned, doomily.

"Yeah," chirped Ian, "and it's not every day we get to live it up as guests o' Lothian and Borders Police, right?"

"Right," Bob agreed, po-faced, while silently concluding that this would doubtless turn out to be the first and last of any such days. If his boss Bruce McNeill chanced to be a fly on the wall here now . . . No, he told himself, that didn't even bear thinking about. Speaking his mind in no uncertain manner to the bosses was one thing, but playing fast and loose with police expenses was quite another. "*You* won't just swan about on police exies," Bruce had said trustingly to him. And OK, so Julie had offered to pick up the tab if everything went pear-shaped, but he'd never stoop to letting her do that either. Amazing, he pondered, the hang-ups a Presbyterian upbringing can give you. Nah, dammit, he'd already allowed things to start getting out of hand here, so he'd just have to go with the flow now and hope for the best.

The popping of a *Cava* cork behind his back jolted him out of his ruminations.

"Whee-ee-ee!" Julie squealed. "Party time!" She held out her glass to the wine waiter. "Bubbly!" she grinned at him as he poured. "*Viva la vida loca, sí?*"

"*Sí, señorita,*" the waiter smiled back, then filled Bob's and Ian's glasses in turn. "*Salud, señores*!" he said, before placing the bottle in an ice bucket by Bob's side. "*Viva la vida loca*! To the crazy life, no?"

"Crazy life, right enough," Ian commented, looking round at the plush furnishings, then out to the spectacular Bay of Palma, its waterfront bristling with the masts of rank upon rank of luxury yachts. "What prompted the stingy old Edinburgh police to splash out on all this for ye, Bobby? Like, I mean to say, who the hell's been murdered — the Governor o' the Bank o' Scotland or Sean Connery or somebody?"

"Maybe nobody," Bob shrugged, "but all I'm bothered about for now is getting on a cruise ship called the *Ostentania*, as I told you on the phone."

Like a poker player surveying the hand he'd just been dealt, there was a lightly veiled look of intrigue on Ian's face as he took a slug of his *Cava* and settled back into his seat. "I'm all ears, Bobby. Tell me all about it, friend. Tell me a-a-all about it."

Bob began to repeat the details of the briefing he'd been given by Detective Superintendent Bruce McNeill the previous day, but no sooner had he revealed the identity of the figure central to the case than Ian motioned him to hold it right there.

A platter of baby cuttlefish had just arrived. Ian dipped one into an accompanying bowl of garlicky *all-i-oli* mayonnaise, then popped the tiny, sizzling mollusc into his mouth. "Magic them, Bobby," he drooled. He nudged Julie with his elbow. "Come on, Doc, get wired in. Cop for the *chipirones* while they're nice and hot." He then copped for another two himself.

"As I was saying . . ." Bob said.

"As you were saying," Ian mumbled through a mouthful of semi-masticated molluscs, "wee Rab Dykes is the deceased." He gave Bob a sly wink. "I'd add the word *alleged*, if I were you."

Bob eyed him warily. "So, you know him?"

"Wee Rab?" Ian said offhandedly. "Oh aye, I know him fine." He was concentrating on the plate of goby fritters that had now been delivered to the table. "Hmm, magic," he enthused, then pronged one of the crisp little golden spheres with his fork. "Pure magic, by the way, the wee *jonquillo* pancakes." He elbowed Julie again. "Go for it, darlin'. Very rare, the wee *jonquillos*."

And very bloody expensive, Bob reminded himself, before urging Ian to get back to the subject of wee Rab Dykes.

Wee Rab, Ian disclosed between gobfuls of gobies, had been coming on holiday to Mallorca once a year for about as long as anyone could remember. For two weeks every July, he'd book the same modest studio apartment along the coast in the resort of Palma Nova. The apartment block was only a stone's throw from the Hotel Santa Catalina, where Ian, alias Juan the singing Spanish keyboard player, did his regular gig six nights a week. Wee Rab Dykes seldom missed a session during the duration of his holiday. Most nights, he'd be in the hotel's Bow Bells Lounge, propping up the bar and loudly chewing the fat with fellow Brit holidaymakers, while Ian churned out endless medleys of singalong requests for Reg and Dot from Coventry, Alf and Liz from Slough, Gus and Senga from Aberdeen, the golden-wedded Joneses from Cardiff, the honeymooning O'Donovans from Dublin, and so on and so on and so on, ad *Lady In Red*-slobbering, *Birdie Song*-twittering, *Viva España*-bellowing nauseam.

Ian had got to know Rab fairly well over the years, eventually even dropping his "Spanish Juan" veneer for occasional two-Jocks-together chinwags over a lunchtime burger and a beer or two at the Cantina Sol bar on Palma Nova beach.

"What about his wife?" Bob asked.

"What about her?" Ian replied.

"Well, what's she like? What sort of person is she?"

Ian shook his head as a caviare-heaped croute disappeared behind his front teeth. "Search me, man. I've never clapped eyes on her, and neither has anybody else here. Never ever came on holiday wi' Rab, as far as I know. Somebody once said she was a cut above him, though. Married beneath her station, sort o' thing."

"And Rab always stayed in the same simple pad here, you say?"

"For simple, read dump. He invited me back to it for a drink once. No kiddin', I had to fight off a herd o' cockroaches attacking the packet o' Hula Hoops he opened specially for the occasion." Ian nodded pensively during munches of canapé, then said, "Yeah, that's why it struck me as strange the last time he showed up."

"That's why what struck you as strange?"

"Eh?" Ian said, his eyes fixed longingly on the last *jonquillo* fritter on the communal plate.

Impatiently, Bob forked the fritter for him. "Just you have it, for Christ's sake, Crabbie, then tell me what struck you as strange about wee Rab's last visit!"

Ian made a token gesture of offering the fishy nibble to Julie, who made a be-my-guest gesture in return. He accepted the invitation without hesitation.

"So?" Bob prompted.

"So, what?" Ian replied.

Bob's patience tether was stretched to breaking point.

Julie recognised the signs, so she stepped swiftly into the conversational ring before verbal blows were thrown. Keeping Ian sweet, even during a freebie feeding frenzy like this, was of paramount importance, after all. "You were saying, Ian," she said, "that something struck you as strange the last time wee Rab was on the island."

"Oh that? Yeah, well it *was* strange. No doubt about it."

The arrival of the grilled lobsters saved Ian from having Bob force-feed the last remaining angel-on-horseback up one of his nostrils. Dispensing with the formality of making a token gesture to Julie this time, Ian popped the bacon-wrapped oyster directly into his own mouth.

"Wine!" he then gasped, a look of panic in his eyes. "We forgot to order wine for the main course!" He summoned the wine waiter with a snap of his fingers, then turned to his two fellow diners. "No need to see the wine list, eh? I'll just fix us up wi' a bottle o' the *Albariño*. A fantastic white from Galicia, by the way. Great wi' seafood."

Julie looked a tad crestfallen. "Oh," she said, a trace of disappointment on her puckered lips, "I was going to suggest a *Viña Esmeralda* from Catalunya. Fantastic with shellfish. Just right to accompany lobster *a la plancha*, I'd have thought."

"I suppose both kinds are appropriately extravagant?" Bob muttered to two pairs of deaf ears.

A spirited debate about the relative merits of each wine was already under way between the owners of those ears.

"Look," Bob eventually cut in, "why waste time arguing about it? Just damn-well order a bottle of each, why don't you?"

He was being blatantly sarcastic, of course, but Ian took him at his word and started instructing the waiter accordingly.

Bob braced himself to raise an objection.

Ian raised a lobster claw.

"Take it easy, Bobby," he said. "Just relax, huh? I've a hunch your wee Rab Dykes business is gonna work out fine, OK?"

"Yeah, but —"

"Yeah, but let's get the *really* important business out of the way first, right? Let's have five minutes silence!" With that, Ian proceeded, in silence, to dismantle and devour his hotplate-grilled lobster like the true lobster-dismantling and devouring expert he was.

Five minutes later, Ian, with only the crustaceous residue of his expertly devoured main course remaining on his plate, was wiggling his seafood-tainted finger tips in a little bowl of lemony water. Bob and Julie, meanwhile, were still scraping, scooping, pulling, cracking and winkling gamely away at their respective *half* lobsters.

"Aye," Ian burped, a mite critically, Bob thought. And he thought right, because Ian went on to say, "Aye, considerin' the outrageous price, there's not a lot o' eatin' in a lobster these days."

"Still, as long as you enjoyed it," Bob mumbled, a touch testily.

Ian burped again, affirmatively this time. "You bet, Bobby. Yeah, Lothian and Borders Police are doin' us proud, eh?"

Bob choked on a flake of lobster shell.

Julie slapped his back.

Unperturbed, Ian slouched down in his seat, slurped a slug of *Albariño*, smiled the smile of the well-sated and unfastened the top button of his trousers. "Ah-h-h-h," he exhaled expansively, "I'll just let everything settle down a wee bit before we cop for the cheeseboard."

"While it's all in the process of settling down," Bob wheezed, "maybe you'd get back to the subject of wee Rab Dykes."

"Oh aye, that. Yeah, I just about forgot about that for a minute there. What, ehm, what was it ye wanted to know again, man?"

"What we wanted to know," Julie calmly replied, while Bob vented his mounting frustration by ripping off a lobster leg, "was why you thought there was something strange about wee Rab's last visit here."

Ian assumed an air of nonchalance. "Oh, just that his circumstances seemed to have changed, that's all."

"For better or worse?" Bob snapped, then did likewise to the lobster leg.

"Would it answer yer question if I told ye he turned up at the Hotel Santa Catalina on his first night here in a black Rolls-Royce — chauffeur-driven?"

Bob's droll riposte was that it seemed a slightly spendthrift way of getting from a humble studio apartment just a short way along the street — even for a flash bampot like Rab.

Ian gave a smug little smirk. "Ah, but that's where the *really* strange bit comes in."

"Obviously, you're going to tell us he wasn't staying at the humble studio apartment this time," Julie speculated. "Would that be right?"

"On the nose, Doc. Yeah, ye see, Rab could hardly wait to tell me all about it. Came straight over to my keyboard perch in the corner of the Bow Bells Lounge and shouted it in my ear durin' the last chorus of *The White Cliffs of Dover*. Oh, I was singin' that one, incidentally, because there was this reunion o' RAF oldies in the hotel, and —"

"Just cut to the chase," Bob butted in. "*What* could wee Rab hardly wait to tell you about?"

Ian raised a patience-prompting hand. "All in good time, Bobby. All in good time." He lowered his hand and laid it on Bob's forearm. "Listen, old mate, when ye've lived in Spain as long as I have, ye've learned that adopting the *mañana* attitude is the only way. Yeah, absolutely," he nodded sagely, "and ye get there just the same." He poured Bob a glass of *Viña Esmeralda*. "Get that down ye, boy. Get that down ye."

"That's right," said Julie. "When in Spain, do as the Spaniards do. Be *tranquilo*. In other words, chill, Kemosabe, chill."

"My sentiments entirely," Ian concurred, while simultaneously hailing the waiter with a *tranquilo* wave of his hand. "I've just remembered — they do a great lemon syllabub here. Ace for freshenin' up the chops after all that seafood stuff, eh? Yeah, we'll enjoy the cheeses a lot more after a nice lemon syllabub." He noticed Bob's face flushing. "It's OK, Bobby," he said with a soothing smile. "Don't go chokin' yerself again. No need to rush the last wee bits o' your half lobster. Nah, no sweat — it'll take them five minutes or so to fix the syllabubs, anyway. Oh aye, all freshly made, ye know."

By now, Julie was beginning to see that Ian was deliberately stalling — not for any malicious reason, she reckoned, but purely to get Bob niggled. It was working, and Ian was thoroughly enjoying the experience. So was she.

"Listen to me, Crabbie," Bob spluttered, the last wee bits of his half lobster making good their escape through his tightly drawn lips, "this is a murder investigation, *not* a bloody excuse for chomping our way through the entire inventory of the Hotel Palas Atenea's goddam kitchens!"

Slowly, Ian lifted his shoulders. "Gather ye rosebuds while ye may. That's what I always say, Bobby." He turned to Julie and gave her a conspiratorial wink. "Yeah, and if my hunch is right, Doc, this won't be the last Lothian and Borders Police rosebud we'll be gatherin'."

That did it. Bob had been on edge about being assigned to this case from minute one, and all this time-wasting *and* costly stuff from Ian was about to tip him right over that selfsame edge. "Right, Crabbie," he rasped, "enough of the messing about! If you've got anything helpful to say, say it! Otherwise, just order the biggest millwheel of cheese they've got, eat the whole bloody lot, and then bugger off before I've spent the entire annual budget of every police canteen in the city of Edinburgh!"

Ian burst out laughing.

As did Julie. Unlike Bob, she had been keeping up with Ian in the consumption of *Cava* and wine throughout the meal, and the effects were beginning to sparkle in her eyes. "Lighten up, Kemosabe," she beamed, tickling Bob under the chin, "and just be patient. Good wee boys don't open their presents before Christmas morning, you know."

"What the hell are you blethering about?"

"Only that I'm sure Ian will tell you whatever he knows — *if* he knows anything — in his own good time." Theatrically, she swept a hand round their ritzy surroundings. "Meanwhile, just be patient and enjoy." She clinked Bob's glass with her own. "*Viva la vida loca, sí*?"

Bob paid no heed. By now, he had fixed Ian with a steely, silent stare, and no amount of half-tiddly glass-clinking was about to divert him from it.

Ian got the message. "OK, OK, Bobby," he chuckled, "maybe I've done enough o' the mysterious bit now, right enough. It was just a harmless wee leg-pull. A wind-up. No offence, eh?"

Bob didn't even blink. "That depends on what you've actually got to say. As I told you a minute ago, *if* you've got anything to say, come right out and say it now!" He fired a cutting glance at Julie. "*I*'m working

— *not* swanking about on a tennis club picnic by yon bonny banks o' Loch Lomond."

"You've lost me on that one, man," Ian shrugged. "But, anyway, here's how the cookie crumbles . . ."

He began to relate how, as soon as Bob had mentioned the *Ostentania* on the phone earlier in the day, he had put two and two together. The disappearance at sea of Rab Dykes had been reported in the *Majorca Daily Bulletin* that morning, and, as Rab was an Edinburgh criminal and Bob was an Edinburgh policeman, it didn't take Sherlock Holmes to deduce why Bob was keen to get aboard the liner in question. Then, a phone call from Mike Monihan on the *Ostentania* itself had sown the seeds in Ian's mind of how to get Bob to join the cruise, irrespective of the company's stated policy to the contrary.

"Wait a minute. Just press the pause button right there," Bob said. "This is all going a bit too fast for my PC Plod-like brain. For a start, who the blazes is this Mike Monihan?"

Ian explained that he'd got to know Mike when the Irishman had knocked around Mallorca a few years previously. He'd been just one of countless wannabe pop stars who fail to make the grade and end up in holiday hotspots like this, hoping eventually to get their big break by being "discovered" singing in some third-rate tourist bar or club. Like the vast majority of these ever-hopefuls, Mike never did get discovered. He had put together a Status Quo tribute band with three other guys, who also had more optimism than talent, and they'd never managed to climb out of the bottom-league bar and club trap. In fact, the band was so rank that even those last-chance-saloon gigs quickly dried up. Mike was reduced to scrounging a living peddling drugs to silly young holidaymakers on the nocturnal streets of neon-blazing resorts like Magaluf. Then, like so many before him, he got hooked himself on the dope he was pushing, defaulted on his payments to the main dealers, who swiftly arranged for him to have a reality check at the hands of a trio of heavies in a back alley one moonless night.

Mike had then disappeared for a couple years, during which, Ian subsequently learned, he had gone to Balgonia, both to get himself "clean" and to try his hand afresh at making it as a pop star via that country's nascent tourist scene. He had succeeded at the former, but failed yet again at the latter.

So, Bob wanted to know, and urgently at that, what had all this long-winded diatribe about an ex-junkie Status Quo imitator got to do with an investigation into the disappearance at sea of wee Rab Dykes?

"It's the Balgonia connection, isn't it?" Julie ventured, her sharp forensic intellect cutting through the *Cava* and wine-promoted onset of mental fuzziness like a well-honed knife through melting butter.

"The Doc's right on the money as usual," Ian said. "Ye see, the Ulanova Cruise Line's home port just happens to be Grabna."

"Balgonian seaport on the Black Sea," Julie advised Bob in a schoolmarmish way that rankled sufficiently for him to curtly remind her that he wasn't *entirely* uneducated himself!

"All right," he said to Ian, "so Mike Monihan's doing his Status Quo thing in Balgonia, gets in with somebody in the Ulanova Line's office in Grabna and lands a job on the *Ostentania*. I think," he added with a chilly sidelong glance at Julie, "that even my underdeveloped policeman's grey matter is just about capable of working that one out unaided."

"Oo-oo-ooh! Getting all defensive again, are we?" Julie warbled, her generous champers and wine intake propagating a display of her female gift for cattiness.

"Your claws are showing," Bob mumbled.

"*Mee-ee-ow!*" Julie miaowed, then started to giggle.

Bob shook his head, clearly not best pleased. "You're half pissed. Not an attractive image for an educated forensic scientist to present."

"We're all educated, us scientists. Education — science — education — science. The two things go hand-in-hand, see?" Glassy-eyed, Julie grinned as an amusing thought came to mind. "Yes, science and education. I mean, one thing's no good without the other, is it? A bit like a toad without a stool, or a fairy without a cake, or a jock without a strap, or — or — or a pigeon without a hole. Stuff like that." She giggled again, pretending to swipe Bob's face with her claws. "Or even a cat without a suit. *Mee-ee-ow!*"

"Or a policeman without the patience of Job?" Bob tartly suggested.

Julie wagged a woozy finger in his face. "Nup, that doesn't work. Wordplay, see, and you have missed the point cupleely."

"Cupleely?" Bob queried, stonefaced.

"Yup, cu-*plee*-ly!"

While he waited for Bob's temperature to come back down to the simmer, Ian quaffed a leisurely draught of the last of the *Albariño*, then continued . . .

What wee Rab Dykes had been so keen to tell him after arriving at the Hotel Santa Catalina in a chauffeur-driven Rolls Royce was that, as a lifelong supporter of Glasgow Rangers football team, it had been in the hospitality suite at one of the Rangers' home games that he'd first met the man who, it eventually transpired, was the owner of several such Rollers. One thing had led to another, and wee Rab had ultimately been taken into this man's employ as his investments manager. "Oh," Ian added, "and the same man also happens to own the Ulanova Cruise Line, which Irish Mike Monihan —"

"— joined while in Grabna, Balgonia?" Bob checked.

"On the nose," Ian confirmed.

Bob scratched his head. "OK, OK, let's leave the Mike Monihan thing for now. Let's just go back and concentrate on wee Rab Dykes for a moment, right? I mean, why on earth would anyone want to employ *him* as their investments manager? I'd imagine that what that wee numpty knew about stocks and shares would amount to less than I know about do-it-yourself brain surgery."

Ian tapped the side of his nose, then winked a wink of almost Masonic confidentiality. "Ah, but ye see, Rab didn't have to know *any*thing about stocks and shares to be *this* particular man's investments manager — so called."

"Oh yeah? How come?"

"Well, all he had to do was buy the shares he was told to."

"Using his so-called employer's money, I presume."

"Naturally."

"A front, in other words, for an investor not regarded in too favourable a light by those whose shares he wanted to buy, right?"

Ian didn't even have to answer that one.

But Bob was onto the point like a ferret up an unguarded trouser leg. "So, why would those same shareholders want to sell to a petty criminal like Rab Dykes instead?"

"Because wee Rab would only be acting as an *advisor*," Julie put in, the restoration of her composure having been prudently entrusted to a large glass of iced water. "He'd only be the sniffer-out of available shares, while the *actual* buying would be put in the hands of a broker, representing, presumably, a cryptically named investments company." She doffed an imaginary deerstalker. "Elementary, my dear Kemosabe, elementary."

"Kemosabe — the nickname of the Lone Ranger," Ian observed. "Well, well, well — life *is* full of little coincidences, wouldn't you say?"

"And even someone *slightly* squiffy like me," Julie said, "can figure out that it wasn't a *lone* Ranger that the rich Roller man wanted to buy, but an entire team of them."

Bob was already well up to speed in the coincidences stakes. "Glasgow Rangers Football Club," he muttered. "And at their games, wee Rab would be rubbing shoulders with loads of fellow supporters who also happened to be small shareholders in the club. Hmm, the jigsaw pieces are falling into place, gradually." He looked Ian in the eye again. "You know wee Rab's mysterious bankroller, do you?"

Ian hunched his shoulders. "Maybe. Do you?"

Bob canted his head, then replied archly. "I believe I may well do at that." He glanced at Julie. "Wouldn't you agree . . . *baryshnja*?"

"If dey no can makink borscht soups vid *pampushki* dumplinks here . . . ?" she prompted.

"I go eatink some odder fockink place?" Bob responded rhetorically.

"Hey, cut all the double talk!" Ian bristled. "I'm trying to help you guys out here, so what's this borscht-and-fockink-dumplinks-somewhere-else crap all about?"

"Take it easy, Crabbie," Bob laughed. "Nobody's trying to do you out of an extra feed or anything like that. No, it's just a flashback to a recent encounter we had in front of the Castle Inn back home in Dirleton, that's all." Going all business-like now, he leaned forward and folded his hands on the table. "But more of that in good time. First, let's get back to your man Mike Monihan, OK?"

Between chops-freshening spoonfuls of syllabub, Ian proceeded to relate how, since landing the job as de facto Entertainments Manager on the *Ostentania*, Mike had occasionally asked him to go on cruises to fill in for one entertainer or another who'd called off at the last minute. Ian had actually taken up his offer a couple of times, just to have a break from the year-in-year-out routine of his Bow Bells Lounge residency. These *Ostentania* trips had been during the winter months, when things were relatively quiet in the Hotel Santa Catalina, anyway. The management there didn't mind him taking such off-season sabbaticals once in a while, as long as he organised an adequate keyboard player to deputise.

Ian went on to say that, shortly after Bob had phoned today, he had received a call from Mike Monihan on the *Ostentania*, panicking because old Enrique Molinero, the resident cocktail pianist in the ship's Stardust Lounge, had just succumbed (terminally) to the dreaded norovirus bug. As Mike had put it, in typical musicianly terms, old Enrique would now be playing in Gabriel's backing band in the Pearly Gates Nightclub, so would Ian *please* fly down to Gib to take his chair at the Stardust's baby grand for a couple of weeks? Mike's hunch was that the ship would probably be setting sail for the Canaries sooner than originally anticipated, and the London entertainment agent who normally booked the acts for the Ulanova Line had been unable to get a replacement for old Enrique at such short notice. It *was* the height of the summer season, after all. For the same reason, however, Ian had had to turn Mike's request down.

Bob was beginning to fidget, but before he could tell Ian to cut to the chase again, Ian piped up that it was the news of old Enrique's death that had presented him with the perfect plan for how to get Bob installed on the *Ostentania* for the resumption of its current cruise.

Once more, Bob almost choked. "Training for undercover CID work didn't include a course on how to play *Chopsticks*, Crabbie, so forget it. I will *not* be doubling as the new Enrique, even if I *never* find out what really happened to wee Rab Dykes!"

It was Ian's turn to laugh now. "*Tranquilo*, man, just be *tranquilo* and calm down, eh! I wouldn't expect *you* to make an arse of yourself like that." He shook his head vigorously. "No, no, no, it was the *Doc* here I planned to plant as an entertainer on the boat!"

If the ice-cold water hadn't completely sobered Julie up, this last pronouncement by Ian went a long way towards helping it on its way.

"Well, I," she flustered, "I mean, I could, you know, if I was pushed, I could maybe still remember a bit of Debussy's *Claire de Lune* from my days at old Miss McKrindle's piano classes in Whitecraigs. But, well, that was a long time ago — twenty-plus years — and I, well, to play those few bars all night in front of . . ."

Ian was laughing so much he didn't immediately notice the waiter arriving at his side with a trolley laden with cheeses of all shapes, sizes and hues. "Nah, you've got it all wrong, Doc," he chuckled. "I wouldn't expect *you* to make an arse of yerself, either."

"How generous!"

"Nah, the thing is, you're an educated woman. A scientist, right?"

"A toad with a stool," Bob wryly confirmed. "A pigeon with a hole, even. Figuratively speaking in both cases, of course."

Julie was temporarily dumbstruck. A few persistent threads of alcohol-woven cobwebs were still clinging to her normally rapid mental reactions.

Ian stepped in to move things along. "Ye see, Doc, it's old Enrique's *wife* I've planned for ye to replace."

While Bob and Julie's eyes met in looks of total bewilderment, Ian's met the recently arrived trolley and surveyed the cheese selection with keen anticipation.

"Hm-mm-mm," he purred, "magic!" Without diverting his gaze, he said to the waiter, "A wedge of the *Manchego*, a slice of the *Mahón*, a lump of the *Tetilla*." He paused to glance at Bob. "*Tetilla* means 'tit', by the way, Bobby. Good name for a cheese, eh? Cow, milk, tit — see what I mean?"

"It could also be a good name for what you're taking me for," Bob rounded. "And if you think that —"

"Ah-*hem*!" Julie coughed in her usual oil-on-troubled-waters way. "I think you'll find, Ian, that *tetilla* actually translates more accurately as 'nipple', which —"

"Which," Bob interjected, "would mean that he's taking me for a sucker. Same difference!" He turned back to Ian. "So, like I said before, just stuff your guts 'til they're full of all the cheese they can hold, and then do me a favour and —"

"And arrange for both of you to get on the *Ostentania* trip for free?" Ian serenely suggested. "*Plus* cop you a few hundred quid in pocket money? Oh!" — He raised a point-making forefinger — "And neither of you would need to tickle a single ivory, by the way."

Ian savoured a *tetilla*-flavoured moment or two while Bob and Julie exchanged puzzled looks again.

"You see, Bobby," he said, his smile exuding over-the-top congeniality, "don't take this personal, like, but for a sleuth of some seniority, you're a wee bit apt to jump to the first conclusion at times. And that, as we all know, is seldom the best policy." He speared a hunk of *Manchego*, then tapped his temple with the handle of the cheese knife. "Accentuate the devious, eliminate the obvious."

"Get to the point, Crabbie!"

"The point, Bobby, is — eh, wait a minute 'til I grab a handful o' grapes here — yeah, the point is, Bobby, that the Doc here is an educated woman. Right, Doc?"

Bob and Julie frowned the affirmative.

"And geography would be included in said education?" Ian further checked.

An uneasy nodding of heads.

"And," Ian went on, "I presume a well-travelled young lady like yerself will have at least a passing knowledge o' the Canary Islands?"

Suddenly, Julie felt the tension abate a bit. She had, in fact, been to all of the major Canary Islands at one time or another — either on childhood holidays with her parents, or later, during summer jaunts with fellow students from Glasgow University. She told Ian all of this, although still at a complete loss as to what it had to do with the stalled-at-the-starting-gate investigation into wee Rab Dykes's disappearance.

Ian's *Mahón*-munching face opened into a cheesy smile. "Old Enrique's newly widowed wife. See where I'm comin' from?"

Formation shaking of heads.

"So, Bobby, ye didn't bother to study the *Ostentania*'s entertainments programme in the schedule they send to every punter before every cruise?"

Silently, Bob waited for the sting.

"Enrique's wife was the shore lecturer — givin' the punters bags o' spiel in the ship's theatre or wherever about the best things to see and do at each port o' call. Naturally, she's jacked in the gig because o' old Enrique poppin' his clogs all of a sudden, and on top o' that she's got a serious heart condition."

"So?" Bob said.

"So, when Irish Mike Monihan gave me his hardluck story about all this on the blower today, I volunteered the Doc here as a dep for Enrique's old lady." He thumb-flicked a grape into his mouth, then told Julie, "Should be a piece o' cake. She's leavin' all her lecture notes and slides and stuff behind. No probs for an educated woman like you, eh?"

Julie was taken aback. "I, uhm — well, I don't — I don't know quite what to say . . ."

"I do," said Bob. "Where do I figure in this?"

"You go too. Lecturer's partner. Full passenger status for ye both. Outside cabin. All inclusive and free — except drinks, that is, but ye get discount on them." Ian pulled a one-shouldered shrug. "No big deal. That's the way it always is on the boats for the lecturers."

Julie still looked apprehensive.

Ian poured her the last of the *Viña Esmeralda*. "Get that down ye, darlin'. Get that down ye!"

"No thanks, Ian. You have it. I — I think I'll . . . water. I'll just, ehm, stick with the water now, if you don't, uhm . . ."

Bob was thinking fast. "OK, Crabbie, what kind of doctor did you tell this Mike Monihan guy that Julie is?"

Ian shrugged again. "Nothin'. Ye can tell him what ye like yerselves, but he won't give a monkey's anyway. The 'doctor' tag's enough to impress his punters, and that's all he's bothered about."

"Fair enough," Bob replied, "and I take it you didn't give him any hint about what I do?"

"Just told him ye were some sort of hanger-on o' the Doc's, that's all. Yeah, I mean, most o' these intellectual bints who do shore lectures on the boats have got some other boffin type taggin' along." Ian winked at Julie. "A load of them are females as well, of course, so the *Ostentania* crew will think Bobby here is a bit, well, not quite so butch as he makes out."

Bob didn't dignify that with a response.

Julie did. "They wouldn't think that if they knew he'd insisted on me packing my old school uniform."

Ian gave a dirty chuckle.

Bob cleared his throat, loudly, then swiftly informed Ian, "I'm travelling as a freelance journalist, as it happens. Doing research into a magazine feature on cruising."

"Yes, and I'll be helping him with that as well," Julie added.

Ian raised both shoulders this time. "Look, suit yerselves about all that undercover stuff. I couldn't care less." He trowelled another dollop of *Manchego* onto a cracker, then said to Julie, "Just tell me if ye're up for this wheeze or not. Mike Monihan's dependin' on ye, so if ye're gonna bottle out, I'll have to let him know pronto."

Bob looked at her. "Well, it's entirely up to you. I wouldn't want to force you into anything uncomfortable."

"Except maybe her old school uniform?" Ian suggestively proposed.

Bob gave him an exaggeratedly bored look. "All right, all right, Crabbie, you've already had your smutty little snigger about that joke, so drop it, OK!" It was time to swiftly change the subject, and this he did by asking Ian, "Anyway, you said there would be some kind of *fee* involved for this shore-speaking stint?"

Ian nodded. "Six hundred quid nett for the fortnight."

"Nett?"

"Yeah — eight hundred gross, less commission."

"Two hundred quid to the London agent?"

Ian shook his head. "Nope." He tapped his breast bone. "To me. The London agent couldn't fill the bill, remember?"

Bob looked as if he was about to blow a gasket. "You — you mean to *say*," he spluttered, "— bloody oysters, lobsters, bubbly, gob-whatsit pancakes, wine and everything else you've rammed and poured down your cakehole at my expense, and now you're gonna rip me off for two hundred bloody quid as well?"

Ian smiled smugly. “Fancy some port wi’ the cheese, Bobby?” He hailed the wine waiter. “Bottle of *oporto, por favor*. The best.” He held up three fingers. “And three glasses, *gracias*.”

Bob held up two fingers. “Up yours, Crabbie! Cancel the port!”

Julie had been thinking away quietly to herself throughout this little exchange. “Not so fast,” she told Bob with an owlish look. “I take it that the fee, the six hundred quid, I’d earn for this lecturing lark wouldn’t involve Lothian and Borders Police in any way. I mean, it’d be mine to keep, right?”

Bob shifted a little uneasily in his chair. “Well, yeah, but *ours* would maybe be a better way of putting it.”

Any alcohol-spun cobwebs that had still been clinging to Julie’s senses were swiftly swept aside by that suggestion. She held up two fingers. “Up yours as well, Kemosabe! Cancel the trip!”

“So, you get six hundred, Crabbie here gets two hundred, and I get sweet Fanny Adams.” Bob was patently miffed. “Who’s being taken for a mug here? I ask myself.”

“You’re being paid for doing the job you’re employed to do,” Julie came back. “*My* six hundred smackers is for work above and beyond the call of duty.”

“Yeah, but —”

“Oh, I forgot to mention one other wee thing,” Ian butted in, a mischievous smile dimpling his cheeks. “The Ulanova Line’s gonna be making a full refund of the price ye paid for the cruise. Only fair that, considering the Doc's gonna be more or less an employee of theirs for the duration of the trip."

Julie whistled through her teeth. "That's the best part of four grand Lothian and Borders Police will be saving!"

Ian metronomed a forefinger. "Not quite, Doc. Nah, nothin' for nothin', that's the only way to survive in this game."

"Which means?" Bob enquired, a look of foreboding in his eye.

"Which means four grand *less* a fifteen per cent arranging fee."

"Which goes to?"

Ian tapped his breast bone again. "Me. Only fair, right?"

Bob didn't know whether to laugh or cry. Like Julie, his old school chum had him by the short and curlies, and there was damn all he could do about it. "Only fair," he agreed, though with undisguised reluctance. "So," he sighed, "if my arithmetic's right, Crabbie, you come out of this with a two-hundred-pound slice of Julie's fee and another six hundred from my illustrious employers, correct?"

Ian chuckled as he watched a look of pique spread over Bob's face. "Wrong, Bobby," he grinned. "Nah, I'll be making another coupla hundred or so from the Hotel Santa Catalina as well."

Bob's puzzled expression returned. "You've lost me," he scowled.

"Accent the devious, eliminate the obvious," was Ian's reply. He checked his watch, then made to stand up. “Yep, ’fraid we’ll have to leave the bottle o’ port ’til the next time.”

“Time to start your gig at the Hotel Santa Catalina?” Julie enquired.

“Nope — time to go and see my young brother. He’s just arrived on the island and he’s desperate for an earner to provide booze money for his holiday. Student, ye see, but a good keyboard player. He’ll fill in nicely for me in the Bow Bells Lounge for the next fortnight.” Ian surveyed Bob and Julie’s mystified looks for a moment, then said, “That’s where my extra two hundred folders come in.”

“You’d rip off your own brother?” Bob gasped.

“Just savin’ him from himself,” Ian coolly replied. “If he got the whole fee, he’d only bevvy it.” He glanced knowingly at Julie. “Ye know what students are like.”

Bob’s highly sensitive policeman’s nostrils were beginning to smell a rat. “And why,” he asked through a frown heavy with suspicion, “would you want to have another keyboard player fill in for you at a peak time of the year like this?”

Ian stood up, pulled his belly in and fastened the top button of his trousers. “Because, Bobby, my wee brother’s desperate for an earner and my old mate Mike Monihan’s desperate for a piano player — who will cop for eight hundred quid, all found, for the fortnight.”

Bob’s jaw dropped. “You don’t mean that you . . . the *Ostentania*?”

Ian slapped his back. “On the nose, Bobby. Yep, it sounds like a fun trip *and* ye’ll have all those extra expenses to throw about now that Lothian and Borders Police are gettin' the big refund." He looked at his watch again. "Anyway, must rush. See ye here for breakfast in the morning, eh?" He patted his stomach, then winked at Julie. "Like I said, this won't be the last Lothian and Borders Police rosebud we'll be gatherin'. Yeah, lookin' forward to the cruise already."

CHAPTER FIVE

THE FOLLOWING MORNING — ON THE TERRACE OF THE HOTEL PALAS ATENEA . . .

The morning sun was already shining warm and unblemished by even the merest feather of cloud in a sky the colour of a kingfisher's wing. Everything was calm and relaxed. *Totalmente tranquilo*, as the locals would say. Even the tall palms skirting the wide *Paseo Maritimo* boulevard in front of the hotel seemed to add an air of guiltless procrastination to the scene. People strolling in their shade were in no hurry to go anywhere. *Mañana*, it seemed, would be good enough for them. Beyond the *Paseo*, the sails of a solitary yacht were reflected on the shimmering mirror of the bay, while along by the fishermen's quay, two old men sat mending their nets at the water's edge. Occasional puffs of cigar smoke rose from beneath the tattered rims of their straw hats to drift lazily away on the limpid air. It was the type of Mallorcan morning that bestows good humour and contentment upon the most restless of souls. Except, seemingly, that of Detective Inspector Robert Burns of Lothian and Borders Police.

For Bob was looking a tad troubled, a shade bleary, a bit done in. "I didn't get much sleep last night," he said to Julie in tones that were a blend of anxiety and selfpity.

"Don't I know it?" she replied, her expression conveying both amazement and a touch of devilment. "And that was even with*out* me giving you the old-school-uniform treatment!"

Bob chose to let that crack pass without comment. He was too preoccupied with certain facets of the police job in hand to indulge Julie's little flippancies. While she was obviously feeling as fresh as a daisy and none the worse for her overindulgence in champers and wine last night, Bob's comparatively unsullied head was aching, his mind spinning with ifs and buts — and with whys as well, but with few, if any, wherefores.

"All these coincidences," he mumbled, massaging his temples. "Something stinks."

"That'll be the kippers," Julie opined.

Bob wasn't listening.

"Kippers. Sign of a good hotel," Julie resolutely continued. "Not usually found in Mediterranean parts, the old kippers. Imported, obviously. No herring in the Med, you know."

For all that he respected Julie's encyclopaedic knowledge of just about everything (except, apparently, the art of playing piano for the diversion of cruise ship passengers), there were times that this admirable and, on occasion, extremely useful trait could be a right pain in the arse. This was one of them.

"Yes," she continued airily, "no herring in the Med." Her well-educated mind was obviously clicking into zoology-revision mode. "*Clupeoid* family of fish, the herring. Same group as the sardine, you know. Well, sardines we call them, but they're actually just young pilchards. Hmm, no herring in the Med. Plenty of sardines, though. Anchovies too. Hmm . . ."

"Hmm," Bob hmm'd, his hmm-ing overlapping with Julie's, though on a different note entirely. His thoughts were firmly entrenched in things that Ian "Crabbie" Scrabster had said and done the previous evening. And although it struck him that there *was* something fishy about certain aspects of that, it had nothing to do with herring, sardines, pilchards, anchovies or, indeed, kippers. He allowed Julie to get on with her piscatorial musings while he got on with his own.

Coincidences, he pondered. Too many goddam coincidences. There was the brush with Boris Kaminski outside the Castle Inn back in Dirleton, and now it seems that he owns the cruise line that owns the ship that Andy Green just happens to be working on, and from which wee Rab Dykes either jumped or was dumped. Coincidences. Yes, and it also seems that wee Rab just happens to be involved with Kaminski in some financial caper involving the purchase of shares in Glasgow Rangers Football Club, which the two Glasgow Celtic supporters had obliquely alluded to outside the Castle Inn. Coincidences. Then there was this ex-junkie Mike Monihan and his chance employment by Kaminski's Balgonian cruise line. And now, on the very day that Bob called Crabbie for advice on how to get round the cancellation of his vital cruise on the *Ostentania*, Monihan calls Crabbie for help to fill a gap in the entertainments roster aboard the very same ship. Too many damned coincidences. Bob didn't like it.

On top of that, he didn't like the way Crabbie had scoffed all that food and drink last night, particularly when it turned out that he'd sussed all along what Bob's problem was *and* had already gone some considerable way towards solving it by volunteering Julie for the vacant shore lecturer's position aboard the *Ostentania*. That had simply been brass-necked abuse of Bob's police exies on Crabbie's part. No, Bob didn't like that at all, even if Julie's take on the situation was that pandering to his old pal's food fetish was still a cheap way for Lothian and Borders Police to kick-start an otherwise stalled investigation. No, it was the principle of the thing that bothered Bob. Bloody gannet, that Scrabster. And now he'd even wheedled his way onto the cruise himself. "Sounds like fun," he'd said. "Fun?" Bob exclaimed inwardly. Jeez, if this was Crabbie's idea of fun, he must have had a sense-of-humour bypass!

Then there was Crabbie's bare-faced exploitation of Bob's plight in order to benefit financially from it himself. Bob wasn't happy about that either. The best part of two grand would be Crabbie's slice of the action, when you totted up the percentages he'd be copping from Julie's lecturing fee, his young brother's depping money and the refund of the police's original outlay for Bob and Julie's cruise booking. Nah, not right, that sort of thing. Not an ethically acceptable way of going about things at all. Bob thought about that for a few moments, then concluded with a silent sigh that maybe it was just his own straight-laced Presbyterian conscience that was at fault. Maybe Crabbie was quite right to go for the main chance, to hack a pound of flesh off a passing milch-cow whenever the opportunity arose. Yeah, come to think of it, Crabbie would probably end up living in the lap of luxury here on the sunny Med, while Bob saw out his old age huddled over a police-sponsored, single-bar electric fire in some dreary old folks' home overlooking a railway marshalling yard on the outskirts of bloody Edinburgh.

However, that was all speculation — all part of the dim and distant future. Of more immediate concern to Bob was the workaday matter of keeping a mental grip on all the minutiae that drizzle down and mushroom up during any crime investigation. And one such piece of potentially crucial trivia had been Crabbie's somewhat throw-away comment the previous evening that he had a hunch the Rab Dykes business was going to work out fine. What exactly did he mean by that? And how much did he know regarding this "business" that he hadn't let on about so far? "Accent the devious, eliminate the obvious." Crabbie had said that twice last night. Significant? Or just a meaningless piece of his old chum's stock-in-trade bluster? And what about his glib comment that wee Rab was the *alleged* deceased? These were things that Bob knew he would have to work on. He stroked his chin and nodded his head pensively while he pondered those points.

"Hmm," he hmm'd to himself once more.

"Hmm," Julie independently hmm'd, her verbal revision of her own fishy subject still keenly ongoing, irrespective of Bob having turned a deaf ear. "Yes, that's right, no herring in the Med, although I'm sure there *is* a fish they refer to as a herring in the Black Sea. A *kerch* herring, they call it, if memory serves me correctly. Mmm, but I think it's actually more of what we'd call a shad. However, I suppose, if they salted and smoked them in the same way we do with our *real* herring, they'd turn out pretty much like —"

"KIPPERS!"

It was the strident cry of Ian "Crabbie" Crabster, who was now striding boldly onto the terrace, his nose raised like that of a bloodhound working downwind of an escaped jailbird.

"KIPPERS!" he declared again. "Man, oh, man, how many years have I hungered for that yummy hum of home? Hey, come to daddy, ye wee beauties!" He then homed in on a waiter to place his order.

"This'll probably result in revised herring-fishing quotas for the entire EU fleet," Bob muttered to Julie. "'Morning, Crabbie!" he then cheerily called.

"Come and join us," Julie smiled, "once you've done your bit for the kipper curers of the Isle of Man."

"Isle of Man kippers? Nah, they're good, I'll give you that, but I just checked, and what we're whiffin' here is the aroma of genuine Mallaig silver darlings, straight from the west coast o' Scotland in all their browned-off, reekin' glory." Ian sat down at the table. "Yeah, I haven't had a taste o' them since a fellow Jock called Euan Armstrong closed down his Scottish deli here in Palma and shot the crow to the Costa del Sol." He pursed his lips and gave a rueful shake of the head.

"Wild salmon from the Tay and Spey, brown trout from the Tweed, Loch Fyne oysters, Arbroath Smokies, Aberdeen Angus steaks, Dalgetty's clootie dumplings, Scott's Porage Oats, MacSween's haggis, Laidlaw's pies, Tunnock's Caramel Wafers, frozen deep-fried Mars Bars — everything. Oh aye, a sad day for the tartan gastronome when Euan left the island." He smacked his lips, rubbed his hands together and looked longingly in the direction of the kitchen door. "*Viva* the Mallaig kippers!"

Bob shot him a chastening look. "Yes, well, let's just hope they're the only red herrings we come across during the next coupla weeks."

Ian faked a smile. "Oh, very droll, Bobby, *very* subtle! Yeah, kippers — red herrings. A career as a stand-up comedian beckons if ye ever decide to jack in the police."

This was precisely the sort of cocky backchat that had got Crabbie into trouble at school, Bob recalled. It brought back memories of giving Crabbie punishments himself, when he was a sixth-year prefect and Crabbie just a cocky first-year sprog. Mind you, he told himself, no amount of disciplining had had much effect on Crabbie back then. And, when all was said and done, he'd never been a *bad* kid, in the strictest sense of the word — just a mouthy chancer who didn't take kindly to authority merely for authority's sake. Come to think of it, Bob had to admit that he wasn't all that different in this latter respect himself, although he *did* like to pride himself on being neither gratuitously lippy nor prone to the employment of unnecessary flannel. It was a matter of degree, a case of knowing how far to go, why to go there and when. In this respect, Crabbie was devoid of the subtlety he'd just so caustically suggested that Bob lacked himself. But Bob couldn't make him write a hundred lines for being cocky now. He needed Crabbie Scrabster to help him get the investigation of this Rab Dykes mystery underway, so he'd have to humour him, cajole him, pander to his gluttonous ways and parry his occasional thrusts of sarkiness with an aloofness befitting his position as an officer of the law.

With this thought in mind, Bob smiled genially and poured his erstwhile schoolmate a glass of orange juice. "Me a career comedian?" he laughed. "No, I'll leave the corny gags to you, Crabbie. You're the professional entertainer, after all."

"*Miaow*!" is what a socially indelicate person would have been inclined to say to that, and Julie was indeed tempted, but the residual effects of her socially delicate upbringing prompted her to refrain. "We can make that a Buck's Fizz, if you like, Ian," she said instead. "A half bottle of *Cava* isn't going to bust the bank now."

Much as it rankled, Bob backed this offer up with a consenting smile.

To his surprise, though, Ian declined. "No thanks, folks," he said, the firm set to his jaw indictating that he meant it. "No, last night was one thing — a good nosh-up and bevvy at the taxpayer's expense — but this is another day. There's work to do with you guys — and I *never* mix drink with duty."

Bob was temporarily stuck for words.

Ian gestured towards his newly poured glass of orange juice. "I'll down this, followed by a brace o' kippers, a slice o' toast and a cuppa coffee, then, in the immortal words of the Seven Dwarfs, *Hi-hoh, hi-ho-o-oh, it's off to work we go!*"

MEANWHILE, IN THE CAPTAIN'S STATEROOM OF THE CRUISE LINER 'OSTENTANIA', STILL LYING AT ANCHOR OFF GIBRALTAR . . .

Captain Georgi Stotinki was Balgonian — or so he claimed. Shipboard rumour had it, however, that, like his employer Boris Kaminski, his place of origin may well have been slightly nearer the heart of the old Soviet Union, and even farther north than Kaminski's native Ukraine. Latvia was one of the possibilities favoured by those few who had bothered to give the matter much thought. Certainly, his appearance was more typically Baltic than Balkan, if blondness of hair and blueness of eye can be taken as reliable marks of that distinction. Yet there was something of the gipsy about him as well — a mysterious, brooding sensuality so redolent of the swarthy folk who contributed no insignificant amount to the gene pool of Balgonia and surrounding lands following the diaspora of their Romany ancestors from northern India a millennium ago.

Georgi Stotinki was in his late forties, full-bearded and bushy of nostril, muscular and tall, with the air of a born seafarer about him. Here was a man with brine in his blood and far horizons in his eye. His right eye, to be exact. The left one was covered by a black patch, below which a livid scar ran down to the corner of his mouth, lending it the appearance of being drawn into a lopsided smirk, no matter what his mood. The penetrating, roguish look that beamed from that icy-blue right eye could strike both the fear of retribution into the hearts of his subordinates and the prospect of a bit of "rough wooing" into the imagination of a certain type of female cruise passenger. In fact, had he worn a tricorn hat instead of a gold-braided, cruise-captain's cap, he would have been, in the eyes of that certain type of female passenger, the very embodiment of the stereotypical pirate who is depicted looming over a scantily clad damsel in distress on the cover of a certain type of book aimed at a certain type of female reader.

Captain Stotinki knew it, and he also knew that his ship was always more than adequately patronised by that certain type of female reader. At every opportunity, therefore, he used that icy-blue right eye of his to the material advantage of his employer, Boris Kaminski. Pirate-fantasising females were prone to making repeat bookings on *Ostentania* cruises. They were also prone to falling prey to Pedro "Speedy" Gonzales' spiked sherries and, consequently, to contributing, albeit indirectly, to Mike Monihan's end-of-voyage bonuses.

Mike had been summoned to the Captain's cabin this morning, as had Doctor Rupert De'ath.

Doctor Death, as he was predictably referred to by both crew and passengers, was a proud man — seventy, if he was a day, wiry of frame and resolute of facial expression. He described himself as the "ship's surgeon", preferring this somewhat archaic designation to what he considered to be the more mundane title of "ship's doctor". The appellation of *surgeon* elevated him a rung or two above a mere *doctor* in the eyes of the passengers — or so he liked to believe. In truth, however, he was no surgeon, nor was he even a doctor, in the commonly perceived sense of the word. His medical qualification was that of anaesthetist, a profession he had practised for most of his working life in Russia, having defected to Moscow from England as a young man, his mind fired by an anti-capitalist ardour that was stoked by romantic Marxist ideals.

These days, the main type of anaesthetic Doctor Rupert De'ath was involved with was of the self-administering variety; specifically, liberal quantities of vodka, which he was in the habit of consuming in the traditional manner of his adopted homeland — one-hundred-proof and straight down the hatch without touching the sides. Strictly speaking, of course, he was not entitled, as an anaesthetist, to undertake the doctoring duties of a general practitioner on a cruise ship, or anywhere else for that matter. But he *did* have a bona fide medical qualification of sorts, and that was good enough for Boris Kaminski and for the lax maritime regulations of the west African country under whose flag his ships conveniently sailed.

Captain Stotinki had summoned his two "civilian" lieutenants to his presence today for the purpose of drawing the curtain as quickly as possible on the recent embarrassing and costly norovirus outbreak. He'd just had a call from Boris Kaminski himself, and Boris had made it crystal clear that he did *not* want the *Ostentania* to continue languishing in Gibraltarian waters for one single minute more than was absolutely necessary. Having a thousand disgruntled passengers holed up on the ship was doing nothing to justify the port charges he was being lumbered with. He wanted these people ashore, spending money in the carefully targeted retail outlets that gave generous kickbacks to the Ulanova Line for business so generously put their way. Either that, or he wanted the *Ostentania* back at sea, making up for lost time in giving those passengers the type of fun that encouraged them to flash their plastic in the ship's bars, shops and casino as if the day of tab-settlement would never come.

"So, vot iss da latest from da local helse ausority?" Captain Stotinki asked, his accent as thick as his whiskers, his good eye beaming an impatient ray directly at Doctor Rupert De'ath. "Da Gib helse officers dey been wissitink da ship again dis mornink, no?"

Rupert De'ath weighed his words carefully before he answered. He'd already had a few steadying shots of one-hundred-proof in the privacy of his surgery, so he didn't want his brain to come up with a line his tongue would be liable to trip over. The more monosyllables the better — that would be the prudent approach.

"Yes," he said for openers, then paused to consider the next lexiconic option. "Yes, indeed," he then confirmed, before pausing again to weigh another word or two.

The Captain's good eyebrow frowned. "Yes, indeed, vot?"

"Ah-um, yes, indeed . . . *Captain*." Rupert De'ath allowed himself a modest smile of self-congratulation. That was three words in a row — four, if you included "Ah-um", which, technically speaking, was actually duosyllabic. This gave him the confidence to venture a more articulate reply to the Captain's original question. The public health officers from Gibraltar, he carefully enunciated, had concluded that the outbreak of norovirus was now ostensibly under control. Indeed, if the health of those still suffering the latter effects of the illness continued to improve in the anticipated way and no further new cases emerged, then the *Ostentania* would be given permission to dock and its passengers allowed to disembark in —

"Ven?" Captain Stotinki cut in, his patience with the good doctor's plodding dialogue rapidly running out. "Ven ve be allow to dockink?"

The doctor took a deep breath, held it for a moment, then launched himself into a quick-fire volley of words. "In four days from now," he blurted out, the glint that appeared in his eyes indicating a fair level of pleasure at having negotiated five words in a row without a single mishap.

The Captain's eye patch quivered like the lid of a kettle coming to the boil. "FOUR DAYS?" he exploded, steam coming from his ears. "*FOUR* FOCKINK DAYS?"

Meekly, Rupert De'ath nodded his head. "Four . . . uhm . . . days."

Captain Stotinki knew that it would be more than his job was worth to keep the *Ostentania* becalmed in a non-profit-making doldrum like this for anything like another four days. Legend had it that Boris Kaminski was so hard that he used sandpaper to wipe his backside, so doing likewise with an under-performing captain's papers would present no discomfort whatsoever. Georgi Stotinki was looking unemployment in the eye — or, rather, in Boris Kaminski's anus.

"OK, doctor," he said, a twitch of resolve tugging at the non-smirking corner of his mouth, "how long 'til still-sick passengers be gettink all-clear vom you?"

The doctor raised his shoulders. "Twenty-four hours?" he replied, in the speculative manner of a butcher asking a housewife if a larger or smaller slice of meat from an indicated joint would be her preference.

But Captain Stotinki was in no mood to parley. He checked his watch. "OK, dis time tomorrow, ve set sail." His good eye turned on Mike Monihan. "So, you be tellink da passengers on da ship Tannoy and on da ship tee-wee and in da ship noospaper and in da ship theatre, casino, nightclub, bars, svim pools, sun decks, everyplace — ve start da cruisink again tomorrow!"

Mike was already at the door. "Right ya are, sorr," he said, waving a sloppy salute. "Oy'll be after gettin' on wit dat right away, so oy will."

Nervously, Rupert De'ath cleared his throat. "Ah-*hem*, Captain, what if we, er, have any, uhm, *new* cases?"

There was an everlasting second or two of volcanic tension before the Captain erupted.

"DER VILL BE NO NEW CASES!" he boomed, then jabbed a threatening finger into the doctor's chest. "Der vill be no new cases, doctor," he hissed, "because you vill intruct da chefs to load da passengers' soup today vid as much fockink antibiotics as you can get your fockink hands on!"

While all this had been going on, one of the *Ostentania*'s tenders had slipped quietly away from the ship and had headed out towards the open waters of the Strait of Gibraltar. On board were the helmsman, a deck-hand, the ship's chaplain, a small elderly lady, her head, face and stooped shoulders covered in a shawl of black Spanish lace, a younger, demure-looking woman, two suitcases and a coffin draped in a Spanish flag.

In the lee of the headland known as Punta Grande de Europa, the helmsman cut the motor and joined the deck-hand at the stern of the little boat. The two women stood, heads bowed, while the chaplain recited a eulogy over the coffin, first in Spanish, then in English, before motioning the two seamen to commit the body to the deep. As her husband was laid to his final resting place, where once he'd spent boyhood days catching sardines with his fisherman grandfather, the distraught widow of old Enrique Molinero, the late resident pianist of the Stardust Lounge, was comforted by the padre. Discreetly, the younger woman stepped to the rear of the boat and drew a cardboard box from a carrier bag.

"He always said he came from Viking stock," she murmured with a sad smile. "He would have wanted to go this way."

Then, with a nod of assent from the chaplain, she sent the contents of the little cardboard casket to join the coffin in the depths of Davy Jones's Locker. Dabbing her eyes with a handkerchief, she turned towards old Enrique's widow and took her hand in hers.

"Come, Señora Molinero," she said. "Time to take you ashore." She gestured towards the two suitcases. "Time to take you home."

CHAPTER SIX

A LITTLE LATER THE SAME MORNING, OUTSIDE THE "HOTEL PALAS ATENEA", PALMA DE MALLORCA . . .

"Work it, baby! Yeah, show me it!"

Ian Scrabster was circling with his little digital camera, going on bended knee to get a different angle here, clicking off some more shots there, tilting the camera this way and that, feverishly clicking, circling again, all the while urging the object of his photographic skills into ever more alluring poses.

"Sell it to me, baby! Against the palm tree! Yeah, *real* sexy! *Now* you're doin' it, honey!"

"Oh, for crying out loud, Crabbie," Bob groaned, "you said your man Mike Monihan only asked for a couple of mug shots for the ship's newspaper, so what the hell's all this *Playboy* centrefold stuff all about?"

"Gather ye rosebuds, Bobby. That's what it's all about. Never know when this material could be worth a right few quid." Ian continued to click.

"And as for you," Bob said to Ian's unlikely model, "it hardly becomes someone of your professional standing to writhe about like an amateur porno queen with a bee in her knickers. God knows what the folks back home would think if they could see you now."

"Lighten up, Methuselah, we're only having a bit of fun," Julie smiled back, then struck another seductive pose, her head tilted, a shock of hair tumbling over one eye, a forefinger pressed to her cheek. "I'd hardly be likely to offend the old dears in the Dirleton branch of the Women's Rural Institute by being snapped fully clothed in jeans and T-shirt like this, *surely*."

"It wasn't the reaction of the *women* I was talking about," Bob muttered. "And the fully clothed bit wouldn't make any difference to the way those horny buggers in the public bar of the Castle Inn think."

Julie winked at Ian. "Just wait 'til we do a session in my St Trinian's uniform, eh?"

Ian suddenly stopped clicking. "Have ye *really* got one o' them?" he gasped, his eyes popping. "Wow!" He rubbed his forefinger and thumb together. "Hey, I know a Moroccan magazine guy who'd cough up *mucho dinero* for pix like that!"

"Well, that does it," Bob said flatly. He took the camera from Ian. "Photo shoot over. Let's get to a computer and email a couple of head-and-shoulders shots over to your man Monihan on the *Ostentania*. The rest of the stuff we'll delete."

Julie took the camera from Bob. "Don't kid yourself, Kemosabe. I'll be keeping a few of the raunchier *studies* for my CV."

"Oh, yeah? Thinking of switching from forensic to filth, are you?"

"Nothing filthy about it. Everything in the best possible taste, in fact." She looked at Ian and shrugged. "Wouldn't you agree?"

As Ian was about to reply, his mobile phone rang. "Hi, Mike, how're they hangin'? . . . Plumb? Nice one! . . . What's that you say? . . . To*mor*row? Hey, we'll have to get the finger out! . . . Aw hey, that's great, Mike — fantastic . . . Yeah, no probs — I'll sort it all out at this end . . . *Ciao*, man. *Hasta mañana*, huh?"

Ian flipped the phone shut. "OK, Bobby," he grinned, "the *Ostentania* sets sail tomorrow, with us three on board!"

"Great," Bob replied, though not without a little frown of apprehension. "But aren't you forgetting something? We're in Mallorca and the boat's something like six or seven hundred miles away in Gib, so there's the small matter of how we —"

"Get there in time?"

"Get there at all, more like. I mean, are there direct flights or do we swim?"

Ian closed his eyes and shook his head despairingly. "Baw-bee-ee," he drawled, "it's yer old mate Crabbie Scrabster ye're talkin' to here. Would Ah tell ye we were gonna be on board tomorrow if the fine details of how and when weren't already taken care of? Nah, nah, no worries, pal. Me and ma mate Mike have got it all sorted." He tapped the side of his nose. "Never forget, *Be Prepared* was the motto of the Scrabsters long before the first boy scout sizzled a single sausage."

While Bob, still frowning, peered at him sceptically, Ian took him by the elbow and shepherded him towards his car. "Come on, Doc," he called back to Julie. "Don't hang about there. We've got things to do."

The office of the Ulanova Line's agents was situated above the ever-busy Bar Bosch at the top of the *Passeig dels Born*, a broad, tree-shaded avenue that leads up from Palma's seafront to the hub of the city's commercial and shopping areas.

Ian indicated one of the many pavement tables outside the bar, then said to Bob, "You sit there and enjoy the passin' show while I take the Doc up to do the necessary in the office."

"Now, just wait a minute, Crabbie!" Bob was nettled by his friend's sudden take-over bid, and he made no attempt to hide the fact. "Let me remind you that this is a criminal investigation and *I'm* in charge, so don't you go telling *me* what to do!"

Ian was coolness personified. "Ah, but let *me* remind *you*, Bobby, that your criminal investigation won't even start until you're on that tub in Gib, and as far as anyone's concerned, you'll be a guest of the Doc here. That's the only reason you're gonna be on the boat, remember?"

"Fair enough, but —"

"But nothin'! Me and the Doc are about to become temporary employees of the Ulanova Line, so *we* go up to the office to sort out our contracts, email the mug shots to the boat and sort out the travel arrangements to Gib, while *you* sit here and relax."

Bob was about to offer another objection, but Ian waved it aside.

"You're the policeman, and far be it from me to tell ye how to do yer job, but it strikes me that ye want to keep as low a profile as possible on any undercover job, right?"

"Sometimes, maybe, but —"

"Right, so no time like the present to make a start this time. Ye'd only be hangin' about like a spare prick at a hoor's weddin' up in the office anyway." Ian beckoned a waiter and, with a nod in Bob's direction, ordered a beer for *el señor*. Then, once more inviting Bob to sit and enjoy the passing show, he ushered Julie through the door of the office building.

She glanced back over her shoulder, gave Bob a better-get-used-to-it smile, and was gone.

If sighs were silver, Bob mused as he sat down, his pockets would be jingling nicely now, because he had just heaved the biggest sigh ever. He pondered the frothy head forming on the golden *San Miguel* as he poured it from its frosted bottle into a glass. Suddenly, he felt a long way from home — out of place, a fish out of water, something akin to the lonely little petunia in an onion patch his granny used to sing to him about when he was a wee boy.

Bob was feeling sorry for himself.

He sipped the beer, wishing upon wish that it could have been his beloved Belhaven Best and that the table he was sitting at could be magically transported there and then to the front of the Dirleton Castle Inn. Dammit, despite himself, he was actually feeling homesick — and for the first time ever, too. Bloody great fool that he was. But he couldn't help it. It was just the way he was feeling about his life right now. Until a couple of days ago, he'd thought it was about as perfect as any middle-ranking policeman like him deserved. But now? Well, he wasn't so sure any more.

He looked out over the wide *Plaça Rei Joan Carles*, a bustling square formed by the intersection of three of Palma's busiest streets, where a complex system of traffic lights dictates the alternate rights of way between endless streams of converging vehicles, ambling duos of smartly dressed businessmen and clutches of rubber-necked tourists. His eyes wandered over the grandiose Spanish architecture of some of the surrounding buildings. Yeah, very impressive — if you liked that sort of thing. He took another sip of his beer. *San Miguel*? Well, it wasn't too bad a brew, he had to admit. Fine and light and refreshing for the climate here. Belhaven Best wouldn't be the same chilled like this, though. That was because there was no need to. Let's face it, it was usually cool enough in Scotland without needing chilled beer to help reduce your bodily temperature. Well, that was his opinion, anyway, even if all the trendies back home were scoffing bottles of ice-brewed this and that these days. Hell, there was even chilled draught Guinness now, for Pete's sake! Where would all this global warming crap end?

Phew, it *was* warm here, though — even sitting in the shade of one of these big communal parasols. And to think he used to reckon, as a young lad, that he would melt during some of those days when he'd help his father and the other farm workers stack bales of newly made hay in what they regarded as the "searing" heat of a Scottish June. Happy times, for all that; the carefree years of childhood he thought would never end. But end they did, as did his family's contented little world.

Although he'd only been nine at the time, he could still remember, as if it was yesterday, the farmer coming to their cottage door to tell his mother what had happened. A tractor had overturned on the silage heap. His father had been driving it, just as he'd done during silage-making operations for years. But now, for the first time ever, he wouldn't be coming home for tea with his doting family at the end of the working day. From then on, Bob would sit with his mother and younger brother and sister at a kitchen table where one chair would never again be occupied by the person they'd taken for granted would always be there for them. The light of their lives had been extinguished, suddenly and cruelly.

Even now, after all those years, Bob still got a lump in his throat when he thought of how his heartbroken mother had worked so hard to support her three young children alone. And she had succeeded, though not without taking a terrible toll of her own health. That was what had prompted Bob to leave school before his final exams, to put on hold his ambitions of being a lawyer and to take a job as a tractor driver on a local farm to help his young brother and sister complete *their* higher education. And his mother would have been proud of how her little Gilbert and Mary eventually turned out; he a successful accountant in Australia now, and she a former UN interpreter married to one of the brightest young senators in the States.

Bob often wondered what his mother would have thought of his never realising his dream of being a lawyer. Would she have been disappointed that becoming a policeman had been the nearest he'd got to joining the legal profession? He hoped not, and deep down he believed not, since his mother would surely have realised that he had put his own career aspirations on hold — permanently, as it eventually transpired — in order to try and take his father's place, no matter how inadequately, as the linchpin of the family.

Oh, how he now missed those few tractor-driving years between leaving school and joining the force. Hard times, and sad times too, without his father, but happy ones in so many ways as well. Life had been simpler then — a matter of getting up in the morning, doing an honest day's work for a fair day's pay, then spending your leisure hours in familiar places with friends you had known all of your life.

But the police force had beckoned; a temporary career move, he'd thought at first, a stepping stone towards eventually going on to study law. Fate had had other paths mapped out for him, however, and, to be fair, he had been happy enough to follow them — for a while, at least. He'd proved himself to be a really good young copper, the best of his generation in the Lothian and Borders Constabulary, it had been said, albeit that his dour determination to do things *his* way and to fiercely stand up against any superior officer whom he believed to be out of line had made his promotional progress distinctly slower than it should have been. Not knowing when to keep his mouth shut had been Bob's problem in this regard, according to Detective Superintendent Bruce McNeill. But was Bob bothered? Not bloody likely he wasn't. He could still look in the mirror in the morning without seeing a brown dollop on the end of his nose, which was more than many of his more upwardly mobile contemporaries could say. That meant a lot to Bob — a helluva lot more than the size his salary-linked pension might ultimately turn out to be.

A tap on the shoulder jolted him from his silent soliloquising.

"Y'al reet, broothah? This seat free, like?" An elderly man, with Geordie vowels as flat as his white summer cap, was grinning at Bob, while motioning towards the chair at the opposite side of his table. "Ah cannut get anoothah one. Al the rest hereaboots is took, like."

Sure enough, the swiftest of glances confirmed that all the other tables on the pavement terrace outside the Bar Bosch were now occupied. With a gesture of his hand, Bob invited the old chap to make himself comfortable. "Aye, aye, just help yourself, friend."

"Aw, thanks, brootha," the old Geordie panted. "Scotchman, eh? Aye, ya can always depend on a Scotchman." He duly made himself comfortable. "Effin' wimmin, eh!" he continued when he'd got his breath back. "Ah just says t' me missus — aye, that's reet, pet, just you say what ya want us t' be daein', an' we'll dae it. Not a problem at al, pet. Aye, ya're on yar holidays, like, Ah says, so it's not a problem at al, like."

For the sake of courtesy, Bob tried to look interested. "That a fact?"

"Aye, it *is* a effin' fact. Al the way from effin' N'castle t' effin' Mah-jorka for a nice, canny spot o' sun, sand an' sex, and what's the first thing the ald boogah wants t' dae? Nah, ya'll nevah even guess in a month o' effin' Sundays, broothah." With a twitch of his head, the elderly Geordie indicated a large store on the other side of the square. "Effin' C&A's! Ah ask yi — effin' C&A's, eh? Al the way from effin' N'castle t' effin' Mah-jorka and al she wants t' dae is effin' shop! And in effin' C&A's an' al!" He pulled his cap forward, then eyeballed Bob from beneath the shade of its peak. "What the effin' hell was wrong wi' effin' C&A's in effin' N'castle, eh? Aye, ansah me that!" Then, diverting his attention to a passing waiter, he called out, "Eh, when ya've got a minute, broothah — a pint o' the N'castle Broon. An' if ya divn't have the N'castle Broon, which Ah presume ya divn't, then Ah'll just have the same as me friend here's havin'. Aye, the Saint Meegwell, like." Turning back to Bob, he then declared, "Effin' wimmin! Ah divn't oondahstand the boogahs, an' Ah likely nevah will!"

While the old chap wittered on, Bob got to thinking about the observations he'd just made about the idiosyncrasies of the female of the species . . .

There was his Sally for starters. What an unfathomable piece of work she'd eventually shown herself to be. The blissful ignorance of young married life hadn't taken long to nosedive into a quagmire of disillusionment and despair — for Bob, at any rate. All those hours of overtime he'd put in, including months commuting between Scotland and London, just so he could afford to get himself into serious hock by taking out a mortgage on the "dream bungalow" Sally had always coveted in the leafy Edinburgh suburb of Duddingston. Then she gave him all his thanks in one fell swoop by buggering off with an old sugar daddy. And a top lawyer, of all things! As if inflicting insult and injury hadn't been hurtful enough without her adding irony for good measure. Still, the plus side was that Bob had then been free to ditch the millstone of that mortgage he'd had round his neck — although living for the next few years in a manky, top-floor flat in a Stockbridge tenement hadn't done much to enamour him of his reversion to bachelorhood. Yeah, the old Geordie was probably right. Women — you'd never understand them.

Now he had Julie to contend with, and *she* wasn't without her little foibles either. But, Bob supposed, neither was he, if you got right down to it. He could be a bit grumpy at times, though usually only if work and that half-wit Andy Green were getting him down. But, as a rule, he felt he could compliment himself on being basically a good-natured bloke, with a droll sense of humour, which, admittedly, could verge on the sharp side when it came to taking a rise out of said Detective Constable Andrew Green. Yeah, and Julie was never slow to tick him off about *that*. The old maternal instinct. Another female quirk that could be hard for a bloke to appreciate. Unless, of course, he happened to be on the receiving end of some motherly pampering when his spirits were low. As Bob's were right now.

Ah, but it seemed Julie wasn't about to oblige in that department. No, the look she'd flashed him as she disappeared through the door with Crabbie a few minutes ago certainly wasn't of the mollycoddling variety. "Better get used to appearing to play second fiddle for a while, Kemosabe," that's what that look had said. Bob considered the implications of this, and the conclusion he arrived at shouldn't really have surprised him, although it did — a bit.

Having to even *appear* to be playing second fiddle was what was *really* niggling him now — much more than being pissed off about having been assigned to this no-win case in the first place. Come to think of it, he'd never ever been happy about taking orders from anyone, not even during his happy-go-lucky tractor-driving days. At the time, the thought of having the responsibility of standing in for his late father as head of the family had made him resent any farm foreman with his brains in his boots telling him what to do, although prudence had always prompted him to hold his tongue. After all, a pittance from the dole wouldn't have gone far to support the family.

Showing irritation at being ordered about by some of the jumped-up beat bobbies he'd first encountered in the CID had been a different matter, however. In a few cases, the brains of those detective sergeants had been in their boots as well, but the results of the decisions they made in the course of their police duties were always liable to be a lot more serious than a farm foreman judging whether or not a potato drill was straight enough. Bob had never been shy of telling the sergeants precisely that.

"Big-headed young bastard," was the stock response, and now that he thought about it, there could be little doubt that this is how he had come across to certain of his more senior colleagues back then. But that was their problem. If they chose not to take the job as seriously as he did, then he couldn't care less what they called him. He had his own standards, and he wouldn't compromise them for anyone.

"Al them pooah bairns," the old Geordie rambled on, "sewin' away al day for a little-wee bowl o' vindaloo in them sweat shops in the backstreets o' New Delhi, makin' effin' blouses an' bloomers for daft boogahs like me missus t' pay fortunes for ovah heeah." He thumped the table and glared resolutely at Bob. "Ah'm tellin' ya, broothah — al them pooah bairns. Ah was readin' aboot it in me paypah, like, an' it's only a effin' disgrace, that's al! Aye, me missus should dae the right thing," he concluded with a rueful shake of his head, "she should forget aboot Mah-jorca an' take her holidays in effin' India an' buy the effin' stuff at factory prices. Wimmin? Ah divn't oondahstand the boogahs, an' Ah likely never will!"

Most of this diatribe was going in one of Bob's ears and straight out the other, although the old Geordie's reiterated observation about women did help nudge his thoughts back to the subject of Julie . . .

Everyone who knew him said she'd been the best thing to happen to him since the break-up of his marriage. And Bob couldn't deny it; Julie *had* brought a welcome and totally unexpected ray of sunshine back into his private life. Also, she, along with Andy Green, had helped him solve two very difficult cases, which, without their involvement (haphazard though it may have been), could well have resulted in Bob being killed. Consequently, though arguably less importantly, he had Julie to thank, in no small measure, for the recent upturn in his career prospects. Although Bob tried to pretend to himself that such professional advancement meant little to him, he had to concede that the resultant improvement in his finances had helped him realise his dream of owning a roses-round-the-door cottage in his beloved native village of Dirleton. He also had to admit that the times he now spent there with Julie meant more to him than anything he could have hoped for just a few short years ago.

Yet, harking back to the old Geordie's sweeping statement about the unpredictability of women, could Bob really be sure that Julie, sooner or later, wouldn't dump him just as heartlessly as Sally had done? Maybe being involved in these crime-investigating escapades with him were no more than a bit of passing fun for her — the occasional, quick left-right through the "exciting" front line of sleuthery, before settling back into the polite normality of her scientific career, wherever that might eventually take her. He couldn't ignore the fact that, when all was said and done, she came from a privileged, academic family background — a world away from his own comparatively humble upbringing in a farm worker's tied cottage. Bob couldn't dispel a nagging doubt about Julie's long-term commitment to him, despite her regular hints about tying the knot. Those were probably no more than a leg-pull on her part. She was young, after all — a good ten years Bob's junior, and with many lifelong connections with guys of her own age *and* social order. Though he tried hard not to, Bob couldn't help but worry about things like that.

Which brought him back to that look Julie had cast him as she headed into the Ulanova Line's office with Crabbie. Maybe she'd get a kick out of having Bob appear to play second fiddle to her on this damned cruise. And there was no doubt in his mind that Crabbie certainly *would* delight in being the sixth-year "school prefect" to Bob's first-year "sprog", if he got the chance.

But the more Bob thought about this, the louder a little voice in his head yelled at him, "For God's sake, Burns, grow up! Stop being such a neurotic idiot! You've got two good friends — three, if you count Andy Green — about to go out of their way to help haul *you* out of an investigative bog that's really nobody's problem but your own. So, as Julie would say, lighten up, Methuselah." The voice was right, of course. He *was* being a neurotic idiot, and he knew it. "OK, boy," he finally told himself, "what do you want — a medal? Wise up. Give yourself a shake and stop being the I-do-it-my-way Mr Independent for a while. That, Burns, is part and parcel of what you're being paid to do for the next bloody fortnight, so make the most of it. Relax. Enjoy yourself, even if it does mean playing Mr Nobody in the cruising public's eye. Just remember, none of them could give a monkey's about you, your inflated opinion of yourself *or* your holier-then-thou principles, anyway."

Then a car caught his eye, crossing the *Plaça* in a charging scrum of vehicles and turning right into the *Carrer Unió*. It was a black, right-hand-drive Rolls Royce, and behind the wheel sat a familiar figure.

"Rab Dykes!" Bob muttered. "Rab bloody Dykes!"

He slammed his beer glass down and set off in pursuit, navigating his way as rapidly as he could through the lily pond of tables.

"Oy, broothah!" the old Geordie called after him. "Hee-ah! Yar bee-ah! Ya havun't finished yar Saint Meegwell, like!" When no response was forthcoming, the venerable Newcastle gent merely shrugged and poured the residue of Bob's glass into his own. "Effin' Scotchmen," he said to a distinguished-looking Spanish man at an adjacent table. "Ah divn't oondahstand the boogahs, an' Ah likely nevah will!" He raised his glass. "Aye, doon the effin' hatch, Hozay!"

Bob exited the *Plaça* at a gallop, barging his way past window shoppers and ambling sightseers, straining his neck to see above the sea of heads. He was heartened to notice that the Roller had been stopped at lights about twenty metres farther on, but before he could cover even half that distance, the lights had changed and the Roller was heading off as quickly as the procession of traffic would allow. Bob continued the chase, but to no avail. By the time he'd dodged his way through the crowds to the front of the city's old theatre, where the street sweeps left towards a wide avenue called *La*

Rambla, the black Rolls had disappeared into the distance.

Ian and Julie were waiting for him when he returned, breathless, to the *Plaça*. They were sitting at his table, which, he was pleased to note, was now minus his quondam Geordie companion.

"Where the hell have ye been?" Ian asked. "The old geezer that was sitting here said ye took off so fast he thought yer effin' Y-fronts had caught fire."

"Yes, you should avoid such sudden bursts of energy in this heat," Julie blandly observed, before adding with a provoking little smile, "especially at your age."

True to his new resolve to lighten up a bit, Bob gave her a touché-type nod of the head, wiped the sweat from his brow with the back of his hand, then slumped down onto a chair and panted, "You never spoke a truer word, Doctor Julie darlin'. You never spoke a truer word."

"So, where *have* ye been?" Ian repeated.

As Bob recounted the recent turn of events, a knowing grin began spread over Ian's face.

"What's amusing you, Crabbie?" Bob eventually asked.

"Could you see Rab Dykes's hands on the steering wheel?"

"Yeah, one of them, anyway. I mean, the Roller had dark-tinted windows, but the driver's one was open, so I could see his right hand as clear as a —"

Bob pulled himself up, realising that Ian had been one step ahead of him.

So, apparently, had Julie. "Well then, Sherlock," she coyly enquired, "was his right hand bandaged or was it not?"

"That's right," Ian said, "a middle-finger amputee would still be showin' the obvious signs just two or three days after the chop, no?"

Bob was sorely tempted to retaliate by raising the middle finger of his own right hand and inviting Ian, à la Rab Dykes of courtroom vintage, to spin on it. But, instead, he raised a concessionary shoulder and repeated the touché-type nod he had given Julie a few moments before. It may have seemed to his two companions that he'd been caught napping evidence-wise, but that still didn't explain to Bob why Rab Dykes, digitally intact and patently not dead, was driving about Palma Mallorca in a black Rolls Royce identical to the one in which, the day before yesterday, Boris Kaminski had visited the Dirleton Castle Inn back in Scotland.

Ian read the confusion on Bob's face and decided to throw him a lifeline. "OK, Bobby," he said, "you hinted last night that you knew who wee Rab's bankroller was, right?"

Bob said nothing.

"And," Ian went on, "I did the same, right?"

Bob nodded, cagily.

"So," Ian said, "there's no mystery. We both know it's Boris Kaminski, who also owns the Ulanova Cruise Line."

"So what?"

"So, pay the nice waiter man for the two beers."

"Two?"

"Yeah, your old Geordie friend buggered off leavin' his tab on the table here."

Bob sighed as he reached for his wallet. "The gather-ye-rosebuds maxim seems to be catching — and all at the expense of Lothian and Borders Police."

"Don't let it bother you," Ian advised. "No doubt there'll be worse to come."

"Ten minutes ago, it *would* have bothered me," said Bob, "but now, Crabbie, I couldn't care bloody less." He handed the waiter a banknote. "Here, *amigo* — keep the change."

"Hey, hey, take it easy, Kemosabe!" Julie spluttered. "A few bits of loose change would have been fine for a tip, but you've just given the guy about fifty per cent on top!"

"Yeah, well, easy come, easy go," Bob smiled. "Welcome to the new me."

Julie looked aghast at Ian, then screwed a finger into her temple. "It's the sun," she said. "The ever-frugal Detective Inspector here has fried his brains!"

Granting that remark the amount of attention any self-respecting duck would give to a splash of water on its back, Bob flashed Ian a benign smile and said, "Now, Crabbie, you were about to tell me something about Boris Kaminski, yes?"

The estate known as Son Vida lies just to the west of Palma city, on the south-facing flanks of the Sierra de Na Burguesa mountains. Its five hundred hectares of lush, subtropical parkland contains one of the world's most palatial hotels, as well as beautifully manicured golf courses, with fairways overlooked at discreet intervals by unashamedly luxurious villas. Ian gave the security guard at the entrance gate a polite greeting in Spanish as he waved his car through.

"Jeez, how the other half lives!" Bob gasped, his eyes wandering over the sheer opulence of the scene unfolding before them.

"Mmm-hmm," Julie drooled, "this is my idea of home sweet home."

Bob gave a knowing little smile. "Not too ostentatious for you, then?"

Julie didn't bother to answer. She didn't have to. The kid-on-Christmas-morning look on her face said it all.

Bob was tempted to quip that she might want to reconsider her notion of getting hitched to someone on a detective inspector's miserable salary if this really was the lifestyle she aspired to. However, he decided that stating the bleedin' obvious would only show him in a defensive light, bordering on the neurotic, and that was a trait he'd resolved to control. Accordingly, he kept his mouth shut.

"If ye think all this is a sight for sore eyes," Ian advised, "just wait 'til ye see what I really brought ye here to have a gander at."

He followed the road all the way up to the higher reaches of the estate, where natural pinewoods carpet the rolling folds of the mountainsides. There, tucked away on its own in a glade that commanded the most spectacular views over the Bay of Palma, stood what could only be described as a lesser mansion of breathtaking opulence. Built in the classic style of a Spanish hacienda, with wide, overhanging eves, a pillared entrance portico, and arched *porches* running the length of the house's facade, this was clearly a dwelling to rival the very best in Son Vida. A colonnade of tall palms swayed in the breeze on either side of the gravelled sweep, while two peacocks strutted regally on lawns as green and smooth as billiard table baize.

Ian had pulled up outside the main gates, which were set into a high perimeter wall, its rough-hewn, honey-coloured stone draped in billows of purple bougainvillea.

"Take sights," he said, "at the Mallorcan pad of Boris Kaminski!"

Bob whistled through his teeth.

"I want it," Julie whimpered.

"Yeah, but what ye see from here isn't even the half of it," Ian informed her. "Round the back there's a huge swimmin' pool with its own *casita* bar, a floodlit tennis court, a barbecue big enough to roast an ox on, and a vine-draped pergola wi' alfresco dinin' facilities that could accommodate half the population o' Dirleton."

"No kidding?" said Julie, patently awestruck.

"No kiddin'. And get this, there's even a private helicopter pad!"

Pensively, Bob stroked his chin. "And to think all this belongs to a bloke who was hamstrung by communism until a few years ago."

"Yep," Ian concurred, "a financial leper yesterday, and filthy rich beyond most folks' wildest dreams today."

"Hmm, how wonderful," said July, dreamily.

"And ye wouldn't bel*ieve* the inside o' the house," Ian went on, warming to the subject. "Every conceivable luxury — even an entertainin' area bigger than some dance halls I've played in. A sauna, a fully equipped gym, snooker room, indoor heated pool, Jacuzzi, even a state-of-the-art solarium to keep the tan topped up durin' the winter. The list goes on."

"You've obviously seen round in there, then?" Bob said, unable to conceal his surprise.

Ian was the epitome of nonchalance. "Played at a private soiree for a bunch o' Boris's east European buddies. Yeah, got the gig through wee Rab Dykes, as it happens."

"Eastern Europeans, you say?"

"Yeah, well, mainly Russkies, I suppose. Mallorca's crawling wi' them these days. Stinkin' rich, most of them, and well dodgy an' all."

"Dodgy?"

"OK, put it this way, they're not known as the Moscow Mafia for nothin', right? Yeah, the word is that they're into all kinds o' rackets. Smugglin', prostitution, people traffickin', extortion — just like the old Al Capone days in the States, but less in yer face. Ah mean, the Russkies play it all pretty close to the chest. Never seem to get nicked for breakin' the law, whatever they're up to." Ian had a little chuckle to himself. "A wild crew when they're in their own company behind closed doors, though." He gestured towards the house. "That shindig I played at in there — awash wi' vodka, mountains o' caviare, and every one o' Boris's mates well *attended* to, so to speak, by flash young bints — Bulgarians and Romanians, apparently — who don't stoop to earn a coin by hand-harvestin' turnips like their old ladies used to." He gave the side of his nose the customary tap. "Get where Ah'm comin' from, Bobby?"

Bob did indeed get the picture, but he was also doing a bit of lateral thinking. "And you say wee Rab stayed here the last time he was on the island?"

"Certainly did, *and* he was squired about in Boris's big black Roller."

"Speaking of which . . ." Julie said, indicating the far corner of the house, from where the limo in question had emerged and was purring slowly along towards the front doorway.

With a mischievous twinkle in his eye, Ian watched the look on Bob's face run the gamut of several adjectives while he waited for the car to stop.

"Wee Rab Dykes," Bob said in a half whisper, his facial expression switching between confusion and vindication as the driver got out. "Like I told you back in Palma, Crabbie, unbandaged right hand notwithstanding, it *is* Rab Dykes, agreed?"

Ian was non-committal. "Want to speak to him?" he asked, trying to keep a straight face.

Bob's eyes were fixed on the figure now flicking specks of dust off the Roller's radiator grille. "You bet your cotton socks I do," he snarled. "I've been given a king-size run-around because of that wee bastard and his so-called man-overboard stunt!"

"Fair enough," said Ian. "Your wish is my command." He then shouted something in Spanish. The figure at the car looked up, gave a grin of recognition, waved and started to stride towards them.

"I didn't think Rab Dykes could understand Spanish," Bob said. "The bugger has a big enough problem with English."

Ian hid a smile behind his hand. He needn't have bothered. The nearer the figure got to them, the more Bob realised that he'd dropped a clanger. At twenty paces this guy was a dead ringer for Rab Dykes, but at ten the resemblance began to diminish, and at five there could be little doubt that this was another person entirely.

Ian slapped his shoulder. "Never mind, Bobby," he laughed, "I made the same mistake the first time the Roller pulled up outside the Hotel Santa Catalina. I thought wee Rab had landed a chauffeur's job, until he climbed out of the back seat."

Crestfallen, Bob raised his shoulders and mumbled, "Well, they say everybody has a double."

Julie couldn't resist a giggle. "Maybe a visit to an optician's in order, Kemosabe. Old age doesn't come by itself, as the saying goes."

The new, lightened-up Bob Burns responded to that crack with a smile — albeit a cheerless one.

Meanwhile, Ian introduced the Rab Dykes look-alike as Rafael, Boris Kaminski's chauffeur-cum-caretaker-cum-gardener-cum-general domestic factotum here in

Mallorca. They all shook hands through the spars in the metal security gate, then Julie exchanged pleasantries with Rafael in Spanish, while Ian explained to Bob his reasons for bringing them up here today.

Obviously, he'd been banking on a hunch that an opportunity would arise to counter Bob's conviction that Rab Dykes was still alive and kicking, and, thanks to Rafael's timely appearance, that side of things had now worked out perfectly. But he'd also wanted to let Bob see first-hand the other world that wee Rab had managed to stumble into.

"Yeah, it's certainly a long way from flogging hooky DVDs at Ingliston Sunday Market on the windswept outskirts of Edinburgh," Bob readily agreed.

His mind was working overtime, though — the cogs clicking and whirring as he tried to make some sort of sense out of all the things that were happening. He decided to broach the subject of just one of those with Ian now . . .

"Last night, you suggested that Rab Dykes was the *alleged* deceased in this case."

"So?"

"So, what exactly did you mean by that? I mean, if you've got some inside info that'd help me see a bit of daylight here, for Pete's sake spill the beans, Crabbie."

Ian pursed his lips and shook his head. "No beans to spill, Bobby, and that's the truth. No, all I meant was that you're dealin' wi' a right tricky bag o' monkeys, if what I've seen o' Boris Kaminski and his cronies is anything to go by, so I wouldn't take *any*thing at face value."

"Not that I ever do," Bob promptly assured him, then added bluntly, "no matter who I'm dealing with, OK?"

If Ian took that last point personally, he didn't show it. Instead he winked, pulled down the lower lid of his right eye and said, "Accent the devious, eliminate the obvious. That's been the Scrabster motto since before Jesus rumbled Judas Iscariot, and ye'd do well to adopt it yerself while ye're on this case, if ye ask me." He gave Bob a nudge with his elbow and winked again. "Say no more, eh!"

Just then, the dull thwack of rotor blades slicing the air drew their eyes eastward, where a helicopter had just appeared above the pinewoods and was descending towards the Kaminski compound.

Through Ian, Rafael explained that this was the boss arriving from the airport; returning from his visit to Scotland.

"Want to say hello to the man himself?" Ian asked Bob. "Better the devil ye know."

"No thanks," Bob replied. "Mr Kaminski and I have already met, and I think it's safe to say that he wouldn't be rolling out the welcome mat for me here."

Ian looked at his watch. "Yeah, maybe we'd better push off now, anyway. I still have to pack a suitcase, and we check in for the Málaga flight in just over an hour."

"Málaga?" Bob queried. "That's a fair old distance from Gib, isn't it?"

"All the same, it's the nearest place to Gib we can get a regular flight to from here." Then, anticipating Bob's concern about how they'd do the last leg of the journey, Ian said, "But I fixed up with Mike Monihan to have a cab waiting at Málaga Airport. It'll take us the final eighty miles or so along the Costa del Sol to the Rock." Ian then adopted his familiar self-congratulatory mien. "Yeah, like I say, Bobby, *Be Prepared* has been the Scrabster motto since before the first boy scout sizzled a single sausage."

While Ian said his flamboyant farewells to Rafael in Spanish, Julie drew Bob aside and shouted in his ear over the din of the approaching helicopter: "Did you notice anything unusual about the Rafael guy when you shook hands with him?"

Bob indicated the negative.

Julie held the middle finger of her right hand up to his face. "Pardon the rude gesture, but this little piggy, my dear Watson, was missing!"

CHAPTER SEVEN

THAT EVENING — THE BAY OF GIBRALTAR . . .

Whether or not Rafael's absent middle finger was related in some oblique way to Rab Dykes's severed digit was of no immediate concern to Bob. For the present, he was content to presume that, in addition to Rafael appearing on the scene as something of a Wee Rab doppelgänger, his lack of a middle finger may simply have been another of the ever-increasing list of coincidences Bob had been encountering before investigations into this case were even properly under way. If, as his wife was claiming, foul play had been involved in Rab Dykes's fatal plunge overboard, Bob first had to find someone to point the finger of suspicion at, and that, he decided, was the only finger he was going to concern himself with for now.

"So, that's the *Ostentania*," he said, looking out from the prow of the small tender that was carrying them from Gibraltar harbour to where the ship was lying at anchor. "Hardly what you'd call a superliner, is it?"

"Probably all the better for that," Julie suggested. "My old folks do a fair bit of cruising and they prefer the more *intimate* ships to the huge floating cities you get these days. More fun, they say. You get to know more people."

Bob raised a cynical eyebrow and grunted that he could hardly wait.

"It's an ex-ferry," Ian casually informed them. "Same as the other three tubs in the Ulanova fleet. That one there used to ply the Baltic. Present captain was the first officer for years, by the way. Knows that boat like the whiskers on his face."

Bob raised a curious eyebrow this time. "Oh yeah? How d'you happen to know all this?"

"Well, like I told ye, I've worked on the *Ostentania* before. Yessiree, and ye can learn a helluva lot in a coupla weeks aboard a cruise boat, if ye keep yer eyes and ears open and ask all the right questions."

"Which is precisely what *you*'ll be doing, Kemosabe," said Julie, with what Bob thought might *just* have been a hint of her pseudo retirement-home-nurse's manner.

"And so will you," he came back, without rising to the bait. "Don't forget, we'll *both* still be posing as freelance magazine scribes on this trip. Having to do your shore-lecturer thing on top of that hasn't changed the basic plan, you know. *And*," he added as an afterthought, "let's hope I can find something for you to sink your forensic teeth into before too long as well."

Julie gave a little bow. "Your wish is my command, oh great one," she intoned, before asking Bob, in a distinctly less deferential way, to remind her from time to time which head she was supposed to be wearing. "Oh! And keep a long-handled broom handy as well."

"Why?"

"I might need to ram it you-know-where so I can sweep the decks!"

"Ex-ferry, the *Ostentania*," Ian said again, clearly more interested in displaying his inside knowledge of the Ulanova Line's fleet than listening to Bob and Julie jousting over undercover police ploys. "Nicely refitted, though, I must say. Somethin' like a thousand passengers she can take — in some style an' all. Yeah, and they say her sister ships are just as well done out."

Bob was nonplussed. "But that must've cost fortunes! Where the hell did the likes of Kaminski get the money to buy four big ferries and convert them into luxury liners? I mean, as I keep saying, like most of these multi-millionaires from the old communist east, he was more than likely just a penniless prole until a few years ago."

"Well, he's supposed to have developed all sorts of legit business interests back there since the Iron Curtain came down — mining, chemicals, even oil and gas, banking too."

Bob wasn't impressed. "Gangster capitalism is what it's called in the hands of those ex-commies."

Ian gave a little chuckle. "Whatever, the word I got on the boat was that he *is* probably behind a lot of dodgy capers as well. Big stuff. International stuff."

"Such as?"

"Search me, man. I'm only a keyboard player, and Boris Kaminski's money's as good as anybody else's when it finds its way into my pocket at the end of a gig. How he comes by his loot is none o' my business."

"Chances are he didn't buy the ships, though," Julie chipped in.

"How do you mean?" Bob asked.

"Probably leases them from the *actual* owners. Greek shipping magnates, maybe? Quite a few cruise lines work like that — just like some airlines do with planes. I suppose it cuts the finance they have to raise up front."

"Maybe so, but it still means Kaminski's gambling bigtime, and he must've had the collateral to do the deals, even if the ships *are* leased. A bloody mystery man, and no doubt he's as bent as a chocolate frog."

"Which," Julie exhaled, sounding a mite bored, "is what you said the first time you clapped eyes on him back in Dirleton."

"Yeah, and I'm a great believer in following my hunches."

Ian chuckled again. "Well, Bobby, if you think Boris Kaminski was behind wee Rab's high dive into the Atlantic, *my* hunch is that yer chances o' pinning any kind o' rap on him are about as likely as me bein' asked to play in Pavarotti's backin' group. Get real, man — that bloke didn't get where he is today without outsmartin' lawmen that could eat the likes o' you for breakfast. Yeah, none of yer namby-pamby, innocent-until-proven guilty stuff wi' them. One wrong look in their direction and ye would likely have been shovellin' salt in Siberia for the rest o' yer days."

Ian's mischievously provocative remarks tested Bob's new lighten-up resolve to the limit, but the realisation that responding to them in the expected way would achieve absolutely nothing persuaded him to keep his thoughts to himself. It would be better by far, he judged, to sit back and start enjoying the experience of being in places that were a touch more "exotic" than his usual beats in and around Edinburgh.

A quick glance at Julie told him that she had already adopted this approach. She was gazing dreamily up at the towering majesty of the Rock, basking now in the golden glow of sunset. Creeping twilight shadows had already enveloped the *Ostentania*, which was lying only a few hundred metres ahead. According to Julie, the lights shining from her tiered decks were reflected on the surface of the sea like the spangled scimitars of the Moorish hordes, who, she reminded her captive audience of two, had sailed over these very waters from Africa to colonise Spain some fourteen hundred years previously.

"Practisin' yer shore-lecturin' shtick already, are ye, Doc?" Ian quipped.

Julie ignored him. "Isn't it romantic?" she sighed. "The mythical twin Pillars of Hercules guarding the entrance to the Mediterranean Sea. The Rock of Gibraltar right here at the toe of Europe, and, just over the Straight there, the Abyla headland marking the ancient northern outpost of Africa. Hmm, the Pillars of Hercules. And long before the Moors," said she went on, "there was Hannibal and his mighty army, pouring northwards across this same sleeve of sea to claim Spain for Carthage. Ah-h-h," she sighed again, "isn't it wonderful to retrace the footsteps of history."

Bob and Ian exchanged bemused glances. Julie's last observation was one with which they were both content to ostensibly concur without need for further discussion.

Mike Monihan, the Cruise Director, was waiting for them in the *Ostentania*'s otherwise-deserted embarkation-disembarkation area as they stepped through the gangway.

"Holy mother o' Jaysus!" he exclaimed when Ian introduced him to Julie. "Somebody phone heaven and tell dem one o' da angels is missin'! Sure an' Oy'll be a lap-dancin' nun if ya aren't da most stunnin' shore lecturer Oy ever had da pleasure o' feastin' me eyes upon, Julie me darlin'!"

"That's *Doctor* Julie me darlin'," Julie politely corrected as they shook hands. "But in your case I'm prepared to dispense with the formality."

"Ah, but dat's grand," Mike grinned. "Oy always tink it's a good ting ta be dispensin' wid da formalities as soon as possible, darlin', so Oy do."

"Quite," said Julie, "and, in like manner, you can dispense with the familiarities. The letters D, A, R, L, I and N don't feature in the initials of my particular PhD."

Far from being taken aback by such a firm rebuff, Mike half turned to Ian, gave him a hearty slap on the shoulder and guffawed, "Ah, trust you to be bringin' me da spunky one, eh! Oh yeah, mate, Oy like 'em wid a bit o' spirit about dem, so Oy do, like."

Bob seethed inwardly.

"And Oy suppose you'll be da new shore lecturer's com*pan*ion?" Mike said to him, with a less than surreptitious wink in Ian's direction. "A male one's a bit unusual, Oy must say. But . . ." He paused to eye

Julie up and down. “But, in dis case Oy’m not surprised.”

Bob dredged up reserves of self-restraint he never knew he possessed as he offered Mike his hand. “Bob Burns,” he said with a thin smile. “I’m Doctor Bryson’s partner. I, uh . . . I don’t know if Ian told you, but we’re both freelance journalists, researching a magazine feature on cruising holidays.” He gave Mike an enquiring look. “Maybe you’d be kind enough to give us the benefit of your experiences sometime?”

Mike swiftly pooh-poohed that request by muttering into his chest that no cruise experience of his that was worth the telling would ever see the light of day in any decent magazine. He then instructed Julie, Ian and Bob to step over to a desk by the gangway, where an Indonesian crewman wearing a security officer’s badge had appeared. He took their pictures on a small webcam, then began to exchange their passports for swipe cards, to be used, he explained, to verify their identity on leaving and returning to the ship when in port. This, they were assured by the hovering Mike Monihan, was standard procedure in these terrorism-blighted days.

While this formality was being completed, Mike spoke a few words into a walkie-talkie, and almost instantly two porters materialised to take the new arrivals’ luggage to their cabins.

“Youse guys will get yer keys when ya sign in at reception,” he said to Julie and Bob. “Ian here knows where it is, don’t ya, me owld shipmate?”

Ian nodded, then, with the back of his hand held to the corner of his mouth, he reminded Mike, sotto voce, *never* to address him as Ian if there were any passengers within earshot. Juan the *Spanish* Keyboard Man was his professional handle at the Hotel Santa Catalina back in Mallorca, and that was also the way he'd be playing it for the punters here. He stressed this point to Bob and Julie as well. "Accentuate the cake, eliminate the bread, as Marie Antoinette used to say. That's how to get ahead in show business, by the way."

"If it's as easy as dat, maybe Oy should've had *you* as me manager all dem years ago," Mike Monihan remarked, and not without a trace of sarcasm. "Anyhow," he continued, an indifferent, switch-on smile returning to his face, "if ye'll excuse me now, Oy'd better be gettin' away to da night club an' introduce da cabaret. Oh, and if ya don't mind, *Doctor* Julie, make yer way to me office in da mornin' — Ian here will tell ya how to find it — an' Oy'll give ya da lowdown on all da shore-lecturin' baloney." He then checked his watch and said to Ian, "Oh, and if *you* don't mind, me owld mate, yer first gig in da Stardust Lounge starts in half an hour, so ya'd better get changed into yer tux and alter ego kinda smartish-like!"

Bob touched Mike's arm as he turned to leave. "Just one thing. I have a message from his parents in Edinburgh for one of your staff. Andy Green, his name is. Trainee barman, I believe. Can you tell me where he's working?"

"Same Stardust Lounge as yer man Juan here's gonna be workin' in. Nice coincidence, huh?"

Bob shrugged. "Yeah, life's full of them."
"Isn't it, though?" Mike replied as he walked away.
"Right, Crabbie," Bob said with some urgency as soon as Monihan was gone, "get along to the Stardust Lounge pronto and tell Andy Green that Julie and I —"
"Wait a minute!" Ian butted in. "Would this Andy Green be the same young loony I had the misfortune to be involved wi' when you were huntin' that murderer in Mallorca a year or two back?"
"The very same."
"Aw, God help us and save us!" Ian groaned. "What the hell's *he* doin' here?"
"He's working undercover for the UK Customs, but that's not important," said Bob, not intending to waste time on such trifling details. "What *is* important is that you tell him right away that Julie and I are on the ship. Tell him that on *no* account is he to show any sign of recognition when he sees us. If he asks why, just say the initials C-R-A-P."
"Crap?"
Bob dismissed the query with an impatient shake of his head. "It's a long story. Just do as I ask, Crabbie, OK?"

His introduction to Mike Monihan apart, Bob was pleasantly surprised by his first impressions of things aboard the *Ostentania*. Never having been within seven leagues of a cruise liner before, the interior of this particular one wasn't the gaudy monument to ostentation that he'd expected, or indeed that the ship's name suggested. With due credit to Boris Kaminski, his

Ulanova Line's flagship was more of a maritime hotel of understated elegance than some Vegas-style tinsel palace of the high seas. Gilt-framed prints depicting seafaring scenes of yesteryear decorated the wood-panelled walls of the halls and corridors they passed through on the way to their cabin. In an odd way, the sedate ambience reminded Bob a bit of the Dirleton Castle Inn. Yes, to his surprise, he liked it here. He felt at home — well, almost.

"Aha, amidships and not too far above the waterline," Julie said as Bob unlocked the cabin door. "Just right for optimum stability, no matter which way she rolls or pitches."

With a seasickness threshold befitting the devout landlubber that he was, rolling and pitching of any degree did not rate at all favourably in Bob's book. But if, as Julie claimed, the cabin they'd been allotted was in an area of even *reasonable* stability, then that was about the best he could have hoped for. He opened the door and ushered Julie through.

"Well, well, well!" she enthused. "Not bad at all!"

Bob followed her inside. "Yeah," he readily agreed, an approving little smile coming to his face as he cast his eyes about the cabin, "not so bad at that! Yeah, even a desk, a telly, a fridge, a phone, a sofa and, what this in here? Uh-huh — not bad either — a neat wee shower room."

"Yep, could've been a lot worse," said Julie. "At least we've got a picture window instead of a pokey little porthole, although it *would*'ve been better if we had our own balcony."

"Be thankful for small mercies," Bob advised. "Shore lecturers can't be choosers." He then opened the fridge. "Hey, how about this!"

"Wow!" beamed Julie. "A bottle of bubbly!" She took the bottle from Bob and read the little card attached to its neck. "*With the compliments of the Cruise Director*, it says. How thoughtful. Hmm, and I see it's a Cordon Negro Brut from *Freixenet*. One of the best mid-priced cavas. Hey, Kemosabe," she winked, "maybe this Mike Monihan guy isn't such a slimy creep after all, huh?"

Bob nodded towards the opposite end of the cabin, a frown of disapproval creasing his brow. "Putting us into a room with two single beds wasn't so thoughtful of him, though, was it?"

Julie wagged a reproachful finger at him. "Now, now, don't complain. After all," she added coquettishly, "shore lecturer's companions can't be choosers either, *can* they?"

Bob popped the Cava cork and filled two flutes that had been chilling in the fridge. He clinked Julie's glass. "Here's to single beds, then."

Julie gave a little curtsy. "Whatever you say, cap'n."

Bob clinked her glass again, "Aye, aye, shipmate, and here's to a slight rearrangement of the furniture once the sun's dipped below the yardarm!"

The Indonesian girl at reception had informed Bob and Julie that they'd be dining nightly in the Caravel Room, the ship's main restaurant. After informing them that they'd be sharing a table with some of the other "entertainers", she had countered Bob's look of horror by flashing him a reassuring smile and insisting that their dining companions were all people of like intellectual character. Bob and Julie would soon be as good friends with their new tablemates as they had already become with each other during the first week of this cruise.

Bob hadn't been too convinced by what he suspected was more or less a stock spiel trotted out by the girl and her reception-desk colleagues to all seemingly non-gregarious new arrivals. On this occasion at least, his hunch was to be proved correct . . .

"Ah, my dears," a loomingly large woman boomed in plummy tones when the head waiter showed Bob and Julie to her table, "welcome to our joyous little gathering of *bon vivants*."

Bob was instantly struck by the odious thought that she resembled a Wagnerian Valkyrie on steroids. All she lacked was the horned helmet and pigtails.

With a smile as wide as it was fake, the woman extended a hand in Julie's direction. "You must be our new shore lecturer. Oo-oo-oh, my darling," she warbled, giving Julie a disapproving once-over with piggish eyes swimming in a sea of blue eye shadow, "you look as though you've sailed only *just* in time into our little haven of epicurean delights. You're so thin — so *thin*!"

"Pay no attention to her, hen," a dour-looking kilted man sitting opposite the bloated Valkyrie grunted. "She was the original model for the triple-XL *I Beat Bulimia* T-shirts."

Pointedly oblivious to that cutting swipe, the woman pumped Julie's hand. "Allow me to introduce myself. Esme Horrocks-Bunt — Professor." Condescendingly, her eyes narrowed in formation with her smile. "That's Professor of History. Specifically the origins and history of the peoples native to our various destinations, which is the theme of my onboard lectures. Oh yes, my dear, I do several of these cruises every year, you know. Different ships, all over the world. Dozens of different lectures on tap. Each one projection-illustrated, of course. I have literally *thou*sands of slides on CD."

"How interesting," Julie fibbed. "I must make a point of attending as many of your talks as I can."

"Just so," Professor Esme Horrocks-Bunt agreed. "And, uhm, what should we call you two de*light*ful young people?"

"This is my partner Bob Burns — journalist. And I'm Julie Bryson — Doctor. That's Doctor of Biology, Pathology and Medical Law, among other scientific disciplines, none of which have the slightest connection with the themes of my onboard lectures."

"Very wise, my dear," Esme concurred, patently unfazed by Julie's attempted put-down. "The average cruising audience would be bored to death."

Then, switching effortlessly from bitchy to imperious, she proceeded to introduce Bob and Julie to the others already seated at the table. The mousey little man next to her was, she said, her husband Simon, a poet, of whose reputation they would doubtless already be aware. Choosing not to notice Bob and Julie's blank expressions, she introduced a dishevelled, contentedly detached-looking chap as crime writer JP Shand, who, along with Julie and herself, completed the trio of speakers on this cruise.

"And, my lovers, before you ask," said the author, his soft, Bristolian burr blurred by what sounded suspiciously like a drink-promoted slur, "the J's for Jimmy, but folks kep' askin' me where my accordion was, so . . . well, thurr tiz . . . JP Shand I be. Oh, and before you also ask, the P stands for nothin'. No, I just reckons the ol' JP sounds more kinda *crime*-slanted than Jimmy for a bloke that's a-scribblin' the type of books I does for a livin'. Yeah," he chuckled, "that's yer ol' JP as in yer Justice of the Peace, see."

"Very clever," Julie said, smiling courteously.

"Uh-huh, very subtle," Bob vacuously agreed.

The next of this coterie of so-called *bons vivants* to be presented to them was the dour, kilted chap, who, a few moments earlier, had made the disparaging comment about the ample physical dimensions of their self-appointed hostess.

"This is Lex McGinn," said Esme in a throw-away manner. "Featured comedian on this cruise." She gave a derisive little snort. "Yes, 'Laugh-a-Minute' Lex is how he chooses to be billed, although I waited for over half an hour the only time I caught his present act, and not one snigger did his material incite. Lost in translation from the Glaswegian, perhaps?" She contraltoed a Valkerie-like chortle, while looking around for signs of approval for what she apparently regarded as a witty remark. None was forthcoming.

What did forthcome was a notably barbed Glaswegian riposte from the butt of her gibe.

"Fuckin' fat slag," Lex mumbled. "Fuckin' escapee outa *Viz* magazine!" He then addressed Bob and Julie directly. "Tellin' ye, if she ever goes for a swim in the sea, there's gonny be whalers, harpoons at the ready, convergin' on her like flies round a new-laid shite!"

"Coarse boor," Esme Horrocks-Bunt sniffed haughtily.

"First time Ah knew Moby Dick was a fuckin' historian," Lex grumped.

"Thar she blows!" JP Shand quietly burred into his wine glass. "A-a-rr, thar she blows, me hearties!"

With a heavy sigh, mousey little Simon Horrocks-Bunt rolled his eyes and gazed heavenward, as if seeking inspiration for a poetic *bon mot*. All his muse managed to help him produce, however, was a yawn.

What price now, Bob asked himself, the reception-desk girl's assurances of new shipboard friendships being cemented in the dining room? The worst of his cruising nightmares was coming all too vividly true. To be trapped at a table every mealtime with a bunch of people who had about as much in common with each other as Eskimo pacifists at a Samurai warriors' convention was his idea of shipboard hell. And there was more to come . . .

"Ah, there you are, my da-a-a-lings!" Professor Esme beamingly bellowed on catching sight of two lissom but breathless-looking young couples homing in on the table. "Early show in the theatre go fandangoingly well tonight, I trust?" Without waiting for an answer, she started to do the honours for Bob and Julie's benefit.

These were the star dancers of the *Espectáculo Flemenco de Granada*, she informed them, naming the dancers individually as they took their seats at the table. "Always absolutely ma-a-a-vellous when the times of their performances allow them to join us for dinner," she gushed. "So rejuvenating to be in the company of the kids after the final curtain comes down, I always maintain."

"The *kids*?" Bob said to Julie out of the corner of his mouth. "Bit discourteous that, isn't it?"

Julie replied under her breath that it was a pet name in the variety theatre world for the "girls and boys" of the chorus.

"Hmph!" Bob hmph'd. "And how many professors of history would know that?"

Julie gave him a my-thoughts-entirely look, before turning to smile at the male dancer now sitting next to her. He was a swarthily handsome young Spaniard, whom Esme had introduced as José, the leader of the troupe.

How fortunate he was to come from Granada, Julie told him in Spanish. In her opinion, she expanded, it was the most magical of all the cities of southern Spain, if not the entire country. Such architecture! The Alhambra, she reflected, the Generalife, the Alcázar, the Lady Tower and the Partal Gardens. The stunning Moorish beauty of it all, the cool fountain water tinkling into ornamental pools, the snow-capped summits of the Sierra Nevada on the horizon. "*Hombre! Qué sitio más espléndido, eh*?"

"Sorry, chuck, but I haven't a clue what ye're on about," José told her, hunching his shoulders apologetically while fishing an olive from a communal dish of hors d'oeuvres.

"Granada?" Julie hinted, nonplussed. "You know — the jewel of Andalusia?"

"Nah, the only Granada I know anything about, missus, is the TV company in Manchester. I used to deliver pizzas to their studios when I worked for an Italian takeaway around the corner in Gartside Street. Yeah, us in the flamenco team, we're all from Manchester, like." He sat through the ensuing pregnant silence for half a minute, before adding inspirationally that the girl of gipsy-like appearance sitting opposite him — Mags Barraclough, or Margarita Barcelona, to give her her stage name — had once been to Torremolinos on holiday, though.

End of conversation.

"Ah, the wine!" Esme Horrocks-Bunt declared as a waiter showed her the label on a bottle he had just delivered to her side. "I took the liberty of ordering this in advance for us all," she informed the gathered assembly. "I just *know* you'll love it. Delightful young red from the Upper Hunter Valley in Australia. *Excep*tional value as well." She addressed Julie directly again. "Yes, we have a house in New South Wales, you know. On the coast. Divide our time between there and our actual home in the Cotswolds." She sniffed the sample of wine the waiter had poured for her approval. "Mm-mm-mm . . . ma-a-a-a-vellous!"

"Panther piss," Lex McGinn muttered. "More respect for ma teeth than to let that stuff touch them."

JP Shand smiled absently and indicated his already-charged wine glass. "Yeah, and I'll be stickin' with my own and all, my lover. I already 'as 'arf of a bottle of 'im left over from lunchtime, look."

The flamenco troupe also declined Esme's offer. As their leader explained, they had a performance to do a bit later in Crusoe's Palace Show Lounge, the *Ostentania*'s cabaret club, and he didn't want the girls getting shit-faced and falling about all over the place during a paso doble or something.

The two girls made no comment, concentrating their energies instead on looking convincingly Hispanic — even if only from a distance.

"That's right, we've gotta think about our public image," Paco (alias Steve), the other male member of the group confirmed, "so we'll wait an' get bladdered down the crew's bar after hours as usual, like."

Julie gave a polite little laugh. "Pulling our legs, I'm sure. You all look much too physically fit to be big drinkers."

"Don't you believe it, hen," Lex McGinn told her. "They're only dago-ised Manchester clog dancers and they've been breast-fed on Boddington's Beer for generations, the lot o' them. And anyway, everybody looks like Lowry's fuckin' matchstick men in their neck o' the woods. Throwbacks to the days o' dark, satanic mills and all that rickets-riddled stuff — know what Ah mean?"

"It takes one to know one," Esme Horrocks-Bunt growled at the blatantly politically incorrect comedian. "Having studied anthropology, I can verify that your own native city, for like industrial reasons, produced more than it's fair share of emaciated people — some of distinctly stunted growth as well." Like a Trident missile, a piercing look shot from her sea of blue eye shadow. "And you, Mr Laugh-a-Minute Lex McGinn, are a shining example of the mental version of same!"

Lex gave a mocking laugh. "What would you know, ye puffed-up old chancer?"

"How *dare* you!" Esme was incensed. "It would have been a bonus for the rest of us on this cruise if you had followed that equally distasteful countryman of yours into the sea off Portugal — permanently!"

The invisible detective's antennae on Bob's head twitched.

"Not a fuckin' chance, doll," Lex meanwhile scoffed. "Nah, there isnae an ocean big enough for Rab Dykes *and* me."

"What, exactly, do you mean by that?" Bob asked, then immediately wished he'd put the question a tad less eagerly.

Julie dug her elbow into his ribs. "C-R-A-P," she muttered ventriloquist-style, as a timely reminder, if indeed Bob needed one, that his natural policeman's urges would have to be kept firmly in check if he wasn't to risk blowing his cover at the first opportunity.

But Lex McGinn's reply came as a welcome indication that their concerns were unfounded.

"Supported the wrong team, didn't he, china? Aye, ye'd never get me sharin' a bath in the Atlantic wi' a Rangers man." Lex screwed up his nose. "Yeuch! As a true follower o' the Glasgow Celtic, Ah wouldnae want to risk gettin' maself contaminated." He sat contemplating his kilt for a few seconds, then said in a gruff voice, "Wee bastard Dykes is better off feedin' the fishes, anyhow."

"Terminally ill or something, was he?" Bob enquired, trying not to sound too interested this time.

"Fuck knows, pal, but livin' wi' that bloody wife o' his must've been a fate worse than death, anyway. A *right* pain in the neck, she is!"

"And," Esme Horrocks-Bunt retorted, "as I intimated before, Mr self-styled Laugh-a-Minute McGinn, it takes one to know one!"

"Aye," Lex swiftly rejoined, "and as *I* intimated before, Mrs so-called historian *Bollocks*-Hunt, you — by exactly the same token — would be a right dab hand at the whale spottin'!"

A waiter arrived at their table wearing a well-rehearsed, is-everybody-happy? smile. "Ready to order your starters, ladies and gentlemen?" he asked with easy Indonesian grace.

Once again, Bob's tongue was a few seconds ahead of his brain. "Yes, I think I can make it easy for you." he said, patently browned-off with his lot. "Just bring us ten empty bowls, a ladle and a big cauldron of vitriol soup! We'll serve it up ourselves!"

CHAPTER EIGHT

FIVE MINUTES LATER — STILL ABOARD THE CRUISE LINER OSTENTANIA . . .

Bob and Julie were heading from the Caravel Restaurant at one end of the ship to the Stardust Lounge at the other, their purposeful progress indicating that they were in a greater hurry to get where they were going than the groups of leisurely ambling, cheerfully chatting passengers they encountered along the way. If the stormy look on Bob's face didn't say it all, his accompanying words to Julie certainly did.

"Bloody cruise-ship, make-new-friends-at-the-dinner-table tripe!" he grouched. "It's the first and last time I'll join in a bloody chimps' tea party like that!"

"I still don't think you should've walked out before the meal had even started."

"I'd rather starve, and I kid you not!"

Julie was struggling to keep up with Bob's loping stride. She was also struggling to keep a straight face. "Well, you've got to see the funny side of it as well," she panted. "I mean, the look on your face when that Esme woman insisted on having the shrimp chowder instead of the vitriol soup."

"Yeah, well, if she'd been joking, I'd've laughed, but the ignorant old rat bag was being deadly serious.

Professor of History? Professor of *any*thing, my backside!"

"And how about that torn-faced refugee from the golden days of music hall? Laugh-a-Minute Lex? Insult-a-Second more like. What a horrible man! And how about the flamenco *kids*? What a bunch of fakes!"

"Par for the course on Kaminski's cruise ships, I shouldn't wonder. Fill the entertainment bill as cheeply as poss with disgruntled has-beens, no-hope wannabes and brass-necked bullshit merchants, and charge the punters the earth for it."

"Still," Julie grinned, "you've got to laugh as well. I mean, people like that Esme and Lex take themselves so *se*riously!"

"Well, I suppose somebody has to," Bob huffed. "Nah, the old West Country crime writer has the right idea — just get quietly pissed and to hell with everything. Which is what I'll be driven to on this case *very* soon now." He opened the swing doors to the Stardust Lounge for Julie. "Follow your hunches, is what I always say. Yes, ma'am, and I should've followed mine by refusing to come on this lowsy boat trip to purgatory in the first place!"

The announcement earlier in the day that they would be setting sail again tomorrow had spread a sensation of mild euphoria through the ship's complement of passengers — a communal feeling of holiday-time anticipation that had been woefully absent from the *Ostentania* since the recent outbreak of norovirus. Now, the only infectious condition at large appeared to be one of *joi de vivre*. It struck Bob and Julie the moment they stepped into the crowded room.

Tinkling away beneath the general rhubarb of chatter and scattered outbursts of laughter were the bland piano sounds of Ian "Spanish Juan" Scrabster, churning out medley after medley of musak favourites. He gave Bob and Julie a cheesy grin across the empty dance floor as they eased their way through the crush of people milling along the length of the bar.

"I see Green's still on duty," Bob told Julie, then directed her attention to where the hapless rookie detective constable was doing his trainee barman thing for a bunch of impatient customers. "Let's hope Crabbie passed on the C-R-A-P message. You know, *Clandestine* Research And Probing? The last thing I need now is for Green to yell out, 'Hiya, Detective Inspector Burns! Fancy seein' you here!' Laugh if you like, but things as daft as that *have* happened with him before, so keep your fingers firmly crossed."

"Poor Andy. You're far too hard on him," Julie maternally objected. "Just look at the poor kid, trying to cope with everybody badgering him all at once. He looks all of a dither."

"No change there, then," Bob said dryly, shepherding Julie to the corner of the bar nearest Andy's station. "We'll hang about here 'til he notices us. Yeah, but don't hold your breath. He's about as observant as a hibernating hedgehog . . . and very often only marginally more awake."

Only a few seconds later, Julie took evident pleasure in adopting an accusing mien while saying to Bob, "Unjustly maligned, Kemosabe."

"You what?"

"Keep your eye on the ball, laddie. When you were busy observing the rear view of that slinky little Indonesian waitress wiggling past just now, *un*observant Andy Green there gave me a knowing little nod. A nod, for your information, that had C-R-A-P written all over it."

"Let's hope it was cryptic and not literal, then."

Despite Bob's own momentary lapse of concentration, Andy's little nod hadn't gone unnoticed by his current boss. Head barman, Pedro "Speedy" Gonzalez, was on to it like a hovering hawk dropping on a confidently camouflaged mouse with a tic.

"What the fook's your game?" he rasped in Andy's ear. "Know that bird, do ya?"

Andy shook his head vigorously.

Speedy looked him warily in the eye. "No chance you tryin' to pull no new talent before yours fookin' truly, right? That's the fookin' ground rules, right? *Sí*, so just fookin' watch it, skin!"

With a charm-oozing smile, Speedy then presented himself to Julie and Bob. How could he be of service to the *señores*? he asked, making the most of the Mallorcan inflections of his accent.

Julie was first in with a reply. He could be of service by allowing Andy Green to speak to her for a moment, she said, explaining that his mother was her mother's housekeeper back in Scotland and that she had a personal message for him.

Bob was impressed by Julie's slick plugging of a potential hole in their undercover dyke. Not only had she allayed any lingering suspicion of Speedy's that she was known to Andy, but she had also opened the door for their talking to him as acquaintances, albeit once removed, at any future time. Yes, Bob was impressed.

Speedy had been put slightly off his stride, but, ever the professional barman, he smarmed his way through it. "*No problema, señora* — I go serve his customers while you give him message from the *mamá*. *Sí*, for me is *no problema*."

Julie raised a finger. "Ehm, there is actually just *one* problem."

"*Sí, señora*?"

"*Sí*."

Speedy looked apprehensive. Had this foxy lady clocked him slipping a vodka into the old bint's sherry at the other end of the bar a moment ago?

Julie treated him to one of her waiter-melting smiles. "It's actually *señorita*, not *señora*, OK?"

Speedy looked relieved. He also looked delighted. "Hey, OK, *señorita*. *Estupendo*, eh! Speedy Gonzales he gonna be your personal barman here in the *fantástico* Stardust Lounge. Best bar on whole sheep." He nodded as enthusiastically as a randy parakeet. "Now I go get the boy for you. *No problema . . . señorita*!"

"Well," Bob told Julie, "you've certainly got *him* wound round your little finger."

Julie dipped her head in acknowledgement. "And you never know when having him right there will prove extremely useful. Yep, as your chum over there at the piano said, you can find out a helluva lot in a fortnight on a cruise ship, *if* you talk to the right people. And —"

"And," Bob said, hijacking the sentence, "who better to talk to than a cruise ship barman, if you want to know *any*thing on a cruise ship, right?"

"Exactly." Julie batted her eyelashes in mock innocence. "Not that I speak from personal experience, of course."

Bob smiled a wry smile as he inclined his head towards the approaching Andy Green. "Whether or not, the theory is about to be put severely to the test, and I've a hunch it's about to be blown to smithereens."

"To drink, sir — madam?" Green enquired, deadpan.

"A spritzer — rosé, if poss, please," Julie replied.

Bob gave Andy a don't-you-dare-show-a-glimmer-of-recognition glare. "Soda water and lime for me. I want to keep a clear head."

After glancing furtively from side to side, Andy pulled down his lower left eyelid. "With or without C-R-A-P, sir?" he asked, with a look befitting the double agent (of sorts) he was soon to become.

"Cut the crap, Green," Bob muttered behind his hand. "Now," he mumbled to Julie, "introduce me to the offspring of your mother's imaginary Mrs Mop, will you?"

Julie was already on the case. She handed Andy an envelope from her purse, then said for all in the immediate vicinity to hear, "Your mother asked me to hand this to you. Some family news — good, I hope. Oh, and forgive me, this is my partner, Bob. Andy Green — Bob Burns, journalist."

Playing along, Andy shook Bob's hand. "Pleased to meet you, Bob. Written any good stories lately? For adults or just kids' stuff, is it, Bob?"

Julie tittered while Bob fumed. Familiarity breeds contempt, and Bob recognised, much to his irritation, that familiarity from his detective constable was something he'd have to endure on this case, at least in public. He'd kick that familiarity into touch long before it reached the contempt stage, however. He let Andy Green know the fact with one threatening glare right there and then.

Andy got the message. He promptly diverted his eyes from Bob's and concentrated on the contents of the envelope Julie had handed him.

"Here," he frowned, after closely surveying the small sheet of paper for several moments, "this says six toilet rolls, six eggs, six blubbery muffins, Tampax — one packet, mince, bacon — smoked." He shot Julie a confused look. "What's the score, Doc? Does ma mother think Ah can get this stuff cheaper for her in duty-free, like?"

With a beckoning forefinger, Bob invited Andy to move in close over the bar, then said in subdued tones, "It's one of Doctor Bryson's *own* shopping lists, you pea-brained cretin!"

DC Green's frown deepened as he checked the list again. "What's a blubbery muffin, anyway?"

Bob took a slow, laboured breath. "Blueberry, Green, *blue*berry!"

Green shrugged. "Never heard o' them neither. Somethin' like red currants, are they?" He handed the list back to Julie. "Maybe ye'll get them in Tenerife."

Bob groaned. "Tell him," he said to Julie, his eyes closed, his head swaying dejectedly from side to side. "Tell him, before I do a Rab Dykes and take a running jump overboard myself."

Julie, ever the paragon of patience when dealing with Andy, explained quietly that the old shopping list had only been a prop, a sham to make their excuse of giving him a message from his mother appear plausible to Speedy Gonzales.

"Aw, yeah, right, got it now, Doc. But, ehm, what's all this stuff Speedy tells me about your old lady scrubbin' floors for ma mother these days? Bit o' a comedown for a toff like her, intit?"

"Just get the drinks," Bob said through gritted teeth. He faked a happy-to-be-cruising smile for the benefit of others nearby. "Just get the bloody drinks!"

"Certainly, Bob, certainly," Andy breezed. "Enjoy yerself, Bob. Ye're on yer holidays! Now, eh, what was it again, Bob? Oh, yeah, a rosé spritzer for the Doc and a soda and lime for you, Bob, correct?"

"Wrong!" Bob growled. "I'll have a whisky instead. Scotch. Yes, and make it a very *large* one!"

By the time the Sunbeam Band had arrived to take over music-provision duties from Ian Scrabster, the Stardust Lounge was buzzing with bonhomie, and Bob, if not quite three sheets in the wind, certainly appeared to have at least one sail flapping loosely. He wasn't a particularly big drinker at the best of times, and Julie had never known him to get even slightly tipsy when on duty. On this occasion, though, the line between on and off duty was a vague one, and the prospect of being imprisoned on this ship for a fortnight with Detective Constable Andy Green *and* people like those he'd met in the dining room earlier had been sufficient to make him down a few more glasses of whisky than he was accustomed to.

Andy, of course, was wickedly delighted to have the opportunity of making his boss's drinks *very* large ones, and Bob's growing attraction to the shipboard method of payment meant that he had offered no objection. To a thrifty man like him, signing a little piece of paper was a lot less painful than handing over hard cash — even if it would eventually come out of police expenses rather than his own pocket.

"Yer eyes look like piss holes in the snow," Ian blithely informed Bob as he took a seat next to him at the bar. "Been givin' it big licks on the cheap bevvy, have ye?"

"Cheap?"

"Twenty-five per cent discount the Doc here gets as a company employee on the trip. Hope ye're usin' her tab, man."

Normally, Bob would have been somewhat distraught to discover that, by signing for the drinks himself, he had been spending twenty-five per cent more than he should have, but right now he couldn't have cared less.

"Name your poison, Crabbie. Drinks are on me, friend."

"Just a Diet Coke, Bobby, thanks."

"*Coke*?" Bob screwed an eye into focus. "What the hell's wrong with *you*? Told you — my shout."

"Nah, I've got another set to do in an hour. Gotta give the band there a break, ye see."

"So what? Nobody in here listens to you anyway. Have a bloody drink!"

"No, no, like I said, I never drink on duty." He cast Bob an accusing glance. "Not like some folk I know."

"Comes with the territory. All us *journalists* drink on the job." Bob wasn't so tiddly that he'd forgotten what he was there for, as witness his emphasising of the word "journalist" for the benefit of a rather spivishly dressed man in his sixties who had sidled up to them.

"Wall," the man said, introducing himself with an oily smile. "Walter Walter-Wall." He handed them a business card each. "Walter-Wall — with an 'yphen — Floor Coverings of 'Ackney — not to be confused with a carpet company of similar 'andle in the north of England. Oh, yes indeedy, Walter Walter-Wall for all your vynils, linos, tiles and wood laminates. Ware'ouses all over London and the 'Ome Counties." His accent was almost convincingly posh, apart from the dropped aitches, that is. "Floor coverings — what other business could a chap with a name like mine go into, ay?" He let out a raucous, saloon-bar guffaw that opened another crack in his la-di-da veneer. "Walter Walter-Wall . . . wall-to-wall-to-wall. Do you follow me?" He let rip with another bellowing laugh.

No one joined in.

Julie gave him back his card. "That's good of you, Mr Wall, but —"

"Please, my dear, you don't 'ave to be so formal." He patted the back of her hand. "No, no, no — consider me a friend. Yes, just call me Wally."

"Would, uh, that be with or without the indefinite article?"

Julie's acerbic dig appeared to go straight over Walter Walter-Wall's head. "*Def*inite is the only word to describe the items of merchandise I sell, lovely lady. Ah, yes indeedy, *def*inite bargains, every one."

"That's good to know, but as I was about to say, I'm OK for floor coverings at the moment, thanks."

"Ah, but the day will come, my dear." He returned the card to her hand. "The day will come, and that's when you will be glad to make a call to Walter Walter-Wall. Privileged prices for cruising acquaintances, especially on receipt of an up-front deposit, you know."

Julie flicked the card onto the bar. "Many thanks, but no thanks. I live a long way from 'Ackney."

Walter wasn't to be so easily put off, however. "Free delivery," he oiled. "Free delivery *and* free fitting anywhere in the 'Ome Counties, my dear."

Julie gave him a chilly smile and pushed the business card along the bar. "I'm afraid Edinburgh's a long way from 'Artfordshire, Mr Wall."

"It is?"

"Yes, about four hundred miles, give or take."

The glib-tongued Walter finally gave up — but only on Julie. He tried his luck with Ian Scrabster next.

"'Aven't I seen you somewhere before, squire? No, don't tell me." He placed a forefinger to his temple. "Let me think. I 'ave a great memory for faces, you know. Now just let's see if —"

"This is Juan, the ship's cocktail pianist," Julie cut in. "He's been playing in the lounge here for the past hour or so. Perhaps that's where you remember his face from?"

It was clear that Walter Walter-Wall had no immediate answer to that, but just in case he was trying to think one up, Julie headed off the sales pitch that would doubtless accompany it by informing him that Juan lived even farther from 'Ackney than she did. "Mallorca, Mr Wall, to be precise."

"*Sí, señor*," Ian (in Juan guise) confirmed, "and I no speak the Eengleesh so good and I no got no *casa* in London also."

Another dry well for Walter-Wall. That left only Bob as a possible patron. Walter tried a fresh approach.

"And, er, I couldn't 'elp but over'ear what you said as I approached, squire, and I was intrigued to 'ear that you're a journalist. Yes, and I could 'ear from your accent that, like the charming young lady 'ere, you're from north of Watford as well, ay?"

Woozy as he was, Bob was on the point of asking this pushy interloper which of Julie's two key words he hadn't understood — "no" or "thanks". To those, he was of a mind to add "bugger" and "off", but Walter got in before him.

"Well," he said, shoulders raised, palms upturned, "I may open a ware'ouse in your part of the world one day, my friend, but I fear I shan't be able to offer you the benefit of my free-delivery, free-fitted, floor-covering services *just* yet already."

"Good," was what Bob was about to say, but once again Walter's lip was quicker off the mark.

"Newspapers pay good money for exclusives, do they not? Yes, and I may just 'ave a juicy bit of info for you." He tapped his wallet pocket. "*If* a mutually favourable business arrangement can be arrived at, of course."

"Not interested," Bob snapped. "The magazines I write for don't do juicy bits."

Walter Walter-Wall raised his shoulders again. "Fair enough, squire. I 'ad more or less decided to save my info about the man-overboard incident 'ere until we're back in Blighty, anyway." He tapped his breast pocket again. "Might get a nice little bidding war going with the tabloids, ay?"

Bob was sobering up fast. "What, uh, overboard incident would that be, then?" he enquired with feigned vagueness.

"The only one that's 'appened on this 'ere cruise to date, as far as I'm aware," Wily Walter replied. Then, noting Bob's poorly disguised interest, he casually informed him that he'd see him around. With that, he bade the threesome a fond farewell and sashayed off, no doubt to offer the opportunity of bargain floor coverings to what he hoped would be more receptive ears — domiciled, preferably, in the 'Ome Counties.

"Pale blue suit an' brown suede shoes," Ian muttered, reverting to his Scottish persona.

"You what?" said Bob, frowning.

"Wally Walter-Wall. Shifty bastard, that. Aye, never trust a man wearin' a pale blue suit an' brown suede shoes. Especially wi' dyed black hair."

"I wouldn't trust that one, even if he was wearing the crown jewels and an ermine-trimmed cloak," Julie added.

"Even more so," said Ian. "Ye can't trust blue bloods either. Long history o' lyin' and thievin' and murderin'. How else do ye think they got to be blue bloods in the first place?"

Bob was deep in thought — a more sluggish process than usual, thanks to the surfeit of whisky he had downed during the evening. Still, a policeman's mind is a resilient organ, and the pipes in Bob's were still playing, albeit a mite out of tune. Which just happened to coincide with the Sunbeam Band striking up at the other side of the lounge.

"What a bloody racket!" he scowled. "Are these old guys tone deaf or something?"

Ian nodded his head ruefully. "Yeah, probably *stone* deaf as well, a couple o' them. The National Youth Orchestra of Indonesia, as they're referred to by certain non-Indonesian cynics on this tub."

Julie squirmed. "But they're so off-key! How in heaven's name did they land a job on a cruise ship?"

Ian motioned towards the happily smiling passengers now crowding onto the dance floor. “There’s yer answer. Most o’ the punters on these boat trips couldn’t tell their arses from their A-flats — *plus* the Sunbeam Band works cheap. Aye, don’t forget this is the Ulanova Line ye’re on, by the way.”

Bob was still considering the man-overboard bait that Walter Walter-Wall had dangled in front of him. Chances are, he mused, that the sleazy git was only trying to sucker him out of a few hundred quid. Then again, every lead — *any* lead — was worth following up at this fallow stage of operations. He’d have to make a point of bumping into Walter again, and the sooner the better. That said, he probably wouldn’t have to go to too much trouble to do that. A wheeler-dealer like Walter-Wall would make sure that *he* bumped into him, and that wouldn’t prove very difficult, given the confines of life aboard a cruise ship.

Satisfied with this conclusion, Bob ordered himself another whisky. Time to relax. Nobody on the ship would be going anywhere until they reached the Canaries, and that was a day and two nights away. Plenty of time to check out Mr Walter-Wall, and anyone else who happened to be of interest as well.

Andy Green served Bob his next whisky. “Hittin’ it a bit hard, Bob, aren’t ye?” he remarked with obvious glee. “Hope we won’t have to chuck ye out for bein’ drunk and incapable, eh!”

“I *beg* your pardon?” Bob was deeply niggled, and he let it be shown.

Andy Green, on the other hand, was thoroughly enjoying this previously un-dreamed-of chance to talk to his boss in an insubordinate way, particularly as Bob's defences now appeared to have been significantly weakened by liquor.

"Just kiddin', Bob," he grinned. "Just you enjoy yerself, Bob. Drink up, Bob — ye're on yer holidays!"

Bob beckoned him to lean in close across the counter again.

"Make the most of this, Green," he snarled, his nose almost touching Andy's. "Because, if you slip up and call me by my first name any time we meet in private on this case, you'll be joining wee Rab Dykes as fish fodder faster than you can count up to three. That's *if* you can up to three. Do I make myself understood?"

"Y-yeah — perfectly, boss," Green quavered. "Ah mean, Ah never meant to —"

"And *don*'t call me 'boss' in public, you dim-witted bloody sumph!"

"Y-yeah, understood, skipper — aw, shite, Ah mean, Bob, like."

"Ebbryseeng she be OK, sir?" It was the voice Pedro "Speedy" Gonzales, his head appearing over Andy Green's shoulder like a Latin jack-in-the box. "The boy Andee he be geebing you the *bueno* service, *sí*?"

"Yeah, yeah, everything's fine — great service," Bob smiled. "I was, ehm, I was just telling him a dirty Scottish joke there. Yeah, a wee taste of home, you know." He gave Andy's shoulder an avuncular pat. "Away from his mother for the first time and everything. You know how it is."

Speedy said he did indeed know how it was, but the way he said it made Bob wonder.

"Are you *sure* you haven't given that little guy any sort of clue about who we really are?" he hissed at Andy Green as soon as Speedy had retreated out of earshot.

"No, honest, boss — Ah mean, Bob — never. Naw, when yer mate Fats Scrabster came in and gave me the C-R-A-P lowdown about you and the Doc bein' here on yer Rab Dykes undercover stuff, Ah knew Ah had to keep dead shtum to everybody, like." He leaned towards Bob and gave him what was intended to be a confidence-boosting wink. "Candlestein Research and Probing, eh? Yeah, and Ah'm still yer very own Mr Candlestein himself, Bob, never you fear."

Bob shook his head despairingly yet again. "Just pass me the water for my whisky, Green," he droned. "Just pass the bloody water, for Christ's sake."

While this cosy little exchange had been going on, Julie and Ian had become involved in conversations with different groups of passengers a little farther along the bar. Ian's motive was to develop contacts for freebie after-gig drinks. Julie's, on the other hand, was to satisfy her natural appetite for meeting new people and making convivial small talk. Bob, for his part, was happy to leave them both to their chosen devices. Despite the mellow spread of whisky through his veins, his policeman's steely will was still too welded to the case to allow it to be detached by the isn't-it-wonderful-to-be-cruising? glow of goodwill that now pervaded the Stardust Lounge — the fact that they were still anchored off Gibraltar notwithstanding.

He sipped his whisky, tried to close his ears to the discordant outpourings of the Sunbeam Band, made a conscious effort not to make eye contact with the skinny old woman sitting alone and twitching in time to the beat at a nearby table, and concentrated totally on observing and making mental notes.

"Evenin', shag. 'Ow's yer parts?"

JP Shand's soft, Bristolian drawl melted into Bob's whisky-lulled right ear like a spoonful of honey dribbling into a mug of hot toddy. It reminded Bob of childhood days at Dirleton Village School; of characters in Robert Louis Stevenson's *Treasure Island*, his favourite book ever; of Long John Silver and Ben Gunn; of Jim Hawkins and the Admiral Benbow Inn; of salty dogs and pirate maps; of square-rigged ships and creaking timbers; of the flung spray and the blown spume and the lonely sea and the sky. Well, OK, if Bob remembered right, that last bit was from *Sea Fever* by a bloke called Masefield, who probably never even met Robert Louis Stevenson. But there were common denominators, and the sound of JP Shand's voice reminded Bob of them. It gave him a warm feeling.

JP's hand rested gently as a parrot's foot on Bob's shoulder, and a whiff of rum drifted past his nose. Bob half expected to hear him say, "Pieces of eight, Jim lad. Arrgh, and 'em as dies'll be the lucky ones!" But instead he repeated, "'Ow's yer parts, shag? All ship-shape and Bristol-fashion, I 'opes."

Bob hadn't paid a great deal of attention to JP back in the plush petulence of the Caravel Restaurant. He'd been just one of several faces that Bob had seen once and hoped never to clap eyes on again. Yet this middle-aged man, who'd come across as a contented drunk with laugh lines holding up the bags under his eyes like a sea dog's hammock strings in a sailing ship of old, had exuded a kind of freedom of spirit that Bob could relate to. He'd mentioned this to Julie, though obliquely, in the aftermath of their aborted dinner date with Esme Horrocks-Bunt & Co. Bob looked the weathered crime writer in the eye now, and he liked what he saw. The feeling appeared to be mutual.

"Mind if I sits 'ere beside you, my boy?" JP asked, his well-lived-in features wrinkling into a smile as open as the Bristol Channel. "I've been meanin' to 'ave a yarn with you about the indigestive qualities of vitriol soup, so I 'as."

CHAPTER NINE

THE NEXT MORNING — IN BOB AND JULIE'S CABIN . . .

Little Bits and Pieces . . . Bob could remember hearing that record being played over and over again by the uncle of his pal, wee George Tait, some twenty-five years earlier. Back then, Bob had only just started to take his first faltering steps into the grown-ups' fascinating world of alcohol consumption; a gulp or two of cooking sherry, perhaps, from a jam-jarful spirited away by wee George from his auntie's kitchen, or maybe a slug or two of Tennent's Lager from a can one of the lads had procured by means unknown to and uncared about by the others in the little group of twelve-year-old boys, gathered for experimental imbibing purposes in the graveyard of Dirleton village church.

Bob could well recall that, while he and his chums had quite liked the sweetish taste of the sherry, none had truthfully enjoyed the mouldering bitterness of beer. "Horse piss" was what wee George always maintained the taste of beer reminded him of, although it had remained a mystery as to where and when, or if at all, George had slaked his thirst on a sip of urine from, say, an obliging Clydesdale or philanthropic

Shetland Pony. In any case, despite the unpleasant effect of beer on adolescent taste buds, the lads had persevered with their alcoholic explorations, if for no better reason than to ogle the tantalising pictures of curvy babes flaunting their stuff on the Tennent's tins of the time.

Little Bits and Pieces . . . In those days of his only *slightly* sullied youth, therefore, Bob had never quite understood the fascination this song held for wee George's uncle, especially on Sunday mornings. He understood well enough now, though!

His mouth, as George's uncle would declare on those selfsame Sunday mornings of a quarter of a century ago, tasted like Gandhi's jockstrap after a game of elephant polo. While it was unlikely that George's uncle had undertaken any more personal research into the validity of this colourful simile than George had done in relation to his beer-related one, Bob had to admit that he'd be hard pushed himself to think of a more accurately descriptive alternative at this moment in time. His mouth did indeed taste bloody revolting. And, as with the seriously hung over party animal in the song, his recollections of last night's events were only now beginning to return — in little bits and pieces.

He was sitting on the edge of his bed, still fully clothed, his head in his hands, his nervous system in meltdown, his temples throbbing, his tongue like sandpaper, his surviving brain cells doing a casualty count inside his cranium. What was that line in George's uncle's song? Yeah, that was it — "*Did I* really *hit the whisky when the party ran out of beer?*" In Bob's case it had been the other way round, except for "whisky" read "rum", and for "beer" read "whisky".

Not that the bar in the Stardust Lounge had run out of anything, of course. No, it was just that JP Shand, having used his "vitriol soup" intro as a launch pad for a well-worded character assassination of Professor (so-called) Esme Horrocks-Bunt, had picked up on Bob's *Treasure Island* musings. The natural progression of the conversation had led to an in-depth discussion of the origins of the "tot of rum" tradition in the navy. This, in turn, had led to JP's suggestion that Bob should join him in a sample tot of Captain Morgan's Dark, in his opinion a direct rum descendant of the tipple favoured by such swashbuckling buccaneers as Long John Silver himself.

It had seemed like a sensible enough idea to Bob at the time. Perhaps predictably, though, one tot had led to two, two to three, and three to . . . well, that's when the black velvet curtain had closed over the window panes of Bob's memory.

"Whisky and rum," he moaned, while plucking up enough courage to take a tentative peek through his fingers. "Never again. Never *ever* again."

Squinting against the bright sunlight pouring in through the cabin window, he glanced at the small travel clock on the bedside table, which latter item, he noted, was still firmly located in its original position between the two single beds. Ah well, the best-laid plans . . .

He blinked and did a double-take at the little clock. Nearly eleven o'clock. Bugger it — he'd slept in, and how! The sound of heavy chains rattling jarred his brain. The anchor! Shit, they must be getting ready to put to sea. Better get sorted out double quick and tackle the day head-on. Things were happening. The game had started and he wasn't even on the pitch. And come to think of it, where was Julie? He looked across at her bed. Not even slept in! He felt the makings of a hangover-fuelled anxiety spasm coming on. Long time since he'd had one of them. OK then, up and at 'em, Burns!

As he struggled to his feet, it felt as though someone was inserting a red-hot girder through his brain, from the top of his skull downwards. His eyes watered and his eardrums beat in time with his pulse. Something akin to a bossa nova rhythm. Not normal. Not healthy. Whisky and rum? Never again. Not *ever* again! Water. He must have water — fizzy, if possible. Life or bloody death.

Just then, the door knob rattled. Someone was coming in. The cabin steward, or maybe one of the maids doing her bed-making rounds! Bob looked at the state of his clothes, at the state of his bed covers. Both had the appearance of having been attacked by an army of Tom Jones fans. Jesus H Christ, he couldn't let strangers see him like this! Bad for the professional image — even if he *was* supposed to be a journalist. But there was nowhere to hide. Not even in the shower room. Steward or maid, they'd have a pass key for that as well. He was trapped. His anxiety spasm was rapidly graduating into a full-blown panic attack. Never had one of them before. Clasping his forehead, he slumped back down on the edge of the bed, palpitating.

"*Fifteen men on a dead man's chest —*

Yo-ho-ho and a bottle of rum!"

The door flew open, and the singer of the sea shanty swept inside, grinning.

"*Drink and the devil had done for the rest —*

Yo-ho-ho and — Ah, so you've returned to the land of the living? Come on, shipmate — show a leg!" It was Julie, fresh as a daisy and rarin' to go.

Bob breathed a quivering sigh of salvation. "Where the hell have you been?" he groaned, every word a knell tolling against the girder inside his head. "I thought you'd done a Rab Dykes."

Julie placed the brief case she was carrying on the desk, then, with a sprightly clapping of her hands, urged Bob in true seafaring tradition to, "Rise and shine, the morning's fine!"

Bob massaged his brow. "*Don't* clap your hands, puh-*leeze*!" he pleaded. "I've already got Quasimodo knocking shit out of the biggest bell in Notre Dame Cathedral right inside my nut here!"

Julie hauled him to his feet. "Come on — out of those clothes and into the shower. God, what a state your bed's in!" She started to strip the covers off. "I'll remake it before the cabin maid comes along."

"But that's what *she*'s paid to do," Bob objected, with as much interest as he could muster — which wasn't a lot. "Why do her out of a job?"

"It's just a thing I sometimes get about strangers fussing with my bed clothes. I'd rather do it myself."

"But it's not even your bed."

"Well, I made my own when I got up at half-past-seven this morning, so I'm not going to leave yours looking like a dog's breakfast now."

Bob shook his head, carefully. "Posh Glaswegians. Paradoxes personified, every one of them."

He was silently relieved, however, to hear that Julie had actually slept in her own bed. For all he could remember, she might just as well have headed off into the shadows of last night with Speedy Gonzales.

"What's with the briefcase?" he asked.

"Oh, that's all the shore-lecture material the previous incumbent kindly left for me. Mike Monihan handed it over when I went for his pep talk this morning. The job should be a piece of cake, incidentally. Yes, the old dear left all her notes for me to mug up on — even her slides of places of historical interest and stuff like that. Must make sure I tell the punters the *right* places to spend their money in when they go ashore, though." Julie gave Bob a crafty wink as she put the finishing touches to smoothing his bedcover. "The old kickback caper for the Ulanova Line, you know."

Bob wasn't really listening. His mind was still preoccupied with thoughts of avoiding a slow, painful death — his own. "Must have a drink of water," he croaked, meandering over to the fridge with his eyes half closed. "Life or bloody death."

"Talking about your bunk being like a dog's breakfast," Julie said, "you should see the breakfasts you get up in the Crow's Nest Restaurant on the top deck. Self-service buffet, but fantastic choice. Bacon, eggs, sausages, mushrooms, hash browns, baked beans, fried bread . . ."

Her review of the breakfast menu cross-faded with the sound of Bob dry-vomiting his way posthaste into the shower room.

"Yo-ho-ho!" she grinned when he reappeared a couple of minutes later. "Just as well you didn't have the *full* bottle of rum, me ol' hearty!"

"Don't (sniff!) ever mention rum (sniff-burp!) to me again." Bob was choking on the words, his eyes streaming. "*Or* fry-up breakfasts, either. Now, let me at that water!"

No sooner had Bob opened the fridge door than he was making another gagging dash for the shower room.

"I'm surprised you've got so much to throw up," Julie commented, showing a distinct lack of the Florence Nightingale spirit that Bob currently craved, "considering you've had nothing to eat since those two greasy pork pies you scoffed in Ye Olde Rock pub in Gib yesterday afternoon." She smiled mischievously as the inevitable result of the pork-pie recollection echoed from the shower room. The smile faded from her lips, however, when she looked inside the fridge to see what had prompted Bob's sudden compulsion to make a further call to Ralph and Hughie on the big, white porcelain telephone.

Gingerly, she lifted out the small plastic container. "How absolutely disgusting," she muttered. "How on *earth* did this get in there?"

"So it's real, then?" said Bob, on making another rheumy-eyed exit from the shower room. "That's a relief. I thought I'd maybe been having an attack of the heebie-jeebies."

Carefully, Julie removed the transparent lid from the box. "It certainly wasn't in there when I went to grab a glass of milk first thing this morning."

Squirming, Bob peeked over her shoulder. "Judging by the Pluto signet ring, I think it's safe to say that this is the same chopped-off finger as the one in the picture Bruce McNeill gave me back in Edinburgh."

Julie flashed him a chastening look. "If it is, both you and Bruce McNeill have been taken for a right couple of chumps."

"What are you talking about?" Bob retorted. No matter how under the weather he was feeling, he didn't take kindly to having his professional perspicacity rubbished out of hand like this. "I mean, I know you're hot stuff at the forensic science game, but before you cast aspersions on Bruce McNeill and me, you should —"

"Do a bit of DNA matching between the finger and any samples of wee Rab Dykes's profile we happen to find?"

"Yeah, well . . . something like that."

Julie plucked the finger from its cotton wool cradle and waggled it in front of Bob's face. She then rolled it into something resembling a small Swiss roll.

Bob was flabbergasted. "It's a . . . it's a . . ."

"If you were going to say 'joke', you'd be dead right. Yes, Kemosabe, it's a joke finger, readily available, for even schoolkids to buy, from novelty shops everywhere." Julie gave Bob a who's-casting-aspersions-now? look.

Bob got the message. Suddenly, he wasn't only feeling *physically* sick. Someone unknown was taking the complete mickey, and that hurt his pride more than the after-effects of the whisky and rum were hurting his head.

Julie then lifted from the little box a doubled-over piece of paper that had been concealed under the rubber finger. She unfolded the paper and handed it to Bob. "A message for you, I think."

Bob's already wan colouring paled even more as he read the note aloud:

"*Welcome aboard, Inspector Burns. I had a feeling the photograph I sent your boss would bring you on this cruise*."

"And the question now," Julie said, "is who sent Detective Superintendent McNeill the picture?"

"That's easy. It was sent by Rab Dykes's wife — obviously."

"Why obviously?"

"Well, who the hell else would have sent it?"

Julie curtly replied that the answer to *that* question could well turn out be vitally important. "And," she continued, "the next question is —"

"Yeah, I know — I'm not *that* bloody daft. How the hell did the fake finger get into the fridge, right?"

"Absolutely. And if you hadn't been lying there comatose when it happened, you'd know the answer, correct?"

Bob was getting rankled now. "Yeah, yeah, yeah!" he barked. "Don't rub it in, eh! I'm feeling bad enough about all this without you sinking the boot in when I'm down."

Julie maintained a tension-building silence. Bob was indeed down, and she *was* enjoying sinking the boot in — but gently. "Can you remember what happened in the Stardust Lounge last night?" she eventually asked.

"*Little Bits and Pieces*," Bob said under his breath. "I'm now about to get the same humiliating treatment as the poor sucker in the song, drop-by-cringe-making-drop. Typical bloody woman!"

"Talking to yourself again?" Julie smirked. "A sure sign of —"

"OK, OK! I've heard all that stuff from you often enough before, so just drop it, OK?"

"Oops! Getting a wee bit tetchy, are we?"

Bob didn't reply. It's difficult to be assertive when you're shackled by self-inflicted amnesia.

Once more, Julie let the tension build for a few minutes, then repeated the taunting question, "Well . . . *can* you remember what happened in the Stardust Lounge last night?"

Bob was familiar enough with Julie's quirky sense of humour to know that the prime purpose of this goading was more for the benefit of her own amusement than for any sadistic desire to see him suffering any more than he already was. The snag, however, was that, in his present fragile state, this knowledge was blurred by the overwhelming feeling of self-pity that invariably accompanies the condition. There was also a creeping sense of shame associated with what he might actually have got up to in the Stardust Lounge last night. Considerations of Julie's personal amusement aside, then, he was aware that she would make the most of any unremembered misdemeanours on his part in order to rub enough salt into whatever psychological wounds she could open. This, naturally, for the commendable objective of teaching him a lesson — as if he needed one!

But the *Little Bits and Pieces* treatment was already under way, and Bob had no choice other than to meekly endure it, for however long it might take to complete — and he knew enough about the female character to accept that it could be dragged out, drop-by-cringe-making-drop, for an uncomfortably long time. In the interim, shouting his mouth off in defence of actions of which he had no recollection would only run the risk of making himself look an even bigger chump than he already did.

"All right," he said with a sigh of helpless resignation, "let's have it. What *did* I get up to in the Stardust Lounge last night?"

Julie stepped round behind him and began to help remove his crushed jacket. "Would you like me to start the story from before you fell off the bar stool or after?"

Bob's shoulders descended into a droop of abject defeat. "Please, God, no," he moaned. "I didn't, did I? E*spec*ially not in front of PC Andy bloody Green!"

Julie was now unbuttoning his shirt with the cold-hearted brusqueness of the retirement home nurse she occasionally chose to ape. "We'd better get you out of these things and into the shower, hadn't we, deary?" She then started to unbuckle his belt.

Bob offered no resistance. "This is beginning to remind me more and more of the song," he mumbled.

"Oh yes? And what song would that be, deary?"

"*Little Bits and Pieces*. Yeah, and in particular, a line that goes, *Did I take off* ALL *my clothes*?"

Julie unzipped his fly with a flamboyant sweep. "Only your trousers, Kemosabe. Only your trousers."

Just then, the door opened, and Samson, their Indonesian cabin steward, entered. He took one look at Bob standing with his pants round his ankles and assumed the obvious. "Sorry, sir, madam, I thinking you be out. Sorry, please, I go come back later." Bowing penitently, he began to shuffle backwards through the door.

"Not so fast, Samson," Julie called out. "It's all right — you're not disturbing us." With a reassuring smile, she beckoned him to come back in. "I need to ask you a question, anyway."

"Yes, please, madam," Samson nodded, his eyes lowered to avoid contact with Bob's naked nether regions. "I do anything you wanting, thank you very much, please."

Whistling a silent tune, Bob stood staring in contrived nonchalance at the ceiling, while Julie proceeded to quiz Samson on the subject of the fake finger in the fridge.

Samson smiled shyly and explained that he had found the little plastic box on the floor just inside the door of his store cupboard earlier that morning. There had been an unsigned note attached, asking him to deliver it, as a surprise, to this particular cabin. He had knocked at the door, but as there was no response, he'd assumed the cabin was empty. On entering, he'd noticed that the gentleman was still in bed sleeping, so placing the box in the fridge had seemed like the best idea — "for making good surprise, yes please, no?"

Samson then covered his mouth with his hand and giggled in a child-like treble. "Is only jokey finger, madam," he told Julie. "No is being real one, please." He then went all serious. "Samson be looking careful at him in box before bringing." He shook his head gravely. "You no making kick-Samson-up-the-ass problem with boss mans, please and thank you very much, yes?"

Julie assured him that he had done everything absolutely correctly and that there would be no repercussions from his superiors. On the contrary, his actions had been exemplary, and this would be reflected in the end-of-cruise tip she and the gentleman intended to give him.

Patently both relieved and delighted, Samson smiled a final string of pleases and thank-yous while backing out of the door and closing it quietly behind him.

"Nice chap," said Julie. "We're lucky to have such an attentive steward."

Bob had more on his mind, however, than the quality of the staff. Significantly, though, his normal Presbyterian reserve didn't compel him to feel too concerned about the cabin steward having caught him with with his trousers down. He was realistic enough to assume that cabin stewards on cruise liners saw a lot worse than that every day of their lives. No, what bothered him most, in addition, of course, to the black hole in his memory relating to the happenings of the previous night, was that someone on the ship not only knew his true identity but also the real reason for his being on this particular cruise. The thought that he may have compromised his professional position with DC Andy Green by making a drunken fool of himself in front of him sent a shudder of mortification up his spine as well.

Right! It was high time to give himself a shake and get to grips with the whole exasperating business. Kicking off his trousers, he downed half a litre of fizzy water from a bottle in the fridge, belched circumspectly into his fist, then strode resolutely into the shower room.

"Don't you want to know all the sordid details about last night?" Julie called after him.

"They're already coming back to me," he lied.

"And?"

"And none of the little bits and pieces bothers me a jot!" He crossed his fingers as a refreshing jet of tepid water sprayed down on his head. "My conscience is clear," he shouted, "and my reputation remains as pure as the driven snow!"

Julie smiled a knowing little smile.

CHAPTER TEN

LATER THAT MORNING — ABOARD THE CRUISE LINER OSTENTANIA . . .

Julie had discovered the Bosun's Locker, a quiet little lounge tucked away in a corner adjacent to the ship's library, while exploring the various decks during Bob's involuntary lie-in that morning, and it was into its tranquil ambience that she now led him for a reviving cup or two of strong black coffee. The room, like most of the other public areas within the ship, was virtually deserted, most passengers having elected to go outside and watch the Rock of Gibraltar recede into the distance as the *Ostentania* headed for the open Atlantic, bound at long last for the Canary Islands.

Although feeling far from chipper, Bob was putting a brave face on things, while still attempting to give the impression that he was now in full mental possession of all relevant details of the previous evening's events. He settled down with Julie on a comfy couch by a window. Glancing out, he waved his hand and said, "Bye-bye, Gib, and good riddance. If nothing else, I won't forget your pork pies in a hurry."

"Nor the happy evening you spent while anchored off the Rock," Julie smiled, with an almost schoolmarmly note of approbation in her voice.

This punch of velvet-glove sarcasm struck home, but Bob rode it without comment. He had little choice. A white-jacketed waiter approached, bade them a gracious good-day, took their order for coffees, then returned behind the small corner bar to set his espresso machine to work. The sound of its hissing and spitting aggravated Bob's still over-sensitive hearing something bloody terrible, but he pretended all was well. Again, he had little choice.

"Yes," he said in a business-like manner, "it'll be interesting to see what Detective Superintendent Bruce McNeill has to say now. While you were freshening up, I sent him an email from my laptop asking how he came by that photo of the supposedly chopped-off finger."

"Wouldn't a phone call have been more secure?"

"Six and half a dozen. Anyway, an email's cheaper, and that'll keep the bean-counters at HQ happy."

They sat in silence for a while, gazing out of the window as the iconic outline of the Rock of Gibraltar faded into the distance.

"Nice to see you looking bright-eyed and bushy-tailed so quickly," Julie said at length, then took a sip of her cappuccino. "You country boys obviously have fantastic powers of recovery."

Bob responded with a modest smile and a sideways dip of his head, then lifted his espresso from the coffee table in front of the couch. Unfortunately, the rattling of the cup on the saucer and the shaking of Bob's hand as he attempted to find his mouth with the rim of the cup totally blew the fantastic-powers-of-recovery tag that Julie had teasingly bestowed upon him. She suppressed a snigger.

"Yes, and the next thing I'll be doing," Bob blustered, returning the coffee-filled saucer to the table and taking the cup firmly in both hands, "is to set up a meeting with young Green and ask him what he knows about the Rab Dykes incident. I'll then work out a plan of action from there."

Julie let that apparently confident statement of intent hang in mid-air while she took another leisurely sip of coffee. "But you've already set up a meeting with Andy Green," she eventually revealed, only just managing to keep a straight face. "Three o'clock this afternoon in the Stardust Lounge." She paused to savour the confused expression spreading over Bob's face. "Nice and quiet at that time of day, Andy said last night. Remember?"

Bob faked a little chuckle. "Ye-e-es," he said expansively, "of course I remembered. Just checking you did, that's all."

Slowly, Julie bowed her head in an exaggerated show of gratitude. "Oh, well, that *was* considerate of you."

Bob was painfully aware that Julie was watching his every move, so he concentrated all his mental and physical energies into lifting his cup as unshakily as possible to his lips, then swiftly tipping what little coffee it still contained into his mouth. His feeling of achievement was considerable, though short-lived.

"Aren't you going to drink what's in the saucer as well?" Julie asked. She then repeated her retirement-home-nurse impersonation. "It should be cool enough for you now, deary."

Bob knew he was on a hiding to nothing if Julie persisted in taking a delight in kicking him when he was down, but he was spared further immediate ribbing by the arrival in the Bosun's Locker of a vaguely familiar figure wearing a battered Panama and a crumpled linen suit. He was sure he had met this tall, rather gaunt-looking, old chap before. But where . . . and when?

"Ah, how fortunate to find you here, Bob," the elderly fellow beamed. "I was just thinking about our conversation last night, as it happens. Well met, indeed."

Bob stood up to shake the old gent's proffered hand. "Yes, I — I —"

"And we meet formally at last," the old chap said to Julie. "Yes, Bob tried to introduce us last night, but it was so crowded in the Stardust Lounge and your company was being monopolised — perfectly understandably, I may say — by so many others that we never quite managed to connect." There was an almost imperceptible hint of a heel-click as he bowed and raised Julie's hand to his lips. "I'm Rupert De'ath, ship's surgeon. Delighted to meet you, Doctor Bryson. Yes, Bob here was singing your praises to the heavens last night — and perfectly understandably at that, if I may say so."

A sliver of light was beginning to filter through the cobwebs shrouding Bob's recollection faculty. Politics. Politics and drink. Yes, that was it. This old guy had joined in the conversation he was having with JP Shand about rum, and had guided the subject round to vodka, which, Bob now recalled, the old guy was downing like water. Talk of vodka had led, naturally enough, to Russia, and from Russia to the pros and cons of communism. And from this to . . . well, that's when the memory spider had completed the spinning of those darned cobwebs.

In any case, wherever last night's conversation had ended up, one question remained constant in Bob's mind, and that was how the hell this old codger could put away so much vodka and still remain conscious, never mind reasonably lucid. And look at him now! No morning-after doldrums and shakes for him. He was the very epitome of senior-citizen fitness and health. Bob wondered, and not without a modicum of envy, just what his secret could be. He was about to find out.

"It is indeed a great pleasure to have a fellow student of the sciences on our little team," Doctor De'ath said to Julie. "I do hope we can meet occasionally to, uhm, compare notes, as it were. One never stops learning, does one?" He then proceeded to give Julie a potted autobiography, which culminated, to Bob's great relief, before drifting into another dreary lecture on Russian politics. No, Vodka was to be his closing subject this morning.

"I drink *far* too much of it," he confessed, though more with a note of pride than remorse. "A legacy of my long immersion in Russian culture, you understand." With an impish wink, he pointed to a slight yellowing of the skin around his eyes. "First sign of liver damge, which suggests that mine is made of corrugated iron, considering my age and the lifetime of abuse I've subjected it to."

This statement was a conversation killer of the first order, so Bob and Julie could only sit in silence and leave the talking to Doctor De'ath.

"Ah yes," he continued, "it has never failed to fascinate me that alcohol plays such an important part in the culture of so many different countries. It *identifies* many of them, really. Your whisky in Scotland, rum in Jamaica, gin in Holland, your tequila in Mexico, port in Portugal, cognac in France, vodka in Russia." He made a theatrical sweep with his hand. "Oh, but I could go on and on."

Just as Bob and Julie were about to thank heaven that he wasn't going to go on and on, he did . . .

"But a side-issue which has added to my fascination is one that I knew nothing of, until joining this ship and visiting Spanish territories for the first time in my life." His face lit up at the very thought. "And, if I may, I shall now give you a practical demonstration." He turned his head and called to the barman, "The usual *carajillo*, please — there's a good chap. And, uh, easy on the coffee, what?" He turned back to Bob and Julie. "You know the custom of the *carajillo*, I take it?"

"No," said Bob.

"Yes," said Julie, "it's a strong coffee, laced with — well, brandy usually, or maybe a shot of anise. Traditional Spanish way of kick-starting the metabolism in the morning. In fact," she added, her eyebrows elevated to an altitude indicating mild astonishment, "I've seen many an old Spanish farmer having his first one in a bar even *before* he's had breakfast."

"Precisely, Doctor Bryson —"

"Julie, please."

"Precisely, Julie. And, if I may, you are about to witness my modest contribution to the marriage of the cultures of Spain and Russia."

The waiter arrived right on cue, carrying a small tray on which he had placed a cup, containing just about enough coffee to cover its base, and a large glass of clear liquid.

"No prizes for guessing what's in the glass," Bob commented, shuddering slightly at the notion.

"Precisely, Bob, precisely." Rupert De'ath took the glass, emptied its contents into the coffee cup and gave the resultant mixture a quick stir. "Here we have my input to the cultural alliance of two great countries." He held the cup aloft, as if about to propose a toast. "The Molotov *Carajillo*! Cheers!"

Bob and Julie looked on in wonderment while he downed the revolting-looking concoction in one.

Doctor De'ath smacked his lips. "Strong coffee and the hair of the dog. The ideal hangover antidote — minus a touch of vitamin C, admittedly, but the administration of a goodly dose of Bloody Mary a bit later will put that right."

"You've obviously gone into the medical side of this very thoroughly," said Bob, not intending to sound facetious, though realising too late that he had.

He needn't have worried. The doctor had clearly taken no offence. "If medical considerations came into it, laddie, I wouldn't have found myself in a condition that demanded such a cure in the first place." He gave Bob a you're-not-kidding-anyone look, then crooked a thumb in the direction of the bar. "Shall I prescribe the same medicine from the dispensary for you?"

Bob raised his hands into the have-mercy position. "*NO*! I mean, no thanks, Doc, I'm — well, I'm kinda resigned to following a cold turkey out of the abyss, if you know what I mean."

"In which case, I salute your bravery, dear boy, and I wish you the very best of British." Rupert De'ath then signalled the waiter to bring him a refill, quickly adding a vocal instruction to go even easier on the coffee this time. An overdose of caffeine he most certainly did *not* want.

Although every nerve end in Bob's body was pleading with him to go and lie down in a darkened room with an ice bag on his forehead, the policeman in him was bugling up a call to duty. This dipso doctor sitting opposite him could well be a valuable source of answers to the Rab Dykes question, so best to start pumping him before he drowned in vodka . . .

"Ehm, I hope you don't mind me asking, Doctor De'ath —"

"Rupert, please."

"Right, uh, Rupert. Yes, I hope you don't mind me asking," — Bob cleared his throat in preparation for a bit of bluffing — "but you may remember I mentioned last night that I'm researching a magazine piece on cruising, and —"

"I remember everything from last night, my dear fellow, but I don't recall you mentioning anything of the sort."

Julie almost choked on her coffee.

Bob knew he had to think fast here. "Ah, yes, you're absolutely right," he chanced. "You were talking to someone else at the time, I think."

"Indeed?"

"Indeed."

"Oh well, *c'est la vie*." Doctor De'ath made a do-continue gesture with his hand.

With the minimum of preamble, Bob introduced the subject of the Rab Dykes man-overboard incident. Had the doctor any views on the matter? he enquired, in as blasé a manner as he could affect.

"Views?"

"Yes — you know — whether it was suicide, misadventure or even murder."

The doctor chortled into his *carajillo*. "That, laddie, is the question asked *every* time someone goes over the side of a cruise ship. Which, incidentally, happens a lot more often than most people imagine. Hardly ever given much media coverage, you see. Cruise line PR chappies make sure of that." Sudden death, he elaborated, was an everyday fact of life when cruising, anyway — especially if, as was usually the case, the complement of passengers comprised a large percentage of elderly people. Why, he himself had known his little mortuary to be filled to overflowing on several occasions — especially during spells like the recent outbreak of norovirus.

"So," Bob pressed, "you have no opinion on whether this Dykes bloke was bumped off or not?"

Rupert De'ath thought carefully before answering. "Strictly off the record, right?"

"Right."

"Right." He struck a confidential pose, one hand shielding his mouth, as if to stymie any lurking lip-readers. "The particular overboard case you refer to could well have been the near-perfect murder."

Bob and Julie swapped glances charged with intrigue.

"Really?" Bob said, attempting to present an air of insouciance, but not quite managing it. "What, ehm, what makes you think that . . . Rupert?"

"All about timing, dear chap. All about timing, and it was near-perfect in this instance."

"Really?"

"Really."

Bob emulated the doctor's do-continue hand gesture of a minute earlier.

The doctor duly continued. What, he asked, was the essential element in the solving of any murder? He answered the question himself with one word — "evidence". And what, he further enquired, would be the best way of eliminating the type of evidence that could be scientifically analysed? "Fire" was the single word he offered as a reply this time. Except, he went on to qualify, aboard a ship, where "fire" ranked alongside "sunk" in the league table of most loathsome four-letter words.

Bob was already getting cheesed off with all this long-winded stuff, but circumstances dictated that he couldn't show it. Maintaining a patient, casually interested look was essential. Not easy when a darkened room and an ice pack beckon.

The ship's doctor put his next question to Julie. What, in her scholarly opinion, he wished to know, would be the next best thing to fire for the purpose of eradicating evidence of the forensic variety? Not, he promptly appended, that he expected her to have any personal experience of that rather sordid branch of science.

Julie pouted pensively. "The next best thing to fire? Well," she shrugged, "a good, old-fashioned scrub, I suppose."

"Precisely. And when would anyone feel inclined to scrub an entire cruise liner?"

Bob and Julie exchanged glances again — anxious ones this time.

"Ah, I can see that you're abreast of me," smiled Rupert De'ath. "The answer is, of course, following an outbreak of a contagious shipboard condition, such as that so recently promoted by the nasty norovirus on this very vessel. *And*, quite significantly, that outbreak occurred almost immediately following the demise of Dykes." He raised an emphasising finger. "Timing, my friends. Perfect timing — an essential component of the perfect murder."

Bob scratched his head. "Wait a minute, Doc, you *surely* can't be suggesting that someone purposely introduced the norovirus bug so that its incubation period would expire right after this Dykes guy was murdered."

"Yes and no."

"Yes and no, what?"

"Yes, I'm suggesting that the bug *could* have been so introduced. And no, I'm not suggesting that Dykes was murdered. All I'm saying is that, if he *had* been, anyone investigating the crime now would be hard pushed to glean any forensic evidence relating thereto."

Bob scratched his head again. "No offence, but it all seems a wee bit far-fetched to me. A bit like the plot of a bad detective novel I seem to remember reading once."

Doctor De'ath laughed out loud. "But it *is* the plot of a detective novel — although it's as well you didn't refer to it as bad when our friend JP Shand outlined it for us in the Stardust Lounge last night. It's the basis of his new book . . . as, my dear boy, you will doubtless recall."

Julie sniggered.

Bob flustered. "Yeah, well, yeah — I recognised it as JP's plot, but I — I —"

Julie came to his rescue. "As a matter of interest, Rupert, just how thorough was the disinfectant treatment given to the ship at Gib?"

"Put it this way, my dear young lady, I'm surprised there's any paint left on any surface throughout the entire vessel. Yes, as I said, the near-perfect murder — *if* indeed it was a murder."

Bob decided he'd better make immediate amends for his recently dropped memory-lapse clanger. "But if it wasn't a murder, Rupert, how would you account for the severed finger?"

Doctor De'ath looked deeply puzzled. "Severed finger?"

"Yes, you know, the one the woman found in her quiche lorraine."

"Quiche lorraine?"

"Yes — right here, in one of the ship's restaurants."

"A finger in a quiche lorraine?" A fit of silent laughter sent spasms through the doctor's bony body. He stood up, reached over and laid a hand on Bob's brow. "Just as I suspected — cold and clammy." Chuckling, he patted the top of Bob's head. "I think, laddie, that you should sign the pledge forthwith. Yes, for it's my expert diagnosis — gleaned from personal experience — that you're displaying some classic signs of the onset of the DTs. A severed finger in a quiche lorraine?" he laughed. "Well, well, well, I've heard it all now!"

Suddenly, the ship gave a lurch, then began to roll — heavily, in Bob's landlubbing opinion.

"Aha, a slight swell," said the doctor, looking out of the window. "Always the same when we enter the Atlantic from the Strait of Gibraltar. Crosscurrents, you know." He swigged down the last of his Molotov

Carajillo. "Now," he smiled, "if you will excuse me, comrades, I must be heading back to my surgery. A queue will be forming for seasick remedies even as we speak." He saluted, clicked his heels, and bade them a polite farewell — in Russian.

"*Da svidanija*," Julie repeated as Doctor De'ath strode out of the lounge.

"Yeah, dah whatever," Bob muttered, then said to Julie, "How the blazes could an old piss artist like that get a job as a ship's doctor?"

"Probably the same way the Sunbeam Band got hired — by working cheap."

"And I wouldn't be surprised either if all that Russian stuff ties him in with Boris Kaminski somehow or other. Nah, we'll never know what characters like that got up to behind the old Iron Curtain."

"Anyway, more to the point — what now the finger-in-the-quiche affair?"

Dolefully, Bob shook his head. "The fickle finger of fate," he droned. "Yeah, right now, it's dangling in my mind's eye like an upside-down Sword of Damocles, and it's got three little words written on it."

"Not 'I love you', surely."

"No, 'Up yours, mate!' "

"Hey, don't get all brought down," Julie breezed. "Come on — even if it all turns out to be a hoax, at least you can look forward to two weeks on a luxury liner at the expense of Lothian and Borders Police."

"Cosmic. My idea of complete bloody heaven, and I don't think."

The ship had now started to roll a mite more noticeably.

Bob clutched his stomach. "I think I'd better go and join the queue at Doctor Death's door."

"Nonsense! Seasickness is a state of mind. And anyway, there can't *possibly* be anything left in your stomach after all the puking you did earlier. So, come on — let's get some food inside you. You'll feel all the better for it."

Bob was now looking distinctly green about the gills. "N-no, I don't — I really don't think that would be a good idea, honestly."

But Julie was persistent. She grabbed him by the hand and hauled him to his feet. "Lighten up, Kemosabe, you're still *far* from being a candidate for the ship's mortuary, believe me."

"Aye, well, you wouldn't say that if you were looking at the world through this pair of bloodshot eyes, believe *me*."

Julie steered him towards the door. "I discovered a fantastic little snack bar overlooking the indoor tropical gardens in the atrium. Nice and quiet and airy. Nice soups and salads and pastas and little savoury pastries and things like that. *Plus* there won't be any Esme Horrocks-Bunt & Co to get up your nose. They'll all be sparring across their table in the Caravel Restaurant, as usual."

Bob rolled his shoulders. "Well, hm-m-m . . . well, OK, then," he grudgingly conceded. "You've talked me into it."

"Attaboy!"

"Yeah, but on one condition and on one condition only."

"Which is?"

"That they don't serve any goddam quiche lorraine!"

CHAPTER ELEVEN

3p.m. THAT AFTERNOON — IN THE STARDUST LOUNGE OF THE CRUISE SHIP OSTENTANIA . . .

Julie had been right. Bob did feel all the better for having had a light lunch in the Atrium Buffet. Not that he could truthfully call it even a *light* lunch, as all he'd managed to face was a bowl of tomato soup and half a slice of toast. Still, it had stayed down, and that was something, considering his stomach's sympathetic reaction to the heaving of the ship when it first met the swell of the Atlantic Ocean a bit earlier.

Meanwhile, Julie had been summoned to Mike Monihan's office for a programme-revising session with the other two "cruise lecturers", crime writer JP Shand and Esme "Professor of History" Horrocks-Bunt. The themes of their respective talks, which venues they'd be given in and at what times, would have to be fixed now, so that details could be posted in the ship's newspaper, the original advertised schedule having been rendered obsolete by the general disruption caused by the norovirus outbreak.

Julie's early departure from the café had given Bob an opportunity to sit alone for a while, quietly looking down at the palms in the atrium's tropical garden, while nursing a glass of water and setting his surviving brain cells the task of recapping events to date. His brain cells were unlikely to be overworked, however, since details of any significance already on mental file would hardly have been sufficient to fill the cerebral cavity of a gnat.

What, after all, did he *actually* have to go on? A ten-a-penny man-overboard report and a claim by the victim's wife that the insurance company concerned was trying to diddle her out of a possible pay-out (and a suspiciously large one, at that). The location of the alleged incident? A cruise ship owned by a shady east-European with an alleged interest in gaining control of Glasgow Rangers Football Club and a related share-buying arrangement (alleged) with said victim. Forensic evidence of possible foul play? More than likely little or none, thanks to the thorough post-norovirus cleansing of the ship. A body? Definitely none — only the victim's allegedly severed finger, which had now turned out to be a fake, with its alleged discovery in a passenger's quiche lorraine a non-event — allegedly. Suspects? Well, just about everyone he'd met so far on this ship had been an oddball of some kind, but that was no reason to point the finger of suspicion at any of them. Of them all, only Esme Horrocks-Bunt and Lex "Laugh-a-Minute" McGinn had given any indication that they didn't particularly like Rab Dykes, yet this could hardly be taken as grounds for accusing them of anything untoward, either.

Hell's teeth, when Bob thought about it, he hadn't all that much more to go on now than he'd had when leaving his boss's office in Edinburgh three days ago!

And neither had the reply to the email he'd fired off to DS Bruce McNeill this morning yielded anything in the way of help. All his boss's lightly coded message had revealed was that the photograph of the severed finger had been received by email from a London news agency, who declined to reveal their source, as they were perfectly entitled to do in the absence of a court order. DS McNeill had warned that the last-mentioned item would probably be difficult to obtain in this instance, then closed by advising that all appropriate action was being taken to move things forward at his end, and that Bob should continue with investigations at his.

Well, at least, as predicted, the Stardust Lounge was now quiet, and, better still, head barman Speedy Gonzales had decamped to supervise potentially more-lucrative drinks sales in Crusoe's Palace Show Lounge, where an afternoon bingo session was currently taking place. This would be an ideal opportunity, then, for Bob to quiz Detective Constable Andy Green about happenings prior to his and Julie's arrival aboard the *Ostentania*. What's more, with Julie still otherwise engaged in the Cruise Director's office, Bob would be able, subtly, to find out from Green whether or not there was any truth in Julie's defamatory assertions about certain trouser-dropping and falling-off-bar-stool incidents the previous evening.

And then Ian Scrabster swept in.

"Aye, aye, Bobby," he winked. "sobered up now, have ye?"

With a sharp head movement in the direction of Andy Green, Bob shot Ian a not-in-front-of-the-bloody-subordinate glare.

Andy Green, meantime, remained circumspectly aloof, busying himself polishing glasses at the other side of the bar.

Ian slapped Bob on the back. "No sweat, Bobby," he grinned. "I won't interrupt yer C-R-A-P work, or whatever ye call it. Nah, I'm just here to do an unscheduled bit o' ivory ticklin', that's all. A wee bonus, ye could say, for the punters. Aye, all part o' the Ulanova Line's drive to compensate the poor bastards for the inconvenience o' the recent shit-and-honk plague." He winked again. "Suits me, man, even if none o' them come and listen." As was his wont, he rubbed forefinger and thumb together. "I'm now performin' strictly piecework-style on this trip, see, so the more extra gigs the better, get me?"

Andy continued polishing glasses until Ian had crossed to the other side of the dance floor and commenced his first medley of elevator-music standards. Andy then sidled up to Bob and said, "The usual, Bob, is it?"

"Cut the familiarity stuff, Green," Bob grunted. "That's only to protect my cover, and there's nobody near enough us to threaten that right now, understood?"

Andy did a quick survey of the almost-empty lounge, then shrugged. "Fair enough. The usual is it . . . boss?"

"Don't get cute with me, kiddo. Matter of fact, my advice to you is to give your brain a rest and just call me 'sir' at all times in here, right? That way there's less chance of you dropping us in it if the wrong pair of ears happens to be in the right place at the wrong time."

"Whatever you say, boss — I mean, Bob — oops! — sir."

Lightly, Bob stroked his still-throbbing forehead. Then, remembering that he needed to elicit some potentially sensitive info from DC Green, he adopted a more conciliatory manner. "So, ehm, Andy," he said through a laboured smile, "enjoying your role as a barman, are you?"

"Yes, sir. Thank you, sir. The usual, is it, sir?"

Bob was tempted to ask if there was a packet of paracetamol behind the bar, but he girded his perseverance loins, smiled again and said, "Just an orange juice, please, Andy. But first, a word in your shell-like, if you don't mind."

Andy stretched over the bar and cocked his ear. "It's all yours, sir."

"OK, OK, son," Bob grimaced, "don't overdo the formality and confidentiality bits, OK? Just, you know, just act *na*turally."

Andy stood up, turned side-on to Bob and started to polish another glass. "This better, boss — shit! — sir?"

"Yeah, yeah, yeah, that's just fine now." Bob raised his patience level, counted to ten, then lowered his voice. "Now, if you can maybe wear your policeman's hat for a moment . . ."

Andy was bewilderment incarnate. "But Ah never even brought it with me. Ah mean, like, Ah haven't even got one now, ye see. Handed it in wi' the rest o' ma uniform, didn't Ah, when ye took me off the school crossin' patrols to join the CID, like . . . sir"

Images of truck loads of paracetamol appeared before Bob's weary eyes now. He inhaled deeply and open-mouthed, like a drowning man coming up for the third time. "Look, son, I want to bring you in as soon as poss on this hush-hush job I'm on here, but . . ."

Andy went all confidential again, though less conspicuously so than a moment before. "I'm yer Mr Candlestein his-self," he reassured Bob out of the side of his mouth, without looking up for even a split second from the deliberately overt glass-polishing task in hand.

"But," Bob continued, "I need you to give me a barman's perspective on something first. *But*," he swiftly reiterated, while looking Andy Green frankly in the ear, "it's a policemanly barman's perspective I'm after, OK?"

"Perspextive," Andy loosely parroted, clueless, but still polishing, eyes down.

"That's right," Bob persevered. "Perspective, son — of the policemanly barman's variety."

Andy devoted a few moments to silent contemplation, then asked, "Could ye run that past me again — in English?"

Once again, Bob was beginning to understand the type of situation that might drive a man of stable disposition to jump overboard, but he had other matters to clear up with Andy Green before he broached that one. "So," he stoically told himself, "never say die, Bob — yet!" He conjured up another wooden smile. "It's just, Andy, that I hope you're keeping your policeman's head on at all times, as well as your barman's one."

"Eh?"

"You know, keeping a weather eye open for miscreants while doing your cocktail-mixing thing behind the bar there?"

"Miss who? We get a lot o' birds in here and it's hard to remember all their names, like."

Bob caressed his forehead again. "No, no, kid," he groaned, "you misunderstand — or maybe you just misheard. I said *miscreants* — people guilty of misdemeanours."

"A helluva lot o' Misses, Ah'm thinkin'."

"Don't think, Green," Bob muttered, his patience threshold descending rapidly. "It's when you're *not* that you're at your best."

Andy Green took that as a compliment. "Yeah?" he grinned.

"Yeah."

Andy's bright countenance darkened slightly. "But, not wantin' to sound big-headed or nothin', it's not just a common barman's job I'm doin' here, ye know."

"Yeah?"

"No. Ah'm what's known in the hospitality trade as a *mixologist*, see?"

Bob put on a show of surprised admiration. "Well, that's a *lot* different from some of the names you've been dubbed in your other trade back in Scotland, I must say."

"Dubbed?"

Bob made a rapid window-polishing movement with his hand. "Forget it, kid. Just forget it. I'll get you a dictionary for your next birthday, OK?" Then, inwardly, he said, "*If* you make it!"

Andy Green's thoughts were now locked in the complexities of mixology. With a casual nod of the head, he gestured towards Bob's drink. "Are ye, uhm, sure ye wouldn't like me to mixologise yer orange juice for ye, sir? There's one we call *The Valencia Volcano*. We do that one wi' the orange juice, Vermouth — that's somethin' like Martini, like — gin and eh . . ." He placed a forefinger on his chin and raised his eyes heavenward, as if seeking a divine memory-prompt from the Master Mixologist in the sky. "What the fuck is it again? Cointreau or —"

"It's OK, Green," Bob butted in. "It's OK. I really don't want *any*thing alcoholic in my orange juice, thank you very much — honestly!"

Andy Green appeared to be an ice cube or two on the miffed side of crestfallen. "But Ah could give ye double measures and only put it on the tab as a single *Volcano*, mind. No problem that, 'cos we do it most o' the time the other way round. Yeah, so Ah'd be well covered stocktakin'wise an' all."

It was evident to Bob that Speedy Gonzales had wasted no time in drumming into Detective Constable Andy Green the priorities of an efficient cruise ship barman. Green's expenses claim sheets would have to be scrutinised *very* carefully indeed when he returned to his police duties in Edinburgh. But that was a world away from the *Ostentania* and Bob's current concerns. Which reminded him — Julie could come wafting in at any moment.

"Look, I'll come right to the point now, son," he said, displaying a well-balanced mix of professional gravity and avuncular sociability. "I take it that the Ulanova Line have a fairly strict code of behaviour that they expect their passengers to comply with?"

"Fairly," Andy shrugged. "But ye've got to remember they're on their holidays an' all, though."

"Still, I mean, you wouldn't — in your capacity as a mixologist in here, for example — condone unseemly behaviour of any kind, would you?"

"Condone?"

"Try 'allow' for size."

"Unseemly?"

"Yes, you know, breach of the peace, as you and I in the fuzz call it. Or maybe drunk and disorderly. Indecent exposure. Unseemly things like that."

"In here?"

"Yes."

"When?"

"Oh, I don't know, but let's say . . . well, let's say last night, for example?"

Andy's frown was one of confused concern. He leaned his elbow on the bar, hooked a forefinger over his chin, half closed his eyes and murmured, "Are you tryin' to tell me somebody done a unseemly in here last night, sir?"

If Bob hadn't been so edgy about the possible outcome of this exchange, he would have laughed his socks off. Instead, he upheld a demeanour of avuncular professionalism. "Yes, well, I'm more than likely way off the mark, but I thought I overhead somebody — up in the Atrium Buffet it was — telling somebody that somebody dropped them in here last night."

"Ye mean, dropped *one*, right?"

"No, no, definitely *them*."

"Them?"

"Yeah, you know — trousers."

Andy drew himself up to his full height, stuck his chest out and gave a dismissive little snort. "No way, José. Nah, nah, nah, nothin' like that's permitted in here. Down in the crew's bar, for sure — every night it happens. But in here? No way. Nah, the guy that done it would've been threw out — unconspiculous, like, but out all the same."

"So, you're saying that nobody dropped them in here last night. Is that what you're saying?"

"Correct. *Them*, no, but *one*, definitely. Yeah, Speedy reckons it was that Walter Walter-Wall geezer. Was boastin' about havin' two plates o' a chick pea curry last night, so he —"

"That's fine, kid," Bob interjected. "Too much information, OK? Now, ehm, the other thing I overheard was that maybe somebody fell off a bar stool or something. I mean, you'd've noticed something like that, wouldn't you?"

"Certainly! *Fell* off a bar stool?" Andy gave another dismissive snort, then headed off to the other end of the bar to serve a newly arrived customer.

And Andy had snorted only just in time, because no sooner had his snort put Bob's mind at ease than Julie swept in, as bright and breezy as the ocean views that graced the picture windows lining either side of the Stardust Lounge.

"*Hola*!" Ian called to her over his mike. "*Buenos dias*, lovely lydee! Now Juan gonna sing you *especial* lovely-lydee song." With that, he launched his vocal chords into an old ditty called *Did You Ever See A Dream Walking*?

No matter how appreciatively the choice of song might have been received by Ian's usual holiday-hotel audiences, the cheesy connotation didn't go down well with Bob. "Enough to make you puke," he grumped.

"Aha," Julie smiled, "and talking of puke, you look a *lot* better, Kemosabe!" She glanced at Bob's orange juice. "Andy's been looking after your vitamin C replenishments, I see."

"Well, a lot more sensible than old Doctor Death's prescription of a Bloody Mary, and that's a fact."

"And talking of Doctor Death," Julie said, "I mentioned our chance meeting with him to Mike Monihan. Told him about the old guy talking the hind legs off a donkey."

"Uh-huh?"

"Yeah, and Mike said we must've caught him on a good day, because the last time he'd been in the Doc's company, he'd been so stotious he'd hardly been able to string two words together."

"You don't say."

"Yes, and that had been at a sort of health-aboard-ship update with the Captain, no less."

"The mind boggles. You wouldn't want to take ill on this tub."

"Talking of which," — Julie gave him a playful punch on the chest — "your own self-imposed ailment *cer*tainly seems to have been shown the door, huh?"

"Which," Bob said caustically, "is more than can be said for the bloke who dropped his drawers in here last night, right?"

"Sorry? You've lost me."

"Shown the door."

"Shown the door?"

"Yes, which he would have been, *if* he had dropped his drawers."

Julie started to giggle. She was trying her best not to, but she couldn't help it.

Bob's expression, conversely, couldn't have been more humourless. "I checked with Green, all right?" He tapped the side of his head. "Us bozo-brained detectives do manage to winkle out the relevant info occasionally, you know."

Julie pulled herself together — almost. "Well, now you know how crap you'd have felt if you really *had* mooned in public."

Bob shook his head, his lips drawn into a slightly smug imitation of a smile. "You underestimate me, though. That's your trouble, Julie. I mean, I *have* actually got more self esteem than to let myself down in public the way you suggested — even allowing for the effect a couple of drinks on an empty stomach can have on a bloke."

"Really?" Julie replied, trying hard not to start giggling again.

"Yeah, really." Bob noticed Andy Green approaching. "Now," he said to Julie, a revived note of authority in his voice, "can we drop the whole silly subject of what I *did*n't do last night and get on with the job — please?"

Julie gave him a be-my-guest nod of the head.

"Sorry I had to rush away there, sir," Andy politely smiled. "No, what I was about to say, sir, is that nobody fell off a bar stool last night."

"You've already implied that, Green," Bob gruffly replied, a revived note of superiority in his voice now.

"Yes, sir, but what I was about to add was that nobody actually *fell* off a bar stool last night. No, for Ah saw it maself, like. Yeah, that old JP Shand gadgie *shoved* ye . . . sir"

Once the ensuing hilarity had died down and Andy had resumed his mixologist's duties further along the bar, Julie admitted to a markedly unamused Bob that she had trumped up his two purported transgressions of the night before as a leg-pull, and that Andy's part in the mischief-making had been purely a passive one, dictated by Julie herself. Bob's immediate assertion was that making him the butt of ridicule in front of a junior officer amounted to a pretty ill-conceived joke — a daft, schoolgirly prank that had achieved nothing but the potential undermining of his authority. Julie's fairly predictable response was that Bob had set himself up for it by getting half blootered — of his own free will — and that a much more serious outcome than having his leg pulled in private by two colleagues could have resulted.

"It's hardly the point," Bob came back, well aware that what Julie had said was perfectly true, but loath to admit it, nonetheless. "I mean, it's clearly vital that I present a certain image to the likes of Green. That's what maintaining a position of authority over these rookie cops is all about. Lead by example."

"Oh, come off it!" Julie scoffed. "What century have you arrived from? It'll have done your standing with young Andy no harm at all to let him see you're only human like the rest of us."

"You still miss the point."

"No, Kemosabe, *you* miss the point!" Julie was getting right on her high horse now. "You're the one who tarnished your precious *certain image*, and if you want my opinion, it's the best thing you could have done!"

"You're talking rubbish," Bob huffed.

"No, I'm telling you the truth! Unintentional as it may have been, getting yourself steamboats last night was the best possible image you could have presented to anyone who saw you — and plenty did."

Bob was beginning to get rattled. "You're not making any sense, so just give it a rest, right!"

But Julie had her teeth in his ankle and she wasn't for letting go — not until she had nipped a chunk out of it. "Think about it. You're not the great *I am* here, only the anonymous sidekick of the shore lecturer — me."

That stung, but Bob attempted to brush it off. "So?" he said airily.

"So, nobody expects you to act like some self-important detective inspector who never puts a foot wrong in front of his minions. You're just Joe Bloggs now, remember? That's what working undercover is all about, in case you'd forgotten."

"OK, OK, you've made your point, so don't push it. It's bad enough being lumbered with this damned stupid case without being lectured by you when I'm feeling like shit."

"And that's another thing! You haven't stopped moaning since the moment you got Bruce McNeill's phone call outside the Castle Inn back in Dirleton, and I'm sick of it!"

Bob was temporarily dumbstruck.

Julie wasn't. "Face it — most guys in your shoes right now would be absolutely delighted to be handed a piece of cake on a plate like this."

"Piece of cake? What the hell are you on about now?"

"Well, if you were so inclined, you could just sit on your bahookie, enjoy the free holiday, then go back and tell Bruce McNeill that the entire case was a load of bollocks. After the post-norovirus clean-up, finding evidence of dirty deeds is going to be tough enough, anyway. And as for other aspects of the investigation, you could just say that nothing came to light, despite your most *stren*uous efforts. Yes, you'll never have a better opportunity to do bugger all except go through the motions and have a bloody good time without disturbing the moths in your wallet!"

Bob was quick to pooh-pooh the very idea of it. "That's the *last* thing I'd do, and you know it!"

"What — disturb the moths in your wallet?"

An involuntary smile played at the corners of Bob's mouth. She was quite a box of tricks, this Julie Bryson. Cuter than a bag of monkeys. First she lulls you into a cradle of self pity, then worries your nuts off with bogus *Little Bits and Pieces* stuff, stirs up your most egotistical presumptions to the point of over-defensiveness, then lets you see how bloody silly you're being with the neatly timed delivery of a perfect little put-down. Clever.

With a mission-accomplished twinkle in her eye, Julie tweaked Bob's cheek. "Haw, wiz that a wee smirkie Ah noticed sweetenin' up that soor face o' yours, big man?" she said in her usual ersatz version of Glasgow-speak.

Despite his best efforts to continue an air of seriousness, Bob's "wee smirkie" soon blossomed into a full-blown grin, just as Julie had known it would. "Maybe," he said, "but the moths-in-the-wallet crack was well below the belt."

"So, it's lighten-up time at last, is it, Kemosabe?"

"Well, it won't be easy under the circumstances, but I'll try my best."

"And you'll be a bit nicer to Andy Green?"

Bob gathered his lips into a reluctant pucker. "Hmm, well, OK . . . but only until this case is over, mind you."

"Which suggests that you aren't just going to sit on your bahookie and enjoy the rest of the cruise in the lap of pampered luxury?"

"I can't think of a more miserable way of spending a fortnight than sitting on my backside watching a watery horizon drift by in the company of hundreds of Ambre Solaire-reeking sun-worshippers laid out on deck like human sardines. No, I've got a job to do, thank heavens."

"Here's hoping it keeps you smiling, then."

"As I said, I'll do my best, and a bloke can't promise more than that."

Julie cleared her throat and gave Bob a coy, permission-to-speak look, which he returned with an assured, fire-ahead one of his own.

"Well, it's just that, in my capacity as undercover sleuth's assistant, while attending Mike Monihan's meeting in my capacity as shore lecturer, I had a quiet word on the side with my fellow speaker, your old drinking buddy, JP Shand the crime-writer man."

"And?"

"And I mentioned Doctor Death's assertion that wee Rab Dyke's demise formed the blueprint of the plot of his new book."

"Go on."

"And I thought he was never going to stop laughing."

"And did you tell him that Doctor Death claims that he, old JP, told me this book-plot stuff last night?"

"Naturally."

"And?"

"And he said that's a load of old codswallop. Said he can remember everything that was said last night, and talk of the overboard incident being connected in any way to his new book didn't come into it. Most definitely not. He was absolutely adamant about that."

Intrigued, Bob stroked his chin. "Hmm, makes you wonder what Doctor Death's game is then, doesn't it?"

"Maybe nothing. Probably just the mental meanderings of an old lush."

"Could be. Yeah, could be at that, but . . ." Bob pursed his lips, weighing his thoughts carefully.

"But what?"

"I dunno. Maybe nothing." He motioned with a flick of his hand towards the bandstand. "But it just reminds me of what old ivory-tickling Scrabster over there always says."

"Accent the devious, eliminate the obvious?"

"Yeah." Bob stroked his chin again. "Except there's nothing obviously devious to accent, is there?"

Julie hunched her shoulders. "You're the sleuth. I'm only the messenger, so what would I know?"

Bob sensed that Julie had more up her sleeve. "OK, messenger, any more messages to deliver?"

"Just the one."

Bob snapped his fingers. "OK, deliver, deliver!"

"It's on the subject of the chopped-off finger in the quiche lorraine."

"Uh-huh?"

"Yes, it's really strange."

"In what way?"

"Well, only that Doctor Death said the incident never happened, remember?"

"Yeah, I do, but what's so strange about that all of a sudden?"

"Just that I asked Mike Monihan about it after old JP and Esme Horrocks-Bunt had left his office." Julie noticed Bob's sudden look of angst. "No, no, it's all right," she assured him, "I did it in a round-about sort of way, without letting any cats out of bags or anything. No, I just said I'd overheard somebody joking about it and I wondered what was funny about finding a finger in your food."

"OK, fair comment. So, what did he have to say about that?"

"He burst out laughing as well — even louder than old JP Shand did when I asked him about the book plot thing. Said it was all part of the show."

"The finger in the quiche?" Bob frowned.

"Absolutely. Said it happens on every cruise."

Bob lowered his head, shook it slowly and chuckled to himself. "If I wasn't stone-cold sober now, I'd think I was still pissed. Unbelievable — a finger in somebody's grub and it happens on every cruise?" He shook his head again. "Strange, *very* strange."

"Not really."

"Well, bugger me, Julie, *you*'re the one who said it was just a moment ago!"

"Yes, but only in so far as Doctor Death said it never happened."

"But it did, and *that* isn't strange? Come on, pull the other one."

Julie held up two fingers.

"No need to adopt that attitude," said Bob, taken aback. "I was giving you a reasonable enough reaction, surely."

Julie tutted in exasperation. "No, no, I meant two *words*, not 'up yours'!"

"Fine, but I'm not a bloody mind-reader, so get to the point, for Pete's sake!"

"OK, what do the two words 'murder' and 'mystery' conjure up?"

It was Bob's turn to be exasperated now. "Come on, come on," he urged, "I'm not here to play games."

Julie placed the tip of a forefinger on the end of her nose. "Games! You've got it — right on the button!"

But Bob hadn't got it. "Games?" he scowled, scratching his head.

"Exactly! *Murder Mystery Evenings* — as popular on these cruises as pub trivia quizzes, whist drives and bingo." She canted her head enquiringly to one side. "Get it now, Kemosabe? The finger in the pie is just one of the clues in a contest for cruisers who get a kick out of playing detectives."

Bob buried his face in his hands. "God help me," he bleated. "I'm trapped in a floating Sherlock bloody Holmes nightmare!"

CHAPTER TWELVE

A LITTLE LATER — IN THE SHIP'S STARDUST LOUNGE . . .

When Bob finally got round to quizzing Andy Green about happenings aboard the *Ostentania* prior to and after Rab Dykes's disappearance, a steady stream of passengers had started drifting two-by-two into the Stardust Lounge to take advantage of today's "Happy Hour" cocktail special. In thoughtful keeping with the ship's current position off the Moroccan coast, the bargain concoction of the moment had been accorded the evocative name of *Crème de Casablanca Casbah* by its creator, head barman Pedro "Speedy" Gonzales himself. Andy, chuffed to bits that he could remember the recipe, had been keen to divulge its secrets to Bob, but had only got as far as "date liqueur and soured camel's milk" when Bob's still-delicate stomach prompted him to insist that the revelation be abruptly terminated.

Speedy, hot from boosting bingo booze sales in Crusoe's Palace, was now entertaining the gathering clientele with a snappy mixology show of bottle-juggling at the other end of the bar. This allowed Andy Green an opportunity to devote his attention to what his real boss wanted to know about matters relating to his current undercover mission.

The first thing Bob asked him was how wee Rab Dykes had got on with other passengers.

Andy's reply was that he'd never really noticed Rab all that much. He'd just been another face in the sea of faces that ebbed and flowed on the other side of the bar when it was busy. Not that Rab had been a particularly frequent visitor to the Stardust Lounge, anyway. There was always a hard core of regular barflies, who could be relied on to make nightly appearances, but Rab Dykes, like most passengers, had apparently preferred to spread his presence more equally of an evening about the rest of the ship's various attractions. Andy's main recollection of Rab Dykes was that he'd been a cheery, if fairly noisy, wee bloke, who seemed to mix easily and get along well with others.

Only once had Andy noticed Rab deviate from these apparently good-natured ways. That had been when an exchange of views about football with a group of other passengers had become a bit heated, as it inevitably does in bars as the night rolls on and the drinks flow faster. On this particular occasion, the cruise comedian, Lex "Laugh-a-Minute" McGinn, had come into the lounge at the end of his late-night variety spot in the ship's Neptune Theatre. Despite one of the standard terms of cruise-ship entertainers' contracts being that they should never enter into public discussion with passengers on the taboo subjects of politics and religion, Lex McGinn had seen fit to do just that. The political and religious elements of the ensuing debate hadn't been all that profound, as far as Andy could remember, although the sensitive subject of football had been skilfully annexed by the two main protagonists. For openers, McGinn had stated that all supporters of Glasgow Rangers were Union Jack-waving Proddie shites, with wee Rab Dykes replying to this motion with an intimation that all supporters of Glasgow Celtic were Papist Fenian bastards.

"Just another Glasgow Saturday night," Bob casually concluded.

"Aye," Andy agreed, "and then the subject was dropped and everybody just ordered another drink."

"No threats of violence between McGinn and Dykes?"

"Nope. Nothin'. It just kinda seemed they both needed to get that out o' their systems, like, then it was back to normal, as if nothin' had even been said."

"*Not* just another Glasgow Saturday night, then," Julie wryly observed, "— otherwise it would've been, 'right, ootside, ya fuckin' baw bag!' "

Bob couldn't resist a little smile of admiration for well-brought-up Julie's ability to borrow so effortlessly, when the notion took her, from the more "colourful" vernacular of her native city. "You could be right," he told her, "but the fact that they didn't threaten to have a go at each other at the time doesn't mean they didn't square up in private later on."

Julie gave him a sceptical look. "And wee Rab ended up overboard?"

"Well, it's a bit pat, I admit, but you never know. And before you say it, it doesn't necessarily mean that McGinn would have skinned knuckles."

Julie's look was even more disbelieving this time. "You mean, Rab could have taken a swing at *him*, missed, overbalanced and toppled over the rail?"

"OK, it seems too obvious to be true, I know, but stranger things happen at sea, as they say."

Julie conceded that, improbable as it was, it was a scenario that could be worth looking into all the same. And, she ventured, the easiest way for Bob to do that might well be to eschew, at least once, his declared intention never to darken Esme Horrocks-Bunt's dinner table again. She countered Bob's instinctive balking at the idea by cannily suggesting to him that, in the course of past policemanly duties, he had doubtless been subjected to many more unpleasant and hazardous experiences than dining in relative luxury with a pair of backbiting oddballs, a drunken author, a hen-pecked poet and a quartet of fandangoing clog dancers.

Bob elected to remain noncommittal about this observation, although realising that, once again, shrewd-thinking Julie had spoken with more than a modicum of good, old-fashioned common sense. For the moment, though, he preferred to leave the idea in abeyance and to continue his quizzing of Andy Green . . .

Of the sparse case notes that Detective Superintendent McNeill had given him, there was one particular aspect that Bob hoped Andy would be able to enlighten him about, and that was the alleged shipping of contraband cigarettes aboard the *Ostentania* — which related directly, of course, to Andy's own undercover presence on the ship. As wee Rab Dykes had been known to flog hookie ciggies around Edinburgh in the past, had Andy and his colleague from HM Customs managed to establish a common denominator, perhaps?

"Contraband?" Andy checked. "Denominator?"

"Yeah, a link between the two."

"The two what, sir?"

While Bob did one of his slow-inhalation, counting-to-ten exercises, Julie stepped in to rephrase his question in terms she considered Andy would feel more comfortable with:

"Did you find out if wee Rab was involved in any kind of fag-smuggling caper on this boat?"

"Aw, that? Yeah, Ah just asked Gentleman Jim —"

"Gentleman Jim?" Julie queried.

"Yeah, that's the nickname for Customs Officer James Alexander — posin' as one o' the dance hosts on the cruise. Male hoors, Speedy calls them, and —"

"OK, OK, Green," Bob butted in, "you can spare us these little details for now. You were about to tell us what you asked this Gentleman Jim guy, remember?"

"That's right. Ah asked him about all that fag-smugglin' stuff this mornin', matter o' fact. Yeah, 'cos Ah was wonderin' maself, like — what wi' him never cluin' me up on nothin' since Ah teamed up wi' him on the boat here an' everything."

"And?"

"And he just says he sorted out that wee bit o' business a few days ago. No problem, says he. A walk in the park."

"So, I take it he's reported his findings back to his HQ in Leith?"

Andy raised his shoulders. "Search me. He's never told me nothin' else about it."

"But didn't you ask him? I mean, as far as he knows, the reason you're here at all is to get some wrinkles about the workings of the Customs Service. Part of your police training, supposedly."

Andy dropped the corners of his mouth. "He just says he couldn't give a monkey's. Says he's done his bit now, then says he's gonna enjoy the rest o' the trip at the government's expense, and stuff the Customs Service and Lothian and Borders Police an' all."

Julie tutted a reproachful little tut. "Well, well, well, a *very* cavalier attitude for a public servant, I must say. If only the UK taxpayer knew."

"A damned poor example to be setting a junior member of the law enforcement agencies as well," Bob opined, realising too late that he had probably shot himself in the foot.

Julie made no comment, but turned her head away and rolled her eyes ceilingward. "People in glass houses," was the phrase she silently mouthed.

Andy began polishing a glass, his head lowered to hide a smirk.

Moving things quickly along, Bob then asked him what he knew about Rab Dykes's wife — or, perhaps more accurately now, his widow.

He'd seen even less of her than he'd seen of Rab, Andy admitted. In fact, she'd probably only come into the lounge once in Rab's company, as far as he'd noticed, anyway. He reflected for a moment, then continued, "Quite a smart-lookin' bint, though — for her age, like."

"And what age would that be?" Bob enquired.

"Oh, gettin' on a bit. Yeah, pushin' forty, I'd say. Gettin' past it, like."

Ignoring Julie's fake coughing fit, Bob asked Andy Green what else he could tell him about Mrs Dykes.

"Bit o' a toff. Well, thinks herself one, anyway. A lot different from the wee Rab bloke. Dead rough, him. Aye, but she's a bit o' a snob. Kinda posh Edinburgh accent. Morningside. Says things like, 'Meh, meh, Endrew, theht's an *awfully* large one you've poured me, theht.' Stuck-up stuff like that, know what Ah mean?"

"Just because she talks nicely doesn't mean she's a stuck-up snob," Julie objected.

"Oo-ooh!" Bob flippantly exclaimed. "Getting a wee bit defensive about that now, are we?" He'd been waiting to chuck that one back at Julie since she'd made the same observation about his reaction to her ageist quip back at the Dirleton Castle Inn.

"Aye, an' you can fuck right off, pal!" Julie rounded, Weegie-style.

Bob was starting to enjoy himself. Nothing like a little interrogation session and a bit of offensive banter to cheer up a down-at-heart policeman.

"Anyway, Green," he continued, "back to Mrs Dykes. Has much been seen of her since Rab disappeared?"

Andy shook his head. "Nah, not in here, anyway." He nodded towards a quiet corner table at the opposite side of the room. "She sat there for a wee while havin' a coffee wi' the padre after the funeral the other day, and that's the last Ah seen o' her in here."

Bob pricked up his ears. "Funeral?"

"Yeah, she went out in one o' the ship's tenders wi' old Enrique the pianist's widow when we were still anchored off Gib. Went to bury the old gadgie at sea, ye see. That's what he wanted."

"But why did Mrs Dykes go along?"

"Dunno — somethin' about her doin' her own burial thing for wee Rab at the same time, somebody said."

Bob's expression was a mix of surprise and suspicion. "But Rab Dykes had been buried at sea off Portugal a few days before — either voluntarily, forcibly or accidentally — so who the hell was his missus burying off Gib?"

"Nah, not who — what," Andy replied.

"What?"

"Yeah, what. Something wee, somebody said. A wee box. Some kinda souvenir o' her late husband inside it, maybe."

Bob pulled a facial shrug. "Well, nothing illegal about that, I suppose. I might check it out, though. You mentioned a padre. Who's he?"

"I can answer that one," Ian Scrabster said, having taken a short break from piano-playing duties to join them at the bar. "The Reverend John Pearce — ex-Royal Navy chaplain. Did his vicar number for the Brit expat community in Mallorca for a few years after he retired. Been doin' these cruise ship gigs for the Ulanova Line since his wife left him a while back. Gets him away from the memories, he says. Plus, he loves the sea."

"You know him, then?"

"Yeah — met him a few times in Mallorca." Ian gave Bob a crafty wink. "At the hand-shakers socials, ye know."

"Hand-shakers socials?"

"The Masonic lodge. Oh aye, ye get a lot o' these Holy Willie guys in the hand-shakers."

Julie looked puzzled. "Shouldn't you be keeping it a secret — I mean, that he's a member?"

"Gerraway," Ian laughed. "No, no, ye don't want to believe all that secret society guff. For instance, if ye want to check the identity o' the hand-shakers on this trip, all ye have to do is stand outside the Bosun's Locker lounge at eleven o'clock tomorrow mornin' and watch them all trippin' in for a wee meetin'. It's even advertised in the ships' newspaper. No secrets."

"And will you be there, Crabbie?" Bob asked.

"Is the Pope a Catholic? Oh yeah, you bet. Gotta keep in touch wi' the brothers wherever ye are. Never know what ye might learn or who ye might meet."

"OK — would it be possible, then, to ask the Reverend Pearce if he knows what was in the wee box Mrs Dykes buried at sea?"

"I'll see how it goes," Ian replied, a mite cagily. "Fact is, though, even if he knows, he might want to keep it confidential."

"Fair enough," Bob shrugged. "It's maybe not that important, anyway."

Now that Bob was feeling almost human again, Julie suggested that they return to their cabin "by the scenic route", as she wanted to show him some features of the ship that she had explored herself while he was still out for the count in bed that morning. Landlubbing Bob was pleasantly surprised by what he saw. No need to feel shipbound and cloistered when there was a promenade deck that ran all the way round the vessel, with direct access, at regular intervals, back indoors to some of the main congregating areas, including bars and the shopping "malls"; on the one hand, handy havens of rest and refreshment for promenading male cruisers, and on the other, irresistible bazaars where their female companions could re-charge their own batteries while rummaging through a plethora of "bargain-priced" luxury goods.

Then, on the upper decks, there were the obligatory swimming pools, surrounded by acres of sun-worshipping, Ambre-Solaired bodies. There was a netted golf-driving range, an open-air gym, facilities for tennis, quoits, deck boules, even clay pigeon shooting. And, of course, there were more bars, each serving snacks as well as drinks. Although none of this added up to Bob's idea of the perfect holiday (particularly at the price these punters were paying!), he had to admit that he could now see why so many people *were* attracted to cruising. If having easy and unlimited access to all sorts of entertainments and gourmet food, in addition to a wide choice of leisure and shopping facilities, happened to be your bag, and if the right boxes were ticked for you by dressing up for "gala" occasions, having impeccably mannered staff permanently at your beck and call, and a plush bar never farther than a stagger away, then cruising would surely be your thing. And the advantage a cruise liner had over a hotel with similar assets was, of course, that the liner delivered you to a different "exotic" location almost every day.

Yes, Bob could see why so many people regarded cruising as their idea of holiday heaven. But, for him, it was that very "so many people" aspect that palled. In this case, there were about a thousand of them, together with more than half as many crew and staff, all living in a relatively restricted space from which there was no escape — at least while at sea. To a country-bred lad like him, this was the antithesis of what he regarded as heaven. Even now, for all that he was surrounded by more luxury than he could ever have dreamed of as a farm worker's kid back in Scotland, he'd still rather be sitting outside the Dirleton Castle Inn, looking out over the wide sweep of the village green, content in the knowledge that, only a short walk away, lay one of the most beautiful stretches of shoreline anywhere. And it was a shore that, more often than not, had little or no people on it. *Plus* it had views, with little offshore islands and rocky reefs and the hills of Fife rolling into the distance on the far side of the Firth of Forth. But what views were there here? None — except the sea, but without an island, a distant hill or even another ship in sight.

Bob drew in a great lungful of air, which was more a wistful sigh than anything else. Yet he couldn't help but notice that there *was* something magical about that air; a strange quality that you could never catch on the banks of the Forth. It was the mysterious aroma of Africa; the hot breath of the Sahara Desert, that most romantic of all wildernesses, reaching infinitely into the vast, dark continent that lurked just a mile or two over the eastern horizon. Yes, he was beginning to see what attracted folk to cruising. Maybe he could even get to like it himself, with a bit of perseverance . . . if only he didn't feel so uncomfortable at being in close proximity to so many people he didn't know, even in such a beautifully appointed sardine tin as this one. Deep down, he knew that this reluctance to be coerced into the company of strangers, this *shyness*, for want of a better word, had been a contributory factor towards his drinking more than he should have done last night. Dutch courage. Not that it would do any good trying to convince Julie of that. A dearth of social confidence wasn't a component of *her* character. Quite the contrary.

Bob looked at her now — already deep in animated and cheerful conversation with a clutch of poolside sunbathers. Julie was just one of those people who had the great gift of being able to feel instantly and totally at ease with others, even if, like those she was talking to now, she had never met them previously or was ever likely to meet them again. He envied her that quality, and, he sometimes suspected, she probably lamented his lack of it.

"A penny for them, squire. 'Aving a late-afternoon constitutional, are we? Certainly a nice one for it." It was Walter Walter-Wall, the irrepressible floor-coverings "magnate", who had materialised at Bob's side during his solitary musings.

Bob had no trouble in remembering *him* from last night, when, as it now turned out, he had been correct in predicting that he would be sought out again before too long by this eye-for-a-quick-buck spiv. The same oily smile was on Walter's face, the same fake hoity-toitiness gilding his accent. But gone were the pale blue suit and brown suede shoes that Ian Scrabster had taken such an aversion to. For Walter was now kitted out in sun-deck garb of yachtie's navy blue cap with *Rule Britannia* emblazoned on it, a DayGlo orange T-shirt announcing *Surf's Up*, red tartan Bermuda shorts and a pair of heavy-duty leather sandals with soles that would have seen a Roman Legionnaire good for a march from one far-flung corner of the empire to the other. If Walter was making a fashion statement, Bob decided, it must have been a short one. Indeed, "Frightening!" was the statement that came immediately to mind.

Walter lowered his mirror sunglasses so that Bob could see the sincerity in his eyes as he muttered the words, "I'd, uh, rather sell my story to a fellow cruiser like you, Bert."

"It's Bob, actually, and I told you — the magazines I write for don't do juicy bits. You'd be better offering your story to the London tabloids, like you said you were going to do last night, remember?"

Walter took Bob by the elbow and led him a few paces away from any eavesdroppers who might be loafing in the nearest sunbathing rank. "No, no, no, squire, you misunderstand me," he oiled. "No, no, the information I 'ave about the recent man-overboard incident is by no means of the *juicy bits* kind — in the strictest sense, you understand."

Bob thought he'd play this weasel at his own game; string him along a bit in the hope of winkling a bit more out of him. "No, I don't understand, Mr Wall —"

"Oh, *plee-ee-eez*, Bob, it's Wally, OK? No formalities between shipmates, ay?" He let out a smarmy chortle and gave Bob a punch on the shoulder that was intended to be taken as playful, but which Bob took as bloody familiar — and painful, too.

"No, I don't understand, *Wally*. I'm a freelance, so I'm not in a position to do any kind of financial deal with you, no matter what information you have."

"But you do 'ave the right press contacts — contacts that, to be honest, squire, I myself do not 'ave — contacts with the ability to do financial deals with someone who 'as a good story to sell."

Bob gave a dismissive little laugh. "The story's dead, Wally. It hardly got a couple of column inches in the papers when it happened, and nobody's gonna part with any dosh for some vague angle on a bit of old news. I mean, these man-overboard things are a dime a dozen in any case."

Bob could see by the look of dismay on Wally's face that his ploy was working. Chances were that this creep had already been on the blower to the news desks at the London tabloids, and had been summarily knocked back. After all, no hard-bitten news editor would commit money to some opportunist he didn't know, without concrete evidence that there was something worth buying. Bob imparted the gist of this to Walter Walter-Wall.

"Ah, but the thing is, Bob," he smarmed, "that's where you would come in, simply because you *are* known to these 'ere editors."

Bob made to leave. "Forget it. Same rule applies. I don't get involved with anything that's mere hearsay." He returned Wally's "playful" punch on the shoulder. "See you around . . . as you also said last night, remember?"

Wally grabbed him by the arm, a little too vigorously for Bob's liking.

"You'll change your mind when I show you this, squire." Wally half turned his back to the sunbathers, then dipped a hand into the pocket of his Bermuda shorts in a way that made Bob suspect that he was about to be offered a selection of dirty postcards. But what emerged was a wallet. Wally pulled out a banknote and showed it to Bob. "Know what this is? 'Ere take it." He shoved it into Bob's hand. "'Ave a good look."

Bob gave the note a cursory glance, then handed it back. "American hundred-dollar bill. So what? I mean, what exactly's your point?"

Wally held the note up to the light in front of Bob's eyes. "Look all right to you? Look genuine enough?"

Bob's patience was being tried. "Look, to be honest, that's the first hundred-dollar bill I've ever seen, so no point in asking me. Now, if you'll excuse me . . ."

Wally grabbed his arm again. "Ah, but I '*ave* seen 'undred dollar bills before — plenty of them." He glanced over his shoulder to make sure no one was likely to hear, then added confidentially, "Currency trading, you see. Makes a nice sideline. Yes, and even I would be 'ard pushed to tell this 'ere note from the real thing."

"You're saying it's a fake, is that it?"

Wally held it up to the light again. "Can't tell if it is, can't tell if it isn't. And *that*, squire, is my point."

"Very interesting, I'm sure, but what's all this got to do with the man-overboard business?"

Wally replaced the note in his wallet, smirked slyly and said, "'Ow would you like to buy a bundle of such notes . . . for only 'alf price, plus a small 'andling charge, as we say in the trade?"

Now, this *was* getting interesting, Bob thought, but feigning *un*interest, he made to leave again. "Look, mate, there are all kinds of Monopoly money scams going on all the time, but I haven't just arrived on a banana boat, so try this one on somebody else, OK?"

Still holding Bob's arm with one hand, Wally patted his wallet pocket with the other. "No scam. The

’undred dollar bill — a Benjamin we call them in the, er, *bureau de change* business — was given me, as a sample, you understand, by the man-overboard victim ’imself. Plenty more where this one came from, ’e said. As many as I want, ’e said, and all at ’alf price yet.”

“So, ehm, you saw proof that he had more of these notes, did you?”

But all of a sudden, the bait was about to turn angler. Wally gave a knowing chortle. “Enough, my friend — enough already.” He zipped a forefinger and thumb from one corner of his mouth to the other. “My lips I seal, until you make a deal.”

Bob shook off Wally’s determined grip on his arm. “Sorry, my friend — no deal. Now, if you’ll excuse me . . .”

Wally raised his hands in mock submission. “It’s all right, it’s all right. No deal, no problem. See you around, ay?” He pushed his mirror shades back up his nose, turned to leave, then paused and said, “But here’s something for nothing — one hour after he gave me the Benjamin, friend Dykes was dead. Yes, squire, and *I* know who did it!”

Bob stood contemplating all of this while he waited for Julie to finish her conversation with her new-found poolside chums. Even if he’d wanted to join her, which he didn’t, he was being paid to do a job, and having a good think about what sleazy Mr Walter-Wall had just revealed was as relevant a part of it as any . . . for the moment.

So, what was in this particular can of worms? The “bundles” of banknotes involved — if, indeed, such bundles even existed — either had to have been forged or stolen. Why else would they be changing hands at half their face value? But who would be stupid enough to try and flog such hot crinkle to someone who was, presumably, a complete stranger, and within the no-getaway confines of a cruise ship at that? Well, Wally Walter-Wall had answered this question . . . none other than the man-overboard victim himself, wee Rab "Mickey Mouse Rings" Dykes. At least *that* detail of Wally's claim did have a ring of truth to it. But where had Rab come by the money, and what was the link between that and his mysterious disappearance? Did Wally Walter-Wall really know things that were pertinent to the case, or was he really only fishing for an easy earner — or maybe just a bit of free press publicity for his floor-coverings business?

Bob felt a tap on his shoulder. He turned to see the yellow-encircled eyes of Doctor Rupert De'ath glinting at him from beneath the rim of his battered Panama.

"Aha, well met again, young man," the ship's doctor said through a zephyr of vodka fumes. "I was sitting in the shade under the awning of the bar there — having a post-siesta eye-opener, you know — when I noticed you being accosted by that dreadful man. He represents capitalism at its lowest and most despicable level, but such are the gutter nouveaux riches that floating temples to hedonism like this attract, I'm afraid."

Bob was inclined to ask what had attracted a redundant old purveyor of ultra-socialism like him to just such a temple, but thought better of it. His policeman's nose smelled something in the air — and it wasn't just the whiff of vodka. There are times, when trying to make the most of an opportune investigative situation, that approaching the subject like a bull charging a fence is the subtlest option. The surprise element can help elicit the most useful of responses, and Bob decided that this modus operandi was the one to employ on this occasion.

"Yes, I know what you mean," he began. "I'm inclined to mistrust people who make financial offers that are too good to be true, but —"

"Financial offers?" Doctor De'ath's ears were twitching like those of a rabbit that had just heard the rustle of a snake in the grass.

"Yes, you probably noticed him flashing a banknote about?"

The doctor feigned insouciance. "No, I — I can't actually say that I did, my boy. I, ehm, a *bank*note, did you say?"

Bob's verbal bull was now up to speed and galloping headlong for the fence. "Hundred-dollar bill — American. As many as I want to buy, and all at half price."

But the experience of living for so long in Russia, where the interrogative lunges of the secret police would have made Bob's "bullish" methods seem namby-pamby in comparison, had rendered the rejecting of this carrot as instinctive as breathing in for the doctor. "Half-price American dollars?" he laughed, with not a trace of pretence in his expression. "Well, how absolutely unbe*liev*able!" He gave Bob a mischievous look. “I take it you agreed to buy loads of them?”

“Of course,” Bob replied, deadpan. “No Scotsman could refuse an offer like that.”

The humorous expression, fake though Bob suspected it had been, faded from De’ath’s face. “Indeed, he could not, my friend,” he murmured. “Indeed, he could not.”

Bob decided to give his bull another run at the fence. “And it would be even more unusual for a Scotsman to actually *make* an offer like that, no?”

Rupert De’ath frowned. “I’m afraid I don’t quite follow.”

“Rab Dykes was a Scotsman, and Mr Walter-Wall claims that he was the source of the cut-price dollars.”

The doctor’s frown deepened. “Rab *who*?”

“Dykes — the guy who went missing, presumed overboard, a few days ago.”

A smile returned to the doctor’s face — a slightly condescending one this time. “Oh, my dear young man,” he said with a dismissive shake of his head, “I meet so many people on these cruises. I can’t remember the names and nationalities of them all, nor am I interested in the silly capers that some of them indulge in.” He then glanced at the rows of sunbathers and checked his watch. “Well, I suppose I must now head back to my surgery,” he sighed. “Soon be the time of day for these loafing lobsters to come seeking remedies for mild sunstroke and frazzled flesh.”

With that, he doffed his Panama in gentlemanly fashion, clicked his heels and was gone.

"You'll never guess what *I*'ve just been told," Julie jauntily declared, having torn herself away at last from the bosom of her new-found friends.

Bob was deep in thought, mulling over the significance of the two consecutive conversations he'd just had. "No, you're right," he muttered. "I'll never guess."

"Well," Julie grinned, scarcely able to contain herself, "I've just been told that — wait for it — Rab Dykes's widow has been having it off with the ship's chaplain!"

CHAPTER THIRTEEN

THE FOLLOWING MORNING — IN THE CROW'S NEST RESTAURANT ON THE SHIP'S TOP DECK . . .

News of Walter Walter-Wall's death had spread through the ship like a fire in a candle factory. "Choked on his own vomit while sleeping" was, according to rumour, the cause of death established by Doctor Rupert De'ath. As Walter had been travelling alone and had made no friends on board, none of his fellow passengers were unduly bothered about his passing, and they were even less concerned about what had induced it. He had been universally regarded as a pushy, irritating wide boy, and his absence would come as a welcome relief to all who'd had the misfortune of being subjected to his intrusive sales pitches.

"What'll happen to his body?" Julie asked Bob over her bowl of muesli.

"I suppose it'll be stored in Doctor Death's little morgue until the next of kin — whoever and wherever he or she may be — decides what should be done with it," Bob replied between sups of porridge. It was a bit hot off the African coast here for such a cold-climate dish first thing in the morning, but Bob had been brought up to believe in the curative qualities of the humble oat, and his maltreated system still deserved all the recovery aids he could bestow upon it.

"Mind if I join ye?" asked Ian Scrabster, already in the process of sitting down in front of the plated mountain of fry-up favourites he'd served himself over at the buffet. "Somethin' funny about that Wally Wall guy supposin' to have choked on his own puke," he said. "'Scuse the unappetisin' subject," he apologised to Julie, while bursting the yolk of a fried egg with a hunk of sausage already plastered with baked beans, "but there's somethin' dodgy about the cause o' death that's bein' put about."

"Common enough cause," Bob said, "— especially among piss artists, so I'm sure it crops up often enough on cruise ships like this."

"Yeah, but that's what's dodgy about it," Ian replied as he trowelled a splodge of sausage, egg and beans onto his fork. "Ye see, that Wally guy didn't drink. That's what Mike Monihan told me, anyway, and he says he's seen him cruisin' on this boat a few times before."

"Ah, but you don't have to be drunk to choke on your own puke," Julie pointed out, clearly not in any way put off her breakfast by such an unsavoury topic of conversation. "A burp of digestive juices inhaled while sleeping on your back can do it, even if you haven't had even a sniff of booze before hitting the sack." She patted her tummy. "Hydrochloric acid, you know — essential for the digestion, but lethal if it gets into the old windpipe."

Bob was relieved to note that such colourful verbal intercourse hadn't resulted in his own involuntary throwing up, which most certainly would have been the case twenty-four hours earlier. "It's a common cause of death among winos and down-and-outs, though," he said, matter-of-factly. "Easy enough to diagnose as well, no doubt."

Julie puckered one of her pensive pouts. "Hmm, well, superficially at any rate, yes."

Ian pronged a piece of black pudding and decked it with a button mushroom. "I see what ye mean, Doc. Easy to fabricate the evidence, right?"

"Fabricate the evidence?"

"Yeah, ye know — ram some half-chewed stuff down his cake hole and leave a few bits dribblin' out the side o' his gob, sort o' thing."

"Wouldn't stand up to much forensic analysis, that," Bob scoffed.

"Which is why I said 'superficially'," Julie came back. "To be certain that it *is* the deceased's vomit, you'd have to do the obvious tests."

Bob nodded his head in agreement. "Otherwise it, the vomit or whatever, could just be a smokescreen to conceal the real cause of death, correct?"

"You said it," said Julie. She stood up. "Fancy a fry-up, Kemosabe? I'll put one together for you while I'm grabbing some more hippy mix for myself."

Bob glanced warily at Ian's mound of cholesterol on a plate. "No thanks," he gulped. "I'm already getting more than enough grease by osmosis."

While Julie trotted off to the buffet for a second helping of muesli, Ian washed down a forkload of bacon-topped hash browns with a slurp of tea. "Nah, Bobby, somethin' tells me there's somethin' dodgy about that choked-on-his-vomit bollocks."

"Yeah? What makes you say that?"

"It's like I told ye — never trust a man dressed in a pale blue suit and brown suede shoes."

"I don't get it. Are you implying that Walter-Wall covered up the true cause of his *own* death? Come on, Crabbie," Bob laughed, "get real."

"No, no, I'm not *that* fuckin' stupid, man. Nah, what I'm sayin' is that a bent sleaze like that is hardly likely to have met a *straight* death. I mean, worms like him can't even lie in their beds straight."

"Fair enough, but I still don't get what you're on about."

Ian tapped the side of his nose. "Accentuate the devious, eliminate the obvious — that's what I'm on about."

Bob considered the latest happenings for a few moments. First there had been his "chance" meeting with Wally Walter-Wall. During that, a connection between Rab Dykes and counterfeit or stolen dollars had been inferred and a claim made that Dykes had been murdered by someone known to Walter-Wall. Then the ship's doctor, the presumed signatory to Wally's subsequent death certificate, had immediately arrived on the scene, advising Bob to pay no heed to Wally's spiels. And this was the same Doctor De'ath who had spun them a yarn about Dykes's death being almost the perfect murder. Maybe Crabbie was right. Maybe it was time to eliminate the obvious — or at least the *obvious* as presented by the ship's doctor.

"OK, Crabbie," he finally said, "I think a visit to Doctor Death's wee morgue is called for, don't you?"

Ian left a forked fried tomato hovering in mid-air. "How the hell do ye think ye're gonna manage that, for Christ's sake?"

Bob winked one of Ian's typical winks of Masonic confidentiality, then leaned in close. "Right, here's the plan . . ."

It had been noted in that day's edition of the ship's newspaper that the dress code for dinner in the evening would be "formal", much to Bob's disinterest. He had resolved to try and put his re-exposure to Esme Horrocks-Bunt's dining ordeal on hold for a while yet and to grab an informal bite in the Atrium Buffet instead. No black-tie poncing about would be required there. But there was a sursprise in store for him.

"Well, well," Julie smiled pop-eyed as she read the card that was waiting for them when they returned to their cabin after breakfast.

"Been given a raise, have you?" Bob asked.

"Sort of. Well, my profile has, anyway." She handed the card to Bob.

He gave it a swift scan. "Dammit," he said, then read aloud: "*Captain Georgi Stotinki cordially invites Dr Julie Bryson and partner to join him for dinner this evening in the Caravel Restaurant. Dress formal.* Dammit," Bob said again. "I'd have to wear a bloody tuxedo. How the blazes do we tell him to get stuffed — politely, of course?"

"We don't — of course! Re*fuse* an invite to dine at the Captain's table? You must be joking, Kemosabe! It's the be all and end all of most people who go on cruises to get the call to nosh with the skipper, and precious few ever do." She raised a cautioning finger before Bob could attempt an objection. "*And* it'll provide you with the ideal opportunity to do your pseudo-journo bit by casually pumping the head honcho himself about the Rab Dykes affair."

Much as Bob tried, he couldn't immediately think of a plausible way out of that one.

"Right," said Julie, sliding open the wardrobe door, "where's that old dinner suit of yours? I'll get Samson to have it dry-cleaned and pressed in time for this evening."

Bob faked a little cough. "I, ehm — I think I maybe forgot to pack it," he meekly suggested. "Didn't think I'd sort of need it. So," he continued, suddenly glimpsing a glimmer of hope at the end of the tuxedo tunnel, "maybe *you*'ll have to do the pseudo-journo bit for us both tonight, huh?"

Five minutes later, Bob's glimmer of hope was being resolutely snuffed out by Julie, while she marched him into the appropriately named Savile Row Boutique within the ship's shopping "mall". Ten minutes after that, he was completely, if somewhat reluctantly, kitted out with the requisite clobber for tonight's formal dinner at the Captain's table.

"That's the thing about cruise lines," Julie chirpily told him as he slouched out of the shop in front of her, "— apart from maybe a trombone-laying elephant on roller skates, they've thought about everything anyone might need in order to feel at one with the happy throng. And they've made sure it's available to buy, right here on the ship." She flashed him an impish look. "I mean, why do you think most women forget to bring so many *essentials* on these trips?"

Glumly, Bob glanced down at the two large carrier bags he was lugging. "Yeah, but think about the cost of this lot. It's gonna look bloody marvellous on my expenses sheet, I must say — especially since Bruce McNeill told me to bring a tux in the first place."

He wasn't about to get any sympathy from Julie, however. "Serves you right for trying to pull a fast one. And let it be a lesson to you," she curtly added, "— *never* try to out-devious a woman if there's even the *slight*est chance of a shop entering into the scheme of things."

All Bob could do was sigh a penitent "Amen" and remind himself of the old Newcastle Geordie's words back in Palma de Mallorca . . .

"Effin' wimmin! Ah divn't oondahstand the boogahs, an' Ah likely nevah will!"

With this being the *Ostentania*'s only full day at sea before reaching its first port of call on the Canary Island of Lanzarote, there was much activity on board ship. The entertainments programme was packed with things to keep the minds and bodies of non-sunbathing passengers occupied, and one of these events would be Julie's first shore lecture.

Crusoe's Palace Show Lounge was like something straight out of a Hollywood movie to Bob's unaccustomed eye. Descending in wide, semi-circular tiers from the vast bar area between the two entrances, the "room", to use the American showbiz expression, was big enough to accommodate perhaps three or four hundred customers, all seated in plush comfort at tables arranged in random precision along the length of each level. The focal point was a large curtained stage, separated from the "front line" tables by an oval dance-cum-cabaret floor. Even now, with shafts of mid-day sunshine bathing its interior in a warm glow that lent the place an atmosphere distinctly different from that of the dimly lit nightclub it became every evening, Bob could envisage Frank Sinatra in *Pal Joey* mood, sitting on a high stool at the bar, trilby pushed to the back of his head, one hand clasping the jacket casually draped over his shoulder, the other holding a cigarette and whisky glass. He'd be crooning a wee-small-hours ode to lost love and loneliness. Here, Bob realised, was yet another reason why people became hooked on cruising; ships like this were actually floating manifestations of "how the other half lives", but all within convenient and affordable reach of, well, much of the *other* other half.

He ambled over to the bar and perched on the stool just vacated by Ol' Blue Eyes, ordered himself a soda and lime, then settled down to watch proceedings. Suddenly, he could actually see himself in the *Pal Joey* part — well, up to a point. Certain items, like the trilby, singing voice, cigarette and glass of whisky would have to remain figments of his imagination. Still, it was a change from sitting with a mug of over-brewed tea in the spartan canteen of Gayfield Square Police Station back in Edinburgh, which is probably what he'd have been doing at that very moment, under normal circumstances.

With only a few minutes to go until the scheduled start of Julie's lecture, the lounge was filling up rapidly, everyone dressed in suitably smart daytime casuals, a lot of them with that tell-tale, straight-from-the-mail-order-catalogue look. It was the awkward, better-appear-relaxed demeanour of the wearers that gave the hint that they felt like fish out of water without the lifelong familiarity of city suit or tradesman's overalls to mark them as occupants of their own secure little pigeonholes. Bob could kinda sympathise with them, albeit that his own "casual" attire of beige safari shirt and beige chinos (referred to by Julie as prison kitchen fatigues) didn't really click with the "ship ahoy" feel of other more *de rigueur* ensembles on parade.

Julie hadn't shown any sign of nerves at the prospect of delivering her debut lecture. Neither had she spent all that much time mugging up on today's subject, the island of Lanzarote. The notes left for her by the widow of old Enrique Molinero the pianist were, she'd said, comprehensive and succinct. Also, she'd already spent half an hour or so with young Fu, the Indonesian "lights and sound man", going through the running order of the relevant "visuals" in Señora Molinero's

Canaries collection. So, combining those elements with her own previous knowledge of the islands, this shore-lecturing stint should be, in Julie's opinion, a complete doddle.

There was an air of keen anticipation about the folks talking their seats, some with notepads at the ready, others with Canary Islands guide books to refer to, others (perhaps arriving hotfoot from the sun decks) more immediately interested in ordering a cool drink from the team of diligently circulating waiters. Tomorrow, though, would mark the long-awaited resumption of the port visits that had been interrupted so unexpectedly and, for many, so uncomfortably by the recent norovirus outbreak. Everyone present, therefore, was ready to hang on every word uttered by the new shore lecturer.

And Bob noticed that it wasn't only passengers who were taking an interest in Julie's maiden performance. Standing discreetly in corners by doorways at opposite sides of the lounge were Professor Esme Horrocks-Bunt and Lex "Laugh-a-Minute" McGinn, while crime writer JP Shand had adopted his own version of a Frank Sinatra pose on a stool at the far end of the bar. Bob pretended not to have seen any of them.

The canned Mantovani-style music that had been playing in the background faded, blinds descended electrically over the windows, a spotlight focused on a lectern at the front of the stage, and the curtains opened to reveal a screen with a back-projected view of what Bob assumed was a typical Canarian landscape. Then, to the sound of a fanfare that would have been more suited to the commencement of a bullfight, Mike Monihan, the Cruise Director, sprinted onto the stage from the wings and did a short warm-up routine of enjoy-yourselves-or-else banalities, interspersed with a few corny jokes that evoked more groans than laughs. It struck Bob that this was the type of over-the-top intro that would have encouraged a hail of raspberries from a less long-suffering audience than this, and quite what it had to do with a preamble to an "educational" lecture was beyond him. Monihan reached the climax of his build-up for Julie by declaring that she was a doctor of something, although he knew not what. What he did know, however, was that she could feel *his* pulse any time. Then, with a bellowed, "Ladies and gentlemen, Oy give yaz da new shore lecturer and da sexiest one yaz has ever clapped yer owld eyes on — DOCTOR JULIE BRYSON!" he exited stage left, as Julie entered stage right.

Bob had to admit that, after all that cringe-making claptrap, Julie's unruffled and smiling entrance took more guts and poise than any normal academic could have mustered. But then, he reminded himself, Julie wasn't really *normal*, was she? Her appearance certainly didn't conform to the popular image of a stuffy intellectual.

She stepped pertly into the limelight in her slingback stilettos and a summery polka-dot frock that left just enough of the right bits exposed and covered to make the most of her undeniably admirable physical attributes. "Small(ish), but perfectly formed" was how Bob liked to think of her. In this glitzy setting, he fancied that Ol' Blue Eyes himself, had he been here, would have been prompted to exclaim, "Hey, hey, hey, ring-a-ding-ding, baby!" And Ol' Blue Eyes, as Bob knew, knew a ring-a-ding broad when he saw one. So did most of the males in the audience, as far as Bob could see. And he could see that Julie already had them eating out of her hand, even although she had yet to speak a word.

With a touch of paradox that Bob could have taken as being well-rehearsed, if he hadn't known it to be totally natural, Julie's delivery of her lecture, when it began, was as sedate as her appearance was frisky. And she certainly knew her stuff — or appeared to. A short history of the volcanic origins of the island was illustrated with appropriate "slides" of its lunar-like landscape — young Fu, discreetly stationed in an open control booth at the side of the lounge, taking nods from Julie as cues to project the appropriate images onto the screen behind her.

A virtual tour of Arrecife, the capital of Lanzarote and the port where the *Ostentania* would dock tomorrow, was followed by detailed descriptions of the island's various attractions to be visited on accompanied shore excursions. An expedition to the crater of the Mountain of Fire; a camel ride up the side of a dormant volcano; a trek through dramatic volcanic caves and tunnels; a visit to the amazing subterranean "lava bubble" art gallery that was originally the home of Lanzarote's most famous son, the artist, sculptor and architect, César Manrique; a "voyage of aquatic discovery" aboard a mini-submarine; a "jeep safari" tour of the island. These and several other not-to-be-missed excursions were described by Julie in ever more enthusiastic vein, as she emphasised the wisdom of purchasing advance tickets aboard the ship for the accompanied tours, as opposed to the potentially less rewarding, though cheaper, alternative of "going it alone".

Bob noticed that Mike Monihan, who was watching Julie's performance from an inconspicuous position to the side of the stage, smiled delightedly at her stressing the importance of the punters opting for the pre-booked trips, from which, of course, he and his team of shore guides earned a commission. He smiled even more delightedly when she drew the punters' attention to leaflets on their tables that listed the best shopping, sightseeing, eating and drinking places to visit for those intent on "going it alone". The presentation of the leaflet at any of these venues, she said, would entitle the holder to an attractive discount. Naturally, she omitted to mention the small detail that the Ulanova Line also received an attractive kick-back from every one of the establishments on the recommended list. Not that the punters were likely to be overly concerned about such machinations, anyway. As long as they *believed* they'd be getting a preferential deal, then everyone was a winner.

Yes, Julie was doing a great job, and even when she invited the audience to lob questions at her, Bob was amused to note that she parried any that he suspected she wasn't too sure about answering by deftly inviting someone (*any*one) in the audience to answer the question for her. She'd told him earlier that this was a trick she had learned from her father, a university lecturer of lifelong experience and, therefore, a past master at passing the buck and letting some show-off patsy take the heat off the learned one.

A whiff of vodka heralded the silent arrival at Bob's side of Doctor Rupert De'ath. These slightly creepy materialisations in the vicinity of the ship's bars were beginning to make Bob wonder if this old guy was actually the genie of an ancient Smirnoff bottle. The doctor was gazing down at the stage with an almost hypnotic glaze to his eyes. Bob guessed that he was either already half blootered or that Julie's slick presentation had him spellbound. Then again, maybe he was just letching her. Bob had certainly noticed a trace of infatuation in the doctor's attitude towards Julie when they'd met in the Bosun's Locker Lounge the previous morning, and this suited Bob's present purpose just fine.

"Ah, well met again, Rupert," Bob smiled, borrowing the old fellow's own favourite form of greeting. He inclined his head towards the bar. "Can I tempt you?"

But old Rupert was lost in a world of his own. "Ma-a-a-velous!" he drooled, his eyes fixed on the stage. "What wonderful, uhm, *talents* that girl has."

"Yes," Bob brightly agreed, "she certainly is the mistress of many, and no mistake." He elbowed the doctor's arm to attract his attention. "Which reminds me, Rupert . . . *Ru*pert . . . *RUPERT*!"

Startled, Rupert stirred. He tore his gaze away from the stage and looked blankly at Bob. "Ah, uhm, ah . . .

well met, young man," he blinked. "Nice of you to join me." He inclined his head towards the bar. "Can I — can I tempt you?"

Bob showed him his glass of soda and lime. "I'm OK for now, thanks. But, please, allow me. What'll you have yourself?"

Doctor De'ath scowled slightly and gave his head a rapid little shake. "Much too early for me, old boy. *Much* too early for me."

This was rich, Bob considered. Judging by the smell of his breath, which was potent enough to fuel an intercontinental ballistic missile, the old bugger had obviously had a few large eye-openers already this morning. Still, that might prove to be no bad thing, when combined with his current state of enthralment with Julie. Time, then, to put "Plan A" into action . . .

"Julie was wondering, Rupert —"

"Julie?"

"Yes." Bob gestured towards the stage. "Julie — Doctor Bryson."

"Ah, yes, of course. Just as I thought. Wonderful, er, *talents*."

"Yes, well, Julie was wondering, Rupert — recalling, as she was, the invitation you extended to her in the Bosun's Locker Lounge yesterday morning —"

"Yesterday morning?" Doctor Death wore a shocked expression. "My dear young chap, I can hardly even remember *this* morning!" Then, as if suddenly realising that he had a professional image to uphold, he qualified his last remark by adding that he had been so busy in his surgery during the past hour or so that his head was in a bit of a spin. "The life of a ship's surgeon can be a very stressful one, you know."

"Yes, I suppose the aftermath of Wally Walter-Wall's sudden death *will* have been pretty stressful for you, at that."

The doctor showed no reaction.

Undaunted, Bob decided he'd grab the chance to do a bit of sly, policemanly snaring. "Choked on his own vomit, they say the cause of death was."

But the doctor still wasn't about to be drawn. "Death, whatever the cause," he said with a stoical smile, "is all part of a doctor's life, Bill."

"Bob."

"Pardon?"

"Bob — it's Bob, not Bill."

"Really? Well, I'll be damned. You look uncannily like a Bill I met in the Bosun's Locker Lounge yesterday morning. Yes, terrible hangover the poor chap was nursing."

Bob decided to give this developing conversational maze a swerve by cutting directly to the chase.

"As I was saying, Rupert, Julie was wondering if it would be convenient for her to take you up on your kind offer . . . tonight."

"Offer?"

"Yes, to compare notes, as you put it in the Bosun's Locker yesterday morning."

The glaze cleared from the ship's doctor's eyes, as though a light had just been switched on inside his head. Then a smile gathered the wrinkles of his face into a look of prune-like joy. "How absolutely ma-a-a-vellous," he enthused. "Tonight, you say?"

"Let's say just after ten in the Stardust Lounge?"

"Capital, young man, capital! Stardust Lounge — a mere hop, skip and a ricochet along the deck from my surgery. Couldn't be better!"

Bob inclined his head towards the bar again. "Can I tempt you?"

Doctor De'ath beamed and gave Bob's shoulder a sociable slap. "Thought you'd never ask! A large Smirnoff, if you don't mind — in a small *café solo*. Based on an old Spanish drinking custom, you know. A mixture of alcoholic spirits and coffee, which they call a *carajillo*. Yes, I call my version the Molotov variety. Fascinating story — mix of Spanish and Russian traditions, you see." He diverted his attention back to the stage and Julie's closing words, then said distractedly. "Remind me to explain it to you sometime, Bill."

"It's Bob."

"Precisely."

CHAPTER FOURTEEN

THAT EVENING — IN THE SHIP'S CARAVEL RESTAURANT . . .

"I feel a right numpty," Bob mumbled, shepherding Julie through the restaurant door. "Having to wait in line there to squirt that slimy gloop on our hands before they'd let us in. Bloody farce!"

"The antiseptic gel's for a good reason, as you well know, considering the recent norovirus problems. Anyway, it's the same for everybody, and you had to rub it on your hands every other time you went into one of the ship's eateries, so why all the complaints now?"

"Nah, it's not that — it's this." He spread his arms. "Look at me. I feel like a thistle in a barley field."

Julie was taking a delight in Bob's embarrassment. "Nonsense!" she grinned, then stepped back to run an appraising eye over him. "The new white dinner jacket and the black bow tie and velvet cummerbund and everything — worth every penny to Lothian and Borders Police. You look like James Bond."

"Yeah, one of a coupla hundred," Bob grumped. "Look at them all. It's like a goddam head waiters' convention in here. All duded up exactly the same."

"That being the case, you shouldn't be feeling like a thistle in a barley field, should you now?"

Just then, the real head waiter (wearing a *black* dinner jacket) stepped up to them. "Good evening, sir, madam. Your table number?"

"Table number?" Bob frowned.

Julie nudged him. "The card! Give him the card!"

Feeling as awkward as he was convinced he looked, Bob fumbled in his breast pocket, then handed over the Captain's dinner invitation.

"Ah, yes of course, Doctor Bryson and partner." The waiter gave Julie a polite little smile. "Captain Stotinki is expecting you. This way, please."

Bob sensed that all eyes were on him as they walked the gauntlet between table after table of beaming passengers, most of them clearly as thrilled to be formally attired for dinner as he was pissed off. At first, he couldn't understand why he was attracting such approving looks and inspiring so many whispered comments, as well as a few deferential nods of recognition. Then the truth dawned — it was actually Julie who was the object of all this attention. Her first shore lecture and subsequent interview by Mike Monihan on the ship's TV station had already turned her into something of a personality, it seemed. What's more, Bob could see that she was lapping up the adulation.

"Ah, there you are, my dears!" Esme Horrocks-Bunt bellowed as they approached her table, which was occupied, not unsurprisingly, by only herself and her mousey little husband. "We've missed your company since that first unfortunate evening with the Scotch comedian and his *dreadful* manners. Thank heavens he has now reverted to eating with the crew — where he belongs."

Julie and Bob paused beside her.

"I've actually been a bit under the weather," Bob half-lied. "That's the main reason we haven't been joining you at mealtimes. Sorry about that."

Ignoring him, Esme gave Julie a sickly smile. "Caught a bit of your talk today, my dear. Very promising, but —"

"But?" Julie butted in, a pugnacious look in her eye.

"Oh, nothing much really. Just a few little pointers I'd like to give you, in order to — how can I say it? — well, to take the *rough* presentational edges off." Esme hauled her face muscles into another grudging smile. "But please do sit, my dears. We can discuss all that over dinner."

Julie returned her smile with an equally curdled one of her own. "Thanks for the invitation." She nodded in the direction of the head waiter, patiently hovering a few paces away. "However, we do have a prior engagement — my dear."

"Oh?" Esme queried.

"Yes. With the Captain, as a matter of fact."

"Oh!" Esme gasped.

"Yes," Julie confirmed. She prepared to leave, then paused again and flashed Esme another smile — a sugary one this time. "By the way, you just dropped something."

"Oh?" Esme said yet again. Confused, she looked down at the floor, then up at Julie. "What was it?"

"Oh, nothing much really — just your bottom jaw."

Bob gave Esme a "gotcha" wink, then walked away, smirking contentedly in Julie's wake. For the first time since being saddled with this case, he was actually enjoying playing second fiddle to this little vixen.

The first thing that struck Bob about Captain Georgi Stotinki was that he could out-ogle any two-eyed man with that single ice-blue peeper of his. Bob knew that Julie had noticed this too, and, as he expected, she went straight into Jezebel mode, though of a demure kind befitting her "Doctor" handle. It was immediately obvious that this appealed to their host — a lot.

In addition to the Captain, there were already five people seated at the table. They were introduced as Joe and Mrs Annie Lannigan, the Reverend John Pearce, the Misses Jane and Margaret Brambleberry, and the ship's First Officer, Janusz Nijinsky. Over ice-breaking glasses of champagne, the stilted small talk eventually revealed that the portly Joe Lannigan was a retired multi-millionaire builder from the north-west of England, the schoolmarmish Brambleberry sisters were retired schoolmarms from Oxford, and the Reverend John Pearce was, as Bob and Julie knew, the ship's chaplain. Ian Scrabster had already told them that he was an ex-Royal Navy padre, who, according to grapevine info recently harvested by Julie, was currently bedding Rab Dykes's widow.

At first, this seemed a fairly unlikely mix of dinner guests, until it became apparent that one thing all of them (apart from Bob and Julie) had in common was an attachment to the *Ostentania* — the Captain, his First Officer and the Chaplain for obvious professional reasons, the Lannigans and the Brambleberry sisters because they were among the most loyally frequent and, consequently, most valued of the ship's cruise passengers.

This formal dinner date with total strangers was the sort of social occasion that gave Bob the creeps, but he had a job to do, so it was now a matter of getting on with it and trying to lace the cross-table waffle with a bit of crafty research and probing whenever the opportunity arose.

As might have been expected, Joe Lannigan's sole topic of conversation was how he had started as a penniless apprentice bricklayer in a rundown backwater of urban Lancashire, had branched out on his own at the age of twenty (by that time "'itched to 'er 'ere and wi' three bread-snappin' brats t' support an' all!"), had prospered by putting in the hours and taking a few chances with the bank's money, had eventually bought out his old boss's business, had made the right Town Hall connections ("a few quid 'ere, a few quid there — nudge-nudge, say no more, lad!"), and had ended up making a right bloody mint out of big-budget municipal construction contracts.

His devoutly tanned wife nodded in agreement, all the while fingering, in a continuous process of inventory-taking, her Linus blanket of heavily jewelled gold rings, bracelets, earrings and necklaces. Only occasionally would she interrupt Joe's vocal autobiography by dropping in little punctuations like, "Aye, an' that's when we bought us first villa in Eyebeeza, like," or, "Opened by t' Queen, it were, that sports stadium. Aye, an' 'im 'ere standin' alongside 'er Majesty in 'is mornin' suit when she's cuttin' t' ribbon, like. Oh aye, touch o' class, were that."

It didn't take Bob long to deduce that it would be highly unlikely he'd glean much information relevant to Rab Dykes's disappearance from this narcissistic pair. They were so wrapped up in themselves that they probably wouldn't even have noticed a human body dropping like a sack of bricks past the balcony of the suite, which — "complete wi' exclusive open-air Jacuzzi an' yer personal butlerin' service, mind you," — they'd come to regard as their own, at least three times a year.

For their part, the two bird-like spinsters were so enthralled by Captain Stotinki's presence that they were incapable of doing much besides giggling girlishly any time he uttered a word, which wasn't often. In return, he would fix them with his Cyclopean leer for just long enough to ensure that they lowered their eyes, whimpered submissively, shifted nervously in their seats, and generally gave every confirming signal that they'd be borrowing a couple of pirate books from the library first thing in the morning and, consequently, booking another *Ostentania* cruise long before they'd completed this one.

If the Captain didn't say much, and he didn't, First Officer Nijinsky said even less. Inscrutable to the point of sullenness, this Vladimir Putin look-alike only opened his mouth to put food in it, apart, that is, from muttering "*Da*" or "*Nyet*" in response to his skipper's brief contributions to the collective dialogue, meagre though this already was. Every so often, Nijinsky would scowl and look furtively over his shoulder. Bob felt that it was as if he were expecting a KGB raid any minute. On the other hand, perhaps the guy was only concerned that the food may not have been coming quickly enough. For, despite his slight build, the First Officer could put grub away with the unbridled zeal of a refugee from a famine in the Urals. And, for all Bob knew (or cared), he might well have been just that.

Anyhow, one way or another, this was shaping up to be a *right* jolly evening, in Bob's sardonic opinion. Talk about your pregnant silences. Even Julie, whose gift for garrulity could generate chit-chat in a Trappist monastery, was struggling to make the Captain's table anything other than a launch pad for conversational damp squibs. Only when the effects of a requisite intake of wine had loosened the Reverend John Pearce's tongue did matters begin to improve. And, as Bob was sitting next to the padre, it seemed at last that an opportunity for a bit of crafty research and probing might now have arisen. Bob decided not to beat about the bush.

"So, John," he said, "you must get some pretty depressing jobs to do — you know, working as a man of the cloth on a ship like this."

"Depressing — on a ship like *this*?"

"Yes, I mean, with so many elderly people aboard, there's bound to be a fair amount of funeral work to do."

John Pearce was a tall beanpole of a man, with tightly cropped white hair and matching designer stubble, and with an expression of face that conveyed as much worldliness as piety. No doubt, Bob reckoned, a lifetime in the Royal Navy would have put that distinctive stamp on him. It would be hard, after all, to be wholly holy when holed up within the grey confines of a warship packed with testosterone-loaded young sailors for weeks on end at sea. There wouldn't be many weakness of the male flesh on which this minister hadn't had to give counselling, or (who knows?) to administer occasionally as well.

It was his hand lighting on Bob's knee under the table that had prompted this last conjecture. Bob removed the wandering mitt with alacrity.

The Reverend Pearce's resultant smile was as innocent as that of a stained-glass saint in a church window. "Funerals, Mr Burns, no matter where or when," he gravely droned, "are sad occasions. That's only natural. But they can be uplifting as well, if you believe. And my calling has committed me to the furtherance of those two positives. Challenging?" He nodded his head solemnly. "Yes. But depressing?" He shook his head determinedly. "No."

"So, committing the ship's old cocktail pianist to the deep recently would've been just another day at the office for you, would it?" Bob knew very well that there was an acrimonious edge to the way he'd put that question. And it had been intentional. He didn't like perverted old gits groping him under the table, no matter how "godly" their front above it.

But the Reverend Pearce was made of sterner stuff than to show any sign of irritation at being on the receiving end of a caustic little gibe like the one Bob had just aimed at him. The saintly smile returned to his face. "A day at the office?" he said with an indulgent little chortle. "My, my, you journalists do have an *inventive* way with words."

Tiny as they were, these ripples of antagonism instantly spread to the opposite side of the table, where Julie was seated next to Captain Stotinki. Neither of them, as far as Bob knew, was privy to the reason for his sudden change of mood from passively bored to openly aggressive.

Julie fired him a what-the-hell's-got-into-you? look.

It was, however, a look that Captain Georgi Stotinki had no need to emulate. Whatever his monocular limitations, they seemed to have been more than compensated for by an extremely acute sense of hearing.

"Funeral at sea beink no big deal," he told Bob, the scar on his face seeming to tug one corner of his mouth into an even more cynical sneer than usual. "I be doink many time ven ve no havink priest on sheep."

Julie was quick to grab this chance to expand the membership of the debate. She gave the Reverend Pearce a smile that radiated apparent interest. "Ah, so I take it from what the Captain just said, John, that you aren't, as it were, a permanent fixture aboard the *Ostentania*?"

The Reverend dipped his head modestly. "No, I — well, I suppose you could say I spread the word evenly between the four ships of the Ulanova Line."

Bob looked diagonally over the table to where Joe Lannigan was absentmindedly picking his teeth with a dessert fork. "Still, I suppose a quarter of a word is as good as a whole bible to a drowning man, eh, Joe?"

"Aye," Joe shrugged, "'appen it might be an' all." With those few words, his leg of the conversational relay began and ended.

Captain Stotinki picked up the verbal baton. "Drownink man?" he said to Bob, his good eye narrowing, his eye patch twitching. "Vy you sayink drownink? Is bad luck sayink drownink on sheep!"

Julie held her breath while she waited for Bob's reply. She sensed that it would be about as subtle as an earthquake, and she sensed right.

"Oh, drowning isn't popular with seafarers, isn't it? Silly me — I should've realised. Still, seems to be quite a common occurrence on cruise ships, doesn't it?"

"Vot you gettink at?" The Captain's good eyebrow was gathering itself into a solo frown.

"The man-overboard thing."

"Vot you meanink man-overboard thing?" The Captain's eyepatch was now quivering like a drain cover during a dysentery epidemic.

"Oh, just that I hear from your own ship's doctor that it happens a lot more often than the general public realises."

Julie coughed a prudent cough. "Bob speaks as an inquisitive journalist, you understand. Making generalisations. Nothing personal, you know." She then shot Bob a "have-you-gone-right-off-your-tiny-trolly?" kind of look.

Another pregnant silence descended upon the table.

The two Misses Brambleberry fidgeted in unison.

Eventually, Annie Lannigan released a silence-breaking burp — a cultured one, emitted into a lightly clenched fist, its gold-dripping little finger raised in butler-impressing elegance. "Ee!" she said, "that man-overboard business fair scares the number twos outa me. Aye, 'appened once before when 'im 'ere an' me was cruisin'!" She addressed her husband now. "Gets us thinkin' maybe we're a coupla Joneses, like — dun't it, chuck?"

"Aye, does that, chuck. Aye . . ." Joe sucked the tooth-pickings off his fork. "Waste not, want not."

Bob turned to the Reverend Pearce again. "Apart from the sad ones, I suppose you must have a few amusing tales to tell about funerals at sea as well, hmm?"

"Amusing?" John Pearce arranged his lean features into a look of shocked puzzlement. "Hardly an adjective one would consider appropriate to such solemn occasions, I must say."

"Let's say *unusual* instead, then," Bob proposed.

"Unusual?"

"Yes, for instance, the recent funeral-at-sea off Gibraltar — old Enrique the cocktail pianist's funeral, where Rab Dykes's widow is said to have buried the contents of a little box along with the main one. A bit *unusual*, no?"

Unfazed, the ship's chaplain raised a shoulder. "Absolutely not. Why, it's a custom as old as the history of sailors — certainly as far back as the Vikings — sending something, a small item that was close to the shipmate lost at sea — sending something to join him in the hereafter."

"And do you think someone in the hereafter would have the medical skill to join a severed middle finger to the lost shipmate's right hand?" Bob was well aware that this last probe amounted to putting two and two together and coming up with a presumptive twenty-two, but he was past caring. He wasn't being paid to be polite. He was being paid to investigate a possible crime (or crimes), and he'd rapidly come to the conclusion that pussy-footing about at this sham social gathering would get him absolutely nowhere in that respect. Neither, unfortunately, would being wantonly blunt, as he was about to find out.

The Reverend Pearce simply blanked him. No reply, no revealing change of facial expression, no reaction whatsoever.

What's more, the look that Julie now cast Bob left him in no doubt that she was convinced he'd either been slipped a Mickey or was having some kind of mental breakdown. What, in heaven's name, was he hoping to achieve by being gratuitously derisory towards the religious convictions of the ship's chaplain — and in public at that?

While Bob could sympathise with her feelings, *she* wasn't the one who'd been on the receiving end of an under-the-table grope from an AC/DC high-seas preacher. So, in for a penny . . .

"Also, it's kinda intriguing," he resolutely continued, "that anyone who goes overboard from a cruise ship stands little or no chance of being rescued."

"Vot you gettink at?" Captain Stotinki reiterated. "Vy you sayink no chance vom cruise sheep beink rescued?"

"Oh, just that you obviously can't stop one of these things on a matchbox. So, even if the alarm's raised quickly, the guy in the water would have to be a pretty good swimmer to survive until you managed to head back for him. And that's given that the water isn't freezing cold, or" — Bob inserted a dramatic pause here — "or that the victim was actually alive when he went over the side."

Automaton-like, the Captain reeled off the section from the book of maritime rules and regulations that covers such happenings. He explained with parrot-like fluency that, on this occasion, a manoeuvre called the Sharnow Turn was the one he had employed to bring the ship about. This particular turn — essentially a wide, looping diversion from the existing course that brings the vessel back to the point of the incident — is acknowledged as the best when a man-overboard alarm has been quickly raised, as had been the case in this instance.

"That's absolutely correct," chirped little Jane Brambleberry, suddenly inspired to lend support to her one-eyed sex symbol. With regular backup from her sister Margaret, she revealed that they had been dining over by one of the windows in this very room, when they saw the poor victim plunge past. They had both screamed, they admitted, hands clasped to their breasts (or to where their breasts would have been, if they'd been so blessed), and then they'd heard the "Man overboard!" call from the deck above. It ultimately emerged that it had been that "rather obtrusive" Mr Walter-Wall who had shouted the alert, they said, then quickly added that the Captain's "Search, search — man overboard!" announcement came over the ship's Tannoy only a matter of a minute or so later.

"*Da*," First Officer Nijinsky agreed with a decisive nod.

"Aye," Joe Lannigan concurred. "Me and t' missus was sittin' just a coupla tables away from t' ladies 'ere, like, an' that's what 'appened."

"You saw the victim falling as well, did you?" Bob asked.

"Nah, too busy eatin'. Yeah, just 'eard t' ado, like."

"I saw it, though," his wife uninterestedly offered. "Reckon it were nowt but a wet T-shirt flappin' off t' sun deck. Summat like that, like."

Captain Stotinki picked up the verbal baton again by trotting out what seemed to be another pat account, this time of how the appropriate notification had been radio'd to the Portuguese coastguards, who had immediately put the statutory search-and-rescue procedures into operation.

"Yes," Margaret Brambleberry chipped in, her cheeks flushing with enthusiasm, "and even a

Portuguese police helicopter arrived and landed on the sun deck." She nudged her sister. "Smart young men in uniforms, weren't they Jane? Yes, and they asked us questions and took notes and looked all over the ship and everything."

Annie Lannigan popped an indigestion tablet and shook her head sagely. "Aye, but they never found nowt, though." She then addressed her husband, but without bothering to look at him. "Never do, chuck, do they?"

"Nah," Joe agreed, swallowing a yawn, "not in us experience, any road up."

Captain Stotinki and First Officer Nijinsky swapped almost imperceptible glances, though not sufficiently imperceptible to go unnoticed by Bob's keen investigative eye. That said, he had no idea of what the glances had signified, particularly in the Captain's case, since his glances only revealed half the clue, the other half being concealed behind that impenetrable black eye patch of his. However, Bob's suspicions were sufficiently aroused to make him speculate that this pair of east European tars had more concealed in their metaphorical sea chests than emergency rations of garlic sausage and pickled cabbage.

In order to winkle out whatever useful information the gathered company of guests might actually be harbouring, Julie decided to try a gentler, more feminine approach than the bull-at-a-fence method Bob had just employed. She targeted her feminine winkler first at the Reverend Pearce.

"John," she said, her mien oozing the milk of female empathy, "it must be a *terrible* situation for the widow of the latest overboard victim to cope with. And so brave of her to stay on board the ship after losing her husband in that *horrific* way."

The Reverend Pearce dipped his head modestly again. "Whatever succour one can give, one does, and one can only hope that a gift of solace helps ease the pain."

Bob couldn't resist another charge at the fence. "Yes, John, and it's common knowledge that you've been giving her one."

The Misses Brambleberry sucked air in concert.

The Captain and his First Officer smirked, inscrutably.

The glare that Julie gave Bob would have chargrilled a garlic sausage at fifty paces.

The Reverend Pearce scowled at him. "*Giving* her one?" he intoned.

"Yes," Bob smiled, "— a gift of solace, I mean."

A soft chuckle of the condescending variety gurgled in the Reverend's chest. "I'm well aware of such smutty gossip, Mr Burns. For your information, groundless tittle-tattle like that is endemic on cruise ships."

"Just as norovirus outbreaks can be *epi*demic?" Bob countered, while glancing over at the Captain for any sign of uneasiness.

Georgi Stotinki gave no such indication. Instead, he repeated, deadpan, what had now emerged to be his favourite English-language phrase: "Vot you gettink at?" He then expanded the question to enquire why

Bob appeared to be linking the recent man-overboard incident with the norovirus episode.

Bob hesitated before quoting Doctor Rupert De'ath's assertion that the bug may have been deliberately introduced so that forensic evidence of the possible murder of Rab Dykes would be destroyed during the subsequent sanitisation of the ship. There were two reasons for his hesitation. Firstly, he had no desire to land the dipso doctor in unnecessary strife with his employers. The second reason, which was linked to the first, was that he believed deep down that the doctor's allegation was just too preposterous to be even remotely plausible. However, considerations for the career prospects of drunks or the potential validity of preposterous suggestions never solved a mystery, so, hesitation over, Bob answered the Captain's question without qualm.

The response was more or less as Bob had anticipated . . .

The Captain guffawed, his guffaw dutifully echoed a few seconds later by the First Officer.

The Misses Brambleberry tittered behind their hands and exchanged nudges.

The Reverend Pearce smiled patronisingly and suggested to Bob that he must have been reading too many Agatha Christie books recently.

"What ya just said," Joe Lannigan grunted at Bob, "— it sounds like somethin' that were once on telly, like. *Columbo* or somethin' far-fetched like that."

"Aye," his wife agreed, while counting the gems on her necklace with an inventory-taking finger and thumb. "Loada detective's godswollop!"

Julie feared that Bob was on course for making a complete fool of himself *and* simultaneously blowing his cover. She produced a jolly little laugh. "Yes, really, Bob," she said with as much whimsy as she could contrive, "you'll have everyone thinking we're researching an article for *The Police Journal*, instead of *The World Vacation Gazette*." Aware that the Reverend Pearce was a much-travelled man, she promptly met his questioning frown with, "It's a new Canadian magazine — based in Vancouver — first issue coming out next month — the emphasis on cruising — all nice, feelgood-factor stuff."

Bob didn't share her concern for prudence, however. His objective was to get on with this damned investigation, and acting the hard-nosed journalist was the only effective tool in his kit. What the hell, then, if his approach ruffled a few feathers or generated a mocking laugh or two? He released his fence-charging bull again, pointing its horns once more in Georgi Stotinki's direction.

"So, Captain, you say that you undertake quite a few funerals at sea yourself?"

Stotinki combined a nonchalent nod with an insouciant shrug.

Bob arched a presupposing eyebrow. "I presume that, in the main, the deceased are elderly people, right?"

The Captain repeated his mute affirmation.

"Travelling alone, a lot of them?" Bob prompted.

Another nod, another shrug.

"And the cause of death determined by the ship's doctor alone, right?"

This time, the Captain's head and shoulders remained still, but his good eye narrowed and his eye patch twitched again. "Vot you gettink at?"

"The cause of death is determined by the same ship's doctor whose theory about a possible link between the recent man-overboard and norovirus affairs you scoffed at a moment ago, right?"

"Vot you gettink at?"

"Oh, just that someone who comes up with *imaginative* man-overboard-cum-norovirus theories could possibly be an equally imaginative judge of the cause of a passenger's death. Tie that in with the convenience of a funeral at sea, from which you can't exhume the body, and —"

"You talkink crazy stuff," the Captain cut in, crumpling his napkin on the table and preparing to get to his feet. "I no understandink vot you gettink at."

"Ah, but I think I do." The Reverend Pearce had been listening intently to all of this, his expression growing darker all the while. He glared at Bob. "And I must say that, even allowing for the rudeness for which your *profession* — for want of a better word — is renowned, your outrageous insinuations are both an insult to your host and an embarrassment to your fellow guests. Shame on you!"

"Oo-er, I say!" the Misses Brambleberry quavered, all of aflutter.

"What's for puddin'?" Joe Lannigan muttered.

His wife handed him the menu card. "The *Creeps Suzettes* is worth a go. That's them set-on-fire crumpet things wi' syrup we 'ad on t' Queen Mary Two last time, 'member?"

"Aye, Caribbean, it were. Capri."

"Please enjoyink rest of meal," said Captain Stotinki, expressionless. Clicking his heels, he gave a little nod to each of the ladies in turn. "My pleasure to entertainink you, but now ve must goink. Excuse, please."

Upon which, he exited the restaurant with a swashbuckling swagger, his First Officer and the ship's chaplain following grim-faced in his wake.

"Nice can of worms I opened there," Bob flippantly remarked, in an attempt to break the silence that had once more descended upon the table.

"'Appen it is," Joe Lannigan mumbled. He was still studying the menu card. "But Ah think Ah'll be plumpin' for t' *Creeps Suzettes* all t' same, like."

CHAPTER FIFTEEN

THIRTY MINUTES LATER — IN THE SHIP'S STARDUST LOUNGE . . .

Bob and Julie were sitting alone at a quiet corner table on the opposite side of the lounge from the bar, where Andy Green was busy doing his trainee barman thing under the watchful eye of Pedro "Speedy" Gonzales. On stage, away to their right, Ian Scrabster, in Spanish Juan guise, was providing tinkling piano music to welcome the clutches of formally attired passengers drifting in from the ship's dining rooms. The passengers were all looking blissfully content.

Julie, however, was not. She still hadn't got over Bob's behaviour at the Captain's table.

"Frankly, I just do *not* know what got into you. I mean, honestly, it was almost as if you were enjoying yourself, being downright rude and provocative like that."

Bob smiled smugly. "That's because I *was* enjoying myself. Being downright rude and provocative is meat and drink to a policeman in the course of his investigative duties, you know. Well, at times, anyway, and that was one of the times."

Julie shook her head testily. "I really don't know what you're getting at."

"To paraphrase Captain Stotinki?"

"Yes, precisely! I doubt if the man will ever have been so affronted — and totally without justification!"

"He's lucky I didn't mention the fake hundred-dollar bills the late Wally Walter-Wall told me are being bought and sold on this ship."

"No, *you*'re lucky you didn't mention them! You haven't a jot of proof that they even exist, so you could very easily have been putting a cat among the pigeons for absolutely nothing."

"Aha, but how else do you think us clumsy coppers get info? Sometimes there's an interesting pigeon to put the wind up, sometimes there isn't, but we have to put the cat in there all the same."

"Clumsy's the right word!" Julie harrumphed. "And what, pray, has your offensive performance at the Captain's table achieved pigeon-wise?"

"It showed that the good Captain isn't at all easy about the whole man-overboard business, *and* a possible link with the recent norovirus thing really bugged him."

"Well, *I* didn't see any of your metaphorical pigeons flapping about — only an extremely insulted host flying the coop, and who wouldn't have!"

Bob was in his element now — thoroughly relishing the fresh atmosphere of confrontation that the long-restrained detective thrives on. "What you forensic boffins seem to forget is that you wouldn't have anything to swirl about in your test tubes and dip your litmus paper into if it wasn't for us poor sods at the sharp end risking the shape of our noses by sticking them in where they aren't welcome. Rattle the suspects' cages, by insulting them if necessary, that's how we flush the interesting pigeons out."

Just as Bob had hoped, this really put Julie on her high horse. "*Sus*pects' cages?" she soprano'd. "And what crime, if I may ask, is that poor ship's chaplain suspected of committing? The way you spoke to him was appalling, to say the least."

"He's damned lucky I only *spoke* to him," Bob muttered. "Groping me under the table like that. Slimy old perv."

Julie glowered at him in utter disbelief. "Groping *you*? Huh! Don't flatter yourself, Kemosabe! He spent most of the evening trying to play footsie with *me*!"

"Well, you know what sailors are. Experience has taught them it pays to keep their options open."

"*And*," Julie continued in high dudgeon, "I had to put up with the Captain's knee rubbing against mine most of the evening as well!"

Bob hunched his shoulders. "Yeah, I kinda expected something like that. I mean, he has that randy look about him, so you should've been wise to it instead of playing up to him the way you did when we arrived at his table."

Julie was flabbergasted. "And *why* do you think I played up to him?" She pointed a finger at Bob, revolver-style. "No, don't even *attempt* to answer that one! The truth is that, unlike you *clumsy* men, we females use more subtle, refined ways of exacting information. And don't you forget that it was to help *you* in your precious damned investigations that I put up with all that footsie-under-the-table, knee-rubbing crap tonight!" She tossed her hair defiantly. "*I* don't get my jollies from the closet advances of dirty old men with more wishful thinking in their dirty old minds than lead in their dirty old pencils!"

Bob started to laugh. This was going beautifully. "Nothing personal in the lead-in-the-pencils dig, I take it."

"You can take it any way you want," Julie snapped. "Just don't take my sacrifices for granted, that's all!"

Bob sat smiling while the dust settled, then enquired with exaggerated calm, "And how much information did you exact by sacrificing the chastity of your feet and knees tonight, Doctor Julie darlin'?"

Julie was patently unamused by that crack. "You miss the point," she said, tossing her hair again, this time dismissively. "It's not what information I gleaned tonight that's important, it's what I may be able to find out in the future."

"Really?"

"Yes, and that's why *I* didn't respond in an aggressive way to those closet advances."

"Not closing any doors, eh?"

"Exactly!"

"Keeping your options open, huh?"

"Precisely!"

"Letting them know you're — well, let's say *approachable*, right?"

"Absolutely!" Julie was still nettled and was making no effort to disguise the fact.

Bob sat back, his arms folded, a self-satisfied grin on his face.

"And what are *you* looking so smug about?" Julie rasped. "*You*'re the one who made an arse of himself at dinner tonight, so I'd have thought a bit of humility would've been in order!"

"No, no, far from it. In fact, I couldn't be more chuffed."

"*Chuffed*? You're *chuffed* at making an arse of yourself?"

"One hundred per cent. Yeah, so far this evening, things couldn't have developed better if I'd worked them out with a slide rule."

Julie cast him an explain-please scowl.

"It's easy," Bob shrugged. "Two of the people who *might* be in a position to throw some light on this case — namely the Captain and the ship's padre — now regard me with respectful caution and —"

Julie wagged a rectifying finger. "Uh-uh, for 'respectful caution' read 'a suspicion of lunacy', I think."

"Suit yourself. It comes to the same in the end, and I couldn't be more delighted."

"De*light*ed?" Julie reached over the table and felt Bob's forehead. "Now I *know* the sun's addled your brains!"

"And that's just another example of how out of touch with reality you boffins are."

"Oh yes? And would you care to explain that highly offensive remark, please?"

"It means," Bob said, with a deliberate note of cockiness, "that I've managed to engineer the perfect investigative partnership. I rough 'em up and you follow up with the *simpático* bit. Yep, classic cops-versus-robbers stuff." Knowing that it would annoy Julie, he puffed out his chest and, with theatrical conceit, added, "Oh yes indeed, many bulky police manuals have been written on the subject of forming the perfect investigative partnership, yet I've managed to achieve the same goal by simply being rude at the right time."

Julie was ready to spit nails. "You — you," she stammered, "you mean to say that your embarrassing performance at the Captain's table was actually preconceived?"

With exaggerated nonchalance, Bob raised his eyebrows. "Nope. Just ad-libbed as I went along. Just assumed the Captain would come on to you and you'd be the coy little strumpet."

"You swine!"

"Hmm, I must admit the old chaplain playing footsie with you under the table wasn't bargained for, though. But, hey, let's regard that as a bonus, eh?"

Bob was spared what the look on Julie's face forecast would be a spirited volley of retaliation by the arrival of Doctor Rupert De'ath at the bar over at the far side of the lounge.

"Right on time," Bob said, checking his watch. He stood up. "OK, Julie, fun's over. Are you all set to put the plan into motion?"

"I honestly don't know if I am," Julie huffed. "Really, this is all getting a bit bizarre, if you ask me."

Bob tweaked her cheek. "Bizarre's the name of the game, darlin'. Enjoy it. I am — immensely." With that, he strode off over the empty dance floor.

Whereupon Ian Scrabster reprised his vocal rendition of *Did you Ever See A Dream Walking?*, with a spoken interjection of, "Nice dinner jacket, *señor*. Hey, you looking *mucho* like James Bond, *amigo*!"

While the cruisers round the bar laughed heartily, Ian responded to Bob's frosty glare by blowing him a kiss.

That little cameo returned a smile to Julie's naturally sunny face. Bob had been brought back down to second-fiddle size, so things were looking up again.

IN THE CAPTAIN'S STATEROOM, MEANWHILE . . .

Mike Monihan had been summoned with some urgency to Captain Georgi Stotinski's presence. The Captain was sitting behind his desk as Mike entered.

"And what can Oy be doin' for ya, Captain sor?" Mike breezily enquired. He gave a cursory nod to the First Officer, who was standing by the Captain's side.

Captain Stotinki twirled his beard pensively with the fingers of his right hand, while drumming a meditative tattoo on his desk with the fingers of his left. His good eye was lowered, staring thoughtfully at his drumming fingers.

"How much you knowink about man vot accompany new shore lecturer — fockink Bob Burns guy?"

Mike admitted that he knew absolutely nothing at all about the new shore lecturer's partner, nor even about the shore lecturer herself, for that matter. Doctor Bryson had been recommended to him by his friend Ian Scrabster and, under the critical circumstances that prevailed at the time, Mike had been obliged to take a chance on her being up to the job. However, judging by what he'd seen of her work so far, she was a more than capable replacement for Señora Molinero. So what, he asked the Captain, was the problem?

"Yeah, yeah," the Captain said impatiently, "I no beink vorry about new shore lecturer. She werry nice lady. No, is fockink Bob Burns guy I no likink. He askink too many question about stuff vot no his business."

"OK," Mike shrugged, "if ya like, Oy'll be after askin' Ian Scrabster ta tell me all about him. Sure, and dat won't be a problem at all at all, so it won't."

The Captain promptly vetoed Mike's offer. "I never trustink vord of fockink musician. Dey only beink interest in money. *Da*, vould sellink own fockink mother for price bottla fockink booze. No, no, I havink better idea." He then instructed First Officer Nijinsky to proceed forthwith to the ship's reception office, to dig out Bob Burns' passport and to email the details, including the mug shot, to Boris Kaminski in Mallorca. "*Da*," The Captain nodded with a sly smile, "boss vill doink check on Bob Burns guy. Boss vill findink out for sure who nosey fockink baster *really* beink!"

BACK IN THE "STARDUST LOUNGE", MEANWHILE . . .

"Ah, well met, young fellow," Doctor De'ath grinned as Bob approached him at the bar. He slapped Bob's shoulder. "Name your poison, laddie."

Bob drew the doctor's attention to where Julie was sitting at the other side of the room. "We're actually OK for drinks at the moment, thanks. But let me order one up for you while you join Julie."

Doctor De'ath looked over at Julie and gave her a cheery wave. "Ah yes," he said, "she does have wonderful, uhm, *talents*, that girl."

"Yeah," Bob agreed sotto voce, "and not a bad pair of pins, either, wouldn't you say?"

If the ship's doctor heard that leading remark, he wasn't for letting on.

Bob's reading of this was that the doc was either dead leary or half deaf. Probably both. Anyway, more importantly, there was a plan to put into motion, and the first phase was to get the old boy tanked up.

"So, what's it going to be, Rupert? One of your Molotov *Carajillos*, is it?"

Doctor De'ath shook his head. "Oh no, a bit late in the evening for those, my boy. All that caffeine, you know. I'd never sleep. No, no, straight vodka will do splendidly, thank you. No ice, no lemon — just as it comes from the well." He slapped Bob's shoulder again, chuckled and headed off to join Julie.

Bob beckoned Andy Green with a wink. "OK, boy," he said softly, "did Crabby Scrabster give you the lowdown on what's happening?"

Andy nodded the affirmative. "Ah wait for his signal, then we go —"

Bob shut him up with a sharp "Sh-h-h-h!" He looked anxiously around. "For Christ's sake, keep it shady, will you!" he hissed. "You'll blow the whole bloody scheme if you let the cat out of the bag." Then, adopting a more relaxed mien, he smiled genially and proceeded to order a drink for the ship's doctor. "Make it an extra large one — Smirnoff Blue Label — and tell the waitress girl to keep 'em coming every time I give her the nod, all right?"

Andy assumed a professional, straight-backed pose. "And will I make it the same for you and your good lady, sir?"

"Yes, but only ostensibly."

Andy half turned and ran an eye along the gantry of bottles at the back of the bar. "Austin Siddley — Austin Siddley — Austin Siddley," he muttered. "No, sir, 'fraid we appear to be out of that brand, sir. But if the Smirnoff isn't to your taste, may I suggest the Vladivar, the Red Square, the Absolut or the —"

Bob tapped him on the shoulder, then signalled him to lean in close. "I'm not gonna waste time going into to any detail, Green, except to say that if you had a brain you'd be dangerous."

Andy grimaced self-reproachfully. "Aw, right enough, Ah remember now — an Austin Siddley's an old make o' motor car, intit?

"That was an Armstrong Siddeley," Bob grunted through clenched teeth.

Andy's forehead corrugated into a frown of confusion. "So, eh, what was that Austin-somethin' word ye said?"

As was his wont on such occasions, Bob took a slow, deep breath. "I didn't. I said 'ostensibly', which means 'seemingly', 'on the face of it'. In other words, I want you to charge the glasses intended for Doctor Bryson and myself, not with vodka of *any* brand, but with water."

This produced a smile of enlightenment on Andy's face. "Aw, well, ye should just've said so. And, eh, will that be the sparkling ostensibly or the still ostensibly you'd prefer, sir?"

"God give me strength!" Bob muttered. "Look, boy, just make sure you put ice and lemon in the water glasses and none in the vodka glass, OK? That way Doctor Bryson and I will stay sober while Doctor Death over there gets blootered. Got it?"

Another smile of enlightenment lit Andy's face. "Oh aye, Ah'm with ye now. The old doctor gadgie thinks you two are drinkin' vodka as well, but little does he know it's only water ye're drinkin' all the time, eh?" Andy put a finger to his lips and winked. "Ah'm yer Mr Candlestein himself, so ye can rely on me to keep it shady . . . sir."

Bob had serious misgivings about entrusting *any* part of tonight's plan to his gormless sidekick, far less the most vital element of all, but there was nothing else for it. Much now depended on the ingenuity (or lack of it) of Detective Constable Andy Green.

To Bob's relief, however, the initial stages of the exercise did go perfectly to plan. Julie strung the ship's doctor along by "comparing notes", as he'd originally put it, on matters scientific, while Andy Green, via one of the Indonesian waitresses, kept the drinks coming steadily. As Bob had anticipated, the more Doctor De'ath drank, the more his fascination with Julie intensified. Here was a man besotted, and by the time Ian Scrabster handed over the evening's music-making to the dreaded Sunbeam Band, the next stage of Bob's plan was ready to be put into motion.

After edging his way across the dance floor, which had quickly filled with formally attired couples keen to flaunt their formal attire in every way possible, Ian, as per Bob's script, joined Bob, Julie and Doctor De'ath at their table. Ian was still in "Spanish Juan" mode.

"*Hombre*!" he puffed. "Phew! Moses he get more easy job for to parting the sea than for me for to swimming through that lot! *Dios mío*!"

Bob offered Ian a seat, which, also as per script, he politely refused. He would appreciate it, however, if he could impose upon Bob to join him at the bar for a few minutes "for to explaining somesing about the cruise *musica* you wanting to know for the *artículo* you writing, *sí*?" He went on to apologise to Julie and the ship's doctor, saying that the information he had to convey to Bob was very boring and he didn't want to interrupt their ongoing conversation, which he was sure would be much more *interesante*.

"Absolutely," the doctor concurred. Without diverting his gaze from Julie's face, he made a dismissive flick of the hand. "Feel free to head off to the bar, dear boys."

Julie laid her hand on his. "Oh, Rupert, but we *can't* ask Juan to stand at the bar — not after such a tiring session at the piano."

"We can't?"

"No."

"But why on earth not?" (The doctor's Hippocratic concern for the welfare of fellow humans clearly did not extend to musicians.)

Julie gave him what appeared to be an inspiration-induced smile. "Because, Rupert, I have a much *better* idea!"

"You do?"

"Yes! I suggest that you and I leave Bob and Juan to discuss their dull old music stuff here at the table, while you take me off and show me your —"

Doctor De'ath choked on his vodka. "Yes?" he squeaked, his eyes watering, his obvious need for air seemingly much less urgent than his desperation to have Julie complete her enticing proposition. "Please . . . do con(splutter)tinue . . . my (wheeze) dear."

Julie fluttered her eyelashes. "Well, you know that I share your scientific background, albeit from a slightly different perspective, but of all the things I've seen in my career, one thing I haven't seen, but would love to, is . . ." Julie dipped her eyes coyly.

"Is?" Rupert De'ath urged, his breath coming in short pants now. "*Is*, my dear?"

Julie raised her eyes and hit him with one of those melting smiles that she had practised for so long on waiters and barmen. "Is, dear Rupert," she crooned, "a ship's surgeon's surgery."

CHAPTER SIXTEEN

FIVE MINUTES LATER — IN THE SHIP'S SURGERY . . .

"My, my, it *is* a dinky one, isn't it?" Julie observed.

Doctor Rupert De'ath was already over at his dispensing cabinet, eagerly dispensing two large vodkas. "Yes, well, like every other *office* on this ship, my dear, it's really just a standard passenger cabin adapted for a specific purpose."

"Yes, I noticed that about Mike Monihan's as well. Quite tiny, really, although you would never guess from looking at interviews on the ship's telly that they're actually shot in a tiny corner of that same tiny office."

"Really?" Doctor De'ath was too preoccupied with the important task in hand to indulge in such mundane small talk. "I, uhm — I could have sworn I had a lemon in here somewhere."

"Yes, I did an interview on the ship's telly from there this afternoon myself, you know."

"Really?" The ship's doctor was now bent over, rummaging in the fridge. "Dammit," he griped, "the nurse must have used the last of the ice before she went off duty." He stood up, red in the face, either from the strain of stooping or due to exciting anticipations of *entertaining* Julie. "I, uhm — I'm dreadfully sorry, but I seem to be out of ice and lemon, my dear."

"Oh, that's quite all right," Julie smiled. "I think I've had more than enough vodka tonight, thanks all the same. Any more," she giggled girlishly, "and I'd be totally squiffy. I wouldn't know *what* I was doing."

"Re-e-e-eally?" Rupert De'ath drooled. He swiftly pulled himself together. "I — uh — I mean, I'm sure it wouldn't affect you like that. N-not at all, in fact." His hand shaking slightly, he presented her with a half tumbler of neat vodka. "One teensy-weensy nightcap will do you good."

Julie giggled again. "Do you *really* think so?"

"Trust me, I'm a doctor," the doctor replied, with a grin that was intended to convey reassuring frivolity, but did little to conceal the lechery that lurked behind his yellow-fringed eyes.

Julie sniffed the contents of the glass, then screwed up her nose. "Pee-ee-*yoo*! No, no, I really can't take it neat like this!"

But the ship's doctor was not to be dissuaded. "Tell you what, my dear — why don't I just pop back to the bar and fetch some ice and lemon? It'll only take a moment. And, uhm-ah . . ." he indicated his examination couch ". . . and you can lie down — that is, I mean *sit* down there and make yourself comfortable in the meantime, hmm?"

Julie did as invited, then raised an eyebrow teasingly. "Oo-oo-ooh, I hope you're not trying to take advantage of me," she said in a husky voice, "— now that you've got me alone in your little den."

That did the trick. In the blink of a bloodshot eye, Rupert De'ath was out of the door and swaying urgently barwards.

Julie was quick to her feet. "Right," she said to herself, "not a moment to lose! Let's see what a good rake about in here will uncover!"

BACK IN THE "STARDUST LOUNGE", MEANWHILE

The reappearance of the ship's doctor came as a complete surprise to Bob, who was now standing at the bar with Ian Scrabster, all set to put into motion the plan for gaining access to the ship's surgery and whatever secrets it might contain. Although it hadn't been in the script, Bob got the picture as soon as the doc stated his order to Andy Green. This was something of a windfall, and no mistake, so best make the most of it to allow Julie as much time as possible to rootle out whatever she could on her own.

Bob nudged Ian. "You go over and keep the old geezer talking, and I'll get Green to stall the ice and lemon order for as long as he can."

"But what the hell am I gonna find to talk to that old lush about?" Ian objected.

"Russian politics should do for a start."

"But I know fuck all about Russian politics."

"Perfect. Now just bloody well get to it."

Bob beckoned Andy. "Make a meal of the ice-and-lemon order for the ship's doctor, OK?"

Andy frowned one of his more confused frowns. "A meal? Ice and lemon? Funny meal, eh? Got the recipe on ye?"

Bob sighed, profoundly. "Just take as long as you can with the order, right? Tell him you're waiting for another iceberg drifting up from the Antartic or something."

Andy's frown deepened. "This was never in the master plan Fats Domino Scrabster there told me about, was it?"

Bob groaned, self-pityingly. "Look, just get on with it, Green. I'll let you know when we're about to revert to Plan A, OK?"

"Well . . . OK, if you say so, like."

Another improvisational brainwave then rolled into Bob's mind. "Oh, and give Doctor Death an extra large vodka to keep him sedated in the meantime. Yeah, and just put it on my tab like all the rest of the booze the old bugger's scoffed in here tonight."

Like a seasoned cruiser, Bob was already succumbing to the day-of-tab-reckoning-will-never-come syndrome. Fair enough, he knew his own pocket wouldn't suffer anyway, but the same might not eventually be said for his career. At this moment in time, however, he couldn't have given a monkey's. The exotic island of Lanzarote was now only a few hours away, but he might just as well have been preparing to land on the moon as far as making any progress with this case was concerned.

Things were about to change, though . . .

By the time Andy finally produced a lemon and a little bucket of ice, a yawning Ian had been on the receiving end of a potted lecture on the finer points of Marxism, ten minutes had passed on the clock, two more extra-large vodkas had passed the doctor's teeth, and signs of his getting blootered were (at last!) beginning to show.

Bob carried the tray containing the ice and some lemon wedges along the bar to him. "Got your order here for you now, Rupert."

"Ah, well met," said the doctor, focusing sociably with half-shut eyes. "Fancy seeing you here, Bill."

"It's Bob," said Bob.

"No, I'm Rupert," said Rupert. He indicated Ian with a sideways wobble of his head. "*This* is Bob."

"Hi, Bob," Bob said to Ian. "Fancy seeing you here."

"Yeah, uncanny, man," Ian mumbled, his Juan guise long since blown away by pro-Soviet hot air. "Fuckin' cosmic!"

Now fully focused, the ship's doctor said to the real Bob, "So, Bill, you were saying?" He then caught sight of the tray. "And, uhm, what's that you have there?"

This was going better than Bob could have hoped for in his wildest dreams. "It's just the ice and lemon you ordered, Rupert," he smiled heartily.

The ship's doctor gave him a limp pat on the shoulder and looked frankly into his eyes. "Aha, but I fear you have me mistaken for someone else, dear boy. I take it straight from the well."

Five minutes and three more fingers of straight-from-the-well vodka later, the doctor gave a little shudder, regarded Bob and Ian as if he'd only just met them, then anxiously exclaimed, "My God, I almost forgot — I have a patient waiting for me!"

"Yes," said Bob, redirecting the doctor's attention to the ice and lemon on the tray, "and I have her medicine here. Like me to carry it to the surgery for you?"

"Splendid suggestion, young sir," slurred the doctor. He hooked his arm through Bob's. "And I'll steady you as we go. Ship's rolling a bit tonight, what?"

Bob gave Ian a surreptitious wink. "OK," he whispered in his ear, "tell Green to put Plan A into action exactly three minutes from now."

Over on the stage, the Sunbeam Band played discordantly on, while delighted-to-be-formally attired cruisers danced the blissful night away.

BACK IN THE SHIP'S SURGERY, MEANWHILE . . .

Julie was draped seductively along the examination couch as the doctor ricocheted through the doorway. He was closely followed by Bob, who was carrying the ice-and-lemon tray and wearing an all's-going-well smirk.

The doctor stopped in his tracks when he saw Julie. He blinked rapidly, leered ambitiously, then zig-sagged directly over to his dispensing cabinet. "Just leave the, uhm-ah, on the table there, Dick," he said to Bob without turning round. "And, uh, that'll be all. Diss*missed*!" Then, his back to Julie, he grabbed the vodka bottle and glugged another swift finger or two of the contents into just one of the glasses.

"Oo-oo-ooh!" Julie squealed, rising slightly from the recumbent. "I hope you aren't going to give me a big one, Rupert!"

The doctor chuckled expectantly. "Just — just compensating for evaporation, my dear," he croaked. He wheeled round, vodka glasses in hand, took a step forward with his left foot, a step back and forward again with the same foot, steadied himself by shuffling it sideways, then remarked, "Bit of a heavy swell going tonight, hmm?"

"I thought it was maybe a new version of the *Hokey Cokey*," Bob quipped.

Re-focusing, the doctor leaned backwards, squinted at Bob and grunted. "Who the blazes are you two? Surgery's closed. Take a seasick pill each and go to bed. And, uh, shut the door behind you when you leave."

Bob and Julie traded nervous glances. Plan A should have kicked in by now. They realised that urgent stalling tactics were called for.

"Don't forget my ice and lemon, Rupert," Julie purred.

"Yes, and a bottle of seasick pills for me," Bob demanded.

"Surgery's closed!" the doctor barked.

"No it isn't," Bob retorted sharply. "How do you think I got in — through the air-conditioning duct?"

Confused now, the doctor took a clarifying gulp of vodka, then lunged towards the telephone on his desk. "Damned impertinence," he muttered. "Closed means closed. I'll call security."

At a stroke, the ice-and-lemon bonus Bob had been handed was turning sour. A visit from the ship's security boys certainly wasn't in the master plan. Gripped by a sudden paucity of bright ideas, he fired Julie a do-something-for-Pete's-sake look.

"Now, now, Rupert," she obligingly cooed, "there's surely no need to interrupt our cosy little twosome, is there?"

"But the twosome's now a foursome," Rupert declared, lifting the phone and pointing it at Bob.

Slinkily, Julie peeled herself off the couch, sashayed over to the desk and placed her finger on the phone's disconnect button. "And if you call security," she pouted, "how many will there be in here then? Much better to give these two gentlemen their seasick tablets now and let you and I continue to, er, *compare notes* in private, hmm?"

It was clear from the constipated expression distorting the doctor's face that something was telling him he should sober up fast here. Easier said than done, however.

And that, at least, was something in Bob's favour. He pulled back the cuff of his white dinner jacket and looked at his watch. Over six minutes had passed since he'd told Ian to get Andy Green to launch Plan A in three minutes flat. What in hell's name was that useless young twonk playing at?

Mumbling ripe expletives, the doctor was now going through the contents of his dispensing cabinet in a fashion that could more accurately be described as a ransack than a search. "Damned seasick tablets!" he cursed. "Damned nurse must have hidden them!" Finally, he spun round, brandishing a small packet. "Eureka!" he beamed. "Seek and ye shall find!" He handed the packet to Bob. "Name and cabin number?"

"Why?" Bob queried.

"So we can charge you for the consultation and pills at the end of the cruise, of course."

This hinted that the old Marxist doctor, no matter how inebriated, hadn't lost his basic instinct for capitalism. It also suggested that, perhaps, he wasn't as inebriated as he purported to be. Bob was understandably concerned that his master plan might now be going ever so slightly wonky.

Just then, and not a moment too soon, the sound of a woman screaming rang out from somewhere in the direction of the Stardust Lounge. Spot on cue, though a few minutes later than originally envisaged, Ian Scrabster appeared panting in the doorway of the surgery.

"Quick, Doc!" he gasped. "Along in the Stardust Lounge! Somebody's collapsed! Looks bad!"

Doctor De'ath was clearly unhorsed. "Dammit!" he huffed. "The best-laid plans of mice and men!" For a moment, it appeared as if he was contemplating an abdication of duty. However, overcome by a sudden flurry of conscience, he laid down the two glasses of vodka and fetched a battered Gladstone bag from behind his desk. "Lead on, McDuff," he instructed Ian. Then, smiling the sorry smile of the cruelly deprived, he told Julie, "Hold the fort until I return, my dear. Shan't be long." Finally, he did a double-take at Bob, gave him a jovial thud on the back and said, “If you have any sense, young man, you’ll take your seasick tablets and follow your twin brother off to bed — immediately!”

“I hope to Christ I never have to be treated for anything serious by that drunken old bampot,” Bob said to Julie as soon as they were alone. He closed the surgery door. “OK, did you manage to find out anything of interest in here while Doctor Death was away on his ice-and-lemon expedition?”

“Coupla things.” Julie made her way with some urgency over to the desk and produced a sheet of paper from one of the drawers. “It’s a schedule of small shareholders in Glasgow Rangers Football Club.”

Bob gave the list the once-over. “Well, well, well, coincidences will never cease. As you’ll doubtless recall, Rab Dykes was supposed to be a front for Boris Kaminski in his efforts to buy out shareholders in Rangers.”

“That’s exactly why this caught my eye.” Julie indicated several names on the list. “And I wonder why the name ‘Ben’ has been pencilled in opposite these.”

Bob shook his head. “Ben?” He thought a bit, then shook his head again. “Nope. Means nothing to me.”

Julie produced a diary from the same drawer. “I had a quick flick through this. Look.” She pointed to an entry. “It says, ‘Lisbon — drop Ben off at Restaurante Farol de Santa Luzia’.” She turned a few pages. “Then it’s repeated, more or less identically, under tomorrow’s date.”

Bob looked over her shoulder. “Same entry, different location.”

“That’s right — ‘Puerto del Carmen, Lanzarote — drop Ben off at Restaurante La Lonja’. Weird, huh?” Intrigued, Julie gave Bob an enquiring look. “I mean, who the blazes is Ben?”

Bob stoked his chin. “I’ve a feeling I *may* know him.”

“Yeah? Tell me more, Kemosabe!”

“All in good time, and we’ve precious little of that.” Bob was still peering at the diary over Julie’s shoulder. “Turn back a couple of pages, will you?”

Julie obliged.

Bob smiled. “The Doc must have been *really* blootered when he wrote this. His writing’s even worse than his profession’s noted for, but it definitely looks like ‘Rab Dykes — Ben’ to me.”

“Looks like that to me too,” Julie agreed, with a look in which confusion and suspicion were evenly balanced.

“So,” Bob reasoned, “maybe Rab Dykes had an appointment with the Doc on that date, which just happens to be the day of the man-overboard drama.”

“Even if he did, what’s this Ben guy got to do with it?”

“Flick over another page or two,” Bob said.

Julie obliged again.

“There!” Bob said. “Just as I thought — the entry for two days after Lisbon.”

“Palma Mallorca? But the ship never got there, as *we* know only too well. Diverted to Gib because of the norovirus outbreak.”

"Exactly, and there's the related entry, duly scored out. 'Palma de Mallorca — drop Ben off at Restaurante La Bodeguilla'."

"Poor old Ben," said Julie. "Sounds as if Doctor Death wants to get rid of him pretty badly, but without much success so far. A bad penny, do you think?"

"Keeps coming back, you mean?"

"Something like that."

"Hmm, I doubt that somehow, and if my hunch is right, I may well have met him, and with dipso Doctor Death observing the entire event from the wings."

Julie was all ears. "Come on, come on — tell me more, tell me more!"

"All in good time." Bob stretched forward and turned the diary pages to the previous day's date, the date the ship had finally set sail from Gibraltar. "Two entries," he said. "Both the same."

Julie read the scribbled words aloud. "Looks like, *solitudo, casus*, N-dash-V." She looked enquiringly at Bob. "Remember any Latin? They still taught it at school back in your era, didn't they?"

"You bet!" Bob resolutely affirmed. "And that was when the quality of Scottish education was *still* admired by the world and his wife."

"Don't get all uppity with me, Kemosabe. Although it wasn't compulsory by the time I went to school, I actually took Latin for a bit as well, you may be surprised to know."

"I'd've been surprised if you hadn't," Bob muttered. "You seem to be an expert on just about every other language."

Julie allowed that dig to pass without reaction as she pondered the meaning of the two Latin words scribbled in the diary. "Well, *solitudo* — that's obvious enough — 'solitude'. And *casus*, if I remember right, is the word for 'accident' — the direct derivative, of course, being the obvious one, 'casualty'."

Bob gave her a reproachful, schoolmasterly look. "Eliminate the obvious, accentuate the devious, as Crabbie Scrabster always says."

"Come again?"

"Latin — in translation, the words don't always mean the first thing that comes to mind when you look at them."

An uncharacteristically puzzled frown wrinkled Julie's brow. "Sorry, I don't follow."

"Obviously, but just think about where you are. In a doctor's surgery, right?"

Julie nodded, trying not to look too taken-down-a-peg.

"So," Bob continued, trying not to look too superior, "another meaning of *solitudo*, if *I* remember right, is 'isolation', whereas *casus* also means 'death'. While Julie mulled over the possible significance of that, Bob pointed to the page again. "Now, what does 'N-dash-V' suggest to you?"

The light of perception glinted once more in Julie's eyes. "Considering we're in a doctor's surgery aboard a recently plague-ridden ship, how would 'norovirus' grab you?"

"Bingo!" Bob said. "And if our interpretation of Doctor De'ath's cryptic Latin note is correct, it would appear that the bug claimed another two victims just one day after the ship was given a clean bill of health by the Gibraltar inspectors."

Pennies were now dropping in Julie's mind like enlightening hailstones. She indicated the *solitudo* word in the diary with her forefinger. "And if the victims were in isolation somewhere, it could be that they'd been hidden away from the inspectors."

"Could be," Bob conceded with a shrug. "But another interpretation of *solitudo* might suggest that they'd simply been travelling alone."

"Or hidden away and *also* travelling alone?"

"Maybe. Now, shove that diary back in the drawer and show me what else you've sussed out in here. If I'm right, Ben and a few of his brothers will be hiding in here somewhere."

"Not a chance!" Julie scoffed. "I mean, look at the size of the place. A matchbox. No, I've had a good rake around, and you couldn't even hide one of Snow White's Seven Dwarfs in here."

Bob gestured towards a door at the far end of the room. "What's through there?"

"Just another ex-cabin like this one, and that one's been converted into what I suppose is meant to pass for the ship's hospital — all two beds of it."

"Any patients?"

Julie shook her head.

Bob walked across, opened the door and stepped inside. He gestured towards a door facing the one he'd come through. "And what's in there?"

Julie raised her shoulders. “Dunno. The door’s locked.”

“Well, this is where my years of police experience come in handy.” He reached up to the ledge above the door. “Some people never learn,” he said, brandishing a key. “Now, let’s have a look inside.”

BACK IN THE “STARDUST LOUNGE”, MEANWHILE . . .

Behind the bar, Andy Green was lying on his back at the opposite end from Pedro “Speedy” Gonzales. Andy’s legs were twitching wildly, his body raked by convulsions, his unblinking eyes staring rabidly at the ceiling, his gaping mouth oozing white froth. He was moaning. As a counter attraction, Speedy was gamely trying to maintain a business-as-usual atmosphere by performing some of his more spectacular mixology juggles for a huddle of customers who were clearly more interested in watching Andy writhing about in the throes of whatever ailed him. Over on the stage, the Sunbeam Band played tunelessly on throughout, while dancers in their finery danced delightedly by.

Doctor Rupert De’ath was on his knees by Andy’s side, listening through his stethoscope to whatever rhythms his patient’s heart was beating out.

“Still alive, is he?” Ian Scrabster mumbled incuriously from his vantage point at the other side of Andy’s flailing limbs.

The ship's doctor raised his head, frowned at Ian and pointed impatiently to the earpieces of his stethoscope. "Can't hear you," he mouthed.

Ian bent down, lifted the business end of the stethoscope from Andy Green's chest and yelled into it, "IS HE STILL ALIVE?"

"VODKA!" the doctor shouted, throwing the stethoscope aside in agony. "PULSE IS WEAK!"

"I think you'll find that brandy would be more beneficial to the victim," an onlooking gentleman well-meaningly ventured.

"It isn't for him — it's for ME!" Doctor De'ath declared. "This man is a fake!" He lowered his face to within an inch of Andy's, sniffed his breath, then swiped a dollop of foam from his mouth and tentatively tasted it. "Just as I thought," he grimaced. "Cappuccino!"

"Not so fast," said Ian, anticipating a sooner-than-bargained-for return of the doctor to his surgery. "Don't you think you should do a few more tests here and then maybe put him in the ship's sick bay for the night — for observation, sort o' thing?"

Andy thought he'd also better do his bit to keep Plan A on course. "That's right. Ah've got a history o' takin' fits," he volunteered, spitting coffee-flavoured froth everywhere. "Ah'm epidermic." He threw another limb-twitching spasm to drive the point home.

But the ship's doctor wasn't impressed. "I'll see to it that the Captain knows about this, young man," he told Andy with a righteous nod of his head. "Drunk on duty. Absolutely disgraceful." He gave Andy a nudge with his foot. "Now get up and serve me that vodka I asked for. Yes, and no ice or lemon. I take it straight from the well!"

Ian breathed a sigh of relief. At least Bob would have a *few* more minutes to complete his rummage through the surgery. Plan A, as far as Ian was concerned, had now been accomplished, even if not entirely as conceived. He made his way over to the stand to give the Sunbeam Band their next scheduled break and the ears of the more musically aware punters a well deserved rest.

"What the fook's your game?" Speedy Gonzales snarled in Andy's face as he struggled to his feet behind the bar. "First rule o' the barkeepin' — never fookin' fall down while the fookin' customers is still standin'!"

"Sorry," Andy said weakly. "Ah must've slipped on somethin', like."

BACK IN THE SHIP'S MEDICAL CENTRE, MEANWHILE . . .

Bob opened the door at the opposite side of the "ward" and, with Julie in close attendance, stepped into a short corridor with yet another door at the far end.

"There's a sign on it," Julie observed. She looked closer. "*Mortuary*, it says."

"Well," Bob shrugged, "we may as well pop in for a look while we're here."

The first thing they noticed inside the tiny, windowless room was that there were two "slabs".

"One for each of the beds in the ward?" Julie cynically suggested.

Bob suppressed a shudder. "Yeah, and each one with an occupied body bag on it." Gingerly, he pulled down just enough of the first bag's zipper to allow him to peep inside. "You were asking who the Ben in Doctor Death's diary is," he said, glancing up at Julie with a surprisingly unsurprised look on his face. "Well, here he is — and a bunch of his brothers as well." Unceremoniously, he whipped the zip fully open.

Julie's eyes popped. "Good heavens!" she gasped. "I've examined some pretty well-endowed stiffs in my time, but this one's in a class of its own!"

Bob peeled a banknote from one of the countless wads stuffed into the bag. He handed it to Julie.

"Wow!" she marvelled. "A hundred dollars!"

"A Benjamin, as they're popularly known in the States, I believe?"

"After one-time president Benjamin Franklin, whose mug shot is right here on the bill," Julie confirmed.

"Yep, and each one a 'Ben' for short, maybe? Thousands of them in this one sack. A million dollars, more or less?"

Stunned, Julie nodded dumbly.

"I refer to Doctor Death's diary," Bob stated in a summarising courtroom manner. "Drop Ben off in Lisbon, it said, then in Palma — aborted — and tomorrow in Lanzarote." He proceeded to the next slab, ran his hand over the body bag and said, "A bit lumpy for a corpse, unless he died from swallowing bricks." He unzipped the bag to reveal another stash of Benjamins. "Snap!"

"Wait a minute," said Julie, lifting one of the wads from the bag, then running her thumb over the edge of the notes. "I thought they looked a bit less tidy than the ones in the other bag. Look — all newspaper, except for the note on top."

Bob pulled out several more wads at random. Each one was the same as the one Julie had checked. "Somebody's been at the fiddle — bigtime. Bits of paper replacing thousands of one-hundred-dollar bills."

"Which begs the question," Julie concluded, "— why did Wally Walter-Wall just happen to choke to death on his own vomit right after he tried to flog you a batch of Bens?"

"An attempt that was seen from the wings by Doctor Death, don't forget."

"And the Benjamin old Wally attempted to flog you had been slipped to him by the overboarding Rab Dykes, right?"

"*Allegedly* overboarding," Bob qualified, doing up the zipper. "As of now, I'd gamble that squire Walter-Wall has a better chance than Rab of being at the bottom of the sea."

"What makes you think that?"

"Simply that, having just died, you'd have expected him to be bagged up on one of these slabs in here."

"OK, but maybe he's bagged up somewhere else, along with the two *solitudo* corpses. After all, old Doctor Death did tell us in the Bosun's Locker yesterday that his little morgue gets full to overflowing occasionally."

"Mmm, that got me wondering at the time, I must admit, and it's got me wondering even more now." Bob shepherded Julie towards the door. "Anyway, let's get the hell outa here before the old bugger comes back from the bar. I'll make a point of paying a visit to the morgue-overflow area as soon as poss, though."

"You mean you know where it is?"

"No, but I know where it *should* be."

CHAPTER SEVENTEEN

LATER THE SAME EVENING — IN BOB AND JULIE'S CABIN . . .

Bob had just emailed a report on his latest findings to Detective Superintendent Bruce McNeill back in Edinburgh, when he and Julie were joined by Ian Scrabster following his final piano-tinkling session of the night.

"So, how did the master plan go, Bobby?" he said, flopping down into a chair. "Ye had plenty extra time to sleuth about in the surgery, 'cos Doctor Death was still standin' at the bar in the Stardust Lounge when I left five minutes ago. Out o' his skull, but still standin'."

Bob winked at Julie. "Jezebel came second place to Smirnoff after all, then, huh?"

"Suits me," Julie replied, shrugging. "He'll never know what he missed."

"Should've worn yer school uniform," Ian advised, only half joking.

"I think that would have defeated the purpose," Julie came back loftily. "You'd never have got him to go and tend to your frothing-at-the-mouth patient in a month of Sundays."

"Aye, maybe ye're right," said Ian, staring dreamily at the wall as he savoured the St Trinian's gymslip visions appearing before his mind's eye. He gave himself a shake. "Anyway, Bobby, ye were gonna tell me if ye found anything when ye were sleuthin' about in the sick bay."

"Let's just say the sleuthing about was *interesting*," Bob replied, not giving anything away.

"Please yerself," Ian mumbled, then sank into a minor huff. "Ye can stuff yer bloody police secrets where the squirrel sticks its nuts. I'll think twice before actin' as yer flunky next time."

"Don't worry, Crabbie, no secrets," Bob laughed. "I'll tell you all about it if you take us down to the crew's bar."

"No can do, man. Only crew, entertainers and musicians allowed in there. Ship's lecturers and their companions are barred." He turned to Julie. "Check the Ulanova Line contract ye signed in Palma. It's all in there."

Bob was already at the door. "Yeah, and the Ulanova Line can stuff their bloody contract where the squirrel sticks its nuts as well. So, come on, Crabbie, lead the way! We'll be your invited guests, *if* anybody bothers to ask." Then, reading the look on Ian's face that had turned from huffy to panic-stricken, he promptly appended, "And worry not, mate, I'll pick up the tab . . . as usual!"

"*Viva* Lothian and Borders Police!" Ian grunted. "Talk about high livin'!"

A FEW MINUTES LATER — IN THE CREW'S BAR . . .

It took Julie but a glance into the room to appreciate the irony that Ian had injected into his last comment. "Now I know where they got the inspiration for that freaky outer-space bar in *Star Wars*!" she said, hesitating in the doorway.

Bob was standing by her side. "Yeah, but they obviously toned down the freakiness for the movie. Jeez, if all those formally attired punters upstairs could see where a cruise liner's working class gets its kicks."

Ian was quick to agree. "Now ye know why the company only allows musicians and entertainers to share all this with the crew. Aye, minstrels and jesters have always been less fussy than Earth people — like toffee-nosed ship's lecturers, for example."

"Present company excepted, I hope!" Julie vehemently objected. "Believe me, this is no worse than most of the Students' Union booze joints I frequented in my socially formative years. Matter of fact," she grinned, commencing another more thorough survey of her surroundings, "I actually feel quite at home in here."

Bob followed her appraising gaze round the room. It reminded him of the bowels of a submarine as depicted in a film called *The Hunt For Red October* — grey-painted steel walls and a claustrophobically low ceiling, exposed rivet heads and pipework spaghetti, mesh-covered bulkhead lights with low-wattage, red bulbs. All that was missing was a periscope, a couple of torpedo tubes and a mural-sized blow-up of Sean Connery's eyebrows.

Compensating for the absence of those adornments was a bustling bar, an ancient juke box grinding out vintage Presley, and a shoulder-to-shoulder crush of customers, a few of them only marginally less weird (in Bob's cynical opinion) than their *Star Wars* counterparts. There were also the Indonesian stewards and cabin maids that you bumped into every day as they went about their respective shipboard duties, there were ship's officers of junior rank and unremarkable Caucasian appearance, there were the Mancunian Flamenco dancers, and there was a knot of reefer-sharing corner-boy types, who, Ian disclosed, were members of the pit orchestra in the ship's Neptune Theatre. So far, all pretty much as you'd expect.

But Bob noticed that there were others who didn't quite fit in with the *normal* crowd here. One group in particular caught his eye; three shifty-eyed, scruffily dressed young men of swarthy complexion, huddled furtively round a table in a dark corner of the room. They were sharing a solitary bottle of beer.

"Who are those guys?" he asked Ian.

"Dog's bodies. The bottom o' the food chain. They do jobs down here in the guts o' the ship that nobody else would do. Poor buggers never even see the light of day. Never mix wi' anybody, either. In fact it's very seldom ye even see them in here. Who knows — maybe they've been savin' up their wages for weeks to buy that bottle o' beer."

"How awful," said Julie, genuinely concerned. "Are there many more like that?"

Ian hunched his shoulders. "Haven't a clue. They all look the same to me. But I've noticed them, or blokes just like them, on previous trips I've done on this boat. Mind you, sometimes it's black guys instead. Aye, but always sittin' at that same table by the door over there."

"And where does it lead?" Bob asked.

"The door?" Ian hunched his shoulders again. "Don't ask me. It's a rabbit warren o' corridors and stairways below decks here."

At that, one of the trio drained the dregs of beer from the communal bottle. He stood up along with his two companions and, without as much as stealing a glance in anyone else's direction, they slouched, heads bowed, through the adjacent doorway.

"OK," Bob said to Julie, "barge your way over and grab their table before someone else does. Crabbie and I will get the drinks."

"Hope you've got some cash on you, then," Ian warned.

"How come?" Bob scowled. "What's wrong with sticking it on my tab?"

Ian let out a mocking little laugh. "Do ye honestly think the company would trust any of this lot wi' credit? No way, it's strictly cash on the counter in here, man."

"Fine, no problem, as long as I get a receipt."

Another laugh from Ian. "A *receipt*? Aye, fat bloody chance, by the way! There's scams goin' on behind this bar that would make even Speedy Gonzales green wi' jealousy. Nah, nah — cash on the counter — no receipts — no questions asked." He gave Bob a consoling pat on the back. "Still, never mind, ye get huge measures."

"Oh, that makes me feel a *lot* better," Bob griped. "I'm still on the water wagon, remember?"

"Well, ye can't win 'em all." Ian started to snowplough a path through the motley crush. "Anyway, Bobby," he called over his shoulder, "what the blazes did ye want to come down to this sweaty hell hole for in any case?"

When they reached the bar, Bob gave Ian an account of his findings in the ship's medical centre. Ian's mouth fell further open with each revelation, but then he said that he still didn't understand why this had made Bob want to come down to the crew's bar, of all places.

"Simple," Bob replied. "If something stinks, check the drains before you sniff the window boxes."

"Aye, I get yer drift, but ye'll never get any inside info from the crew, *even* if they've got any to offer. Too scared o' losin' their jobs and bein' sent back home to the paddy fields or salt mines or wherever. And as for as the musos and entertainers, well, most o' them are never on one ship long enough to pick up *any*thing, except maybe a dose o' the clap."

"No doubt, but it's getting access to parts of the ship that passengers don't see that I'm interested in right now, not straight-from-the-horse's mouth info. In other words, I trust my own eyes more than other people's tongues."

"Fine, so what is it ye want to see?"

"I won't know 'til I've seen it, but a hunch tells me the kitchens might be a good place to start."

"The *kitchens*? What the hell for? Turned cockroach detective now, have ye?"

Bob felt a prod in his back. He turned to find himself looking into the hangdog face of Lex "Laugh-a-Minute" McGinn, the cruise's star comedian. The face was attempting to smile.

"Aye, aye, son," Lex droned. "Glad to meet ye outa the company o' that fat windbag, Esme Horrocks-Bunt."

"Yeah, I suppose she *is* a bit overpowering right enough, the Professor."

Lex's attempted smile dissolved into a scowl. "Professor, my arse!"

Bob feigned surprise. "You don't mean she's not *really* a boffin, do you? I mean, my partner Julie caught one of her lectures, and she said old Esme knew her stuff. Put on a first-rate performance, Julie reckoned."

"Aye, performance is right."

Bob inclined his head enquiringly. "I don't quite, ehm . . ."

"She's an ex-hoofer," Lex announced with undisguised glee, then swivelled round to acknowledge an oil-smeared crew member's back-slapping salutation.

"I'll just take the drinks over to the table," Ian muttered in Bob's ear. "I can do without that old git's gossip about the golden age o' music hall. Bores the tits off ye. And anyway, I see Doc Julie's attractin' a swarm o' oriental Klingons, so I'd better go warp factor two and energise the deflector shields."

"Yeah, OK, Crabbie" Bob nodded, "I'll be right with you."

"Aye, as Ah was sayin'," Lex said to Bob after he'd satisfied his engine-room fan with a suitably smutty joke, "the Professor, so-called, was a hoofer years ago. 'Esmeralda, Exotic *Notre Dame* Dancer', she was billed as. Coupla ostrich-feather fans coverin' her thrup'nies an' Azerbaijani an' that. Exotic *Notre Dame* Dancer? More fuckin' grotesque than a female Quasimodo! Aye, and about as exotic as a bucket o' shite, as we say in showbiz circles. Used to bump into her on the old Moss Empires variety circuit. Claimed she once did a tableau turn at the Moulin Rouge in Paris. Wi' a bahookie the size o' hers? Ah don't think so! Christ, ye could play a game o' dominoes on that arse! In fack, the first time Ah saw it Ah thought she was wearin' a bustle, an' Ah kid ye not!"

Lex went on to say that Esme had, however, always had a hankering for history, avidly reading books on the subject, even back in her chorus line days. The backstage word, when she was eventually "plucked from the boards" by her present wimpy husband, was that she had used some of his inherited money to go to the States and buy herself a professor's "certificate" from a bogus university, at which the specialist discipline was the while-you-wait printing of fake degrees.

"Is that right?" Bob said with a distinct lack of enthusiasm for the subject. "And a sham qualification like that is good enough to get work as a lecturer on cruise ships, eh?"

"On the Ulanova Line, anyway," said Lex with a distinct lack of esteem for his current employers. "Tellin' ye, son, ye get all types o' chancers lecturin' for this outfit. Some o' the poets they rope in is the worst. Poets? Ah don't think so! Some o' them would be hard pushed to compose a filthy limerick for a lavvy wall, never mind a proper pome. Which reminds me — ye wanny see the shite that snivvelin' wee Simon Horrocks-Bunt passes off as pomes. Tellin ye —"

Bob held up a hand. "Very interesting, Lex, but not the kind of material I'm needing for the magazine article I'm writing, I'm afraid."

"Please yerself," Lex grumped. "Just markin' yer card, that's all."

"Yeah, and I appreciate that, thanks very much, but I'm kinda concentrating on the man-overboard angle right now."

"Still on about the Rab Dykes thing, are ye?"

"Yup, and I'm told there's a lot more overboard incidents on cruise liners than the public get to hear about — some of them happening in suspicious circumstances as well."

Lex raised to the light a glass of amber liquid the barman had just poured from a Scotch whisky bottle. "Look at this," he said to Bob. "Scotch? Don't kid yersel'. Naw, the nearest this stuff ever got to anything Scottish was when Ah wrapped ma fingers round the glass just now. Bootleg gnats' piss, that's what it is — good enough and cheap enough for this low-life drinkin' pit, but exackly the same stuff's bein' served out o' Chivas Regal, Glenmorangie, Johnnie Walker and

Famous Grouse bottles in all them swanky bars on the passenger decks. Aye, and the punters' tabs are bein' charged top dollar for it an' all. Suspicious circumstances, ye say? Hey, tell me somethin' on these boats that isnae, son!"

"Honestly?" Bob said, striving to sound sceptical.

"Aye!" Lex replied, sounding adamant. "An' if there was anything suspicious about that Rab Dykes business, ye can bet it'll have been well covered up long before the Portuguese polis dropped in on their helicopter." He prodded an emphasising finger into Bob's chest. "Ah've been on enough cruises in ma time to see it all. Aye, and then some. Think about it — a multi-billion-dollar caper the cruise business is these days, and growin' all the time." Lex shook his head scornfully. "Ye're no gonny tell me the money-grabbin' buggers that runs them companies is gonny let a few punters takin' a dive overboard damage the floatin'-paradise image they've built for cruisin', are ye? Naw, all the man-overboard stuff's covered up, son, and don't tell me money disnae change hands in the process, especially if the foreign polis is involved. Suspicious circumstances, ye say? You bet yer fuckin' life!"

So warmed to the theme had Lex become that Bob reckoned the time was right to put his bull-at-a-fence questioning technique into operation. He recalled that Andy Green had told him that Lex, being a Catholic, was a fervid supporter of Glasgow Celtic Football Club, whereas Rab Dykes, a Protestant, had been a staunch follower of Celtic's arch rivals, Glasgow Rangers.

"Did you know," Bob asked Lex, "that Rab Dykes was working for Boris Kaminski, the owner of the Ulanova Line — helping him buy shares in Rangers — hopefully enough to gain control of the club?"

"Doesnae surprise me," Lex mumbled. "So it serves Dykes right if he's went and drowned. Turds don't float."

"Yeah, but seriously —"

"Ah'm *be*in' serious!"

"OK, but do you think anyone aboard the *Ostentania* would have been so concerned about a moneybags like Kaminski buying Rangers that they'd have —"

"Shoved Dykes over the side?" Lex pulled a facial shrug. "There's always *some*body daft enough to try and do a King Canute."

"King Canute?"

"Aye, shite happens, and ye cannae hold it back. Like, when one Rab Dykes disappears, another one just pops up. That's life when money and football's involved, son, so what's the point in gettin' too excited about it?"

"Excited enough to commit murder, you mean?"

Lex gave a knowing chuckle. "Listen, boy, if ye've spent a lifetime doin' ma stage act, comedy bagpipes an' all, ye've committed enough murders, believe me. Naw, naw, Ah can tell ye nothin' about Rab Dyke's disappearance, but if ye want to get a story about the sleazy side o' cruisin' for yer article, Ah'm yer man."

"Wouldn't do your career much good, that, would it?" Bob said leadingly.

"Career, ye say?" Lex peered reflectively into his whisky glass. "Aye, well, that was fucked years ago. Once the old variety theatres got turned into bingo halls, that was it for the likes o' me. Yeah, it was either stay on land and go fast down the cludgie in the workin' mens' clubs, or go to sea and die slowly in luxury. *And*," Lex promptly tagged, "Ah say 'die' in the theatrical sense, just in case ye were gettin' any daft ideas. Oh no, boy, there's plenty life in this old trouper yet."

"So, why expose the unsavoury side of the cruise business in a magazine article?"

"Because this is Laugh-a-Minute Lex McGinn's last boat trip. After this, me and the missus is retirin' to a static caravan doon the Clyde coast somewhere. Somewhere about Greenock maybe. Watch these cruise liners goin' past and thank fuck Ah'm no on them."

"Having copped a few quid for the inside info in the magazine article, right?"

"On the nose, boy! Like Ah say, Ah'm yer man."

Resuming his bull-at-a-fence thrust, Bob then said, "Would it surprise you to know that the last man to make me an offer like that is now dead?"

Unfazed, Lex looked Bob in the eye. "Oh aye? And who would that have been, like?"

"The name Wally Walter-Wall mean anything to you?"

Lex started to chortle. "Him o' the bargain floor jobs?" He downed his whisky and prepared to leave.

"Aye, ye get all kinds o'chancers on these boats, and it wouldn't be the first time one o' them faked his death."

"*Faked* his death?"

"Aye, easy. Take somebody like the Walter-Wall guy, right? Right, and he wants to start a new life somewhere, OK? OK, so he hides away somewhere in the ship one night and the ship's doctor issues a death certificate in the mornin'. With me? Right. Then he just goes ashore at the first port o' call and disnae bother comin' back on board when the ship leaves. Like Ah said — easy!"

Bob couldn't help laughing. "*Too* easy," he said. "Where's the dead body, for a start?"

"Who needs one? Think about it. The guy's travellin' alone, right? So, none o' the other punters on board could care less about a body. Naw, the whole thing's forgotten about in no time flat."

"And the death certificate?"

Lex took a sip of his whisky, then pinged the rim of the glass with a finger nail. "Booze, son. Ye get a piss-artist doctor like the one on this boat, and he'll issue a death certificate for the price o' a fortnight's worth o' bevvy. Not a problem."

Bob laughed again. "Aren't you forgetting that every passenger has his swipe card checked by the ship's security on the way off and back onto the ship, wherever it docks. And there's an automatic head count before the ship leaves again. That's all in the rules and regulations posted in every cabin."

"Oh aye," Lex readily agreed, "and on top o' that, yer face is checked wi' the mug shot they take o' ye when ye first come on board. But so what?"

Bob shrugged. "You tell me."

"Money," Lex said sagely. "Everybody has a price, and the so-called security guys they've got on this line would turn a blind eye to somebody jumpin' ship for about the same money it'd take to buy their old mother a set o' false teeth back in the jungles o' Borneo or wherever."

Smiling tolerantly, Bob scratched his cheek. "Yeah, well, fine in theory maybe, but there's got to be more to it than that, no?"

Lex gave him the customary parting pat on the shoulder. "Ah'll tell ye all about it any time ye want, son. But, hey, bring yer cheque book, eh? Yeah," he said, an afterthought sprouting, "and ye can forget about tryin' to tie the Rab Dykes business in wi' Esme Bollocks Hunt, if that's what's on yer mind. OK, the bitch hates men — ye can see that by the state o' the miserable specimen o' manhood she married — but she'd never get involved in bumpin' one off. Naw, doin' her highfalutin lectures on cruise ships is the nearest to showbiz stardom she's ever gonny get, and she'll never do *nothin*' to screw that up. Nothin!"

"Well, well, well," Bob said to himself as he watched Lex disappear into the crowd, "the strange things that happen at sea — allegedly."

He was about to start making his way through the crush to the table where Julie and Ian were sitting, when he felt another nudge in the back. He wheeled round to be confronted by an elderly, silver-haired man of distinctly well-groomed appearance. Suave, tanned and athletic-looking, he was dressed in immaculate white shirt and slacks, the former open a few buttons too far for his age and exposing a gold medallion on a chain.

He offered Bob his hand. "So," he smiled, "we meet at last, Detective Inspector Burns." He glanced around to double-check that no one was listening, then said in confidential tones, "I'm Officer Jim Alexander of Her Majesty's Customs. As you know, I'm working undercover on this cruise with your sidekick, Detective Constable Andy Green — thick as a plank and a useless waste of space, in my frank opinion."

Bob was temporarily dumbstruck. How the blazes did this bloke know who he was? And, oddly, he felt aggrieved by his disparaging comment about Andy Green. Decrying your own subordinate was one thing, but hearing a complete stranger rubbish him was quite another. Bob's first impressions of this fellow were that he was just too flash and wrapped up in himself for comfort; a typical, shining-knight womaniser in over-polished armour — that was Bob's opinion. So much so that, if he had been of the female gender himself, he would have pulled up the drawbridge smartish and barricaded himself in a turret. Old guys with open shirts, gold chains and medallions made his flesh crawl!

"I take it you got my calling card?" Alexander asked presumptuously.

"Calling card?" Bob echoed, frowning.

With a lopsided smirk, Alexander held up the middle digit of his right hand. "The finger in the fridge?"

"You? *You*? But — but, I thought — I could have sworn it was Rab Dykes's wife who . . ."

Bob was in a quandary. His thoughts in turmoil, he looked more closely at this man who had appeared from nowhere and had immediately blown one of his instinctive theories to smithereens. What, exactly, could this slick-looking bastard's game be?

Gentleman Jim Alexander's smirk developed into a self-satisfied chuckle. "I *knew* you'd jump to the conclusion that Catherine was behind the chopped-off finger ploy."

"Catherine?"

"Rab Dykes's wife — or widow, depending on your point of view."

"Point of view?" Bob's frown intensified. "What do you mean by that? And *ploy* — you said *ploy*. What the hell are you talking about?" Bob was not a happy policeman. He lowered his voice to a menacing snarl. "If you've been pissing me about, *Officer* Alexander, I'd advise you to make an urgent dental appointment!"

Gentleman Jim apparently felt more amused than threatened by Bob's attitude. "Oo-oo-ooh, getting all aggressive, are we?" He gave a disdainful shake of his head. "No, no, I think my charming smile will be intact a while yet, and without help from a dentist."

This bugger's cockiness was really getting up Bob's nose. "You referred to Dykes's wife as Catherine. Know her well, do you?"

"Not as well as I'd like to, but I'm working on it." Jim flashed Bob a man-to-man wink. "*Very* attractive piece of stuff, huh?"

"I wouldn't know, and I couldn't care bloody less!" Bob pointed a finger straight between Alexander's eyes. "Now, wipe that smart-arsed look off your face and tell me what the hell this is all about!"

Jim Alexander was coolness personified as he began his explanatory narrative . . .

The sole reason for his (Alexander's) presence on the *Ostentania*, he reminded Bob, was to ascertain how significant quantities of contraband cigarettes happened to be circulating in Edinburgh every time the ship arrived from the Canary Islands. This, despite the fact that no such cigarettes had ever been uncovered during the local Customs' searches of the vessel. To add to the confusion, those searches had always been sparked by telephone tip-offs from a supposed crew member prior to the ship docking. Rab Dykes's record of having been involved in the peddling of hooky cigarettes in the city had, Jim Alexander guessed, prompted Bob's boss Bruce McNeill to suspect that Dykes's mysterious disappearance from the *Ostentania* may have been related in some way to the cigarette smuggling affair.

Bob granted him that with an affirmative nod.

"But that matter would have been left in HM Customs' hands," Jim Alexander surmised, "if it hadn't been for the suspicion of foul play against Rab Dykes, agreed?"

Bob nodded again.

"So, that's where the idea of sending your boss the picture of the finger in the quiche lorraine came from." Jim Alexander added that, without the threat of such a sensational twist being picked up by the media in Edinburgh, it would have been likely that Superintendent Bruce McNeill would have readily let things rest in the hands of his Portuguese counterparts.

Bob conceded that these assumptions were all fairly accurate so far, but they still didn't explain why Jim Alexander had gone to so much trouble to get Lothian and Borders Police involved.

Officer Alexander responded by revealing that there were two reasons. The first was that he had "taken a shine" to Rab Dykes's wife and, to help her get what she was entitled to from her husband's life insurers, he'd wanted to do what he could to ensure that his plunge overboard wouldn't be summarily adjudged as having been suicide. He knew from collaborating with Bruce McNeill in the past that he was the type of assiduous policeman who'd want to get to the bottom of a quirky case like this. He also knew, from studying background files on Rab Dykes at the onset of this assignment, that Bob had been responsible for putting him behind bars on a few occasions. So, it was a reasonable bet that McNeill would assign Bob to this investigation, and that pleased Jim Alexander fine, as he knew Bob from reputation to be someone who wouldn't treat the exercise as merely an excuse to loaf about on a cruise to the Canaries.

"Thanks for the compliment," Bob said coldly, "but I wish you'd aimed your admiration at somebody else!

Anyway, you said you had two reasons for dragging me into this caper."

His second reason, Jim Alexander proceeded to explain, was that, since early in this cruise, he had suspected that the alleged cigarette-smuggling activity was actually a smokescreen to cover a much more serious contraband hustle. However, as he'd already got to the root of the cigarette business, he felt he had accomplished the mission he'd been sent on and was, therefore, under no obligation to dig into anything else, irrespective of how momentous it might eventually prove to be.

"Oh really?" said Bob, his hackles rising. "And, according to DC Green, you probably haven't even reported your findings to your HQ yet. Is that correct?"

"My, my, very perceptive of Green," Alexander smirked, "— for such a useless waste of space."

Despite himself, Bob chose not to respond to that snide remark — for the moment. "Some might say," he growled, "that you're sitting down on the job. In fact, Officer Alexander, if it was up to me, I'd cancel your bloody pension!"

"Ah, but then, not all of us are so blindly dedicated to our mundane careers as you are, *Officer* Burns!"

Bob was seeing red now. "Dedication's got bugger all to do with it, mate. I'm paid to do a job — mundane or otherwise — and my conscience wouldn't allow my arse to sit on it."

"How virtuous."

"No, it's called self-respect! Yes, and even waste-of-space Andy Green could lend the likes of you a barrowload of that and still have more than enough left over for himself!"

Jim Alexander smiled condescendingly. "Not that it's any of your business, Bob — I take it you don't mind me calling you Bob? — but when my wife died after a long illness a few years ago, I decided that, given the opportunity, I'd make the most of what's left of my own life."

"I'm sorry about your wife," Bob said with genuine sympathy, "but we all have our private sorrows to nurse. However, that doesn't give us —"

"I know, I know, I know. That doesn't give us a right to free lunches."

"My point exactly. You're being paid by HM Customs to do a job on this cruise, and if there's more than one worm in the can you've opened, you're duty bound to have a damned good look at it."

Officer Alexander shook his head. "I used to subscribe to all that duty-bound stuff once, but not any more. And without boring you with the details, I can assure you that, during forty years in the service, I've more than earned the pension I start drawing a week from now. And that's *my* point exactly! Now, if I may go on?"

Bob instinctively knew he wasn't going to like what he was about to be told, but he was obliged to listen anyway.

Jim Alexander confirmed that his way of thinking was that he'd completed the task he'd been set, namely getting to the truth of the cigarette smuggling mystery. He now intended to enjoy the rest of the cruise and, as he'd already told Andy Green, "stuff the Customs Service and Lothian and Borders Police as well!" What's more, he continued, he'd actually been having the time of his life acting as a "dance host", and he was seriously tempted to take up the occupation full-time. Admittedly, there wasn't much money in it, but there were many worse ways of earning a crust than waltzing about on luxury liners with well-off widows. And, who knows, there might even be a chance of hooking one with enough money in the bank to give him the class of life that his measly civil service pension most certainly wouldn't. After all, he concluded with a self-approving glance in the mirror behind the bar, he had the necessary appearance *and* charisma to pull the right one when she eventually came along.

"Call me cynical," Bob said, "but it could be suggested that you've already targeted the *right* one in Rab Dykes's widow."

"Nothing cynical about it," Jim Alexander nonchalantly replied. "Given half a chance, I'll be right in there, and I make no bones about it."

"Yeah, except I'm told there may well be competition from the ship's chaplain, no?"

"Ha! Don't make me laugh! He'd have to decide which way he swings first. Yes, and I can tell you for nothing that Catherine Dykes doesn't like her porridge stirred with a pendulum, if you get my drift."

"Yeah, I think I can grasp the 'oats' analogy as well," Bob squirmed, thinking drawbridges and turrets again. "Anyway, more importantly, the contraband cigarette thing — you say you've cracked it."

"Absolutely." The smug smile returned to Jim Alexander's face. "A piece of cake, and my HQ will get a full report when this ship docks at Leith in a week or so. But, as I can see your nose is bothering you, I can let you know now that the long and short of it is that the cigarettes come on the Ulanova Line's ships from the Black Sea to Spain, and from there by road — vans, trucks, cars, whatever — to Portugal, and from there by certain means to the south of England."

"Certain means?"

But Jim Alexander wasn't prepared to be drawn. "It'll be in my report. I overheard it all being talked about in a bar in Lisbon when we docked there. All I'm prepared to say for the present is that I was already onto one particular member of this ship's company. I tailed him to the bar, where he met and started talking to another man, in pidgin Russian. My late wife was Russian, as it happens, so I understood enough of what they were saying."

"And how does the south-of-England delivery tie in with the glut of hooky fags in Edinburgh every time the *Ostentania* arrives there? I mean, there's something like five hundred miles between the two points."

Jim Alexander's look suggested that Bob might recently have absconded from a banana boat.

"All right, all right," Bob conceded, raising his hands to the don't-shoot position before Officer Alexander had time to fire a broadside of ridicule. "I've got it, I've got it — smoke screens and mirrors and all that stuff. In short, they've always got a forward stash of fags somewhere near Edinburgh — delivered, presumably, by road from the south of England — which they release onto the city's streets whenever the *Ostentania*'s paid a visit."

"Well done. But even your boy Green, dense as he is, would have been able to figure that one out, eventually."

Again, Bob resisted the temptation to give this puffed-up smart alec a good reason to seek urgent dental treatment. Instead he calmly asked, "But why all the cryptic stuff with the finger in the fridge? Why didn't you just introduce yourself to me when you found out I was on the ship? Yeah, and come to that, how *did* you know I was on the ship?"

"Which begs the question — why didn't your mob advise my mob you were coming?"

"Not something they discussed with me during the pre-trip briefing, I'm afraid. In fact, I hardly had time to pack a toothbrush before I was whisked onto a plane."

Jim Alexander's expression had now turned to one of mild derision. "Don't give me any of that too-much-of-a-hurry claptrap!"

"OK, maybe they just assumed I'd make contact with you through Andy Green when I thought the time was right."

"Yeah, that's more like the police. Suspicious of the day they never saw. Your plan was to keep me in the dark about your presence until you'd had a chance to check me out, correct?"

"Don't flatter yourself, chum. And you can spare yourself the paranoid stuff at the same time, because the only way you'll come under suspicion from me is if you do something to deserve it."

"Like helping Catherine Dykes get a pay-out from her late husband's insurers, for instance?"

"There you go being paranoid again," Bob replied, while thinking to himself that the open shirt front and gold medallion had already made him suspicious enough of this character to treat him with extreme caution.

Sensing Bob's distrust, Jim Alexander asked, "So, then, why *didn't* you make contact with me through Andy Green from the outset?"

Bob fixed him with an icy stare. "I more than likely would have done, until I heard from Green that you'd totally blanked him out of any involvement in your Customs investigations here."

Officer Alexander responded with a sniffy little chuckle. "No point in casting pearls before swine."

"Yes, well, we've yet to find out just how valuable your investigative *pearls* turn out to be, haven't we, mate? But come what may, your couldn't-care-less attitude towards the training of a young colleague will gain you bugger all brownie points from either my mob or your own."

Alexander snapped his fingers in Bob's face. "*That*'s what I give for brownie points! I aim to sail, literally, through my last few days in the employ of Her Majesty's Government by enjoying myself to the full at their expense and by *not* getting involved in any cloak-and-dagger business that would risk me spending one day longer than absolutely necessary as one of Her Majesty's *servants*."

"Nice to know I can depend on your support," Bob said. "Anyway, back to my question — how *did* you know I was on the ship?"

Jim Alexander resumed his imperious manner. "Oh, nothing stays secret for long on a cruise liner, particularly with a sharp barman like Speedy Gonzales keeping his eyes and ears open. The very first night you came aboard I just happened to pop my head into the Stardust Lounge to see if any of my lonely old damsels in distress needed a bit of comforting company, and my eyes lighted on the stunning young woman who was obviously the centre of attraction at the bar. Doctor Julie Bryson, the new shore lecturer, Speedy told me she was. Then he pointed out her companion, Bob Burns — journalist."

Bob knew what was coming next, and it obviously showed.

Alexander smirked knowingly. "Hmm, you were somewhat tired and emotional, shall we say, in the company of our two resident drunks, Doctor Death and crime author JP Shand."

"Yeah, well, I'd had a rough couple of days getting here," Bob offered lamely.

"Hmm," Alexander repeated with a sardonic nod of the head.

"And the finger in the fridge?" Bob urged in an attempt to steer a course towards less choppy waters. "You still haven't told me what the hell that was all about."

"Not too hard to fathom, really. When it became obvious from your, let's say, *relaxed* demeanour in the Stardust Lounge that night that you were in no hurry to make contact with me, I decided to play you at your own game. I thought it'd be an amusing idea to check *you* out by setting you a little clue-solving test — which, as it now transpires, you failed."

As Jim Alexander had anticipated, that last remark niggled.

"Yeah," Bob retorted, "and it may or may not surprise you to know that I've got more to do with my time than play silly bloody parlour games. But, just as a matter of interest, why the severed finger angle in the first place?"

"Just a happen, that's all, although it did link with Rab Dykes . . . in an oblique sort of way."

"*Oblique*? What the blazes is that supposed to mean?" Bob's patience was being sorely tried now. "Come on, come on — as I just told you, I'm not into silly bloody parlour games!"

"You take yourselves too seriously, you police types — that's your trouble."

"Like I always say, somebody has to. Now, just get on with it and tell me how a joke-shop finger is linked *obliquely* with Rab Dykes."

"I take it your preliminary enquiries have revealed that the owner of this cruise line is one Boris Kaminski?"

Bob indicated the affirmative.

"And did your investigations also reveal that he has a minder who's a dead ringer for Rab Dykes?"

"You mean the Spanish guy with a finger missing? Yeah, yeah, yeah, I've got all that sussed. But so what?"

"Well, Kaminski and his Spanish sidekick visited the ship back in Scotland when it called in there last week. I noticed the sidekick's similar appearance to Rab Dykes, and I also noticed he had a finger missing. So, after Dykes went overboard off Portugal, I went to offer my condolences to his wife, she confided her worries about the insurance implications of his death being regarded as suicide, and as the Portuguese police had already washed their hands of the matter, I offered to do what I could to find a way to bring your lot in. Then, by pure chance, it happened that, on the very same night, there was one of those murder-mystery contests for the passengers, the main clue being a severed finger in a quiche lorraine." Picking up the vibes of Bob's growing annoyance, Jim Alexander smiled smugly, then said, "I can see you're ahead of me now, eh? The *oblique* link I mentioned, right?"

Bob started to count to ten, but only reached two. "You mean to say," he snarled, "that I've been press-ganged onto this damned case on the strength of nothing more concrete than a couple of airy-fairy connections straight out of *Cluedo*?"

"Airy-fairy or not," Jim Alexander grinned, "they worked, and to prove it, you're here. Anyway, I told you I intended to enjoy the rest of this cruise, and I'm lapping it up more by the minute — thanks, in no small measure, to the look on your face. Hey, talk about the end of the laughing policeman!"

"Yeah, well, *you*'d better laugh it up while you can, friend, because if I find out you're involved in anything fraudulent with Rab Dykes's widow, I'll make a point of seeing to it that you spend the next few years waltzing with screws in Saughton Prison."

"Oh, I don't think so," Jim Alexander pooh-poohed. "No more chance of that than needing a dentist to fix my smile."

Bob looked him up and down disdainfully. "It may come as a surprise to a conceited ponce like you, but I'm actually pleased you won't be getting in my way on this job."

"Not as pleased as I am, I assure you."

"Fine, but there's a couple of things you can do for me before you spend your last week in Government employment swanning about with rich old widows instead of earning your corn."

"Uh-huh?"

"Yeah! Number one, you can introduce me to Mrs Dykes at the earliest opportunity."

"But that goes without saying," Jim Alexander smirked. "After all, that's why I went to so much trouble to get you here."

"And it also goes without saying that nobody except her, and I mean *no*body, gets to know my real identity, right?"

"Another no-brainer." Alexander fanned a yawn with his hand. "I hope your second request is a bit more original."

"That depends on you."

"Oh really? How intriguing!"

"You said you reckoned the cigarette smuggling thing was probably only a tactic intended to divert attention away from something more serious."

"That's how I took it to be. But I repeat, I'm not interested in getting involved in something that I'd probably have to follow through beyond my retirement date. It could well turn out to be more of a police matter anyway, so you're welcome to it."

"How kind! And I suppose some sort of lead is equally out of the question?"

Just then, a squabble broke out a bit further along the bar. A burly crewman had become involved in a shouting match with one of the barmen. They were arguing in what Bob assumed was Indonesian, and he could see that the object of their dispute was an American one-hundred-dollar bill.

Gesturing towards the rumpus, Bob leadingly asked, "Could it be, in your opinion as a customs officer, that the big guy might have tried to pass a counterfeit c-note?"

Pursing his lips, Jim Alexander raised a shoulder and said, "That'd be my guess, and if he did, he's just given you the very lead you were looking for."

"OK, and can you tell me, then, the connection between Rab Dykes and counterfeit —"

Jim Alexander cut Bob off with a determined snap of, "No chance! If you're worth your salt, you probably know as much about this forged banknote thing as I do, and you're welcome to get on with it, *if* you're so inclined. As from right now, *I* am well and truly not interested!"

"Thanks a million," Bob muttered. "Remind me to return the favour sometime!"

"That won't be necessary, I promise you." Jim Alexander looked at his watch and yawned again. "Well, I value my beauty sleep, and it's already *way* past my bedtime." He laid his glass on the counter, then said to Bob as a parting shot, "Oh, and just to show goodwill, I can tell you that the big guy trying to fob off the fake banknote along there is Jojo, the *Ostentania*'s head of security."

No sooner had Bob given Julie and Ian a summary of recent happenings at the bar than they were joined by a distraught Andy Green.

"Ah've been fired," he whined. "Speedy says Ah'm worse than a man short at the best o' times, but writhin' about on the floor and foamin' at the mouth in front o' the punters was the last straw, he says."

"Ye *did* overact just ever so slightly, son," Ian remarked.

"Ah was only doin' ma best," Andy quavered, his chin trembling. "Ah mean, Ah thought that doin' the complete epidermic turn would keep the old doctor gadgie occupied for longer, like — give the gaffer and Doc Bryson here more o' a chance for snoopin' about in the ship's infirmary an' everything, like."

Julie gave his knee a consoling pat. "You did well, Andy, never fear. Mission accomplished, as far as your contribution goes, anyway."

"Aw, thanks, Doc. Ah could do wi' a nice wee rest, right enough."

"Don't kid yourself, Green," Bob countered. "You're still being paid by Lothian and Borders Police, and you're still *very* much on the case, believe me!"

"Suits me," Andy shrugged. "We better be quick about solvin' whatever we're supposed to be solvin', though, 'cos Ah'm bein' stuffed on the first plane back home from Lanzarote by the Ulanova Line. Aye, and they're chargin' me for the ticket, so it'll be goin' on ma Lothian and Borders Police expenses."

Before Bob could blow a gasket, the security man and bartender who had been having the altercation about the hundred-dollar bill came barging through the crowd and went out through the door close to where Bob & Co were sitting. The two men were still exchanging heated words in Indonesian, although three of those words needed no translation.

"They said 'Bastard Walter-Wall'," Bob noted.

"Yeah, and they looked as if they were gunnin' for him," Ian chipped in.

"But Wally Walter-Wall's dead," Julie protested.

"That remains to be seen," Bob replied. He swiftly got to his feet. "Right, Green," he said, "you and I are heading off in hot pursuit, so give yourself a shake."

"What about Ian and me?" Julie asked. "Don't you want us for backup?"

"Better not make it look like a mass exodus. Give us ten minutes and then come looking."

"But we'll never find you," Ian objected. "Like I told ye, it's a rabbit warren o' corridors and stairs down here."

"Just follow the screams," Bob said on his way through the door. "I'll be putting Green in first if there's any sign of trouble."

However, it wasn't Andy's screams that echoed through the dimly lit passageways as Bob and Andy stealthily followed the voices of the two bickering Indonesians.

"Did you hear that?" Bob whispered.

"Sounded like a pig squealin'," Andy whispered back.

"More like a baby crying — which is very strange indeed."

"Strange? What's strange about that? All sprogs bawl, don't they?"

"Yeah, except this is a child-free cruise. Says so in the propaganda."

"Aw, well, strange right enough then, eh?"

Andy followed close behind as Bob edged further along the corridor. The drone of the men's voices grew fainter and fainter, before disappearing altogether.

"Dammit," Bob muttered, peering into the shadows. "Lost the buggers."

"Must've gone left round that corner up ahead," Andy proposed. "Or turned right round the other one. Or maybe went down them stairs along there."

At that, a child's cry rang out again — this time from behind a door next to where they were standing. Bob tried the handle, then gingerly pushed the door open and looked inside. It took a few moments for his eyes to adjust to the near-dark conditions, then but a second to take in the wretched scene. Perhaps a dozen bunk beds were lined up on either side of a narrow room that was every bit as spartan as the crew's bar, but even more squalid. It was tantamount to a windowless, steel-walled dungeon. Several ill-defined faces, their eyes like those of frightened animals, stared out from the gloom. Bob thought he recognised one of the three young men who had been sharing a single bottle of beer back in the bar. He was kneeling on the floor beside a girl who looked to be no more than in her late teens, her back propped against the wall, a tiny baby in her arms. An older woman was fussing over her with much wringing of hands and tearful whimpering.

The young man stood up and approached Bob, his palms outstretched, his expression imploring. "Please, sir, my wife she make new baby," he said in faltering English. "She must have doctor very quick, please. Many blood coming."

Bob assessed the situation in an instant. There would be no point in summoning the ship's doctor. According to Ian Scrabster, he'd already been "out of his skull" in the Stardust Lounge an hour ago, so he'd hardly be in a fit state now to administer medical help to the young woman and her newborn child.

"OK, lad," Bob said to Andy Green, "find your way back along to the bar and bring Doctor Bryson here pronto."

"But she's a doctor o' forensic stuff," Andy objected. "Are ye suggestin that sprog's a test-tube baby or somethin'?"

"Doctor Bryson's a woman," Bob sighed, "and that's good enough for now, so just *get* her down here! Yeah, and while you're at it, tell Crabbie Scrabster to come along as well. We may need strength in numbers before the night's out, and Crabbie's worth at least two men . . . weight-wise, if nothing else."

During Andy's absence, Bob, laying on the sympathy thick and fast, managed to glean from the fretful new father that he, his wife and their companions were from the Republic of Malgravia, one of the ex-Soviet satellite states which lie landlocked to the north of the Black Sea. Harsh economic and social conditions had prompted the group to flee their native land in search of a better life abroad.

Bob hardly needed the young chap to tell him the rest of his story, so typical was it of refugees being duped by unscrupulous people-traffickers who relieve them of what little money they have in exchange for forged papers and "a ticket to freedom". The young man went on to say that, after an arduous overland journey, they had been spirited aboard the *Ostentania* at the Balgonian port of Grabna, one of the conditions of passage being that they would have to undertake unpaid manual work on the ship as part of the deal to keep the cost of their fares low. They were bound for America, hence their projected landfall in the Canary Islands, where, they'd been promised, they would be transferred to another cruise ship at the start of its transatlantic voyage to Florida.

Although hardly surprised at the callousness of whoever was behind this obnoxious trade, the gullibility of the victims — certainly this one — took Bob's breath away. The young chap was actually trusting enough to divulge all this self-incriminating information to a complete stranger, presumably in the belief that the "good and free" people of the new world he was about to enter would welcome oppressed asylum-seekers like himself with open arms. This, as Bob knew only too well, might prove to be an extremely naïve presumption. However, he chose not to disillusion the poor fellow, who clearly had enough to cope with as it was.

"Water — hot water, soap and clean towels," Julie demanded of him as soon as she arrived on the scene. She then prepared to set about the task in hand, without any apparent regard for the squalid conditions surrounding her.

By the expression on the young father's face, though, even normally taken-for-granted items like hot water, soap and clean towels might prove difficult to obtain in this below-decks cattle pen.

"You guys can make yourselves scarce," Julie told Bob. Then, after taking a couple of seconds to weigh up the situation, she changed her mind. "On second thoughts, better leave Andy with me. He can always run back to the crew's bar if I need anything." She crouched down beside the mother and baby and took a closer look. "Hmm, yeah," she conceded, "I can see I'm gonna have to improvise here."

"Fair enough," Bob said. "In the meantime, Crabbie and I may as well see if we can pick up the trail of the two Indonesian blokes who were muttering curses about Wally Walter-Wall."

They didn't have far to go. No sooner were they back out in the corridor than the sound of raised male voices came reverberating up a companionway dead ahead. Cautiously, they descended the metal steps, the throb and smell of diesel engines increasing as they went. They were now well and truly in the intestines of the ship, in a passageway where the walls and ceiling were a clutter of pipes and ducts, and with a series of doors, each with a sign designating one kind of store or other. One door was slightly ajar, and as Bob and Ian approached, they could hear an eerily familiar voice resonating from within:

"You 'ave my word upon it, squire — I most certainly did *not* know that I 'ad paid you in dodgy banknotes!"

A shiver ran up Bob's spine. "Wally Walter-Wall," he said under his breath. "The slippery old snake!"

"Don't talk ill o' the dead," Ian muttered. "They'll come back to haunt ye!"

"Seems like this one already has," Bob replied.

Then, what they took to be the irate voice of Jojo the Indonesian security man was heard to say: "No real money por me, no secret way to island in morning por you!"

"Yes," added another Indonesian voice, which they assumed to be the barman's, "and if you no gib back real money I gib you other day in change por dodgy money, I going bloody kill you!"

That threat produced an unconvincingly reassuring chuckle from Wally Walter-Wall. "Come, come, my friends," he oiled, "we're all businessmen 'ere, and we businessmen 'ave to —"

"I no bloody businessman!" the security man hotly interrupted. "I poor bloody sailor man!"

"Yes," the barman agreed, "me too! And if I no put real money back in till instead of dodgy money you gib me, Speedy Gonzales going bloody kill *me* before I bloody kill you!"

Bob and Ian listened intently as the three-way conversation gradually narrowed down to some serious two-way negotiating between Wally and the security man, whereby it was ultimately agreed that, provided Wally left his passport with him as surety, Jojo would arrange for Wally to be covertly transported onto the island of Lanzarote as originally arranged. Once there, Wally vowed, he would obtain legitimate funds and have the agreed payment "for services rendered" delivered to the *Ostentania* before it sailed away the following evening. Deal done.

"Wally's forgotten about gettin' his passport back," Ian whispered to Bob. "Daft twat."

"Fat chance! Nah, if he's gone to all this trouble to do a disappearing act, he'll already have fixed up a new identity with passport to match. Take it from me, the only daft twat here is the security guy."

Wally's voice rang out again — altogether more confident and convivial now. "So, there we go, Jojo my friend — I get myself along to the Marina Deck service area at eleven a.m. — suitably attired, of course — and we take it from there. Ah, yes indeedy, squire, yes indeedy indeed."

Wally's mention of the Marina Deck rang a bell for Bob. Julie had told him earlier in the day that the first item on the ship's schedule for the following morning would be to drop anchor for a few hours by the small island of Graciosa, off the north-west coast of Lanzarote. This was intended to give those passengers so inclined (Julie included) an opportunity to indulge in water sports from a pontoon floated out from the sea-level Marina Deck. Ian now divulged that this facility was actually a throwback to when the ship had been a ferry. The large sea doors at the stern had been retained during her conversion for cruising purposes, and those doors would now be opened, when itinerary and weather permitted, to reveal what had originally been nothing grander than the ferry's vehicle loading/unloading bay, but was now described in the Ulanova Line's brochures as "the *Ostentania*'s unique Aquatic Leisure Centre".

"Right, Crabby," Bob said out of the corner of his mouth, "we'd better get outa here smartish and see how Julie's doing in the post-natal department. Yeah, and let's hope she's got everything stitched up or whatever. We could all do with some shut-eye. It's been a long day, and tomorrow looks like it's gonna be a busy one."

CHAPTER EIGHTEEN

THE FOLLOWING MORNING — IN BOB AND JULIE'S CABIN . . .

The final stages of Julie's impromptu midwifery stint in the early hours had reminded Bob of scenes he'd witnessed as a kid back on the farm in Scotland, but his likening her efforts to those of a cattleman "tidying up" after a heifer's first calving had met with a predictably frosty response. The average cattleman, Julie advised him, would probably have had better medical means at his disposal than she'd had, although she did concede that the surroundings were indeed reminiscent of a byre, if not quite a pigsty. Still, the important thing was that mother and child had survived the ordeal and had been left in as comfortable a state as was possible in such appalling conditions. The only casualty, in fact, had been Andy Green, who had mistaken the placenta and its attached umbilical cord for a deformed, one-legged twin of the newborn baby and had promptly fainted.

Bob was now crouched over his laptop computer on the bedside cabinet, while Julie sat at the dressing table mirror, putting on her face for the day.

"I thought I'd be able to wheedle more info out of that young Malgravian guy and his wife about who's behind this people-trafficking racket," she said, delicately brushing mascara onto her eyelashes, "but they genuinely don't know. Every contact along the way simply hands them over to the next one, then disappears. They don't even know who's pulling the strings on the ship here. One of the Indonesian crewmen, who's probably not much further up the food chain than they are, gives them their working instructions each day, their meals, such as they are, are brought to them by another downtrodden menial, and that's it. They don't even know how they're going to be transferred to the next ship for their voyage to the States."

"That's because it'll probably never happen," Bob said vaguely, preoccupied as he was with his laptop. "Yeah!" he suddenly exclaimed, jabbing a finger at the computer screen. "Just as I thought!"

"What you on about now?" Julie garbled gape-mouthed as she applied her lipstick.

"This email from Bruce McNeill. I asked him to run a check on Walter-Wall's business, and it says here it's a goner. Totally bust, with a list of creditors as long as a roll of Wally's bargain linoleum."

"Surprise, surprise!" Julie gibed. "Who'd have guessed?"

Pensively, Bob stroked his chin. "Hmm, an absconding bankrupt, a bent security officer, an ex-junkie Cruise Director, enough counterfeit money in the drunken doctor's morgue to undermine the economy of a banana republic, exploited refugees and a missing-presumed-dead smalltime Edinburgh villain. Quite a ship, the *Ostentania*."

"Mm-hmm," Julie agreed, putting the finishing touches to her eye shadow, "and don't forget about the smuggled ciggies."

Bob started pounding the keyboard of his computer. "Yeah, you're right, but I'm leaving that one to Gentleman Jim. However, considering I only came aboard this tub to find out what happened to Rab Dykes, I reckon we need reinforcements to help pick the rest of the mushrooms that have popped up since."

"Reinforcements?"

"Yup. I'm gonna ask Bruce McNeill to bugle up the local cavalry."

"You mean the Guardia Civil, the Spanish police?"

"Exactly. We'll be conveniently inside Spanish territorial waters when we anchor off Lanzarote this morning, and it looks like the island's gonna be on the receiving end of at least *one* uninvited immigrant, so —"

The phone on the bedside table rang. Bob answered it.

"Hello . . . Yes, this is Burns . . . A-a-ah, good morning, Officer Alexander! I'd like to say what a great pleasure it is to hear your voice again, but I'm just a bit *too* honest . . . Catherine? Who the hell's she? . . . "Oh, yes of course, the *reclusive* Mrs Rab Dykes . . . OK, her cabin, it is. Tell her we'll be there in ten."

TEN MINUTES LATER — A LUXURY SUITE ON THE SHIP'S TOP DECK . . .

Catherine Dykes led Bob and Julie through her spacious lounge and onto her private balcony. "Make yourselves nice and comfy," she said in an oh-so-awfully genteel Edinburgh Morningside accent. "I'll just go and call the butler to fetch some coffee. Freshly milled City-Roast Colombian Primero will do you, I take it?"

"Common-as-muck Nescafé will do me." Julie smiled primly as she lowered herself into a chintzy cane chair. "Can't stand the grounds of that posh stuff between my teeth."

Oops, Bob thought — instant animosity as well as coffee. Julie had clearly taken a dislike to Mrs Dykes, whose look of disdain in response to Julie's chilly rebuff suggested that the feeling was entirely mutual.

"But the posh stuff *will* do me," Bob said. "I'm on a self-improvement drive."

"Really?" Catherine Dykes replied, patently unamused by Bob's droll riposte. "How fascinating."

Bob eyed her rear elevation as she wiggled back through the patio doors.

"Hmm, I can see why she has her admirers," he told Julie. "Quite attractive, in a bookish sort of way. You know, sort of Nana Mouskouri-ish, with the long, dark hair and the horn-rimmed specs and everything."

"More like Gothic vampire-ish, in a Morticia-from-the-Addams-Family sort of way," Julie snorted. "I mean, what's with all the ankle-length black gear?"

"Mourning?" Bob asked, sceptically.

"Yeah, right!" Julie answered, mockingly.

Bob craned his neck for a peek back inside the lounge. "Anyway, mourning or not, she's well fixed up in this pad. The last word in extravagance, and you could fit four cabins like ours into that one room alone."

"Fur coat and nae drawers, as we say in Glasgow," was Julie's take on that observation. "All that City-Roast Colombian Primero bullshit. If she knew *any*thing about coffee, she'd know that 'Primero' relates to the size of the bean, *not* its quality."

"I'll take your word for it, but even if she isn't the real-deal, top-rung article, she's still a helluva lot higher up the social ladder than Rab Dykes. Yeah, I'd never have imagined that pair as an item."

Catherine Dykes reappeared at the patio doors, her expression suggesting that she had overheard Bob's last remark. "I met him in prison, if that's what you're wondering about," she said haughtily.

"Ah, so you were a screw?" Julie enquired, smiling primly again. "I mean in the *custodial* sense, naturally."

Catherine Dykes looked fleetingly down her nose at her, then addressed Bob again. "I was — *am* — a psychologist, specialising in criminology. I was with the Social Work Department in Edinburgh for a while after I left university. Making case studies of Saughton Prison inmates was part of my brief."

Bob couldn't resist a smile. "And your fascination with the young Rab Dyke's villainous mind, albeit a small and incompetent one, blossomed into love and marriage, eh? And they say the age of romance is dead!"

"Be facetious if you like," Catherine Dykes shrugged. "Such *apparent* mismatches do occasionally happen." She looked at Julie, then critically at Bob, then back at Julie. "Don't they, *Doctor* Bryson?"

"You pays your money and you takes your pick," Julie said offhandedly.

"Fortunately," Catherine Dykes sneered, "I've never been reduced to paying."

Bob was already beginning to sympathise with Lex "Laugh-a-Minute" McGinn's and Andy Green's views of this woman, except that he was now inclined to add "catty bitch" to their "stuck-up" and "pain in the neck" assessments. If only like poles attracted, she and Gentleman Jim Alexander would be joined at the lip. Which reminded him . . .

"Why, Mrs Dykes, did you get Jim Alexander to go through all that finger-in-the-quiche palaver just to get the Edinburgh police in on the case?"

Catherine Dykes wafted a hand airily. "Oh, let's just say I've always had an interest in amateur dramatics — though strictly back-stage."

"Make-up department?" Julie ventured.

Bob glared at her. What the hell was she thinking about? This "catty bitch" stuff was obviously highly contagious.

Catherine Dykes seemed to catch his train of thought. "No doubt you're also wondering about the shipboard gossip regarding myself and the Reverend Pearce," she stated blandly.

Bob shook his head. "None of my business — unless, of course, he's implicated in your husband's disappearance."

Catherine Dykes laughed quietly into the button-up collar of her black dress. "No wonder so many criminals get away with it. Honestly, it never fails to amaze me how the workings of the average policeman's brain are so, how can I say, so *guile*less in comparison."

"Maybe that's why your husband never got away with *any*thing," Bob retorted. "I've got a dim-witted rookie detective who's got more guile in one nostril than Rab Dykes has in the vast emptiness of his entire skull."

"*Had* in the vast emptiness of his entire skull," Catherine Dykes corrected. "My husband is dead, remember?"

Sighing, Julie stood up. "Mind if I use your loo?"

Catherine Dykes made another airy waft of her hand. "On the left — far end of the lounge."

With Julie in her present confrontational mood, Bob hoped she'd be kept occupied for quite some time by whatever call of nature had beckoned. The sarky Catherine Dykes was going to be difficult enough to handle without Julie rubbing her up the wrong way.

"So, Mrs Dykes, your friendship with the Reverend Pearce is purely platonic — that's what you're saying, is it?"

"Look, I've known John for ages — since I worked for the Navy in Portsmouth back in the early Nineties, in fact. We've remained good friends since, but that's all." She gave another patronising little laugh. "Let's just say I'm not John's type."

"Too *feminine*, perhaps?" Bob speculated, pouting.

Catherine Dykes attempted a coy look. "I couldn't *possibly* comment."

"And Jim Alexander — what's your relationship with him?"

"He's been extremely supportive since Rab's death, and there's absolutely nothing more to it than that." Catherine Dykes noticed Bob's sceptical look, then added, "OK, he has this reputation for being a bit of a ladies' man, but there's no law against that, and all I can say is that he's been a rock for me over the past week. I mean, look no further than yourself — you wouldn't be here investigating Rab's disappearance for me if it hadn't been for Jim."

"Yeah, I really owe him one," Bob muttered, before looking Mrs Dykes in the eye and asking her bluntly if she knew that Jim Alexander was interested in developing a more permanent relationship with her.

Far from being even in the slightest way fazed by Bob's unsubtle approach, Catherine was the epitomy of self-assurance. "No attractive woman is ever surprised by that sort of mistaken notion, Sergeant Burns."

"It's Inspector Burns, as it happens, but no flat-footed policeman is ever surprised by that sort of mistaken notion, *Mrs* Dykes."

Another condescending little laugh from Catherine Dykes. "No need to emphasise the 'Mrs', *Inspector* Burns. Rab and I have lived our separate lives for years, but I never forgot that I was still his wife."

"Especially after he insured his life for two million quid, no?"

It was now Catherine Dykes's turn to look Bob in the eye. "Again, I couldn't *possibly* comment," she stated flatly.

Bob emulated her airy wafting of a hand. "And what about all this?"

"All what?"

"This suite. It must be costing a fortune. Where did the money come from? I mean, let's not beat about the bush, it would've taken a helluva lot of hooky DVD sales at Ingleston Sunday Market for a low-league crook like Rab to earn the dosh for a trip to the Canaries in this pad."

"Not that it makes a whit of difference, but the trip was actually a gift from the owner of the Ulanova Line, whose private suite this just happens to be."

"And why would Boris Kaminski be so generous to a bum like Rab Dykes?"

Catherine Dykes smiled indulgently. "Rab was a business associate of Mr Kaminski, as I'm sure your preliminary investigations will have already shown."

"By 'business associate' I presume you mean he was helping Kaminski infiltrate the shareholdings of Glasgow Rangers FC?"

Still Catherine Dykes maintained her composure. "Rab's business was none of mine," she shrugged. "He phoned me up out of the blue and asked me to come along on this cruise, and that's all there is to it."

"Except that he'd just insured himself for two million smackers and then did a disappearing act somewhere in the Atlantic Ocean off Portugal."

"And I'm saying it's your job to prove that he disappeared in suspicious circumstances."

"Or," Bob thinly smiled, "that he didn't disappear at all."

Catherine Dykes was about to object to that speculation, but Bob cut her off . . .

"You see, I happen to know that the head of security is prepared to take bungs in exchange for spiriting wide boys like your husband off this ship when it docks."

Catherine Dykes laughed out loud. "Don't be absurd! This ship hasn't docked anywhere since it left Lisbon, and Rab disappeared *after* that. Yes, and if your next obvious hypothesis is that he's hidden away somewhere here on board, then think again. For all their apparent lack of interest in the incident, the Portuguese police did at least check every nook and cranny in the ship, and that was at *my* insistence. I went with them, as did Captain Stotinki, who, having served on this vessel since it was launched, knows it like —"

"Yeah, yeah, I know — like the whiskers on his face. I've heard all that before, but I've no more reason to believe Stotinki than I have to believe you."

"Meaning *what*, precisely?"

"Meaning that the Captain obviously bypassed the people-trafficking dungeon in the hold when he was giving you and the Portuguese police a guided tour of the ship's nooks and crannies."

Catherine Dykes flicked her hair dismissively. "I haven't the slightest idea what you're talking about."

"And if he bypassed that, it follows that he could also have conveniently swerved the rat's nest where your husband's probably holed up."

"Typically, your policeman's thought process is putting two and two together and coming up with the first number it thinks of, no matter how ludicrous."

"Maybe, but unless you can come up with something concrete to back up this 'suspicious circumstances' claim of yours, I won't be wasting any more time than I already have on this *alleged* man-overboard case. In fact, nothing would give me greater pleasure than to get off this tub when it ties up at Lanzarote and catch the first plane back to Edinburgh."

"Well, as far as concrete evidence is concerned," Catherine Dykes bristled, "you've got your forensic scientist ladyfriend in tow, so why doesn't she pull her finger out and —"

"And stuff it in a slice of quiche lorraine?" Julie interjected, emerging jauntily through the patio doors.

Now Catherine Dykes did look as if she was about to lose her cool.

Bob grabbed the chance to get in fast with another annoying little barb . . .

"On that very subject, how come Rab's Mickey Mouse signet ring was on the dummy finger, if he'd already gone over the side before the quiche caper was dreamed up by Gentleman Jim and you?"

"*Pluto*, not Mickey Mouse," Catherine Dykes said impassively, then stood up and went back inside, returning a few seconds later with an enamel trinket case. She opened it and handed it to Bob. "See for yourself. Rab had duplicates of *all* his rings."

Bob handed the case back without bothering to look inside. "Yeah, or these could have been taken off him before he went AWOL . . . or *after* he was bumped off."

Catherine Dykes gave a mocking little laugh. "An impressively original idea, I must say."

"Sometimes the hackneyed ones turn out to be the best," Bob came back. "But, to digress a bit, what was your relationship with the widow of the ship's late cocktail pianist?"

"Señora Molinero?" Catherine Dykes lowered her eyes, then said softly, "Such a lovely old lady. We were two women united in grief. I'd struck up a friendship with her quite early in the cruise, but the common denominator of bereavement brought us even closer."

Bob and Julie exchanged pass-the-sick-bag glances.

This didn't go unnoticed by Mrs Dykes. She turned her displeasure on Julie. "Instead of mocking my feelings of loss, Miss Bryson, you would be better employed doing what you're paid to do, and that's to gather forensic evidence to support my assertion that my husband did *not* commit suicide."

Julie was quick to respond by firmly reminding Catherine Dykes that the thorough decontamination of the ship following the recent norovirus outbreak would have cleared any evidence of a clinical nature from the spot from which Rab Dykes was reported to have taken his plunge. Julie also pointed out that she had already made a thorough visual inspection of the deck area from where the Misses Brambleberry *thought* they had seen someone fall, and not a trace of anything relevant had been found. The same had applied to any rails and obstructions on lower decks that a plummeting body might have come into contact with. “The fact of the matter, Mrs Dykes,” she concluded, “is that there’s absolutely no evidence of any kind to support your claim that your husband went overboard at all.”

“And so,” Bob swiftly chipped in, “in the absence of a body or anything more substantial than your assertion that your husband wasn’t the suicidal type, it seems crystal clear that your insurance claim will be kicked right into touch.”

But Catherine Dykes wasn’t about to be so easily put off. “That may be your policemanly reading of the situation, Inspector Burns, but I happen to have a less hidebound view of such things. As far as I’m concerned, if the police can’t perform their duty competently on my behalf, then I’ll simply turn the tables by putting the onus on the insurance company to prove that my husband *did* take his own life.”

It was all Bob could do to stop himself from bursting out laughing. Instead, he politely offered the opinion that, if Mrs Dykes wanted to pursue that line of action, then he wished her the best of luck, adding pointedly that he reckoned she’d need it. At the same time, however, it was going through Bob’s mind that an intelligent woman like this surely couldn’t be so naïve as to believe that attempting to prise two million pounds out of an insurance company by such tenuous means would have even the remotest chance of success.

No, there was more to all of this than met the eye, and Bob was inclined to believe that the astute Catherine Dykes had a real finger in the associated pie, just as much as she'd been involved in concocting the ploy of stuffing a fake one into a wedge of quiche lorraine.

Over the balcony rails, the barren expanse of a sun-soaked island came into view only a half a mile or so distant. As the *Ostentania* slowed gradually to a halt, Bob checked his watch. Ten o'clock — almost time to see if he could gatecrash Wally Walter-Wall's sneaky farewell party.

"Well, Mrs Dykes," he said as he got up to leave, "all I can do is repeat that, unless you can come up with something concrete to support your allegations of foul play against your husband, I'll be closing the book on this case and returning to Edinburgh at the first opportunity." He extended his hand. "Thanks for the hospitality. Oh, and in case it had slipped your unhidebound mind, I'd better caution you that wasting police time *is* a criminal offence."

As soon as they were out of the suite and a few paces along the corridor, Julie slapped Bob's back. "Well done, Kemosabe!" she giggled. "Your parting shot was a cracker. Yeah, just what that arrogant cow had been asking for."

Bob's response, however, was a tad less appreciative than Julie might have anticipated. "That's all very well," he snapped, "but why the hell did you try and put her down with that crack about the make-up department being her attraction to amateur dramatics. I mean, she's obviously dead vain about her appearance, so why the blazes stick an insulting dig like that in? Hell's teeth, she was a prickly enough customer to deal with without you going out of your way to provoke her!"

"Provoke nothing!" Julie retorted. "I was simply referring to a bona fide observation I'd made."

"Observation?" Bob scowled.

"Yes!" Julie scowled back. "I could see them through her bedroom door when she led us into the lounge. Right there, plain as daylight on her dressing table, they were."

"There what were?"

"A selection of wigs and enough make-up to stock the dame's dressing room in the London Palladium for an entire pantomime season. You should keep your eyes open, Sherlock!"

Bob was slightly taken aback. "You mean your make-up crack wasn't actually a —"

"A crack at all?" Julie rolled her shoulders, a mischievous twinkle in her eyes. "Well, I have to admit there was a *wee* bit of snideness in there, but it was based on fact, so she could take it whichever way she wanted as far as I was concerned."

Bob allowed himself a wry smile. "Now you come to mention it, I did think bits of her face looked as if they'd been applied by a plasterer. You know what I mean — just a smidgen too much Polyfilla slapped on the wrinkles here and there."

Julie was delighted. "Exactly! And I bet that long, raven hair wasn't her own either. Yes, and I noticed the Nana Mouskouri specs only had window glass in them too. No, take it from me, that Catherine Dykes bitch isn't just *two*-faced. She's got enough stuff on that dressing table to create a different face for every day of the week!"

They stopped at the end of the corridor, where Bob pressed the "Down" button on one of the two neighbouring lifts, then pensively stroked his cheek. "Hmm, which makes you wonder if she really has been as reclusive as everyone thought since she went on that burial-at-sea jaunt off Gib with the Reverend Pearce and old Enrique the pianist's widow."

"Which brings me to my confession of guilt," Julie said, faking a remorseful look while dipping into her purse.

"Confession? Guilt?"

Julie gave Bob a sly wink. "Come on, Kemosabe, you surely didn't think I wasted my time having a pee when I went to her loo — supposedly."

"Supposedly?"

"Absolutely! No, I went straight to her bedroom for a rummage about in her drawers — the storage variety — and I came up with this." She handed Bob a printed leaflet.

Bob gave it a quick look, then passed it back. "It's in Russian or something. Double-Dutch to me."

"Well, I'm not sure of all the details myself," Julie confessed. She pointed to the title. "But this says *Satellite Radio Beacon*, and I'm pretty certain of that."

"I'm none the wiser," Bob shrugged.

Julie drew his attention to the photograph on the front page. "It's just like the one my dad has on his yacht. It's a marker thing for the rescue services to trace you if you capsize or sink or whatever. Neat little gadgets."

Bob shrugged again. "OK, so she's into amateur dramatics — make-up a speciality — and she's into yachting and doesn't fancy being drowned if her boat sinks. Nothing too suspicious about that, is there?"

"Maybe not, but how about this?" Julie dipped into her purse again and took out her mobile phone. She showed Bob a picture on the screen. "I found that in the same drawer."

"A bottle?" Bob frowned.

"Yes, but look at the name on the label."

Bob squinted at the screen. "*Thallium*. That's poison, isn't it?"

"Yup — in this case in the form of salts. Tasteless, colourless, water-soluble and highly toxic. Very handy for a sneaky murder, which is why it's sometimes referred to in the skulduggery books as 'inheritance powder'."

"Well, well — I wonder who Mrs Dykes is thinking about bumping off."

"Whoever it is, the deed could well have been done by now. The seal on the bottle was broken and half the contents were out of it." Julie pointed at the image on her phone. "You can't quite make it out on the photo, but the label's in Portuguese. It's got the name of a pharmacy in Lisbon on it."

Bob was deep in thought. "Lisbon, which was this ship's last port of call — just a day or so before Rab

Dykes went missing." He looked at Julie. "This thallium stuff quick-acting, is it?"

"No, it's actually a very slow and unpleasant death, although the first reactions happen within a few hours."

"What kind of reactions?"

"Oh, vomiting, diarrhoea, headaches, things like that."

"Not unlike the symptoms of a norovirus infection, then?"

"I suppose not," Julie conceded, "but that's where the similarity ends, because being poisoned isn't contagious."

The lift doors pinged open.

"OK," Bob said, "we'll tackle Mrs Dykes about the thallium thing when the time's right, but in the meantime, let's assemble the troops and get ready to head down to the Marina Deck. With luck, we'll find out how Wally Walter-Wall fits into this jigsaw puzzle — if at all."

CHAPTER NINETEEN

MINUTES LATER — OFF THE CANARY ISLAND OF GRACIOSA . . .

When Bob and Ian Scrabster arrived in the Marina Deck's "Aquatic Leisure Centre", the wooden pontoon that had been extended out from the *Ostentania*'s open sea doors was swarming with people eager to take part in the various water sports at their disposal. The sun was blazing down from a cloudless sky, but a fresh breeze served both to temper the hot Saharan air and to provide just the right conditions for those already windsurfing in the narrow strait called El Rio, which separates the little island of Graciosa from its largest neighbour in the Canaries archipelago, the breathtakingly bleak volcanic island of Lanzarote.

In the hangar-like area that had originally been the stern segment of the ship's vehicle deck, all the miscellaneous items of aquatic equipment available for hire had been laid out in neat order. There was everything from scuba diving gear to jet skis and from pedalos to sailing dinghies. A dozen or so swimmers were already in the water, while moored to the pontoon were a couple of water-ski boats and, for the less adventurous, a few little inflatables with outboard motors.

In order not to look too conspicuously "together", Bob had instructed Julie and Andy to follow Ian and him down to the Marina Deck a few minutes later. The plan, such as it was, was simply to keep their eyes open for any sign of Wally Walter-Wall being covertly taken from the ship. If Detective Superintendent Bruce McNeill back in Edinburgh had been successful in alerting his counterparts in the Spanish Guardia Civil to the imminent illegal entry of an alien from the *Ostentania*, then it was likely that Wally's presumed new identity and escape from reality would be short-lived.

As previously arranged, Bob and Ian split up to wander about the covered area of the deck, ostensibly taking a casual interest in the various items of water sports equipment on display. After a couple of minutes, Ian sidled up to Bob, then, in a typically corny effort to make himself appear inconspicuous, turned his back on him.

"Take sights to yer left," he said out of the corner of his mouth. "What do ye see?"

"A lot of people jostling about in bathing costumes and wet suits?"

"Yeah, but the one standin' all awkward-like by that bulkhead door back there . . ."

"The one wearing the rubber balaclava, scuba-diving mask and snorkel?"

"That's the one."

"What about him?"

"Well, he came through that door with the balaclava, mask and snorkel already on."

"So? You're the one that's always spouting the 'Be prepared' motto."

"But check his feet. Are these flippers he's wearin'?"

Bob gave a little gasp of surprise. "Brown suede shoes!" he quietly exclaimed.

"Exactly," said Ian. "And what do ye see stickin' out o' the bottom o' the legs o' his baggy diver's suit?"

"The cuffs of a pair of light blue trousers?"

Ian smiled smugly. "Another one o' ma favourite mottos, and the very one I quoted the first time I clapped eyes on Wally Walter-Wall — 'Never trust a man wearin' a light blue suit and brown suede shoes.' Now I can add, 'especially if he's wearin' them wi' divin' clobber,' right?"

"OK, we've got our man," Bob nodded, then motioned towards an alcove on the other side of the deck, where he'd caught sight of a lanky young man struggling into a wet suit. "I wonder what young Green there thinks he's up to?"

Ian was already ogling Julie as she helped Andy get kitted out. "The Doc certainly fills out the rubber gear better than him," he drooled.

"So would a stick insect," Bob grunted. "Anyway, I'll go and have a word with them, if you just have a wander about keeping your eye on Mr Walter-Wall. But, for Pete's sake, Crabbie," he cautioned, "don't let him know he's been rumbled. I've a hunch a *lot*'s gonna depend on that!"

Bob gave Julie and Andy Green the critical once-over as he approached them. "What the hell's the idea of you two getting togged out in wet suits as if you were on holiday like the rest of these characters?"

"Jet skiing," Julie chirpily volunteered. "I told Andy I was going to do a bit if there was time when you were finished with us here, and he asked if I'd give him a few lessons. Well, you know, me being a bit of an expert and all that."

"I don't suppose you've got a license to pilot a space shuttle as well, have you?" Bob caustically enquired.

"Not yet, but never say never, Kemosabe. Daddy always said versatility should have been my middle name."

"Well, NASA will have to wait, but you can book yourself a jet ski as soon as you want. It could well come in handy before too long."

"And Andy?" Julie asked.

Bob pulled a wry smile as he patted his young detective constable's back. "Let's just say I've got a slightly less spectacular mode of transport in mind for this lad."

"A *ped*alo?" Andy Green squawked, when Bob broke the mode-of-transportation news to him. "A piggin' *ped*alo?"

Bob nodded, deadpan.

Andy, the palms of his hands upturned, looked down disconsolately at his wet suit. "But all this 007 kit," he moaned. "The macho-man, jet-ski gear an' everything. And ye say ye want me to go fartin' about out there among all them water-skiin' and wind-surfin' folk on a piggin' *ped*alo? Ah'll look bloody stupid!"

"All part of an undercover policeman's lot," Bob said nonchalantly, "as, of course, you recently found out for yourself."

Andy raised his head and gawked at him. "Eh?"

Bob returned his subordinate's blank look with a coy one. "For example, an over-acted epileptic fit in the Stardust Lounge, perhaps?"

"Oh aye, that. Yeah, but at least Ah wasn't wearin' a bloody wet suit at the time, like."

Bob shrugged. "Your choice. It was dress-optional as far as I was concerned."

With a look of desperation in his eyes, Andy glanced in the direction of the pontoon. "A wee rubber dinghy, then? One o' them ones there wi' a wee outboard motor. Kinda better image for an undercover dick than a piggin' pedalo, no?"

Bob tried to suppress a smile. "It isn't about image, Green, it's about being unobtrusive. C-R-A-P. *Clandestine* Research and Probing, remember? And, uh, for the record, 'dick' was your word, not mine."

Andy's head and shoulders sagged into the "why me?" position. "Yeah, but that's *exactly* what Ah'll look like — a total dick, fartin' about on a pedalo out there, an' all duded up like *The Lady Loves Milk Tray* gadgie an' all!"

Bob's mobile phone rang. "Hello! . . . Who? . . . Sorry, you're breaking up . . . No, I didn't catch that . . . Look, hang on, OK? . . . Yeah, hang on. I'll go outside and see if there's a better signal. Just hold the line, OK? . . . *Sí, sí, momento*!"

He took Julie by the elbow and hustled her towards the pontoon.

"Somebody Spanish on the line. Crap reception in here, but I think it could be the Guardia Civil." He handed her the phone as they emerged onto the landing stage. "You can speak the lingo, so see if you can pick him up any better out here."

She did pick him up better — perfectly, in fact.

While Julie dealt with the phone call, Bob took in as much as he could of the surroundings. On one side, the looming cliffs of Lanzarote shimmered in weird volcanic tones of black and pink, while on the other, golden sand dunes undulated gently towards the naked hilltops of the sleepy little island of Graciosa. This close to the coast of west Africa, the sunlight reflected from the Canaries' lunar landscape generated a dry, fiery heat. Bob could understand now why so many passengers were keen to take to the water. Under other circumstances, he would have joined them without hesitation. But there was work to do.

A muted splash and the slow chug of a diesel engine starting up drew his eyes to one corner of the *Ostentania*'s stern, where what he took to be one of the ship's tenders-cum-lifeboats had just been lowered into the sea. He could only see its bow, and that quickly disappeared as the boat was reversed out of sight, tucked tightly beneath the curved overhang of the ship's hull.

He walked over the wooden decking to where Andy Green was easing his gangly frame down onto the moulded contours of a pedalo, while trying to look as macho as it's possible to look while assuming command of a tiny, plastic catamaran, even (or, perhaps, especially) while wearing a wet suit.

"Pedal your way round that corner of the ship there," Bob instructed, "and take a sneaky peek at what's going on with the tender that's just been launched."

Buoyed up by the call to duty, Andy Green saluted. "Aye, aye, sir! Chocks away!"

Bob cupped his hand to his mouth. "And remember, C-R-A-P, right?"

Deftly manipulating the little tiller, Andy pumped his knees to set the pedalo's paddles surging like those of a mini Mississippi river boat. "Cap'n Candlestein at yer service, admiral!"

While Bob drew in a worried man's sigh, a short, sharp whistle from inside the Marina Deck caught his attention. He wheeled round to see Ian Scrabster beckoning him with a come-hither jerk of his head. Things were hotting up. Suddenly, there were three fronts to cover at once. He left Julie and Andy to their allotted tasks and nipped smartly back inside.

"OK, Crabbie, what's up?"

"See that door where the incognito Wally Walter-Wall was lurkin' about?"

Bob looked in the indicated direction. "Yeah, except he isn't there any more."

"That's because a hand appeared round the door a minute ago and hauled him inside. It was like somethin' out o' one o' them Scooby Doo spoof horror cartoons."

Bob's head bobbed up and down impatiently. "OK, fine, but whose hand was it?"

"Search me, man. Without a body and face attached, they all look pretty much the same to me."

"And what's behind that door, anyway?" Bob pressed.

"Search me again, man. And before ye ask, don't bother askin' me to have a look. I'm only here as a passive observer, so if ye want a hero, better find yerself a non-musician."

Just then, a shrill "Coo-ee-ee!" rang out from the vicinity of the pontoon. Bob turned to see Julie waving to him, then frantically pointing at the mobile phone in her hand. So much for clandestineness! With another sigh, he hurriedly made his way back outside.

"Just as you reckoned, it was the Spanish police on Lanzarote," Julie informed him in hushed tones.

"Better late than never," Bob dryly remarked.

"What is?" Julie asked.

"The hushed tones."

"You mean the *coo*-ee-ee?"

Bob nodded.

Julie gave an umbrage-induced harrumph. "What in heaven's name did you expect me to do — send a carrier pigeon?"

"OK, OK, don't get your jet-ski breeks in a fankle. Just tell me what the guy said, all right!"

With exaggerated calm, Julie informed Bob that an officer called Pedro Valbuena, a *Comandante* in the local Guardia Civil, had been tipped off by Lothian and Borders Police that one Walter Walter-Wall, a supposed dead man, might be attempting to disembark on Lanzarote with a false passport, and possibly in possession of counterfeit American dollars. Julie had already given Valbuena an accurate description of the suspect, and Valbuena had assured her in turn that there would be an adequate plain-clothes police presence at the port to identify and apprehend the law-breaking *británico* the moment he set foot on Spanish soil.

"And which port, precisely, did he mean?" Bob enquired, an onset of angst wrinkling his forehead.

"The port of Arrecife, of course," Julie snapped. "The place where this ship's due to dock this afternoon. Where the blazes else?" She held up a hand. "Yes, yes, I know and *amigo* Valbuena knows that there's no guarantee Wally's gonna be conveniently delivered onto the pier at Arrecife. But Lanzarote's a big island, with something like two hundred kilometres of coastline — much of it deserted — so there's no way the local police can cover every possibility."

"Which is precisely why runaway villains choose islands like Lanzarote for their disappearing acts."

"Obviously. But why should you care now? I mean, you've passed the buck to the local fuzz, so why not sit back and let them get on with it? It's their patch, after all — not yours."

Bob shook his head. "Except that the possibility of our man Wally being involved in passing forged banknotes could, according to his own admission, link him to Rab Dykes, and I'm still very much on *that* case, don't forget."

"But you told his wife less than an hour ago that, unless she could come up with some concrete stuff about his disappearance, you'd be chucking in the towel and heading back to Bonnie Scotland on the first available flight."

Bob treated himself to a little chuckle. "Yeah, and if you believe everything a sleekit polisman says in the course of his enquiries, you'll believe anything."

"Pss-sst! Pss-ss-sst! Excuse me, sir!" It was the hushed tones of Andy Green's voice that were caressing Bob's ears this time. While Bob and Julie had been talking, he had pedalled his pedalo back round the corner of the ship and was now berthed at the edge of the pontoon, right behind them.

"What's with all the 'sir' stuff?" Bob grumped. "Nobody here knows your real job, remember?"

"That's right. They still think Ah'm a barman, and that's why Ah'm callin' ye 'sir' . . . sir." Andy winked a confidential wink. "C-R-A-P, remember . . . sir?"

Smirking, Julie dug Bob in the ribs. "The word *touché* leaps to mind, Kemosabe."

Giving that remark the total lack of acknowledgement he felt it deserved, Bob asked Andy Green what he had managed to find out about the significance, if any, of the seemingly furtive launch of one of the ship's tenders.

Andy revealed that, from casual meetings in the crew's bar, he knew Rudi, the young Indonesian seaman who had been put in charge of the little boat today. Rudi's orders were to take several lower-order crew members to a neighbouring island "for a break".

Another "party" would be waiting at the same location for transportation back to the ship. This latter instruction had left Rudi somewhat confused, but orders were orders, and he wasn't about to risk his job by querying them. His family back home depended for survival on the share of his wages, paltry as they were, that he sent back to them every month.

Finally, a few crucial pieces of the jigsaw were beginning to fall into place for Bob. "Was there any sign on the tender of a man wearing a rubber balaclava, a scuba diving mask and a snorkel?" he asked Andy Green.

"How could Ah miss him? Skulkin' at the back o' the boat like some kinda perv, he was." Andy shuddered. "Aye, no wonder the rest o' the passengers was givin' him a wide berth when they came through the gangway."

"The rest of the *passengers*?"

"Aye, ye know — them MacGrannians or whatever that was holed up in the bilge pit where the Doc here sorted out the newborn chavi's mother."

"The Malgravians?" Julie checked, concern writ large on her face. "You mean *they*'re the ones being sent 'for a break' on one of the islands?"

Andy raised a rubber-clad shoulder. "Seems like it. Yeah, there must be more than a coupla dozen o' them stuffed into that wee boat wi' their brown paper parcels and stuff."

Julie shook her head in dismay. "Brown paper parcels — all their worldly goods. What a dreadful, dreadful shame." Moist-eyed, she turned to Bob. "You were right, weren't you? They're going to be dumped like so much garbage and left to whatever fate has in store for them now?"

Bob was no less appalled, but he wasn't surprised and he was thinking fast. He addressed Andy Green again: "You said your mate Rudi was told to take them to *an* island, right?"

"That's what he said."

"And there are a few smaller ones lying off the main island of Lanzarote here, aren't there?" he asked Julie.

Julie gestured towards the sandy beaches of Isla Graciosa just over the strait from where the *Ostentania* was lying at anchor. "There's that one, which is inhabited, but there are one or two others beyond that. Tiny ones without any people on them at all."

Andy pressed a finger to his temple. "Ehm, Ah could be wrong, but Ah think maybe Rudi mentioned somethin' like Mount Clarty. Could that be right?"

"Montaña Clara?" Julie suggested. "Could he have said that?"

"That's the one," Andy affirmed, a smile of admiration lighting his boyish features. "Right on the button as usual, Doc!"

But Julie was in no mood at present to show appreciation for praise of her knowledge of geographic trivia. "So," she pondered, "unless whoever's behind this people-trafficking racket decides to do the right thing by picking up these wretches on Montaña Clara and sending them on the next stage of their journey, they'll be castaways there, literally."

"That's the chance they took when they signed up for the trip," Bob said, his words sounding unintentionally more callous than pragmatic. "Also," he continued, "it looks as if Jojo the security man has turned the tables on Wally. He must have figured he'd never get the real money he was owed, so he's decided to do a Ben Gunn on him instead."

"Serves the creep right," said Julie. "He's supposed to be dead already, so he's lucky Jojo didn't just make a truth out of the lie."

"Yeah, he could well have got away with murder at that," Bob acknowledged. "Anyway, you'd better get on the phone to your Guardia Civil *Comandante* in Arrecife and tell him to get a reception committee over to Montaña Clara pronto."

"But Arrecife city's on the south coast of Lanzarote and Montaña Clara's away off the north coast here. There's fifty kilometres of volcanic mountain range, another island and two stretches of sea dividing them."

"That's his problem. All we can do is pass on the info and leave him to get on with it as best he can. If he wants to catch a bunch of illegal immigrants in the act, he'll have to move it."

Now that things were coming to a head, Julie's instinctive reaction was to tell Bob that, although she had no sympathy for a sleaze like Wally Walter-Wall, it was cruel to cut off the escape to freedom of the Malgravians, who had invested everything they owned and had already gone through untold hardships in the hope of realising their dream. No matter how reluctantly, however, she eventually came round to agreeing that, as Bob had bluntly stated, there had never been any guarantee that the Malgravian asylum seekers would get any further than one of the Canary Islands, anyway. Heartless as it might seem, then, the prime objective now had to be the obstruction of this particular instance of people-trafficking and, if at all possible, the exposure of those responsible.

From Bob's point of view, although such a goal was beyond his remit of getting to the bottom of a man-overboard claim and any connection this might have with a cigarette-smuggling caper, he'd never be able to live with his conscience if he didn't at least pass the baton over to the Spanish authorities now.

Accordingly, Julie made the phone call to *Comadante* Valbuena.

"Any chance of your mate letting you tag along on the jaunt to Montaña Clara?" Bob asked Andy Green. "You know, like some kinda volunteer help — him thinking you're still a member of the crew and all that."

Andy looked doubtful. "That wee boat's loaded to the gunnels already, but Ah can always ask."

"Pedal back round there and do just that, then. We could do with a witness on board."

The sea in the immediate vicinity of the *Ostentania* was now swarming with water sports enthusiasts enjoying the various items of equipment hired from the ship's Aquatic Leisure Centre. Adding to the jamboree atmosphere, a few little motor boats had set out from the island of Graciosa to join in the fun. A suitably chaotic scenario, Bob thought, into which to dispatch a boatful of refugees, with precious little chance of anyone taking the slightest notice. And that's precisely what happened next; except that an element of farce was added by the spectacle of the ship's tender setting off through the seaborne melee towing a pedalo, on which its pilot was lying back, his lanky legs spreadeagled in the air, while his tiny craft's pedals spun below in a spontaneous blur.

"I might have known," Bob groaned, "when I told that bloody idiot to see if he could tag along, that that's exactly what he would do."

"It's bound to end in tears," Julie anxiously predicted, handing Bob his phone back.

"He'll end up blowing the whole operation," Bob lamented.

"I'd better provide some rearguard backup," Julie said, "just in case." With that, she sprinted across the pontoon, straddled a jet ski, fired up its motor and set off in hot pursuit, leaving a train of foaming spume in her wake. Typically, no one seemed to pay much heed.

Simultaneously, a powerful motor launch homed in on the other side of the ship, having headed out from the main island of Lanzarote, though without attracting undue attention either. However, Bob did notice it as it finally nudged alongside the pontoon, and he recognised its two main occupants as well.

A large, expensively dressed man disembarked, followed by a Rab Dykes look-alike with the middle finger of his right hand missing. The digital-amputee was rolling his eyes heavenward. The expensively dressed man was having a rant . . .

"I tellink you, Rafael, I been havink hunch ven I seeink him in Scotch willage hotel place vot no can makink borscht soups vid *pampushki* dumplinks. And now Kapitan Stotinki been sendink me photo, and hunch is true. Secret contact in British passport office tellink me Bob Burns is fockink Scotch KGB baster!" Boris Kaminski was purple in the face with resolve, his beard bristling atop hidden goose pimples of rage. "Now, I must squashink him like fly before he go spoilink my beesness vid his nosey fockink nose!"

"Shit!" said Bob, as he tried to make himself look as small as possible behind a gaggle of people waiting their turn to do a bit of water skiing. He said "Shit!" again when he noticed who was stepping out of the aqua-sporting throng on the pontoon to welcome the Ulanova Line's head honcho. Her hair was blonde and bobbed instead of raven and waist-length, and her dress was summery and revealing instead of black and all-concealing, but her haughty mien and affected Morningside accent were dead giveaways . . .

"My, my, Boris, fancy seeing you here," she said with a coquettish flutter of her false eyelashes.

"Ah, Katarina, *dorogaya moya*!" Boris growled. Hungrily, he took her hand in his and pressed it to his whiskered lips. "My leedle dahlink, for this moment I am gaspink since last ve been meetink!"

"Likewise, I'm sure," Catherine Dykes purred.

As he witnessed this touching little liaison, Bob was torn between throwing up and making himself scarce. Erring on the side of discretion, he opted for the latter. Stealthily, he edged his way back inside the Marina

Deck to where Ian was still standing by the bulkhead door through which Wally Walter-Wall had disappeared.

"Yeah, I saw all that," Ian muttered. "Bear Man meets Wolf Woman. Fuckin' frightenin', man."

"And they're heading this way," Bob observed. He gave Ian a frank look. "All things considered, Crabbie, I think it would be prudent if I avoided Boris Kaminski for the moment."

Ian gestured towards an adjacent companionway, down which Captain Georgi Stotinki and First Officer Janusz Nijinski were briskly tripping, their faces wreathed in servile smiles of welcome for their newly arrived master.

"All things considered, Bobby, I think you're right," Ian freely conceded, gesturing now towards a dark little corridor that branched off at right angles to where he and Bob were standing. "We'll nip in there until the coast's clear."

Once their eyes had grown accustomed to the gloom inside the passageway, they could see that it was only a few paces long, with a sign at the end saying, *Service Elevator — Aft Galley Cold Store — No Unauthorised Use*.

Bob looked at Ian.

Ian looked at Bob. "Well, you said you wanted to see the kitchens . . ."

Bob grinned. "Yeah, but this is even better. The freezer was what I really wanted to get into all along."

"You've lost me, man," Ian said. "But whatever turns you on."

They entered the lift, Ian punched the "Up" button, and they eventually emerged into yet another corridor — this one no more than a small, enclosed chamber isolating the elevator from a heavy steel door. On the door were the expected words: *Cold Store — Aft Galley*.

"Shall we?" Ian asked.

Bob nodded. "No time like the present."

Ian yanked the locking lever down and hauled the door open. Just as would happen with a domestic fridge, lights automatically came on inside. But this was no domestic fridge. This chiller was big enough to accommodate small herds of cattle, sheep and pigs, all cut in half lengthways and suspended from hooks like row upon row of frosty, pink stalactites.

"Just as Doctor Death told me," Bob said grimly.

Ian squinted at him. "Carcasses o' meat? Ye surely didn't need anybody to tell ye that's what ye'd find in a cruise liner's freezer, did ye?"

"No, what the ship's doctor told me was that his little mortuary was occasionally filled to overflowing." With a sideways twitch of his head, Bob indicated a huddle of dark shapes lying in a corner away to the left of the door.

"Christ!" Ian gasped, slack-jawed. "Body bags! Four o' them, and they're all occupied!"

Bob stepped towards the grizzly find. "Yeah, and if Doctor Death's diary tells no lies, two of them will contain the *solitudos*." He responded to Ian's puzzled look by explaining that the diary entry, written in a sort of shorthand Latin, suggested that two late victims of the norovirus outbreak may have been hidden away somewhere to avoid detection by the Gibraltar health inspectors. "After all," he continued, "when the heat's on, where better to preserve dead bodies than in a cold store?"

"Which is why you wanted to snoop about the kitchens," Ian deduced.

"You got it," said Bob. He kneeled down beside the body bags. "Now, let's see who's in here."

Ian swallowed hard. "Ye reckon one o' these stiffs could be Rab Dykes, don't ye?"

"Nothing would surprise me," Bob confidently replied, though not without an undertone of apprehension.

The first two zippers he lowered, however, revealed the ashen faces of two elderly people recognised by neither himself nor Ian.

"The *solitudos*, maybe?" Bob suggested in a solemn whisper.

Speechless, Ian merely stared blankly at the two lifeless masks.

However, when Bob opened the third body bag, Ian caught his breath and, his knees buckling, steadied himself against the wall. "Jesus Christ Almighty," he quavered, "it's Señora Molinero — old Enrique the cocktail pianist's widow!"

The hairs rose on the back of Bob's neck. "But, if this is Señora Molinero, who was the elderly lady who buried old Enrique at sea?"

Ian looked on, whey-faced, while Bob slowly undid the zipper of the fourth bag.

"It — it can't be!" Ian gasped, horrified.

Bob looked up at him. "What can't be?"

"Him," Ian said, his eyebrows high in disbelief. "It's impossible!"

"*Nothing*'s impossible," Bob barked, his nerves fraying, "so just tell me who this *is*, Crabbie, will you!"

Ian took a deep, shuddering breath, then, his lips trembling, he whispered, "Enrique — it's old Enrique Molinero."

"You mean . . . the ship's late cocktail pianist?" Bob said, scowling incredulously.

Ian nodded his affirmation.

Bob looked down at the old man's wax-like features. "So, if he wasn't in the coffin that was committed to the deep off Gib, who was?"

Ian had turned his eyes away and was staring at Señora Molinero's exposed head, his expression now combining shock with confusion. "What do ye make o' this, Bobby?" he asked. "Look, some o' her hair's fallen out — wee tufts o' it lyin' inside the body bag there."

A chill ran up Bob's spine. "Thallium," he muttered, unable to hide his revulsion at the possibilities now entering his mind. "Thallium — a tasteless, colourless poison. And hair loss, according to Doctor Julie, is one of the characteristics of having been on the receiving end of a dose of it."

But something didn't quite add up. Julie had said that death from thallium poisoning was normally a lingering one — very often taking several weeks — and the symptom of hair loss didn't usually occur quickly either. He related this to Ian.

"Yeah, but I told you back in Mallorca, when the port lecturer's gig was bein' set up for Doc Julie, that the old dear had a serious heart condition, remember? Maybe that could have speeded up the effects of this thallium stuff. And — well, I don't know — but maybe the poison gettin' mixed up wi' whatever heart medication she was on could've advanced the hair loss thing, no?"

"Who knows? Maybe an autopsy will give us the answers, though." Gently, Bob closed the body bag.

Ian was nonplussed. "But who'd want to murder a harmless old soul like Señora Molinero — particularly when she was still grievin' for her husband?"

Bob stood up. "I reckon the person best qualified to answer that question would be another woman whose husband had also just died — allegedly."

Scepticism now joined the looks of shock and confusion on Ian's face. "Ye *sur*ely don't mean Rab Dykes's own wife, do ye?"

Bob shrugged. "At this moment in time, she's the only one I know who was present at the non-burial of old Enrique *and* also has a stash of thallium in her cabin."

"But what about the Reverend John Pearce?" Ian queried. "I mean, he conducted that funeral."

Bob stroked his chin. "That's right. And what about the little-old lady who posed as Señora Molinero at the funeral and was then deposited ashore at Gibraltar? And who, or what, was in old Enrique's coffin? And why did Rab Dykes visit Doctor Death's surgery on the day of his disappearance? And does that have any connection with all the thousands of fake hundred-dollar bills that are missing from one of the two body bags in Doctor Death's morgue? And what were the contents of the box that Catherine Dykes tipped into the water at old Enrique's non-funeral?"

Ian held his head in his hands. "Too many questions, man. Keep it simple, eh? I'm gettin' dizzy here."

But as the clouds of confusion were gathering inside Ian's head, the dawn of denouement had already broken inside Bob's. "An instruction leaflet for a small satellite radio beacon was also tucked away in Mrs Dykes's suite," he told Ian, with the here's-something-for-nothing air of a TV quizmaster. "*And*, as you may have gathered from her appearance on the pontoon deck a few minutes ago, she has a selection of wigs and stacks of make-up there as well. Are those big enough clues for you?"

"Yeah, yeah, I *kinda* get yer drift," Ian frowned, "but why would Rab Dykes and his wife set up a two-million-pound life insurance scam and then settle for rippin' off maybe a quarter o' that amount in fake banknotes — especially involvin' a complicated heist like the one ye're suggestin' now?"

Bob tutted a few reproachful tuts. "You're forgetting your own favourite maxim, Crabbie. Accent the devious, eliminate the obvious, right?"

Ian lowered his head despairingly. "Nah, ye've lost me, man." He shivered, crossed his arms and rubbed his shoulders briskly. "*Plus*, it's fuckin' freezin' in here, and all these dead bodies, human and otherwise, are givin' me the heebies. Let's get the hell out o' it."

While ushering Ian back towards the door, Bob took a piece of paper from his shirt pocket. "This email came in from my boss back in Edinburgh a few minutes before we headed down to the Marina Deck." He offered the note to Ian.

Ian waved it aside. "Nah, nah, just run the highlights past me." Grimacing, he glanced back at the quartet of corpses on the floor. "If 'highlights' is the right word."

Bob proceeded to explain that his colleagues at Lothian and Borders Police HQ had been in touch with the Edinburgh company whose logo was on the letterhead of Rab Dykes's life insurance schedule that had been given to Bob by his boss Bruce McNeill at the onset of the investigation. That schedule had been emailed to McNeill along with the photograph of the severed finger, and it had since been established that the sender had been Gentleman Jim Alexander, the undercover customs officer with a self-confessed case of the hots for Rab Dykes's wife. The hot news from the insurance company now, however, was that no such life insurance policy for Rab Dykes existed, nor had even been applied for. Dykes's record of failed insurance swindles over the years would have rendered such an application useless in any case.

"I'm even more confused than ever now," Ian confessed as he pressed the service elevator's "Down" button.

"That's understandable," Bob allowed, "but this is where your 'accent the devious' bit comes in. You see, although Rab was barred himself, his wife *did* take out insurance with that selfsame company just before the start of this cruise. But not life insurance for two million or even two hundred smackers. In fact, not life insurance at all, but a simple travel policy, covering theft of her personal effects, potential illness, loss of cash, holiday cancellation, that sort of thing. Probably cost her less than twenty quid."

"I *think* I'm beginnin' to get it," said Ian. "She scanned the insurance company's logo from her travel policy into a computer and faked the two-million-quid life schedule that eventually got emailed to your bossman. That it?"

"Could well be. And if it's true, it would explain why she went to so much trouble to raise a storm in a teacup about a man-overboard claim that she must have known would never succeed."

Ian extended his lower lip, then nodded slowly and approvingly. "Hey-y-y, nice smokescreen! And while *you*'re bustin' yer nuts on a wild goose chase, Rab slips out o' his disguise as Señora Molinero and goes trawlin' under a radio beacon in the Straits o' Gibraltar for a coffin stuffed full o' hundred-dollar bills." He nodded again, more animatedly this time. "Hmm, now *that*'s what I call accentuatin' the devious!"

"Yep," Bob conceded, "and all very cunning — even admirable, in a perverse sort of way — until we remember that nice old lady lying in a body bag up there in the freezer."

Ian squirmed at the thought. "So, I take it you're gonna nick Dykes's wife for murder, and bloody smartly at that, huh?"

Bob hunched his shoulders. "Not my call, Crabbie."

Ian shot him a puzzled look. "But you're a lawman, for Christ's sake! Nickin' villains is what ye're for!"

"The only lawmen on a cruise ship, when it's at sea, are the company's own security guys, and we already know what the head security guy on this tub's worth. He was even prepared to take a bung to help a slug like Walter-Wall find a new stone to crawl under."

"Yeah, but we're not at sea any more," Ian objected. "We're in Spanish territorial waters."

"Precisely," Bob agreed. "But I'm not a Spanish lawman, so I carry no authority here either."

A look of panic joined the various others jostling for pole position on Ian's face. "But, Bobby man! I mean, if all these theories o' yours are right, ye could be up against every bent bugger on this boat, from the Captain right down to the kitchen hands, and *includin'* the owner himself now!" He glared at Bob. "What the *hell* are ye gonna do?"

The lift doors opened.

"Well, for the moment," Bob said with an optimistic little smile, "if the coast's clear, we'll go back out onto the pontoon and phone the Guardia Civil in Arrecife. You can give them the lowdown on the frozen people in Spanish and tell them to get their arses out here at the double." He gave Ian a reassuring pat on the shoulder. "Then we'll see what develops after that."

"Aye, and when ye say 'we'," Ian quickly qualified, "just remember that if there's any trouble, I'm a keyboard player, *not* a fuckin' Keystone cop!"

CHAPTER TWENTY

FIFTEEN MINUTES LATER — ON THE BRIDGE OF THE OSTENTANIA . . .

Jojo the Indonesian security man had been waiting for Bob when he arrived back at his cabin. Jojo was carrying an invitation from Boris Kaminski — not in the form of a business card, but in the ominous shape of the business end of a revolver which Bob noticed distorting the side pocket of Jojo's tunic. Jojo was radiating the edgy vibes of a man who'd already had one disappointment too many today. Prudently, therefore, Bob accepted the invitation without hesitation.

When Bob was shown onto the bridge, Boris Kaminski was lounging in the elevated captain's chair at the hub of the ship's command centre. His back to the door, Boris was gazing out through the panoramic sweep of raked windows, one arm dangling loosely by his side, the elbow of the other resting on the arm of the chair, his fist raised to support his chin. He spun slowly round and fixed Bob with a cobra-like stare.

Bob took a fleeting glance round the bridge to see who else had been invited to Boris's reception. Only Captain Georgi Stotinki and First Officer Janusz Nijinski were there. They were standing, arms folded and legs apart, on either side of their boss. The door clicked shut as Jojo left, and if there had been a naked light bulb suspended above his head, Bob could easily have imagined himself in a Cold War interrogation room somewhere deep behind the Iron Curtain. All that was needed to complete the illusion was a total blackout and the distant jangle of balalaika music — and, perhaps, the dull thwack of fist on flesh and the despairing scream of a fellow interviewee echoing along the corridor.

Back in the realms of reality, Boris raised a hand to shield his eyes from the glare of the sunlight pouring in through the windows of the bridge.

"So, Meester *Police*man Burns, ve meetink again," he sneered.

"Life's full of nasty surprises," Bob replied, expressionless.

"Yiss, and maybe soon now you goink get big von." A crepitus chortle crackled in Kaminski's chest. With a snap of his fingers, he indicated that Bob should move, and with a jerk of his head, he indicated to where. "Stop!" he commanded, when Bob's shadow fell over the captain's chair. Boris lowered the hand that had been shielding his eyes. "Last time ve meetink, you tellink me I blockink out sun, you bourgeois baster prole."

"Hmm, bourgeois prole," Bob mused, placing a forefinger to his cheek and looking upwards at nothing in particular. "Classic communist oxymoron, if I ever heard one."

Boris chortled again, a self-satisfied smirk exposing a glimpse of gold tooth. "Absolute, and moron beink you,

’cos now *I* usink *you* as fockink parasol. *Da*, I think is makink werry nice piss-take, *nyet*?”

Boris laughed aloud, as did Captain Stotinki a second or so later. First Officer Nijinski followed suit a further second or so after that. Predictably, another snap of Boris’s fingers brought the group hilarity to an abrupt halt.

He glared at the outline of Bob’s head silhouetted against the sunlight. “Vy you cruisink as yurnalist ven you really beink cop?” he gruffly demanded. “And vy you pokink nose into man-overboard and funeral-at-sea beesness ven Kapitan Stotinki invitink you to table vid odder passengers and company priest? Is makink bad atmosphere, and bad atmosphere is damage my cruisink beesness.”

“Though no more so than inviting a passenger to the bridge at gunpoint?” Bob proposed.

Boris went instantly on the offensive-defensive. “Is absolute legal for security man to carryink rewolwer on sheep!” he snarled. “Is for to guardink terrorism opportunity!”

Stotinki and Najinski nodded their heads in subservient unison. “*Da*, is absolute legal.”

“So, Meester Burns, vy you cruisink as yurnalist ven you really beink cop?” Kaminski reiterated.

“And why is Rupert De’ath cruising as a ship’s doctor,” Bob retorted, “when he’s really a smuggler of counterfeit money?” He stepped sideways so that Boris’s face was once again in the full glare of sunlight. “And why is Jojo cruising as a ship’s security officer when he's taking backhanders to help a so-called dead man enter Spain illegally?"

Blanching, Boris raised his hand against the glare once more. "Get back to beink parasol, Burns, or I squashink you like fockink fly!" he barked.

Bob moved in the opposite direction from the one indicated. "Enjoy the sunshine, Boris," he smiled. "It'll put the colour back in your cheeks."

But the colour was already back in Boris's cheeks and it was intensifying rapidly. "And vy," he roared, "you been accusink Kapitan Stotinki of hidink Malgravian stowavays in hold of sheep?"

"Aha!" Bob said inwardly, giving himself a self-congratulatory pat on the back. "Feed 'em enough rope and they'll always trip over it." He ambled over to Georgi Stotinki and looked him straight in the eye — his good one. "But I didn't accuse you of any such thing, *did* I Captain?"

The Captain's eye patch went into one of its involuntary quivers, but his mouth remained firmly motionless.

Bob turned again to Boris Kaminski. "The only person I mentioned the Malgravians to was Mrs Catherine Dykes, and that was when I asked her why Stotinki here had bypassed their pigsty when he was giving the Gibraltar health inspectors a tour of the ship."

Looking ill at ease, Boris Kaminski made to answer.

Bob got in first. "So, Boris, it seems that Mrs Dykes has been carrying tales to you, eh? I wonder why. Oh, and incidentally, the Malgravians are *not* stowaways, they're helpless victims of a stinking people-trafficking racket that this fine cruise *beesness* of yours is being used as a cover for."

Stotinki and Nijinski stood nonplussed and fidgeting. Their boss rose to his feet. He lurched forward and, in the manner of a football player who has just been spat on by an opponent, locked foreheads with Bob.

"Katarina beink werry goot friend. She tellink me ev'rysink and she tellink me to lookink out for nosey Scotch police baster like you!"

"Oh yeah? How thoughtful of her! And did she also tell you that she'd helped her *drowned* husband jump ship at Gib with a coffin full of *your* fake American dollars — maybe a million of them? Yeah, and did she also tell you how your drunken ship's doctor was in on the scam? And did she mention that the same doctor is storing the corpses of norovirus victims beside supplies of meat in at least one of the ship's freezers?"

Boris Kaminski was now trembling like an about-to-erupt volcano.

Bob decided he'd better get in swiftly with another inflammatory broadside before the lava started to flow. "And did *Katarina* Dykes neglect to tell you how she poisoned an innocent old woman as part of this rotten scheme she'd plotted with her half-wit husband to rip *you* off?" Bob knew he was going well beyond the circumstantial with these, as-yet, uncorroborated assertions, but his bull-at-a-fence technique had served him well in the past, so why abandon it now?

A low growl rumbled at the back of Boris's throat, and his breath rasped in short, staccato bursts into Bob's face.

Bob turned his nose away. "Bugger me," he gagged, "if that's what the after-effects of borscht soup with *pampushki* dumplings smell like, thank Christ they don't have the recipe at the Dirleton Castle Inn!"

That did it. His eyes blazing, Boris spluttered out what Bob took to be a string of damning curses in his native tongue, then cocked a clenched fist in preparation for proving that, at times like this, actions speak more painfully than words. Stotinki and Nijinski stepped forward to give their boss physical support.

Not a second too soon, Bob caught sight of three small craft rounding the northern cape of Graciosa Island, just a few hundred metres distant. They were approaching fast. As a diversionary tactic, he drew his hosts' attention to them.

Stepping over to the window, Georgi Stotinki lifted a pair of binoculars to his eyes. The only words which Bob understood in the fairly anxious-sounding statement that followed were "*Guardia*" and "*Civil*".

Boris Kaminski grabbed the binoculars from the Captain's hands. "Fockink basters!" he murmured, exuding venom reminiscent of a greeting between two groups of rival football fans in Glasgow on a Saturday night. "Lousy fockink polis basters!"

Bob could now just make out with the naked eye that it was, in fact, the rearmost craft, a high-powered launch, that bore the insignia of the Spanish Civil Guard. In front of that was the *Ostentania*'s tender that had set out earlier for the islet of Montaña Clara with Andy Green's pedalo in tow. The pedalo wasn't in evidence now, but Julie's jet ski was. It was leading the little procession, and it was apparent that two people were on board. It was also apparent, from the erratic way in which it was being driven, that the jet ski's pilot was none other than Andy Green himself.

Just then, the thud of a helicopter's rotor blades filled the air above and to the rear of the bridge.

"Is landink on Sun Deck," Boris Kaminski shouted above the din, his contorted facial expression indicating deep displeasure. "Basters is landink on mine private fockink helipad!"

Bob smirked the contented smirk of a condemned man who has not only been given a nick-of-time stay of execution, but has also been given the right to dangle a noose above the head of his would-be executioner. He pointed towards the sound of the descending helicopter as he strode towards the bridge door.

"I think you'll find, Boris," he smiled triumphantly, "that you should also have added the 'polis' qualification to the 'basters' that are landink on your private fockink helipad." He opened the door, stood to one side and, posing like a matator about to entice a confused bull to charge his cape, said, "Prepare to welcome Spanish boarders, *Señor* Kaminski!"

THAT EVENING — IN THE 'OSTENTANIA'S' STARDUST LOUNGE . . .

Near mutiny had broken out among the passengers when *Comandante* Pedro Valbuena of the Lanzarote division of the Guardia Civil pronounced that the *Ostentania* would be held at anchor in her present position and under Guardia Civil control until their preliminary investigations into alleged criminal activity within Spanish territorial waters had been concluded. Furthermore, no one, except those suspected of being implicated in these crimes, would be allowed to leave the ship until the Lanzarote health authorities had given the vessel the all-clear. The bodies of probable norovirus victims being stored alongside food intended for human consumption contributed towards a situation that would have to come under the most rigorous scrutiny.

A degree of stoicism had prevailed, however, following Boris Kaminski's magnanimous announcement (prior to being taken ashore under arrest) that he would personally guarantee that every one of the inconvenienced passengers on the *Ostentania* would be given a full refund of the cost of this cruise, would have their current bar tabs made void, and would be given complimentary vouchers for a future Ulanova Line cruise of their choice. It was a moot point whether the Ulanova Line would even be in a position to carry on cruising following the media furore that would inevitably accompany the forthcoming police investigations, but at least the inconvenienced passengers on this particular cruise could now make the most of the freebie bar concession that the self-preserving Boris had so "magnanimously" put their way. Accordingly, the atmosphere in the Stardust Lounge was distinctly upbeat and was becoming more festive as the evening wore on.

Bob, Julie, Andy and Ian were sitting at a corner table at the opposite side of the dance floor from the bar, where Speedy Gonzales was dispensing drink as usual, although visibly disconsolate in the knowledge that Boris Kaminski's devious gesture of generosity had wiped out his prospective booze-sales bonus for the entire trip. On stage, the Sunbeam Band churned out their usual out-of-tune medleys of middle-of-the-road favourites for circulating swarms of determined-to-enjoy-themselves dancers.

Julie was nursing a sprained wrist, sustained, she had earlier revealed, when helping Andy untangle what was left of his pedalo after he'd rammed it into the rear of the *Ostentania*'s tender when young Rudi had brought it to an unexpectedly sudden stop while approaching the islet of Montaña Clara. Andy's carelessness, however, had unwittingly served to present first-hand and potentially crucial evidence to the Spanish police. The delay caused by the necessity to effect running repairs to the tender's propeller and rudder had provided the extra time required for the Guardia Civil's cutter to complete its journey from Órzola, a fishing village near the northern tip of Lanzarote. The cutter had eventually arrived at Montaña Clara just as the Malgravian refugees were about to wade ashore, where their arrival had been awaited by another group of equally unfortunate souls. Huddled on the beach had been some two dozen people who, it ultimately transpired, had sailed in a tiny open boat from the west coast of Africa, having paid several thousand dollars to people traffickers for the privilege, along with a promise that they would be transported aboard a cruise liner to a new life on mainland Europe. To add to their potential misery, some of the members of this ragamuffin group had also been found to be in possession of significant quantities of drugs, which, they claimed, they were transporting as part of the "escape to freedom" deal. These, then, were the latest batch of black equivalents to the exploited Malgravian "seamen" to whom Ian had alluded that night in the crew's bar.

Naturally, the police had instantly quizzed young Rudi regarding what he knew of the perpetrators of this evil trade. Predictably, though, Rudi's predominant attributes were revealed to be more happy-go-lucky than cerebral, a personality trait ideally suited to the insidious ways of his masters, whoever they might be. All Rudi knew was that he had been given his orders by a fellow Indonesian crew member, who was only marginally higher up the pecking order below decks on the *Ostentania* than he was himself. Here, therefore, was a Hydra, the identities of whose various heads were neither known to third parties nor, conceivably, to each other. A "cell" system of textbook type.

After witnessing the plight of these two groups of hapless people, Julie had considered the injury to her wrist to be insignificant in the extreme, even rendering relatively painless the necessity of riding pillion to jet-ski rookie Andy Green on the return trip to the ship. What did hurt her, however, was the knowledge that all of these illegal immigrants were to be detained in the hold of the *Ostentania* until the Spanish authorities had decided their ultimate fate, which, more than likely, would be repatriation — an ignominious return to their "homelands", with even less to their names than when they'd set out.

The only vaguely lightsome thing to come out of this depressing episode had been the sight of Wally Walter-Wall, minus rubber balaclava, being herded onto the Guardia Civil launch for transportation to jail on Lanzarote, along with Boris Kaminski and the rest of the suspected instigators, aiders and abettors of the various crimes recently associated with the good ship *Ostentania*.

"So, Bobby, what now for the farthest-flung of the Lothian and Borders Police Detective Inspectors and his intrepid undercover sidekicks," asked Ian as he summoned a passing waitress.

"Well, Crabbie, we're officially off the case — or cases. Everything's in the hands of the Spanish authorities now, but we're obliged to hang about here until they tell us they don't need us any more. Yeah, yeah, I know, it's a tough job, but somebody has to do it. What about yourself?"

"Simple. As soon as the purser pays me for services already rendered, plus compensation for cancellation o' the rest o' the engagement, I'll be makin' ma way back to Mallorca and the relative sanity o' ma regular spot at the Hotel Santa Catalina in Palma Nova." He paused to order a fresh round of drinks from the waitress. "Unfortunately, Bobby," he went on, "ye've never had a chance to treat me to all them slap-up feeds courtesy o' yer police expense account like ye promised."

"I think that was like *you* promised, Crabbie," Bob replied good-naturedly. "But never mind, I'll see you're mentioned in dispatches."

"Aye, and ye know where ye can stuff *them*," Ian grunted. He licked his lips. "Mmm, and there's some great eateries Ah could've taken ye to in these Canary Islands an' all . . . *La Cañada* here in Lanzarote, for instance, *La Hierbita* in Tenerife, *Las Trébedes* in Gran Canaria, *El Faro* in La Palma. Oh aye, Ah could go on and on . . ."

"Yeah, well, ye'd better *dream* on as well, Fats," Andy sniggered, "for ye'll get nothin' fancier on this tub than salad and fruit until they de-quarantine the kitchens again. That's what happened durin' the last norovirus scare, and they'd never even discovered *one* dead body in the freezer that time."

"Remind me never to get press-ganged into another cruisin' gig again," Ian moaned. "A man could starve on a diet o' parrot food like that."

Leaving Ian to lament in peace, Julie, who had been uncharacteristically quiet up to now, asked Bob what the latest word from the Spanish police was.

Things had been happening pretty quickly, he informed her. Boris Kaminski, as would have been expected, was denying all knowledge of everything, particularly the counterfeit money caper, which already made the police suspect he might be protesting too much in that regard. To back this up, they had established that Rafael, his right-hand man in Mallorca, was a high-tech printer to trade and had, in fact, lost the middle finger of his right hand in an accident with a paper-cutting guillotine while involved in a botched money-forging attempt several years previously.

So far, Doctor Rupert De'ath had remained tight-lipped about his obvious involvement in the distribution — and possible pilfering — of the fake dollars, and he had also declined to comment on whatever dark motives might lurk behind the secreting of dead passengers in the ship's cold stores. The police were aware, however, that withholding even the smell of a vodka cork from the old lush for a night would doubtless loosen his tongue about those and, they suspected, other related matters marked by notes in his diary. The payment, or intended payment, of fake dollar "sweeteners" to small shareholders in Glasgow Rangers Football Club was one line of enquiry on which they were already collaborating with their UK counterparts, for example.

Cruise Director Mike Monihan, much to his apparent surprise, had also been arrested on suspicion of being implicated in drug-running via the African fugitives who had been picked up on Montaña Clara earlier in the day. Mike's record as a petty drug-peddler in Mallorca some years previously was still extant, which made him an obvious target for the Spanish police now. He had also been grassed up by Gentleman

Jim Alexander as the person behind the comparatively less serious crime of cigarette smuggling, Gentleman Jim now choosing to release this information to the police as a bargaining tool to help diminish his involvement with Catherine Dykes.

Mrs Dykes, for her part, was being held on suspicion of murder, pending the results of an autopsy on old Señora Molinero. The Guardia Civil had already taken the half-empty container of thallium from her suite as potential evidence. Motive? The most obvious one was greed — perhaps playing two men against the middle — a desire to get her claws into Boris Kaminski and his apparent fortune on one side, while contriving to cover her backside by suckering her husband into ripping off a rainy-day fund of hooky banknotes on the other. The Spanish and British police still had a lot of work to do on that one, though.

The Reverend John Pearce, as an accessory to the fake sea-burial of old Enrique Molinero, was now also being held in custody by the Guardia Civil on Lanzarote. Both he and Gentleman Jim Alexander, if they'd had the good fortune to meet the elderly Geordie who'd recently shared a beer with Bob at a pavement bar in Palma de Mallorca, might now have been pondering the significance of his taproom philosophy, if applied to the dangerously attractive Catherine Dykes . . . "Effin' wimmin! Ah divn't oondahstand the boogahs, an' Ah likely nevah will!"

It was a precept, Bob now told Julie, to which the gullible Rab Dykes himself might be inclined to subscribe, given that he had been arrested in Gibraltar dressed as an old woman and in possession of Señora Molinero's passport, while attempting to bribe two Royal Navy divers to help recover a lost coffin from the bottom of the Straits.

This last bit of news finally brought a smile back to Julie's normally sunny face. There was a funny side to most things, she breezily declared, and it was always well worth trying to find it, no matter how gloomy the circumstances. Life, after all, goes on, and she suddenly felt inclined to help it on its cheery way.

"Fancy a party?" she beamed at Andy Green. "The drinks are on Boris Kaminski, remember!"

"Count me in," said Andy.

"Count me out," said Bob.

"What about you, Fats?" Andy asked the disconsolate Ian Scrabster. "You could rattle up some lively stuff on the old joanna. Let's face it, anything would be better than the dreaded National Youth Orchestra of Indonesia over there."

"Nah," said Ian, "Ah'm not in the mood, man."

"We could get all the punters involved," Julie enthused. "You know, make it a theme party. Tarts and Vicars — that would do it."

Ian pricked up his ears.

"Yes," Julie went on, further inspired, "and I could wear my school uniform!"

"Count me in," said Ian, already on his feet. "I'll grab the microphone and make the necessary announcement!"

As Bob exhaled a forlorn sigh, he felt a tap on his shoulder and looked up into the well-weathered face of JP Shand, the tippling West Country crime writer.

"'Allo there, 'ansome," he grinned. "'Ow's yer parts?"

"Intact," Bob nodded. "Just."

"Anyway, Bob my ol' friend," JP said, "I just been hearin' about all this 'ere crime-bustin' stuff you been up to aboard ship 'ere, an' I just been a-thinkin' it'd make a fine ol' plot for my next book, see."

Bob gave the old chap a sympathetic smile and invited him to take a seat. "I'm flattered, JP," he said, "but forget it."

JP looked disappointed. "What's up, Bob? Come under the Official Secrets Act or somethin', does it?"

Still smiling, Bob shook his head. "No, no, nothing like that, JP. It's just that, if you wrote a book about it, no bugger would ever believe you!"

EPILOGUE

THE NEXT MORNING--BY THE JACUZZI ON THE SUN DECK OF THE OSTENTANIA . . .

Julie and Andy were still sitting in the Jacuzzi, Andy holding his head in his hands and moaning the groans of the seriously hung-over, Julie bright as a button and full of the joys. Bob was still lying on the sun lounger, fully clothed and searching, eyes closed, for lost sleep.

"I mean, you've got to admit, Kemosabe," Julie chirped, "that you've been on worse cases than this one. OK, so we're marooned on a luxury liner off a sub-tropical island, all expenses paid and in full receipt of our wages for doing nothing but wait for the Spanish police to solve the puzzles you chucked at them. Rough as it is, you've gotta admit you've been on worse cases."

Bob forced an eye open. "Believe it or not, but I actually agree with you — almost."

"Really?"

"Yeah, and with all the villains that gravitate to places like this, you couldn't blame a Brit copper for jacking in his pension and setting up as some kinda private eye here."

Julie sat bolt upright and stared at Bob in confused optimism. "You wouldn't, *would* you?"

"Maybe better in Mallorca," Bob went on, preoccupied. "At least it's got trees as well as criminals."

"And would there be a sidekick's job in it for a Little Miss Versatile like me?"

Andy Green emerged hesitantly from his in-body exile. "And would there be a trainee dick's job for me in it for me?"

"I couldn't think of anybody more ideally suited," Bob murmured absently.

"You'd *really* do it, Kemosabe?" Julie probed. "I mean, chuck Bonnie Scotland to be a freelance sleuth in the sun?"

Bob closed his eye again, lay back and covered his face with a newspaper.

"Stranger things happen at sea," he yawned. "Stranger things happen at sea."

Also available in ISIS Large Print:

Plum Lovin'

Janet Evanovich

Watch your backs — Stephanie's playing Cupid . . .

It's Valentine's Day and bounty hunter Stephanie Plum needs a relationship expert. One who goes by the name Annie Hart. Because Annie is wanted for armed robbery and assault with a deadly weapon.

Stephanie's shadowy but enigmatic friend Diesel knows where she is, and he's ready to make a deal: he'll help her get Annie if Stephanie plays matchmaker to several of Annie's most difficult clients. But someone wants to find Annie even more than Diesel and Stephanie. Someone with a nasty temper and "unmentionable skills".

With Stephanie in over her head, things are sure to get a little dicey — and a little explosive!

ISBN 978-0-7531-8214-7 (hb)
ISBN 978-0-7531-8215-4 (pb)

Under Suspicion

The Mulgray Twins

DJ Smith is sent to Tenerife to infiltrate a money-laundering organisation run by Ambrose Vanheusen. DJ knows she is in deadly danger from such a ruthless criminal but luckily he has an Achilles heel: his obsession with his Persian cat, Samarkand Black Prince. DJ's passport into Vanheusen's empire comes in the form of Gorgonzola, a moth-eaten ginger Persian and sniffer cat extraordinaire, acting under the pedigree alias of Persepolis Desert Sandstorm.

With drug dealing, money laundering and murder to contend with, not to mention a cat with attitude, DJ has her hands full. So it's not surprising she doesn't realise that the greatest danger lies in Vanheusen's determination to steal her supposedly pedigree moggy. He's prepared to go to any lengths necessary to get his hands on a mate for his brute of a cat, and only a tooth and claw confrontation will determine who survives . . .

ISBN 978-0-7531-8216-1 (hb)
ISBN 978-0-7531-8217-8 (pb)